NEW YORK TIMES BESTSELLING AUTHOR
JOSS WALKER

the BOOK of SPIRITS

JAYNE THORNE, CIA LIBRARIAN BOOK FIVE

The Book of Spirits
© 2024 by J.T. Ellison

Digital ISBN: 978-1-948967-78-5
Trade ISBN: 978-1-948967-76-1

Cover design © The Killion Group, Inc.

All rights reserved. No part of this text may be reproduced, transmitted, decompiled, or stored in or introduced into any information storage and retrieval system, in any form or by any means, whether electronic or mechanical, now known or hereafter invented, without the express written permission of the publisher.

This is a work of fiction. Names, characters, places, and incidents are either the product of the author's imagination or are used fictitiously, and any resemblance to actual persons, living or dead, business establishments, events, or locales is entirely coincidental.

For more, visit Two Tales Press.

PRAISE FOR THE JAYNE THORNE, CIA LIBRARIAN SERIES

"*The Book of Spirits* is a fast-paced fantasy with so many of my favorite things—grimoires, layered character relationships, and a dragon! If you haven't started the Jayne series yet, now is your moment!"

—**Alisha Klapheke,** *USA Today* **Bestselling Author of the Bound by Dragons Series**

"Vivid world-building, a page-turning mystery and a smart, adventurous heroine in the process of discovering her own power and learning from her mistakes makes for another great addition to an outstanding urban fantasy series."

— **Jayne Castle,** *New York Times* **bestselling author of the Harmony series, on** *Master of Shadows*

"Light-hearted books can get a bad rap, as though making readers smile is somehow a weakness on the author's part... Walker has a light touch with [her] prose, and the likable characters breeze through many of their interactions. Which isn't to say that Tomb of the Queen lacks gravitas. No, there's a good story here with real edge-of-the-seat moments... It's fun from start to finish, and I'm going to keep my eye out for more from this "new" author."

—**Charles de Lint,** *The Magazine of Mystery & Science Fiction* **on** *Tomb of the Queen*

"Writer Joss Walker brings the magic back! It will take a witch with heart, humor, and book smarts–plus some killer kickboxing skills–to save the world, and Jayne Thorne is the witch we need now. Hold on tight, you urban fantasy fans, because once you open *Tomb of the Queen*, the action doesn't stop until the last thrilling page."

— **Laura Benedict, bestselling author of the** *Bliss House* **trilogy, on** *Tomb of the Queen*

"A librarian gets recruited by the CIA to help track down rare and magical books... Jayne Thorne has just discovered that magic is real, and the CIA needs her help. After a crash course in Magic 101 she's sent to Ireland to investigate a rare manuscript. The start of this series is everything I love about urban fantasy: a wise-cracking heroine who diffuses tense situations with a joke, plenty of adventure, and an interesting magical world that exists alongside our own. I can't wait for more adventures with Jayne!"

— **John McDougall, Murder by the Book, on** *Tomb of the Queen*

"Joss Walker's debut had me completely under her spell. Part cleverly plotted fantasy and part thriller, I was drawn in by her charming bookworm of a librarian with magical powers, dashing Irish rogue, and the complicated battle between 'good' and evil. Addictive and utterly delightful, this is a book to treasure."

— **Paige Crutcher, author of** *The Orphan Witch,* **on** *Tomb of the Queen*

"*Tomb of the Queen* is a relatable, fun romp of a thrill ride! The characters are lifelike and well fleshed out, and the magic is done in a unique way that I have never seen before. I loved this book, and I'm sure that I will read it over and over again!"

— **Julie L. Kramer,** *USA Today* **bestselling author of** ***Of Curses and Scandals,*** **on** ***Tomb of the Queen***

"This book was just my cup of tea! Or perhaps, my slice of pie? 😉 Jayne Thorne, CIA Librarian is a relatable, lovable, and smart heroine dead set on vanquishing evil. A genius mythology twist, swoony budding romance, and gorgeous library imagery, paired with non-stop action, makes *Tomb of the Queen* a winner for fans of urban fantasy. Stop everything and read this book!"

— **Ashley McLeo, author of the bestselling *Starseed Trilogy,* on *Tomb of the Queen***

ALSO BY JOSS WALKER

Jayne Thorne, CIA Librarian Series

The Scrolls of Time

The Book of Spirits

The Prophecy of Wind

The Keeper of Flames

Master of Shadows

Tomb of the Queen

Novellas

A Betrayal of Magic

The Eighth Road

The Guardians Mini-Series

Guardians of Power

Guardians of Fury

Guardians of Silence

Writing as J.T. Ellison

Standalone Suspense

A Very Bad Thing

It's One of Us

Her Dark Lies

Good Girls Lie

Tear Me Apart

Lie to Me

No One Knows

The Lt. Taylor Jackson Series

The Wolves Come at Night

Field of Graves

Where All the Dead Lie

So Close the Hand of Death

The Immortals

The Cold Room

Judas Kiss

14

All the Pretty Girls

The Dr. Samantha Owens Series

What Lies Behind

When Shadows Fall

Edge of Black

A Deeper Darkness

A Brit in the FBI Series, Cowritten with Catherine Coulter

The Sixth Day

The Devil's Triangle

The End Game

The Lost Key

The Final Cut

*For my parents, who showed me magic exists.
And for Randy, mon véritable amour.*

CHAPTER ONE

The Kyoto National Museum was quiet. No great shock for four o'clock in the morning, but the very essence of the building was peaceful. Discreet. Perfect for a nighttime raid. The Kingdom operative known as Blaine came from the back of the grounds, slipping past the Teahouse Tan'an, and the museum was in his sights. Just needed to get past security, and he was in.

On cue, a guard came clanking around the corner, and Blaine sent a Stunning spell at the man, coupled with an Attack designed to cut off the electrical signals to the man's heart. He was dead before his eyes closed. Blaine caught him before he fell, lowering him gently to the ground so as not to make a sound and give away his position. There would be more, and he was prepared to take them all if needed.

He told himself that he'd taken the man's life because the guard was in his way, that he was human, had no magic, and therefore preserving the life was pointless. His mission, his role as a Kingdom operative, had no room for regrets. But in the back of his mind, he knew he'd done it with the hope that a fresh sacrifice might appease the monsters in the sky. They circled and danced above him, his own personal Air Force. One smelled the kill and swooped down. The guard was gone in a flash. Moments later, the remains of his body fell to the ground with a heavy *thump*.

Blaine cringed but moved forward. He couldn't have imagined the world as they knew it now: Ruth Thorne, overtaken by a Wraith and answering to a dark overlord only she could speak with; more and more Adepts appearing all over the world; magic swirling like a poisonous fog; dark creatures of lore springing forth. The Torrent was breaking free, but not in the way it should have, and it was all that stupid girl's doing.

Getting their hands on the grimoires was more important now than ever. The battle must go their way. The TCO and Jayne Thorne must not prevail.

Blaine moved like the night itself around the side of the building. The air outside was cold and humid, faintly smelling of gasoline and salt. Another scent lurked beneath the entirely nonmagical human ones—a faint burning stench that stuck to the inside of his nose and seemed to rot there.

The grand brick-and-sandstone European-style building that housed the main collection of the National Museum had a portico entrance for visitors, but there was no reason to try the front, where more guards would surely be stationed. Instead, Blaine chose to press his hand to the solid steel door of the employee entrance. He pulled an Unlock spell from the Torrent with an ease that was new to him; he was still getting used to the intense flush of power. Spells that had once drained his power now seemed to invigorate him. *Let my enemies come at me now.* He slipped through the door and down a dark, dry, blissfully bland-smelling hallway. He Cloaked himself, giving the finger—one he knew couldn't be seen—to a security camera.

Blaine reached a simple, wide-stepped stairwell. He closed his eyes, breathed in, and waited for the call of the grimoire. It didn't take long. Power called to power, and his new magic had made something of him indeed.

The tugging felt like a hook in the back of his spine. He headed down the stairs, into the bowels of the museum.

The security became tighter the farther down he went. But what would once have been a challenging puzzle at the edge of his abilities was almost child's play now. Even the magical wards and alarms that blanketed the door at the center of the museum basement could be unlocked with a few moments' concentration.

The room beyond was blacker than black. Blaine called a soft light to him, mindful of any potential artifacts and their sensitivity to brightness. Ruth Thorne, the Head of the Kingdom, had specially selected him for this mission, and he didn't dare let her down. Not now that she was...whatever she was.

There. A large metal safe stood against one corner, locked with a keypad and several magical wards, layered in a tricky calligraphy that commanded Blaine's attention for a few minutes. He carefully separated the spells and disarmed them, one by one. He was barely out of breath by the time he set his sights on the keypad. He grinned again. He felt invincible.

Then he recalled the sight of Ruth Thorne's storm-steel eyes filling up with black, and he remembered there were some powers he still bowed to in this world. He opened the safe with a quiet click.

Something flashed hot. An alarm blared—not in the museum, but in his consciousness, like a neon light flashing from the Torrent. Damn, he must have missed a ward lurking in the mundane lock. He needed to hurry. He peered into the safe, holding his conjured light as close as he dared.

The safe was neatly lined with rows of ancient texts, written on linen and paper, and even papyrus. Each text floated between two plates of glass, protecting it from the outside elements and the oils of researchers' fingers. It also made things easier for stealing. Blaine ran his fingers along the tops of the plates, probing with his mind, waiting for the call of the grimoire. There were only a few known fragments remaining of the original Man'yōshū—the revered anthology of Japan's epic poems. Some didn't believe any originals truly existed, but Blaine could sense magic straining to be released. This was one —or a portion of it, at least.

It seemed to spark against his fingers. His hand closed around it reflexively, and he pulled the glass panel free. Crisp, neat lines of calligraphy sat on a stark white background, the edges torn, half of the poem missing. And the power swirling within—he could almost see it, the glass filling with a fog invisible to the naked eye. This had to be it.

For a brief moment, Blaine considered trying his luck. What if *he* could return to the Kingdom with the Spirit totem bound irrevocably to him?

He thought of Ruth's eyes again and tucked the grimoire safely in a Carry spell. Blaine had survived by knowing his place in the world—knowing when to step forward, and when to fade into the background. Besides, he didn't have time to mess around with the grimoire. He needed to get out of here.

He didn't bother closing the safe or masking his tracks. The Japanese authorities would never be able to trace this back to the Kingdom, and it wasn't like they would admit to the world they'd been burgled. Bad for business.

He headed for the door and the hallway beyond. Extinguishing the soft light, he moved swiftly down the corridor.

He wasn't sure whether he heard the soft exhale of a breath, or the searing whizz of a spell coming at him, but Blaine dropped to the ground right as an Attack spell smashed into the wall next to where his head had been. He swapped the Cloaking spell for a Shield just as a second Attack spell bounced off it. Whoever his opponent was, they were fast.

His eyes adjusted to the light, and he saw a wall of a man.

He wore a loose linen wide-sleeved shirt and wide-pleated trousers. A samurai sword was sheathed at his massive waist. A Disciple of Gaia, Blaine realized with a mental sneer. Well, these magical hippies were an easier enemy than the TCO. He sent an Attack of his own spinning down the hall. The Disciple dodged it with ease.

"You have something that does not belong to you, foreigner," the man said in crisply accented English.

Blaine brought up his broad hands and shrugged. "I guess it's what we do." He fired off another Attack, aimed high. While the Disciple reacted, he sent a second spell to sweep the man's feet, and he fell, hard. Blaine took his chance to flee, running down the hall. A moment before he catapulted himself over the Disciple, Blaine summoned a magical spike that went through the man's thigh, pinning him in place. The Disciple screamed, and Blaine was away.

More Disciples would be coming soon. And more guards. Now that he had the grimoire, Blaine's foremost objective was to get it back to Ruth. The price for making a mistake at this point would be high. He took the stairs two at a time and barreled through the side door of the museum. The cold early-morning air hit him like a wall. He glanced one way, then the other, checking the museum grounds. But he saw nothing unusual, nothing untoward.

Yet. Something waited. He could feel its presence. The chilled air was heavy, and the sounds of the city faded to nothing.

He set off at a dead run, rounding the side of the building and making for the fountain. His partner was waiting for him on a side street nearby; they would portal out together. He picked up the pace.

A spell lifted him off the ground and tossed him like a rag doll. Blaine hit the gray brick pavement shoulder first with a grunt. He rolled over, summoning a Block spell just in time.

Some sort of magical whirling kick spun off his shield. He looked up to see the huge Disciple of Gaia make an inelegant landing. Impressive, considering he still had a spike in his leg.

The Disciple limped toward him, determination written on every line of his face. He drew his sword, and Blaine caught the glitter of magic along its blade. His other hand pressed on the wound at his thigh. Blood soaked his pants.

"You have something that does not belong to you," he said again.

Blaine staggered backward. But this wasn't a reaction to the Disciple.

He'd spotted the thing *behind* him.

Blaine dug into the pocket of his coat. Ruth had given him a new weapon developed for their enemies. The little glass ball seethed with a darkness that rivaled the night. Blaine didn't know what it did, and he didn't care who it hit. He just needed to buy himself some time. He tossed it in the air, then layered both a Wind and Attack spell to send it toward the Japanese Disciple of Gaia.

Then he bolted. The shatter of glass and the burbling cry behind him told him all he needed to know.

He pumped his arms and legs in a panicked fury. He needed to find his partner. If the shadowed creature could be distracted, maybe he could lose it, find the other Kingdom operative, and go home.

He heard a whisper on the air like wings. Though every instinct screamed for him not to look, Blaine turned his head. A choked whimper escaped his throat. His lungs and legs burned, but he spurred himself on. *Faster.* The fear kept him from thinking of anything else. *Faster.*

He was not fast enough. Two claws fastened around his shoulders, and Blaine was swept up into the air.

CHAPTER
TWO

Jayne Thorne stood in the hallway of the TCO headquarters, surveying the wall of polished brass stars that shone down on her. Like the marble wall of stars on the north wall of Langley's lobby, the names of the dead were encased in a vitrine below the stars. Each star corresponded to a magical life lost in service. It was a lot of death—the stars stretched around the wide-open space that acted as a foyer, meeting point, and portal site for going to or returning from nonpermanent locations. Even in the subdued light, the stars glittered almost as brightly as the Torrent itself. *And for what?*

For freedom. Freedom for Adepts to be themselves, neither the masters of nonmagical people, nor hidden from them. And while dying for one's country was noble, it had been the last thing on her mind when she joined the CIA. Of course, a few months ago, that had seemed a much more distant prospect than it did just now. Jayne looked to the end of the marble wall, imagining her name on a star there. Surprisingly, the thought didn't fill her with dread. If she did die, she was doing it to save the people she loved. The people who needed saving.

And if I do, someone had better make sure they don't use my full name, she thought in a flash of annoyance. She would find a way to haunt the TCO forever if she were immortalized as Agnes Jayne Thorne.

Or, I could...live? If they could defeat Odin, the Allfather, could there be peace? Could they find some way to bring down the Kingdom and La Liberté without further unleashing magical destruction on the innocents? Could a woman change the fate bestowed upon her by a multitude of goddesses? Could she wrangle them when she needed their power?

Cheerful voices from down the hall interrupted her reverie, and she tucked the thoughts away for another time. Tristan and Vivienne were back from their coffee date—*taking their good old French time,* she thought wryly—still chatting happily.

Well, Tristan was listening happily. Vivienne was complaining, which she also seemed to enjoy. *She was trapped in a grimoire for years,* Jayne reminded herself. Her Rogue partner had missed out on all the experiences she should have had as a teenager. Instead, she'd been thrust into a life of service to the TCO because she'd bonded as Jayne's Rogue the moment she escaped the curse.

"...but when I want a macchiato, I am not asking for a latte. It's not my fault the girl knows nothing of coffee. It is *her* fault for working in a coffee shop where she knows nothing of coffee. *Beurk.*" This last was directed at Tristan, who had put his arm around Jayne and given her a feather-light kiss on the cheek that sent shivers all down one side.

"Still on the search for the perfect cup of joe?" Jayne said.

Tristan favored her with a lopsided grin that sent shivers down the other side of her body. "We are banned again."

"You're going to get yourself thrown out of every restaurant and cafe in Virginia if you're not careful," Jayne said.

Tristan shrugged. "Vivienne knows what she wants." His smile turned sly, and her heart sped up. "A family trait. You cannot tell me that is a bad thing."

"Yeuch. Time to spar," Vivienne declared, her expression twisting as it always did when she was a little too privy to Jayne's feelings about Tristan. They'd gotten better about putting boundaries down between them; Vivienne was in charge of an emotional barrier that she could erect and dismantle at will. It meant she could keep her distance when things got mushy between Tristan and Jayne but keep a strong enough connection to use her Rogue abilities if they had to spring into action. Vivienne shouldered past both of them, flipping her glossy dark hair behind her head.

"You're the ones who were late," Jayne pointed out as they followed. Tristan's hand trailed down her arm, and they interlaced fingers.

Vivienne flapped a hand. "You Americans. Always obsessed with time."

Tristan leaned in to whisper, "You cannot win." His breath tickled her ear.

Jayne grinned. She disagreed. In fact, she already had won —Tristan's love, Vivienne's friendship, and in this moment, casting one last glance at the marble wall of stars, she couldn't help but think that this victory could make them unstoppable.

The TCO's gym had been modified over the past few weeks as the officer Adepts who trained there accessed more and more power. Magic flowed through the air as it had ages ago, and any Adept genetically predisposed to have magic found themselves with a whole new skill set. A lot of fear, too. And the Adepts who'd already accessed theirs found themselves more powerful than they could have ever imagined.

The room had been magically enlarged, similar to the TCO library, to fit in more equipment and more training devices. The floor pads were softer; the glass and mirrors had Unbreakable spells on them. And to accommodate the Rogues and their innate desire to fly, the ceiling went up another hundred feet. They weren't alone—as the war against Odin progressed and more and more Adepts accessed their magic, decisions had been made as to how to move forward. The TCO's training had hit a fever pitch. There were new Adepts everywhere Jayne looked. Adults who joined up were trained in the TCO gym; the children were sent to her sister, Sofia, and her bonded Rogue, Cillian.

Hector Ortolan had taken over here for the adult training. Jayne sent him a salute in acknowledgment, and in that moment of distraction, an older man with a trim beard managed to launch Hector into the air. There was laughter from that end of the gym, and Jayne caught Hector in midair with an Upright spell. He returned the salute, then faced his recruits, blowing on his whistle.

"Warm up first," Jayne said, heading to a mat and bending over to touch her toes. Vivienne stretched her arms high above her head, then lifted one leg like a ballerina, doing a series of barre moves that made Jayne shake her head in admiration. Vivienne had the graceful movements of a warrior born, but that wasn't such a surprise. She'd been trained by a goddess, after all.

With a fond thought toward Vesta and Freya, and a quizzical one toward Medb, whose silence had become unnerving of late, Jayne gave a punching bag a few rounds until she felt loose and ready.

Facing Vivienne, Jayne squared her shoulders. "Ready?"

"*Oui.*"

"How about we go big? Elephant."

Vivienne changed with ease and trumpeted, loudly, ruffling Tristan's hair with her trunk. Her ears flapped. *Now small?* she suggested.

"Good idea. Mouse," Jayne said. The elephant shrank down, changing color as smooth brown fur spread over her body. She scurried to the edge of the mat. "Now something with feathers. Surprise me."

Color rippled over Vivienne. A moment later, an emerald-and-scarlet parrot flapped over to the punching bag and settled on top. "Now I can converse with Tristan in his own language," she squawked.

Tristan snorted. "What dulcet tones, my sister."

Vivienne replied with something French and impolite.

"Well." He slid off the windowsill where he'd perched himself. "Let's join in the fun, shall we?"

Jayne grinned, backing away from the punching bag. "Get off there," she told Vivienne. "Your claws will puncture it."

Like I care, Vivienne replied, but she took off, soaring up to the top of the room.

Jayne reached for the Torrent, and a moment later, a gleaming brown staff appeared in her hands. Wraith sightings had been increasing over the past couple of weeks, which made it imperative to practice with weapons with both magical and nonmagical components. Tristan countered with a long saber, looking for all the world like an eighteenth-century French courtier. Spells flashed along its edge, some sharpening the blade, some waiting to be released. His smile glinted.

"Ready, *mon amour*?" Tristan said.

"I was born ready," Jayne replied. But before the words finished coming out of her mouth, he was moving. The sword darted forward, but she knocked it aside easily with her staff. She moved back, keeping a good distance between them. "Vivienne, how about a snake? Anaconda, maybe? Something to trip up his fancy footwork?"

"I don't want to get stepped on," Vivienne argued. She had a point. In a real battle, she'd be in danger so close to the ground. Instead, she changed to hawk form, darting at Tristan's head and forcing him to duck and throw up his arms for shelter. A small green circle, the size of an old Viking shield, flashed. Vivienne's claws scraped against it with an unholy *screak*.

"What was *that*?" Jayne said. Most Block spells covered the whole body. At the same time, she took advantage of his distraction to bring the staff between Tristan's feet and sweep out his knees. He hit the mat with a grunt.

"Just a little something I've been working on," he said, scrambling to his feet. He wasn't even out of breath. "A Shield that can bounce spells back in a certain direction. Like a Scottish targe. They're small, protect the arm and hand, and are easier to maneuver than a larger shield."

Without warning, he lunged forward. His sword flashed as it hit her staff. A spell reverberated up the wood, and it went flying from her hand.

Jayne skipped back. Tristan took two quick steps sideways. He was now between her and her staff. "Neat trick," she said. But she had plenty of tricks of her own.

Imagining a javelin, she layered a Knockback spell with a Pierce. It went straight through Tristan's localized Shield and sent him flying across the mat. She ran for her staff, throwing a wider Shield over herself in anticipation of more attacks. "Vivienne, a tiger! I need protection."

The hawk swooped down and changed seamlessly to an enormous tiger, landing on the floor with a feral growl. Tristan backed away, hands up in defeat. When he laughed a moment later, his voice was tinged with nervousness. Jayne could well understand it. The tiger sent a thrill of primal fear through her. Even though her mind knew that Vivienne would never hurt her, her body wasn't quite convinced.

She grabbed the staff and turned just in time to see a jet of water spray over Vivienne. Vivienne backed away, snarling and shaking her head. For a moment, her disgusted expression was so like a regular housecat's that Jayne had to laugh.

Then the water hit her.

The spray was warm, at least. It lifted her off the ground and sent her flying into the padded wall. She hit the floor with a wet thud. Before she could get up, familiar and strong hands closed around her waist. Tristan flipped her over and settled on her lower back, squeezing her gently with his knees. He trapped her wrists. The scent of his magic still clung to him, vanilla and soap and man.

"You layered your spells," Vivienne said in an accusatory tone. She must be in human form now, for Tristan chuckled at that.

Jayne tried to twist around, but his grip was too strong. His thighs tightened in a way she didn't find displeasing in the least. "I thought that was beneath you, Mr. Purist."

"The magic's not so obvious in the training room," he admitted.

"You're better at it than she is," Vivienne observed.

This time, Jayne's struggles were all real. *"What?"*

"More elegant." Vivienne's face appeared right above her. "Your spells are mashed together without any thought for their form. But Tristan's spell forms were...pleasing."

"All spells have different classifications," Tristan said. "I simply put my spells together based on classification, not whatever first springs to mind."

Jayne felt a flash of annoyance tinged with respect. Tristan's greater knowledge of the Torrent had given him an edge, as always. But he'd also taken a leaf from her book. It warmed her that he thought she had something worth emulating.

He bent close to her ear, and she grew warm in an entirely different way. "Now that I have you where I want you, what should I do with you?"

Jayne wriggled, entirely for his benefit. "I think you should let me go, and I'll show you what a real ass-kicking looks like."

His voice deepened to a rumble. "I thought we should get you out of your wet clothes—"

"The two of you make me sick," Vivienne groaned.

Tristan tensed and eased off Jayne. She rolled over with a sigh. *"Boundaries,* Viv."

Vivienne gave her a half-smirk that said she knew exactly what she was doing. "Boundaries go up when we don't have training time. I'm doing this for us." She fluttered her lashes a little. "We started late, you know. We must make use of the time we have."

Jayne pushed down the urge to throttle Vivienne. Was this how Sofia felt about little sisters? "All right." She sat up, regretting what might have been, and peeled her soaked tank away from her skin. "Tell me about the spell classification. Is there a book so I can read up on them?" Maybe if she practiced with that, she could put a few combos together to call up in the fight.

The door to the training room flew open and Ruger's broad form squeezed through.

One look at his face told Jayne that now was not the time for flirtations or even theory lessons. She took Tristan's offered hand and got to her feet.

Ruger was so distracted that he didn't even comment on the water sprayed all over Jayne, Vivienne, and the training room floor. "Crisis time," he said shortly. "Let's go."

Jayne nodded. "Viv and I will get changed and meet you—"

"No time. We're going *now*."

Jayne exchanged an alarmed look with Tristan and Vivienne. "What's going on?"

"I'll tell you on the way," he said.

They went toward the hallway with a series of doors set up as permanent portals to other parts of the world. As they rounded a corner Jayne spotted Amanda, the head of the TCO, looking rattled and even paler than usual. She tried to smooth her red hair when she saw them. Jayne didn't know why; Amanda always looked more put together than she did. "Thorne—well, I suppose there's no time. But the Japanese are very particular about appearances. Try to dry off." She sounded almost accusing.

She turned and started walking again.

"So we're going to Japan?" Jayne asked. That was something, at least. She was trotting after Amanda; for such a short woman, she moved fast when she had somewhere to be.

"To Kyoto," Amanda confirmed. "The Man'yōshū manuscript was stolen this morning."

Jayne's specialization was more in the realm of European artifacts, but she'd heard of the Man'yōshū manuscript. It was a collection of more than forty-five hundred poems, revered as an archive of Japanese history, lore, and culture. "They couldn't possibly have stolen the whole thing," she said.

Amanda nodded. "They only needed a single selection. We've long suspected that the manuscript could be a grimoire, but the Japanese Disciples of Gaia have never let us near it. But this theft makes it almost certain. As is the fact that the Japanese Disciples have reached out to us."

Jayne felt her breath catch. If the Disciples of Gaia were asking for their help, the manuscript must be valuable indeed—and they must be in dire straits.

"So what's the plan?" Tristan said. "Find whoever stole the manuscript and take it back?"

"Yes. And...see if we can negotiate a peek at the grimoire." Amanda stopped at a door and turned, glancing at Jayne's forehead. "I have the feeling our Master here could acquire herself another totem if we play our cards right. Though we'd need a goddess to bestow it, and who knows if this is a portal to another one or not."

Jayne felt her totems warm, her forehead tingling in response. Another goddess, another totem...if that grimoire contained a powerful dead Master's spirit, then what were the odds the Kingdom had accessed it? Was the totem already on its way back to Ruth, making the monster more powerful?

And this particular manuscript...who could the Master be? She wasn't familiar with many Japanese goddesses. Research.

She needed to do research. Her fingers itched to flip through the pages of a library book and figure it out.

"So what if we find the grimoire, activate it, and *then* give back the manuscript?" she suggested.

Amanda closed her eyes and took a deep breath. Jayne could almost hear her thinking *Goddess, give me strength.* "You are not to try activating the grimoire. You are not to cause an international incident. If we can prove ourselves trustworthy to the Disciples of Gaia, we can lay the groundwork for more teamwork. And we need that." She opened her eyes and fixed Jayne with a look that made her insides shrivel. "Our ranks are still too small to take on the Kingdom directly. And don't think for a minute they aren't bringing in their own recruits, just as we are. They have children, too."

Amanda turned her glare on Tristan, then Vivienne. Jayne felt them shrink back beside her. "I'm counting on you two to keep our girl in line. Ruger will liaise with our Disciple contact."

She looked like she wanted to say more but instead nodded stiffly and opened the portal door.

"Good luck, Jayne."

"May the Force be with us," she replied, squeezing Tristan's hand and stepping through.

No one laughed.

CHAPTER
THREE

Sofia Thorne sometimes rued the day she offered to create a magical school for the TCO. Not that she didn't like the kids, quite the opposite. She felt quite warmly toward them. Nor was it the fact that she was teaching them magic; that part she actually loved. It was more the fact that they were in a Time Catch created specifically for the purpose, and that meant anything went. They were limited by only the power of their magic and their imaginations—and the kids had plenty of imagination. She'd been running ragged getting them ready for this afternoon's war games, trying to keep them contained, from the usual magical spats between new Rogues and new Adepts to the overdeveloped egos of the kids for whom this magic came naturally. Not to mention grading them on their efforts.

"Remember to watch your flank," Sofia said into her earpiece. On the field below the cliff, two students exchanged a few hand signals. One turned to keep watch as the rest of the team made their way across the field.

The field was surrounded by a dense wood. Somewhere inside it were Cillian's forces, students led by Sofia's half-brother, Matthew. Beyond the woods were waterfalls, more cliffs, mountains, snowscapes, and glittering cities filled with images of people. Anything Sofia, Cillian, and Seo-Joon could think of that the kids might encounter was stuffed into the Time Catch. *Well, almost anything,* Sofia thought, shivering when she recalled the Wraith that her mother had become. But that memory felt like something she had encountered a lifetime ago.

In many ways, it was. Sofia's hair was now threaded with a few strands of silver. A few days ago, she and Cillian had stepped out of the Time Catch to celebrate their fifth anniversary, by their own reckoning. The endless nature of a Time Catch could be dangerous, but a strict routine helped. A castle worthy of being called Hogwarts (Cillian and Seo-Joon had told her no) housed the students and gave them warm beds each night and breakfast at the same time every morning. They sparred and took classes on theory, tactics, defense, and civilian aid. It was a magical West Point, and they took the responsibility seriously. Fun and big personalities and magic aside, the TCO has them training the kids for war.

Today was their first big test. For the inaugural graduating class, for the teachers in charge, for the entire concept. They hadn't even gotten an approved name for the school yet, though she had one in mind. It was all moving so fast.

She spotted a flash of gold magic from among the trees but held her tongue. Rebecca needed to see it—Rebecca, Amanda's daughter and the leader of Sofia's team. Sofia had left a lot of the planning up to her, in fact. Previous skirmishes had shown that she and Cillian could see too much of each other's plans—their Rogue-Master connection was beautiful in many ways, but not when playing the sort of multidimensional chess match that made up a mock battle. Sofia touched the blue handkerchief tied around her wrist. Her students had been briefed on the terrain and would communicate amongst themselves. She was watching, but she wouldn't interfere. They were on their own.

Rebecca bent her head toward a couple of the other kids on her team, and they broke off to investigate. Rebecca herself kept moving toward the prize. The prize in question was a flag—a big red flag on the other side of the field, through a patch of forest, and in the middle of a lake. Cillian sat with that flag, while the blue flag waved next to Sofia. If one of Cillian's team members got to the top of the cliff, her job was to hand over the flag and call the game.

Another flash of gold in the forest, and Rebecca sent two more. Then a flash of green. Sofia's jaw tightened when she realized what Cillian was doing. It was up to Rebecca and the team to use their tactical lessons and leadership skills to figure out the problem and respond adequately. Nevertheless, it was difficult to watch as Rebecca thinned her forces dangerously in the pursuit of picking off lone magical actors. She made a mental note to discuss the move later.

Something in the forest roared, and the fight was on. Cillian's forces burst from between the trees and set upon the blue team. Sofia bit her lip, hard, when one of her girls went down. The magic here was dampened, softened, and their attacks couldn't really hurt each other. Rogues had a restricted range of forms they could take, and anyone who summoned weapons from the Torrent could only summon wood and could never attack the head.

A tight knot of students formed around Rebecca, protecting her. She had drawn her arms together in great concentration, and threads of golden light were spreading between her hands. At her shout, the entire blue team dove for the ground—and a spell like a shock wave flew out from her hands. It sent the red team tumbling to the grass. In the back of her mind, Sofia could feel Cillian's surprise and dismay—and his pride. Rebecca had power, and she knew how to use it.

Rebecca turned and took off at a run with her splinter team. The rest of the blue team would take care of the hostiles here, preventing any of them from running back to help with the defense of their flag. Sofia watched one of the red team make a valiant effort, turning into an enormous python and slithering toward the cliff. A few moments later, a shimmering gold net settled over it, hooking into the rocks with magical grapples and digging in deeper. The python thrashed, trapped.

Matthew pulled two short wooden sticks from the Torrent, layering them with spells—one side for Block, one for Attack. It was elegant, Sofia noted. He had good form and even better instincts. He faced off against Eduardo, a promising young Adept who preferred to keep his distance from Matthew's staves and Sling spells. Eduardo dodged easily, too, diving like a gymnast rather than summoning powerful Blocks when he wanted to avoid an attack.

Sofia peeked into Cillian's mind to check on Rebecca's progress. She had to wonder if Rebecca had suspected Matthew's strategy or had known of it before the battle. She'd lured Matthew into a perfect false sense of security, making him believe that he was separating out her group when he was really enabling her to reveal a showstopping move.

The showstopper had taken a lot of effort, though, Sofia could see. From Cillian's standpoint, Rebecca was pale and sweaty. Her three teammates—Rufus, Laura, and Medina—were doing most of the heavy work. *The tanks of the operation,* she thought with a small smile, remembering Jayne's short-lived obsession with *World of Warcraft*. They had power in them, though they struggled with the precision of hand-to-hand combat or picking a target in a skirmish. It made them perfect for this sort of advanced teamwork. Medina brought a boulder tumbling down from a nearby slope to splash into the lake, creating a tidal wave that soaked Cillian and distracted his defense team. While they were scrambling, Rufus summoned a Knockback spell that sent two of them flying into the water.

There was just one red team member left. Her name was Zia. She was a fierce brown girl who had proved reluctant to give in, even when she was beaten, and right now, she scowled at the blue team.

"Come on, Zia," Rebecca called. "It's obvious we've won."

Zia's lips pursed. She brought her hands together. Rufus and Medina pulled in front of Rebecca.

But the spell didn't fly toward the group of students. At the last moment, Zia turned and flung it straight at the flag in the middle of the lake.

Cillian dove to the side to avoid being hit. A waterspout sprang up from the middle of the lake, enveloping the flag. The spout writhed and wriggled like some living thing, then took off over the lake and onto dry land, the flag carried up with it.

Sofia burst out laughing. Zia was a genius when it came to movements on the field. Her focus and tenacity would make her an excellent operative.

The battle was nearly finished: most of the red team had been caught off guard by Rebecca's blast and had been quickly subdued. Matthew was surrounded by five combatants; he looked around and threw up his hands in resignation. Cillian's voice came in over the instructor's channel.

"Call it." He sounded amused.

"Your flag's still running away," Seo-Joon pointed out from the control room of the castle. He was clearly amused, too. He could barely keep a chuckle out of his voice.

"Zia," Cillian called and cut the line.

A few moments later Seo-Joon's magically amplified voice boomed out over the training area. "Victory goes to the blue!"

Sofia's team cheered. She pumped her fist from the top of the cliff for all of them to see. They'd acted near-perfectly today. Rebecca's plan had been smart and utilized the gifts they had, and their combat prowess was better than some of the field officers of the TCO—though they'd had the equivalent of five years of training.

With the battle officially over, the students helped each other to their feet and headed off the field, whooping and chatting. Matthew waited until Rebecca had trudged back, soaked and muddy but triumphantly carrying the red flag. He started talking to her the moment she was within earshot, and they walked back toward the castle together, deep in conversation.

"I need a pint," Cillian grumped. "And a towel. I'm soaked. Zia's...enthusiastic."

Sofia laughed. "She never does anything halfway. Come on, we'll bring you in for a cup of tea."

"Only if you put some Jameson in it."

The skirmish students got cake, tea, and cocoa in a rec room designed to help them come down from the fight and be friends again. Sofia, Cillian, and Seo-Joon sat in their library office, a comfortable place with couches and squashy chairs, with some of the more advanced magical theory books in a bookcase behind them, sipping their own beverages of choice. Sofia had taken to calling it the headmaster's office since Seo-Joon was in here most of the time to help students and do research. It was, perhaps, her favorite place in the whole world, with access to everything she wanted: tea, books, and her students. The only thing missing was her sister.

A steaming teapot and a bakery box greeted her when she came in. "You didn't," she gasped. Inside was a perfect peach pie from her favorite Nashville bakery. Seo-Joon smiled and cut an extra-thick slice, which he offered it to her. "There's ice cream in the mini fridge," he said. The mini fridge was hidden under his desk.

"On it," Cillian said.

Sofia narrowed her eyes. Ice cream? The best pie? "What's going on? Are you gearing up to tell me bad news?"

But Seo-Joon just laughed. He laughed a lot these days; it was one of the things she liked about him. And he was good with the kids. He knew how to talk to them about things like girl troubles or if they'd been caught smoking. Sofia was best with the smaller ones, the ones who still thought they needed a mother. "We're celebrating," he said. "That fight went great. I'm going to tell Amanda that we have some potential officers."

Sofia stopped with a bite of pie halfway to her mouth. "Officers?" she repeated blankly.

Cillian's hand landed softly on her thigh, warm and reassuring.

Seo-Joon hadn't noticed her pause. "I don't think Matthew and Rebecca can learn any more in simulated circumstances. And they've both aced their theory exams. Zia's less on theory, but she's incredible in combat. And most importantly, they like each other. We have a tight-knit group of kids here. They know each other's strengths and weaknesses and can protect each other in the field." Seo-Joon lifted his cup in a toast to her. "Good work, Sofia. We have the TCO's first graduating class."

Sofia's pie was still hanging in the air. A warm glob of sugary peach fell off her fork and hit her plate with a *plop*. She stared. Cillian leaned forward for her, gently knocking Seo-Joon's cup with his. "Thanks, mate. I think she just needs a minute to take it all in."

The first graduating class. The cumulation of everything she'd worked for.

Her magic school was working. These kids could go out into the world knowing how to protect themselves, and knowing they weren't alone.

But if her magic school was working...did that mean Matthew and Rebecca and the others would be sent out into danger? Into *battle*?

The world is full of dangers, she told herself and took a bite of pie. It tasted like ashes and mud and worry.

CHAPTER
FOUR

Kyoto was humid and cold with a light spring drizzle and a wind blowing in off the sea. Jayne shivered. Great. She was wet, she was cold, and she had no coat. This had better be a quick mission.

Tristan, Vivienne, and Ruger stepped out of the safe house behind her. They'd portaled in to a dusty two-room apartment with almost no furnishings. Evidently the TCO didn't need to use this safe house often. Ruger had checked the windows and door before ushering them out into the street and taking the lead, walking confidently and ignoring the stares that passersby sent his way. The sight of a towering Black man striding down the street was enough to make the bedraggled white people behind him a lesser oddity. All the same, Jayne found herself wishing for a Cloaking spell.

She got her wish a few blocks away from the Kyoto National Museum. Suddenly, no one was looking at them anymore; people stepped neatly out of their way as they headed down the pavement, without really knowing why they were moving. Ruger led them to a small teahouse on a corner, paused, then ducked inside.

It was clear who the Disciple of Gaia was. He was the only man Jayne had seen so far *not* dressed in a suit. Instead, he wore a loose-sleeved shirt and *hakama* pants. But it was the long-handled sword, the *nagamaki*, that really gave it away.

Also, he was looking right at them, clearly watching for their arrival.

He stood as they approached and bent forward in a slight bow. His eyes were full of suspicion. "Thank you for coming," he said. "I am Akio."

"Anything to help our allies. What's happening?" Ruger said.

"You may as well see for yourself." The Disciple made his way around the table and took the lead with a scowl. He might say the right things, but he made no pretense: he didn't like it that the TCO was here.

He led them out of the teashop and toward the museum, ducking under a familiar yellow-and-black tape. Jayne grimaced. Normally, Adepts and their fights didn't attract the attention of the nonmagical world, even the police. If the Japanese cops were here...

"A guard was found dead this morning, partially eaten," the Disciple explained. "And neighbors reported seeing a *tengu* flying above the museum."

Vivienne and Tristan looked at Jayne in confusion. She shrugged. "What makes you think I know what a *tengu* is?"

"Because you've never met a book you didn't want to make love to," Vivienne grumbled.

Jayne laughed. Her Rogue had a point. "All right. *Tengu* are Japanese demons. They're associated with protecting mountains and forests, but they were once considered harbingers of war."

"Wraiths," Tristan said softly, running his hand along the soft beard lining his jaw. "Harbingers of war. They're not wrong."

Jayne's mirth gave way to a dread that deepened in the pit of her stomach. She hurried after Ruger and the Disciple.

The museum was a long building of red brick and white stone, surrounded by a tidy garden. A portico with three arches proclaimed the front entrance to the museum, but no one was getting near there. A fountain sat at the front of a long walk that led up to the entrance, and in front of the fountain stood the police and their police tape. Tourists and locals alike were turned back with a firm politeness. "The museum is closed," an officer told a disappointed couple.

They all ignored the figure lying prone right in front of the fountain.

Jayne's feet picked up speed. She recognized the man and groaned aloud. *Blaine.* The Kingdom operative was dangerous, malicious, and cruel. No one was bothering to help him.

His shirt was shredded and soaked with blood. Jayne counted at least four long slashes that had parted his skin from cheek to abdomen. His chest moved up and down with shallow, quick breaths. His eyes darted from side to side. He was struggling to see her, she realized. He was dying, and she had a hard time feeling bad about it.

She knelt next to him and gingerly lifted a long shred of shirt. These wounds were deep. How much blood had he already lost?

"Come...to finish the job?" he rasped, coughing blood.

She recoiled. "Of course not. I'm not like you."

Ruger opened a bag, pulling out a length of cloth. "Apply pressure," he said, handing the cloth to Jayne.

She did, knowing it was fruitless. "This isn't what he needs."

"Jayne," Tristan warned.

She ignored him. "He might have valuable information. Whatever attacked him—"

"Could still be here. So it's our job to find the Man'yōshū

manuscript and get out. Remember?" Ruger said. He put a hand on her shoulder. "You can't save them all, Jayne."

Tristan knelt on Blaine's other side and gave her a significant look. She knew what he was thinking. Of all the people to spend power on and risk herself, was Blaine really worth saving?

But that was the problem. Once you started sorting people into who was worth saving and who should be allowed to die, you began a very dangerous descent.

"Don't bother," Blaine said. His eyes were drooping. "It will ...end things..."

"What does he mean by that?" Vivienne asked.

Her question was answered a moment later. Sudden screams split the quiet air around the museum. The air filled with a sick burning, rotting stink. The nearest policeman looked up, pointing, mouth agape. *"Tengu,"* he yelled.

Jayne followed the direction of his gaze, then threw herself against Ruger, knocking both of them out of the way. Gray, scaly claws the size of her head scraped against the gray brick pavement, and Blaine screamed. He was lifted off the ground, then dropped, hard, knocking Jayne to the ground. Dazed, she lay on her back and watched the Wraith flap up, ungainly.

"Merde," Tristan gasped, staggering to his feet. He hadn't been so lucky: a long slash ran down the length of his arm. Blood spattered on the pavement.

"Tristan!" Jayne leapt up.

He put out a hand, smiling, though his eyes were full of pain. "It is all right, Jayne. Focus on finding the manuscript." He took a deep breath and reached out, and a moment later a sword appeared in his hand, dripping with magic and his soap-and-vanilla scent. "It was my wrong arm, anyway."

Her heart hammered against her ribs, making it hard to think. *No one hurts Tristan,* she thought with a sudden fury. Her body longed for action, to kick some Wraith ass. So the faster she found the manuscript—

She spotted a leather satchel lying next to Blaine. He must have brought that to smuggle out the manuscript. She scrambled around his legs, ducking as the Wraith dove for them again. Vivienne changed into a sleek panther and leapt. *We'll lead it away from you,* she said.

Jayne nodded in a sharp jerk of acknowledgment. Ruger stood over her and planted his feet, drawing two knives from the Torrent.

She tore open the satchel. But there wasn't much inside: just a couple of marbles and a weird-looking gun.

If she'd gone after the manuscript, she would have fashioned a Carry spell to hold it in. But Carry spells took a lot of energy, and Blaine was dying. Would he be able to hold on to it?

"Where is it?" she hissed at Blaine. "Did you hide it?"

"The future has wings," Blaine whispered. His eyes were somewhere far away. He was going fast.

Ruger shouted and twisted to the side. Jayne looked up in time to see his knife plunge into the thigh of the Wraith. "Holy —" she shouted. "I thought you were drawing it away!"

"It won't go." Vivienne sounded panicked. "There's something—"

She was interrupted by a deafening crack. Jayne instinctively hunkered close to the ground, hands over her ears. Her eyes squeezed shut of their own accord. The Wraith screamed in rage and pain. When she opened them again, she saw a bullet casing lying on the ground. Off to the side, a police officer had his gun out and trained on the Wraith.

The Wraith shrieked. The policeman's panicked eyes grew wide. He dropped the gun and ran. The Wraith flew after him, gaping maw opening to let out another hideous screech, and within its mouth, Jayne spotted the glint of razor-sharp teeth.

The Wraith was pulled up short. Like it was on a leash. Its wings beat uselessly against the air. Why could it go no further?

"Look."

Jayne looked over to Tristan. He held up his bleeding arm. He was pale, swaying slightly on his feet. And from the bottom of his elbow a long strand of green magic, thin as spider silk, stretched away from him.

It led to the Wraith.

Jayne's heart froze. She spun to Ruger. "We have to go. Now."

"Jayne, the manuscript," he warned.

"Is the manuscript worth the life of two people?" Jayne snapped. She looked back at Blaine. His breathing was even shallower. He wouldn't make it—not unless they portaled him to the TCO hospital or she tried healing him herself.

And if she healed him, she might leave Tristan vulnerable...

Jayne squinted. Now that she was looking for it, she could spot the green glimmer of a magical thread, leading from his chest. It wavered in the air, disappearing and reappearing in the gloomy Kyoto light. She thought she saw it, or something like it, wrapped around the Wraith's claw.

Blaine was bound to the Wraith somehow. And now that Tristan had been attacked, he was bound, too.

Blaine didn't have the manuscript, which meant he'd either hidden it or given it to another Kingdom operative. "What are the odds he's got it in a Carry spell? We take him home, save him, get him to give up the book." Hell, they could even bring their new best friend. "Maybe portaling could sever the connection."

"Or maybe it could bring the Wraith with us," Ruger countered.

"Or maybe, if we stand here deliberating all day, both Tristan and Blaine will *die*." Jayne's voice rose in panic. She clenched her fist.

Ruger's eyes ran over Blaine, assessing the situation. He had dipped his chin in the beginnings of a nod when Vivienne said, in a strangled voice, "It's not in a Carry spell."

Jayne whipped around to look at her. Ruger looked confused, then followed her gaze. The panther's ears were flat, her tail down. "The Wraith. Look what it's holding."

Jayne had been so worried about the claws on the Wraith's feet that she hadn't paid much attention to its arms. But now that Vivienne had said it, she spotted the wide rectangle of glass, carefully sealed with archivist's tape, holding fragile paper and ink within.

That can't be good for the manuscript, she thought.

"Vivienne. Hawk!" The panther was gone in a flurry of feathers, and Vivienne darted beneath the Wraith's massive wing. Jayne reached into the Torrent and pulled out her staff. It was time to make short work of this Wraith so they could go home.

Forgive me, books. She layered a Knife spell over the end of her staff and leaped into the fray. The staff jabbed the Wraith on its inner thigh, causing it to growl. It swiped at her, knocking her staff away—but at least it was distracted from Vivienne. Jayne dove for her staff. *Keep your eyes on me,* she thought. Tristan and Ruger moved in to flank her. Tristan managed to hold his sword steady, even if his steps were slow.

"Now, Viv," Jayne shouted, and the three humans surged forward together. Tristan swiped his sword at the soft underbelly of the Wraith, while Jayne jabbed up in the direction of its abdomen. Ruger stuck a knife through the thin muscle at its wing, pulling down to create a long tear.

The Wraith screamed in agony. Its grip on the manuscript loosened for an instant—and an instant was all Vivienne needed. Her claws clamped to either side of the glass rectangle and she beat her wings frantically, trying to gain altitude.

The Wraith snarled as it spun for her. Jayne slammed the

staff against its claws as it tried to swipe at Vivienne. The Wraith spun back in the air, screaming. Spittle flecked over Jayne's face.

We're not thinking about that. We're not thinking about that. She stumbled back. "Portal time, Ruge?"

"Keep it off us, Agnes," Ruger replied.

Even in battle, he managed to annoy by using her hated first name.

Tristan lunged forward, and the sword pierced high on the Wraith's thigh. He pulled it out and a gout of black tar-like blood spouted out of the wound. He'd hit an artery. The Wraith became more desperate, but it was as though the creature couldn't decide what it wanted most—at first it tried to flap up, after Vivienne; then it swiped at Tristan and Jayne. Jayne swung her staff to give it a heavy *thwack* on the side of its head.

The Wraith's head lolled. Its ruined wing couldn't keep straight, either. It fluttered low to the ground, claws scraping the pavement. The Japanese Disciple moved in and swung his *nagamaki* sword. It sliced cleanly through the Wraith's neck. The creature crashed to the ground, cracking the brick under its enormous form.

"Let's go," said Ruger. "Tristan first. Jayne, you and Akio get Blaine. We'll send someone for the body."

Tristan stumbled past Jayne toward the portal. She resisted the urge to reach out to him—he didn't need the distraction—but sent him a smile then hurried over to Blaine, heaving him by the shoulders as Akio sheathed his sword and came to grab Blaine's feet. "Are we sure we should move him like this?" she said.

"You are the one who wanted to take action immediately. Can we wait for a stretcher?" Akio said.

Probably not. Jayne grimaced, trying to heave Blaine's motionless form. His eyes had gone glassy, and the dread in her stomach deepened.

As they awkwardly hurried toward the portal, Jayne's eye caught on a policeman near the line. He was staring right at them. He must be an Adept. "Akio," she said softly, jerking her head. His eyes darted to the man. "One of yours?"

Akio shook his head. "Must be new. But we will take him in." Then he was backing into the portal and disappearing from view.

"You're going to be all right," Jayne said, in theory to Blaine, but mostly because Tristan wasn't there.

She'd expected Blaine to be too far gone to reply. But he chuckled, a sound like a rusted door closing. "No one's all right."

CHAPTER
FIVE

Utter confusion greeted them on the other side. Two medics rushed forward with a stretcher as soon as Jayne was through the portal. Her shoulders sagged with relief when she let her burden drop onto the stretcher, and he was hustled away. Blaine was a big man.

He'd also lost a lot of blood. She could have helped him. And she wondered again...if he died, how guilty would she feel?

"He chose his side, and he went into battle willingly," said Ruger softly from beside her. Jayne swallowed a sudden lump in her throat.

He looked like he wanted to say more, but Akio touched his arm. "I would speak with you," he said.

Jayne felt Vivienne's presence next to her. She was back in human form, and she still held the grimoire. She also looked more like a little girl than Jayne had ever seen her before. Pale, wide-eyed, watching the hall down to the hospital as though her entire life was at the end of it and on the verge of falling apart.

"Tristan is hurt," Vivienne said.

Jayne took her hand. "Let's go," she said.

They headed down the hall together and through a pair of double doors. On the other side of it, the look of the TCO changed completely: they were no longer in an office but in a hospital waiting room. Adepts and nonmagical nurses and doctors scurried around in scrubs. Jayne spotted Blaine being taken through a door. Tristan must be down that hall, too.

Jayne set off with purpose. But when she reached the door, an Adept in blue scrubs she'd never seen before in stepped smartly in front of her. "I'm sorry, ma'am. You can't go that way."

The door opened and Tamara stuck her head out. Her dark hair was covered in a medical cap and she was also wearing scrubs. "It's all right, Donesh. Jayne, Vivienne, this way."

Jayne tried to spare her a grateful smile, but what came out felt cracked and wrong. Tamara didn't seem to care, though. She strode down the hall ahead of them, all business. "You are a doctor? You have experience in magical wounds?" Vivienne asked, clearly worried.

"Field medic in the army before I accidentally worked some magic. My old commander had had run-ins with the TCO before, so he knew where to send me," Tamara called over her shoulder.

Field medic. At least she had triage knowledge. "What's the prognosis?" Jayne said.

"Physically? Tristan should be fine. It was a shock to his system, but the wound was not deep. He'll need to rest up and get some extra fluids, but nothing scary. The other guy? That's anyone's guess. Are either of you injured?"

Vivienne shook her head. "No," Jayne said for both of them.

She'd expected Tamara to take them to Tristan, but instead they were led into a smaller examination room with a couple of chairs, a bed, and a table with a computer. "Take a seat," Tamara said.

"We were hoping—" Jayne began.

THE BOOK OF SPIRITS

Tamara shut the door and smiled at them in understanding. "I know what you were hoping," she said softly. "You can see him when he's done getting stitched up. But for now, I'll need to examine you. Tell me about the fight."

Jayne and Vivienne exchanged glances. This wasn't part of the usual debriefing process. They got hurt all the time and were basically told to walk it off. Shouldn't Jayne be telling Amanda what had happened? Or, more likely, shouldn't Ruger be telling Amanda? Still, they did their best, and from both Vivienne and Jayne's perspective, Jayne figured they'd covered all the angles. While they talked, Tamara examined their throats, eyes, and ears, and listened to their hearts and lungs.

"Did the Wraith use any sort of magic?" Tamara asked. "Pull down the front of your shirt, please, just over the chest."

Jayne frowned and did as Tamara asked. Wraiths never used magic. Next to her, Vivienne said, "No. Just its claws."

"Did the Kingdom operative use some kind of magic?" Tamara asked. "Back of the shirt now, please. Lift up."

"By the time we got there, I don't think he could have summoned the simplest light," Jayne said. She was shivering, she realized, pulling up her tank top. It was soaked in blood.

"Why?" Vivienne asked.

Tamara's lips tightened. For a moment Jayne thought she'd keep them in the dark, but she sighed. "There's some sort of magical binding. It's holding Blaine and Tristan together, and Tristan said it held the Wraith, too."

Jayne nodded. "That was the line of power we told you about."

"We'll have to test it. And we'll have to test you for it. It..." Tamara bit her lip and looked at Vivienne. "It could be worse than a simple bind."

"But we weren't hit," Vivienne said.

"We need to make sure the binding is only transferred through physical injury."

They sat in the room for the better part of an hour as Tamara tested them, both magically and physically, noting everything down in meticulous strokes on the keyboard. Jayne had to strip and examine herself for any sign of a magical thread, give up a tiny drop of blood, and do half a dozen mundane spells before Tamara said, frowning, "I *think* we can let you go."

Then it was Vivienne's turn. She also had to test her Rogue abilities, and in her hawk form, Tamara insisted on examining her claws for any sign of damage the Wraith might have done to her.

Something beeped at Tamara's waist. She checked her phone and scrubbed her face with a hand. "I'd better go. Tristan's out of the operating room. And no, you can't come. I'm sorry. But you can be discharged."

"Blaine was saying that no one's all right," Jayne began as Tamara opened the exam room door.

"Dying men say a lot of strange things," Tamara replied. "Don't put too much meaning in it."

She led them back to the waiting room and left them at the door. "I'll keep you updated," she promised. "But for now, you've got a boss to see. Once you're finished there, call me. If I pick up, you can come back."

As Tamara walked away, Jayne felt as though part of her heart was getting farther and farther away, too. Her last sight of Tristan had been of a pale and sweating man. What magic might be ravaging his body now? Damn it, she couldn't lose him. Not when she'd just found him.

She heard a soft snuffle beside her and cursed herself for a fool. Their connection would make Vivienne sensitive to this sort of thing. She stared down the hall, twisting a lock of dark hair in her fingers. Her face was drawn and pale, and tears shimmered in her bottom lashes.

"We'll see him soon. I promise," Jayne said. She took Vivienne's hand again and gently led her back through the doors.

∼

AMANDA NEWPORT WAITED FOR THEM. She was pacing back and forth, pale with anger, red hair escaping from its tidy bun. Next to her stood Ruger, looking slightly guilty.

"There you are. *There* it is." She strode forward and seized the grimoire from Vivienne. "What were you thinking, running off with it?"

They hadn't been thinking. Jayne looked at the ground. But her fearsome Rogue lifted her chin. "I was thinking that my brother is in mortal peril. My brother, whose life should be safeguarded by *you*. Do you dare to tell me that I should not have followed him here?"

Amanda swelled. She looked like she very much did dare. But then she seemed to see Vivienne, to remember that she was a seventeen-year-old girl, and she deflated somewhat. "There are some things we have to do, even if we think we need to do something else with every fiber of our being. Tristan risked his life for that grimoire. We can't afford for it to get lost in the scramble. And more than anything, we need to access it."

"Did we get permission?" Jayne asked, excitement flaring through her.

"Come." Amanda led them to a small meeting room off the side of the waiting room, where a gray table sat with ample blue chairs for them. She shut the door. "Akio has agreed to look the other way in exchange for our help. He seems like he'd like any excuse to change his mind, though, so we need to act quickly." She cast Jayne a significant look.

By quickly, she evidently meant *right now*. Jayne swallowed. Vivienne laid the glass plate down on the table, and they all crowded around to get a good look.

Jayne was no expert on Japanese calligraphy, but this was done by an elegant hand, with lines that swooped and swirled almost joyfully across the page. Whoever had written this leaf had taken his time and enjoyed his craft. It was simple and unadorned by gilt or paint or drawing. Jayne took a deep breath. *Ready?* she asked the other totems silently. She hadn't really expected them to answer. Nevertheless, she felt a prickling of anticipation. She set her hand on the glass and opened herself up to the grimoire.

She breathed deep. She reached down.

And she hit...a door.

At least, it felt like a door. It was a way into the grimoire, she was certain. It felt like a space she ought to slip through, like a cat who knows he belongs everywhere. But the magical door would not open at her touch. She called on her totems and the other goddesses. *A little help here? Medb? Vesta? Freya?*

More silence. They could be maddening sometimes.

She pushed, but it was like trying to open a safe vault with her bare hands. And from behind the door, she got a strange, tickling sensation. Like amusement, like feeling the way a tinkle of laughter sounded. A scent drifted to her, of water lilies and salt.

There was definitely something within this grimoire. And it was holding her at arm's length—deliberately and with amusement. She pulled back and shook her head.

"Don't tell me it's the wrong one." Amanda's brows came together in a scowl.

"It's one of more than four thousand pages...but I think it's right. But it's as though the Master within the grimoire wants me to—beg, or something. Prove myself."

Amanda stared at her, baffled. "What?"

"If you must beg, you must beg," Vivienne said with a shrug. "Do not let pride get in the way of this. Tristan's life could be at stake."

"It's not as simple as saying 'pretty please,'" said Jayne, frustrated. As though Vivienne would ever beg for anything.

"Then what is it?" Amanda said. She raised a brow and fixed Jayne with a look that demanded answers.

But Jayne had none to give. She put her face in her hands. Maybe she was too tired, or too worried about Tristan, or too worked up from the fight...and she couldn't suggest any of these things, because Amanda would call them excuses, and she'd be right. "All I know is that it's waiting for something. Maybe I need a special power or spell. Maybe I just need to prove that I'm worthy. I haven't even figured out who might be contained inside. I need more time."

Amanda looked like she was going to object. But Ruger touched her arm and shook his head, and she heaved a sigh. "I suppose we can always talk to the resident techies about it. And Ruger, see if you can get any more information from Akio about it."

"I'll try. But I'm afraid he'll try to take the manuscript back with him to Kyoto when he goes, and our failure will just be more fuel for that fire."

"Can the Japanese Disciples handle more problems right now? Especially if the Wraiths are after the Man'yōshū?" Amanda pointed out.

The big man shrugged, looking at his hands. "The real problem is that people aren't logical like that. The manuscript fragment belongs in Japan, and they want it in Japan. Even if the risk of another theft is high."

"So that's how we convince them to let us keep it," Jayne said, tapping the edge of the manuscript. "It's safe here, hidden, until they can get rid of their Wraith problem." She looked at Ruger.

Ruger bobbed his head, considering. "Maybe. I can sell that. The Wraith problem, as you put it, is bad, very bad, in Japan. Wraiths have been spotted throughout Tokyo, more than we've seen in any of our operations before. It looks like a spreading plague. The current theory is that latent Adepts whose powers have awoken don't know how to control their powers. Anyone with the potential to be a Master also has the potential to be a Wraith. Which means that anyone with power should take extra care. The untrained can easily burn out." He raised an eyebrow at Jayne significantly. She tucked her arms behind her back, fingering the edge of the leathery patch of skin she'd hidden beneath her sleeve. Her Wraith patch hadn't spread at all in the past few weeks. She had a handle on her power.

Her phone buzzed. A text had come in from Tamara. *He's asking for you. You can come on back WITH CAUTION.*

Jayne showed the message to Vivienne and they stood up together. "This meeting's not over," said Amanda, nostrils flaring.

"Tristan's awake," said Jayne, putting a hint of steel in her voice and in her gaze. But it turned out she didn't need to get into a battle of wills with Amanda. The director stood, too, and they filed out of the meeting room together.

Jayne had hardly gone three steps when she heard a shriek, and something barreled into her from the side. "Oof," she grunted, staggering back and spitting out a mouthful of blonde hair. Sofia's arms crushed her in a rib-creaking hug.

"I just came out to visit Quimby, and then they said you were in the hospital—"

"It's all right." Jayne made a sound somewhere between a laugh and a sob. She rubbed Sofia's back, trying to calm her sister down. "I'm fine."

Sofia drew back. Her blue eyes shone with worry. "I hate being out of the loop. What did you do to yourself?"

She sounded so fierce and motherly that Jayne had to laugh again. Her sister had dozens of surrogate children now, but Jayne suspected she would always be the one Sofia mothered the most. "I'm fine," she repeated. "Clean bill of health from Tamara."

"But my brother is not. We must go," Vivienne declared, and strode off with a flip of the hair.

"Age doesn't mellow her, does it?" Sofia asked in a low voice as they followed the procession down the hospital hallway.

Jayne had to laugh again. "What age? No one here is older but you, sis."

It was weird to think that her sister and Cillian were living in a Time Catch. To stabilize it, to make sure the school was as safe as they could make it, the TCO had worked with her dad, Henry Thorne, to manage a nifty bit of magic that allowed them to stay for extended periods of time. Like, years. It was important for the children to grow up, to be educated in battle and magic, and to emerge from the Time Catch as warriors, not kids. But that also meant Sofia and Cillian were aging, too, and when they came back to the real world, it showed. She could see it in the light wrinkles around Sofia's eyes, in the assured way she moved. When Cillian was with her, she saw it in their relationship, too—they were out of the honeymoon phase, settled comfortably into a life of companionship together. It was nice, seeing Sophia like that. But it also made Jayne ache—for the years she was missing at her sister's side, and for the same comfort with Tristan. That time would come, she tried to assure herself. Tristan was going to be fine.

Tristan and Blaine had been put at the end of a large room, alone but for the honor guard of Adept doctors and nurses. Blaine's bed was surrounded by curtains to give him privacy, but Tristan was sitting up in his bed, sipping from a cup of water. He met Jayne's eyes and smiled. His arm had a long, red line punctuated with black surgical thread. He was still pale, too pale. And the hand that held his water glass trembled. A deep dread seemed to root her to the spot.

Vivienne was arguing with Tamara off to the side, though

Jayne noticed Tamara was keeping her distance. "You said we could see him."

"I didn't say you could touch him. And if you don't stop causing a scene, you'll lose visiting rights."

"What's going on?" Jayne asked. She couldn't take her eyes off Tristan.

Tamara held up her left hand and wiggled her fingers, and Jayne forced herself to focus. After a moment, she saw it: a glittering thread of green magic, stretching from Tamara's hand through the curtains around Blaine's bed.

"It spreads," she said simply.

"Great. The Wraith is catching." Jayne made for Tristan, but a beefy Adept moved to block her.

"It obviously didn't spread to you—yet—but it's contagious somehow. And until I figure out how, this is as close as you get," Tamara said.

Amanda and Ruger arrived, and Tamara showed them her new party trick. Everyone was silent for a moment. "Nope," Amanda decided. She motioned to Ruger; he sighed and turned for the door. "Quarantine this room. Everyone out. Once you have more information, report directly to me."

"No!" Vivienne cried.

"What joy do you think you'll bring your brother if you end up in a hospital bed next to him?" Amanda said coldly.

Anger bit at Jayne, anger and determination. "There's no need to isolate everyone," she said. If she'd healed Tristan in Kyoto, they wouldn't be having this conversation. "I can take care of this."

"Jayne," said Tristan softly. His quiet voice was like a hammer striking the bell of her heart.

Don't say it.

"I know what you want, and I think you know what a bad idea it is." He offered her that crooked smile, but it seemed to cost him. He set the water down. How did his arms look so thin?

"I *can* heal you," Jayne said. "Why are we relying on nonmagical solutions to magical problems?"

"Because I am ordering you not to," Amanda said.

"Because using your power to heal would be doing what we just told you not to do," Ruger put in.

"Because healing me might infect you," Tristan said, in that same quiet, even voice that cut through everything else. "And how could I live with that, *mon amour*?"

Sudden emotion flooded Jayne. Her lip was trembling and she had to clench her fists to keep from letting any tears slip out. She had no interest in crying in front of her superiors. She swallowed the lump in her throat and tried for levity instead. "It's so bloody French of you, only thinking of how badly you'll feel if I die. Did you ever think about how I'll feel if you die?"

She dared to look up. The joke had landed; he was smiling, at least.

"I'll be here when you get back. I swear it."

She nodded. "Come on, Viv." *Of all the promises to break, Tristan Labelle, don't let it be this one.*

CHAPTER SIX

Sofia was paying Quimby a visit, too, so once they'd left the hospital, the team split up: Amanda and Ruger went back to Amanda's office, Vivienne went to the apartment she and Jayne shared with Tristan, and Sofia and Jayne took the Man'yōshū manuscript fragment to the Genius wing, as they'd taken to calling it. It was the place where Henry Thorne and Quimby theorized, debated, experimented, and drank a lot more coffee than was healthy.

The Genius wing was a white laboratory with two long tables in an L shape. One table was stacked with books and papers obscuring several laptops. The other table was lined with microscopes and beakers and test tubes and jars. All that was missing was bubbling pots. The whole place smelled like an odd combination of sterile lab and training room, mixing the old leather-and-soil smell of Henry's magic with the scent of cleaning agents and coffee.

"Seven microscopes, two people," Jayne commented. Each microscope had a drop of red fluid in a petri dish beneath its lens, and a ceramic jar sitting behind it. "Have you started employing ghosts?"

Quimby spared her a distracted smile. "That day might come sooner than you think. Try taking a peek." She retied her hair in a messy blonde bun and pushed her glasses back up her nose.

Jayne peered doubtfully down the lens of a microscope. She'd never been much for the biology side of things. She'd rather make a guy bleed than collect samples of his bodily fluids. "Looks like...blood?" she said, examining the little red cells.

Quimby came around to the side of her microscope. The petri dish was removed from beneath the lens, and Jayne watched as Quimby carefully sprinkled a tiny spoonful of powder onto the dish, then slid it back beneath the microscope. Jayne looked again, and gasped. The red blood cells were laced with a sparkling green light that looked like—"The Torrent?" she said.

"Magic flows through the blood," Quimby explained. "So it started us thinking—maybe if we could reintroduce magic, we could strengthen it. Sort of like the blood doping we did with Cillian."

"What are you doping it with?" Sofia picked up the container.

"Careful with that," Quimby said quickly. Jayne and Sofia looked at her with identical raised eyebrows. "Those are the cremated remains of former Masters and powerful Adepts."

Sofia carefully set the jar down and stepped away from the table.

"You want to...put that into people?" Jayne said.

"Why so squeamish?" Henry called from where he was squinting at his laptop.

"I could state the obvious, but I have a feeling it wouldn't make a difference." Jayne sighed.

"We talked to Amanda and Katie, and they gave the project

the green light." Quimby sounded a little sulky. "You seemed on board, too." She looked pointedly at Sofia.

"I am." Sofia pressed her hands together as though trying to convince herself. She offered Quimby a tepid smile. "This is probably one of those 'let's not see how the sausage is made' moments."

Henry stood. His salty brown hair frizzed about his head, and his glasses were askew. He'd buttoned his lab coat wrong, too, making one side of his collar half an inch taller than the other. Jayne didn't even want to ask about the myriad stains on the hem. "The TCO keeps the remains of all Adepts and Masters who have burned, through magical means or otherwise," he explained. "We used to consult them regularly. We could access their memories as long as we had even a small piece of them. When the Torrent closed, the Masters and their memories were lost to us as well. But when you broke it open"—he favored Jayne with a smile—"a lot of things became possible. Think how it could be if you could access the knowledge and power of a Master any time you liked because they were in your blood."

"Well, the blood thing worked for Cillian, so we trust you." Sofia nudged Jayne with her hip, and Jayne nodded. "What else are you working on, Dad?"

Henry Thorne flushed and fiddled with the cuff of his lab coat. "Oh, ah. Torrent research."

"Research sounds like my kind of fun," Jayne said.

"It's not," Henry said quickly. "Snooze-worthy stuff. What did you need from us?"

Henry Thorne never thought research was boring. If it didn't take hold of his mind, he simply moved on to the next thing. Sofia and Jayne exchanged suspicious looks. And if he was trying to change the subject...

Sofia lifted one shoulder in a Gallic shrug, a gesture Jayne was much more used to seeing from Tristan and Vivienne than her sister. Jayne felt a twinge of guilt. Since she'd misused his Time Jumper in the Liber Linteus heist, Henry had been a little standoffish with regard to his research. It pained Jayne that she had failed him, that she had driven a wedge between them. She'd have to work on getting him to let down his guard again. But if they could, he might open up about his project.

Quimby was muttering, peering through a microscope, making notes on a sheet of paper. Jayne held up the panes of glass holding the thin leaf of the Man'yōshū manuscript. "We were hoping to get a little help with this."

Henry looked it over. A line appeared between his brows. "No magical wards. There's some power in there, though. What sort of grimoire is it?"

Jayne explained the events of the morning. Henry scratched his chin and leaned in, studying the script as if he could learn to read Japanese by frowning at the characters hard enough. Light gold magic played along his fingers. He spun a spell, but it fizzled out when he touched the glass.

Jayne resisted the urge to pull the plate to her chest. "What was that?"

"It was a simple Seeking spell," Henry replied. "I thought that if we could find an aperture, we might be able to disintegrate any protective magics at the root and expose our quarry."

Jayne and Sofia looked at him blankly. Even for him, this was obscure. "There are spells acting like some sort of locked door," he explained with a sigh. "I'm looking for a way to pick the lock, so to speak. Or find the equivalent of a cat flap so I can reach up and open the door from the inside."

"And no luck?" Jayne guessed.

"It's not really our specialty," Quimby put in, moving away from the row of microscopes. She went over to a long set of shelves stuffed with chemicals and lab equipment. She took down a Bunsen burner and a variety of jars, setting them on the table behind her.

Henry shook his head in agreement. "If you leave it here, we could run some tests."

"See if we could beat it into submission." Quimby grinned and slid on her safety goggles. She carefully put some of the Master-doped blood into the dish over the burner. Then, taking a dropper, she carefully added an acrid-smelling liquid.

The dish cracked. Red flames leaped a full foot into the air; Quimby jumped back. Jayne gasped at the exact wrong moment and got a lungful of foul-tasting smoke.

"On second thought, maybe we'll just talk to Katie," she said, clutching the manuscript sheaf close.

Henry hurried over to his laptop and shut the lid. "If you set off the fire alarms again—" he threatened Quimby.

"Come over here and help me figure it out," she replied amiably.

Henry started to gather his papers. Jayne spotted a printout on top titled *Quantum Particles and Temporality: The Defiance of Linear Time*. "Time travel?" she said.

Half the stack slipped out of Henry's hands. "Ah, yes. Yes. Dear colleague of mine wanted me to look it over. Peer review, you know. Are you sure I couldn't take another look at that grimoire?"

Jayne checked the date of the paper. It was from 2015. Henry Thorne was not an accomplished liar, and he didn't want her asking questions.

Sofia's phone beeped. She frowned. "I have to go. Quimby, I'll be in touch about the serum, okay?"

"You still want it?" Quimby looked surprised. She was flapping at the air with a dishcloth, trying to disperse the smell.

"As long as it works." Sofia nodded, then reached out to squeeze Jayne's elbow. "I'm never far away if you need me," she said softly. "We're staying at the Nashville apartment tonight. Text me if you want to hang out."

Jayne watched her go, shutting the laboratory door softly

behind her. She should be going, too. Amanda had said that the grimoire was her top priority. But her father was up to *something*. "How *is* the Time Jumper working?" she asked, hoping to angle her way in. "Did you and Quimby manage to make it last any longer?"

"No," said Henry. Jayne waited for more, but he just blinked at her. *Okay.* She opened her mouth to ask another question, but Henry surprised her. "I'm sorry, honey. I'm exhausted. I've been in the lab since four this morning and I've been staring at a screen all day. Why don't we take a break? Pie and rummy?"

Something between nostalgia and longing pierced her heart. She'd loved playing rummy with her dad when she was a kid. She'd gotten good at beating him, too. Henry Thorne was too distractable for his own good. They could drink tea, eat pie, play cards, chat about things that didn't affect the whole world.

She knew he was trying to get her out of the lab and away from his secret research, but she didn't care. Sometimes an ulterior motive could lead to a good thing.

She also knew that Amanda Newport would disembowel her if she caught her taking a break in the middle of a crisis to stuff her face with pie. The fate of the Torrent was at stake, which meant the fate of the world was at stake.

She managed a weak smile and brandished the grimoire. "Rain check? I'd better get this out of here before Quimby blows it up." Quimby stuck out her tongue. "Maybe Katie will know what to do."

"I do think her skill set would be more suited to your dilemma." Henry leaned forward and kissed Jayne on the forehead. His whiskery chin scratched her. He probably *had* been up since four this morning and hadn't bothered to shave. He smiled at her. "Don't be a stranger, Jayne."

She offered him a smile in return, a smile she dropped when she turned toward the door. *Which one of us is keeping his distance, Dad?*

CHAPTER
SEVEN

Toulouse, France, had been swelling with magic for weeks. New Adepts were popping out of cafés and schoolyards, and the Kingdom was always looking for opportunities to recruit. The group's second in command, Lars, was determined to bring as many to their side as possible. One newbie in particular, a surprisingly nondescript boy, was rumored to be more powerful than many of the other youngsters the Kingdom had identified. He held Guardian magic as well as Adept, and they needed him, badly. Lars had come to find him, bringing a team of highly skilled soldiers to help.

Unfortunately, the excess magic meant the Wraiths seemed to be multiplying as well. Any time the Kingdom identified a particularly powerful new Adept, up popped the monsters, too.

So while it seemed Lars was casually sipping a coupe of champagne and munching on olives and potato chips, waiting for a couple of his Adepts to bring the powerful boy to him, minding his own business, really, he was on high alert. He'd just spotted the boy emerging from the schoolyard down the street and being snatched by the two operatives when the first Wraith landed with an unholy shriek. Two more followed in a flurry of snarls and wings. This was becoming a much too common occurrence. It seemed the Wraiths also had a mission, though no one had figured out what that was.

He spun up a Tornado spell, wind whipping in his hand, and held it threateningly toward the lead Wraith. He'd learned they fed on fear, so showing disdain was better. "Shoo. Leave."

The Wraith reached deep into its lungs and roared at him.

"Fine. Be like that, you scaly bastard."

Lars pulled his mace from the Torrent and swung it, hard. It lodged in the side of the enormous Wraith, making the creature scream. A second lunged, turning from its quarry—one of the Kingdom operatives—and took a swipe at him. Lars ducked, sent a beacon into the Torrent for more Kingdom operatives to join him, then spun back to the monster. He connected with the mace. His constant training and readiness was paying off. The Wraith, off balance, scrambled for purchase, its claws raking the shoulder of a Wraith behind him.

The second wounded Wraith lumbered toward him. *Grand,* he thought grimly, *now there are* two *Wraiths out to get me.*

A Wind spell buffeted one Wraith back, and a sword appeared through the heart of the other. Lars pulled his mace free, then dropped, swinging for a Wraith's hind legs. He connected, severing its Achilles and taking the beast down. There was no time to be relieved. No time to think about anything other than his next swing and who was protecting his back. And how to keep their quarry safe.

The young object of their battle had stuffed himself into a corner behind one of the café chairs. The boy had his arms over his head and his knees drawn up to his chest. He was not screaming, or crying, or praying. A good position, and out of the way. Easy to defend...well, relatively easy to defend. Nothing was truly easy against these monsters.

Lars called up a special spell, one he'd constructed from descriptions in old grimoires. Masters had once used it to get water to flow from a dry well. He attached it to the tip of his mace. The next swing connected solidly, and the blood began to flow like a river. The four-legged Wraith bellowed, but the snap it took at him lacked power and punch. Its eyes rolled up in its head, and it collapsed in a pool of its own blood. Dark splashes of it speared across Lars' trousers.

There were five Wraiths still standing now, more than the Kingdom team could take on. When Lars portaled in with his minions, the beasts had already shown up for the boy, so he must be powerful indeed. Wraiths only came to consume those with true ability. And the Kingdom needed soldiers of true ability. Lars had no intention of going back without one more for their ranks.

A ruckus started nearby, men and women appearing with their hands and weapons raised, engaging the wraiths. A man strode toward him, hands up in supplication. He recognized Pierre. His rivals, the French group La Liberté.

When he sent out the magical distress signal at the first sight of the Wraiths, La Liberté must have intercepted it. Would he be fighting a battle on two fronts now?

It seemed not. All around him, across the suburban battlefield, La Liberté operatives fought the Wraiths, pushing back the tide. Lars was nothing but grateful. Without this help, his soldiers would be smears on the floor already, their magic absorbed by the Wraiths. But once the fight was over...who would get the boy?

He spared a moment's consideration for making a portal and grabbing the child. That moment almost cost him his life. A scaly, six-fingered hand lifted him off the ground and shook him like a rag doll. The Wraith's mouth opened wide, unhinging like a snake's to reveal three rows of razor teeth. Lars yelled. A moment later, the shaft of an arrow stuck from the roof of the Wraith's mouth. It dropped him in surprise. Lars punched it in the stomach with the blunt end of his mace, and Pierre swung forward with his sword to lop off its arms.

The Wraith stumbled back. Lars swung the mace again and caught the Wraith square in the chest. It crashed against the café window and fell dead onto the pavement.

Lars paused to look around. All the Wraiths were dispatched. The air was filling quickly with their burnt-rotten stink, becoming cloying and choking. The café had been trashed beyond repair. No horizontal surface remained; the bar counter sloped down from two sides, broken in the middle, while the tables were no more than kindling. Acidic blood was rapidly congealing over the floor, the counter, the scraps of table, leaving scars wherever it went. The bottom of Lars' trousers was done for.

From the other end of the café he heard the spray of running water. A Kingdom Adept crunched over broken porcelain. He was soaked. "Nansen's dead," he said gruffly. "Also, toilet's out of order."

Members of the two factions—the Kingdom and La Liberté—gathered on opposite ends of the room. No one made a move toward the boy. The moment they did, the fighting would break out again.

"We work well together," Pierre said. He looked around, then wiped his sword clean on an upholstered chair.

"That we do," Lars agreed cautiously. His men still held their weapons at the ready, primed to attack. But they looked exhausted. One of them bled freely from his arm; another had to lean against the windowsill. They'd spent their power fighting the Wraiths, and they'd lost at least two men. He knew he had to get them out of here without a fight.

He also knew he wasn't leaving without the boy.

The boy in question snuffled, then hiccupped. All eyes were drawn to him. He put up trembling hands. Twelve, Lars estimated. Maybe a small fourteen. "P-please," he whispered. "I don't want any trouble."

"We want the same things, do we not?" Pierre said. His men held their weapons tip down, ready to defend but not intending to attack. *Relevant,* Lars thought. "A restoration of the natural order."

Barring the Kingdom's stance on Rogues. Lars nodded cautiously. "What is it you're suggesting?" he said. "Allies?"

"We could do better than that." Pierre smiled. "Why not partners? Bring our two organizations together once and for all. We have the same goals. We will be stronger together than apart, fighting for their scraps."

Partners. That would require a lot of trust, and it was trust the Kingdom lacked. *Both within and without,* Lars thought with a grimace. He hadn't even told Ruth Thorne that he was going on this little mission. In fact, he tried to tell her as little as possible these days. He never knew whether the Wraith inside was in control, or the woman.

Then again...perhaps La Liberté could help him with his Ruth Thorne problem. "Tell me more about this partnership," he said. "Do we work together? Are we all part of La Liberté?" He nodded to the boy, who was clearly tired and scared. "Who trains him?"

"Why not both of us?" Pierre said. "We all know what's coming. We'll be fighting on two fronts now, and the TCO has government backing." His lip curled. "We could both build smaller armies with lesser power. Or we could combine to make a force to be reckoned with."

Lars looked at his men again. The Kingdom had never been a democracy, but it had always been about power. He couldn't seem weak to his followers, or they'd seek to replace him. Yet... the acting head of La Liberté was offering the power he so craved. He could be in charge of more assets, more resources. He could work with the intelligence of two organizations instead of one.

They needed a victory. More than that, his followers needed to feel like they were on the right side. With a Wraith for a leader, many of them had faltered. If Lars said no, would they defect to La Liberté anyway? If power was their goal, that was a true possibility.

And if Lars said yes...he could get the power he needed to destroy Ruth Thorne and install himself as the Head of the Kingdom.

He smiled, let his mace drop, and extended his hand. "Let's go somewhere we can drink your fine French wine and talk terms."

Pierre's hand was slick with sweat and blood, but he squeezed firmly. "You will find us to be excellent listeners," he said with a smile of his own.

CHAPTER
EIGHT

Sofia smoothed down the rumpled front of her dress shirt, then stepped into Amanda's office. Cillian was already there, looking comfortable and sexy in a T-shirt that barely held his biceps. He smiled warmly at her when she took the chair next to him. She smiled back, but it was a brief one. No matter how he made her heart flutter, they were facing their boss. Amanda sat behind her desk, looking grim.

"Thank you for joining us." Amanda made it sound like Sofia was late. "Status report for the school?"

Seo-Joon had probably already sent her the results of this morning's skirmish, so there was little point in lying. Sofia squeezed Cillian's hand, borrowing a bit of strength, then said, "It's going well. The children are forming natural bonds with each other, which turns into good teamwork. In completing their tactical assignments they often seek to form groups where a good array of strengths is represented."

"And you've tested these strengths?" Amanda said.

"Repeatedly," Cillian answered.

"Seo-Joon tells me that some of them are old enough and advanced enough to be considered for field positions." Amanda looked away from the report on her computer and regarded Sofia sharply. "Do you agree?"

Sofia exchanged a glance with Cillian. *No.* "Many of them are old enough to make life decisions for themselves," she acknowledged reluctantly. "And they've advanced past the top tier of lessons."

Amanda tapped the top of her desk. "Good. It's time. We need operatives urgently."

She turned her computer monitor around. It showed a map of Europe covered in red dots. Sofia swallowed a sudden tight worry in her throat. That didn't look promising.

"Every dot is a Wraith attack," Amanda said. "They're going after innocents, Adepts whose magic just became apparent. They can often reach an Adept before we even know of them, and wherever they go, they leave bodies behind. We have to take them down."

"Crikey," Cillian muttered.

"Wraiths?" Sofia was already shaking her head. "They are absolutely not ready for Wraiths. We can't do that to a bunch of kids."

"I thought you said they were old enough to make life decisions for themselves." Amanda pursed her lips.

"I thought you meant putting them in TCO headquarters. Research, filing, a few intel-gathering assignments. Not life-or-death missions." She heard her voice go shrill. Cillian squeezed her hand again. She had to keep calm. She couldn't let Amanda think her objections were rooted in hysteria.

Amanda leaned back, folding her arms. "Ruger was recruited to the CIA when he was eighteen," she pointed out. "So was I. Kids join the army when they're eighteen. And right now, eighteen seems to be a luxury. I'm receiving reports of Kingdom and La Liberté operatives being shadowed by Adepts as young as twelve. In the field, fighting. *They* are not worried about their fighters' age."

"*We* are not the Kingdom," Sofia snapped before she could think about her tone. Amanda's jaw twitched. Sofia breathed deep and said again, in a more even voice, "We're not the Kingdom. We're not Ruth Thorne or Gina Labelle. We don't use children to fight our battles. And this"—she tapped the screen—"is exactly why. They wouldn't stand a chance against these monsters. We'd be sending them to the slaughter. How does that help us? After all the work we've done to train them, all the sacrifices we've made—they've made...that would be a waste."

Amanda ran her tongue over her teeth. She looked like she wanted to argue.

Cillian said, more gently, "I agree with Sofia."

Amanda rolled her eyes. "Of course you do."

He was not intimidated. His brogue grew broad. "These kids have developed good battle instincts in simulations, but I think we can all agree that sparring practice has nothing on a real fight. Let's put them on a lighter assignment and make sure we have cooler heads prevailing over the Wraith fight."

Amanda watched them for a moment, assessing. Then she shook her head. "You're right," she said. "You're both right. But these kids are old enough to decide what they want, so I'm going to give them that chance. You assemble a team of your best students and offer them the TCO paperwork. Whoever signs reports to me tomorrow. I'll find an assignment that can test their abilities and teamwork in the field, without putting them up against a Wraith on their first day. Deal?"

It was all too fast. Too soon. But Sofia knew she could do nothing about it. And Amanda was listening to her, at least. "Deal," she said.

"By the way, did you ever cook up a name for that place? If I'm going to have it as a line item in the budget, it might be better to have a department name rather than simply magic school."

Sofia felt a spark of joy—the school wasn't temporary, it

was becoming a true part of the TCO. She glanced at Cillian, and he nodded.

"We've decided to call it Aegis School of Magic. Aegis was the magical shield of Zeus and Athena. These children are our shield."

Amanda nodded. "I like it. But this is a battle academy. The name should reflect it."

"We're trying to teach them more than war, Amanda."

"We are at war, Sofia. I will let the director know."

"But we won't always be. If we succeed, if the kids, and Jayne, and the TCO, and my dad succeed, then we won't be at war forever."

Amanda set down her pen. "Sofia. Yes, we may defeat the Wraiths. Yes, we may take down the Kingdom and La Liberté. We might even vanquish Odin. But you, of all people, know that no matter what happens, there will always be another maniac who wants power. Some twisted person who gets a taste of magic and allows it to go to their head. History shows us we are never fully safe. The world knowing we're openly training Adepts for war will be a true deterrence. Plus, battle academy sounds cooler."

Cillian stifled a laugh.

"You may go." Amanda pulled a stack of papers toward her and began to examine them, initialing each paragraph.

Sofia and Cillian moved toward the door. Sofia found she was trembling, though with anger or sorrow or fear, she didn't rightly know. Cillian put a broad hand on her back.

"Sofia?" Amanda's voice was laced with iron. Sofia turned back. The redhead pinned her with a sharp glare. In her small hands, her pen looked like a weapon. "You *are* training an army. That was always your objective. If you're too soft for the job, you'll be reassigned. Understood?"

Amanda Newport, remove her from these children? Who

had already been abandoned by so many? "I'm not too soft," she replied, in a voice just as hard.

"I'll be the judge of that. First team: tomorrow. Second team: next week."

Sofia opened her mouth to object, but Cillian's hand moved from her back to her shoulder. "Come on, love," he said quietly and steered her out.

CHAPTER NINE

Sofia and Cillian portaled from Langley to Jayne's Nashville apartment. Sofia flopped on the soft green couch while Cillian raided the pantry for dinner. "We're missing everything," he said with a sigh, leaning against the black granite counter. "Suppose that's what happens when you disappear into a Time Catch for years, and your sister is constantly on the move. Shall we get takeaway?"

Sofia offered him a wan smile. "Whatever you like."

She waited while he ordered Chinese food and baked goods over the phone. They'd gone directly from Amanda's office back to the school, where they'd called in Matthew, Rebecca, Rufus, Medina, and Zia. Those five had shown exemplary skills and good thinking on the field. Sofia had already acknowledged that they were ready to graduate. Now, she just had to come to terms with the life they were graduating into. All five of them had agreed to be field officers. Rebecca had even pumped a fist in the air. She had her mother's spine.

Cillian came into the living room, and Sofia moved her legs so that he could sit on the couch. When he was settled, she propped her feet on his lap. She closed her eyes as his strong fingers rubbed her arches, sighing with pleasure. But it was short-lived.

"I don't like it," she said.

"We don't have to like it," Cillian replied softly. "But Sofia... we did everything we could to give those kids a fighting chance. We took them away from a life where they didn't understand their magic and were maybe even considered wrong for having it. We've done well by them."

"Yeah, and maybe now we're sending them off to die," she replied bitterly.

"Every option had a downside," Cillian reasoned. "We made this choice. And so did they. They agreed to join the TCO training program. They agreed to become field officers. The best we can do is give everyone the same choice and let them walk away if they need to."

"But what if..." She couldn't bring herself to say it.

"It's war, lass," Cillian said sadly. "There *will* be casualties. But we've done what we can to teach them."

Cold comfort, Sofia thought. What might have happened if she'd never opened her mouth? If she'd never offered up this idea of a school to train the children whose magic was newly realized?

Then she thought of the child she'd saved from the Wraiths. The children they'd found locked in closets or handcuffed to beds. Why was there no good option for them in the world?

And was her work changing that? *No. You're creating an army.* Her hand went to her belly. *And when your child is sent to war? How will you feel then?*

They had to have peace, soon. They had to win.

Cillian was watching her, a frown pulling his brows together. "Sof? Are you—"

"Am I what?"

Cillian gave her the lazy, wolfish grin that always made her stomach clench. "I'm no expert, but something is definitely up with you. You've been walking around in a daze, and you keep touching your stomach. You're also glowing, like, bright gold right now."

She looked down at her hands, and sure enough, a liminal glow emanated from them. This was magic, but a different kind. "Oh, boy," she said, sighing.

"Boy, is it, then? Or a wee girl?"

Cillian's eyes were shining. Sofia couldn't help smiling back. "It's terrible timing. Amanda is going to flay me alive."

"It's perfect timing, love. And if Amanda says a harsh word I will rip her to pieces. I'm going to be a father." The wonder in his voice, the realization still tinged with question, made her heart sing.

"You are. We're going to be parents, and that's on top of all the kids here at the school."

He gathered her in his arms and snuggled her neck. "You're going to be the most perfect mam. And I'll be a fierce dadaí. And I love you so much right now I might have to shift and do a quick run through the forest so I don't start howling right here. This is grand! Do you think they'll be a Rogue or an Adept? Have you thought about names?"

"Slow down, darling. I haven't even taken a test yet. Let's get confirmation before we plan their whole life."

"Well, Sofia Thorne, I'd been planning to do this in a slightly more romantic way." He stood up. "Stay right there."

He dug in his backpack and pulled out a small velvet box. He moved back to the sofa, dropping down on one knee. He popped open the top of the box. A beautiful diamond in an antique setting glistened up at her. "Tell me you'll let me make an honest woman of ya." His accent was especially broad, the way it always got when he was overcome with emotion. "Will you marry me, Sofia?"

This was really happening. He actually had been planning

to ask her before finding out about the baby. An answering smile crossed her face.

"I—"

The lock on the front door jiggled. Sofia shot up, summoning a spell for each hand. Cillian crouched with a growl, ready to transform.

"...told me she'd be here. So as long as—see?" The door opened to reveal Jayne and Vivienne. Jayne's brown hair was half falling out of her messy bun, and she wore leggings and a tank top still damp with sweat from a late workout. Vivienne was, as usual, impeccable from her curly brown hair to her polished shoes.

Jayne stopped when she saw the two of them in battle-ready positions.

"Um...what did we interrupt?" Jayne asked with a lascivious grin.

Sofia dropped her hands and the spells. She shot Cillian a glance. He had shoved his hand in his pocket. He winked at her. *Our secret for now,* she telegraphed silently. *And yes. A thousand times, yes.* To her sister, "I told you to text me. I thought you were burglars, or worse."

"Sorry," Jayne said. She was obviously distracted.

Cillian cleared his throat and rose to his usual towering height. "We just ordered dinner. Should I get back on the phone?"

"Just tell me you ordered pie," Jayne said.

"And *fromage*?" Vivienne asked. "All your sweets, Jayne."

"There is plenty of both. And we have enough ordered. Cillian always gets way more than we can eat, anyway," Sofia said fondly, squeezing his arm. Then she remembered that Jayne was there and dropped it. She wasn't sure what to do. It felt weird to sit down with Cillian again and plop her feet in his lap while they waited for the food. She knew it was silly, but she still felt awkward sometimes showing her affection for Cillian in front of Jayne. Just wait until she told her little sister she was pregnant and they were getting married. That was going to be interesting.

Jayne, though, seemed unperturbed. She kicked off her shoes and trudged into the living room, collapsing into the leather armchair across from them. Sofia sat back on the couch, this time keeping her feet firmly on the floor. Cillian sat next to her, grinning. The few inches of space between them felt like yards, somehow. Now that he knew what she'd suspected for a couple of weeks, the bond between them felt stronger than ever.

Vivienne was looking back and forth between them. "What is wrong with you?" she asked in her usual blunt manner.

"Er," said Cillian.

"Nothing," Sofia told her firmly.

Jayne seemed to notice the awkwardness for the first time. "Come on." She flapped a hand. "This isn't because of me, is it?"

"Well..." Sofia faltered. For her and Cillian it had been years. But in Jayne's world, she'd been Cillian's girlfriend just a few months. This was perhaps the first time they'd all hung out together since Sofia and Cillian had become an item.

"Forget about it," Jayne said. "Seeing you two happy together makes me happy. Seriously. Okay? Can we move on? Because I really need to talk to you, and I don't need things to be weird." She let her head fall back.

Sofia exchanged a glance with Cillian. She couldn't help smiling. Her sister's dramatic streak was showing tonight. "All right," she said and swung her feet up on Cillian's lap again. Vivienne made a face at that, but Jayne didn't even blink. "What's going on? Boy problems?"

"Among other things. They still won't let us in to see Tristan."

"It is most unfair," Vivienne agreed. "They threatened to remove us by force." She laughed lightly. "As if they could."

Sofia rubbed her eye with one hand. "You did *not* punch an orderly today."

"No," Jayne said a little too quickly.

"She came close. But Tristan told her not to," Vivienne said.

Jayne smiled at Vivienne, but Sofia could see the anguish beneath. Her little sister was trying to keep things together for his little sister. "So they still think he's contagious," she murmured.

"I could heal him. He's just being stubborn," Jayne grumbled.

"Well, some people are worth being stubborn about." Sofia laughed.

"Though why he thinks you are one of them, I'll never know," Vivienne retorted with a little wicked smile on her face. Jayne threw a pillow at her.

Jayne sighed. "So that was my day. Dad couldn't help with the grimoire and is being shifty as hell, and Katie Bell didn't get anywhere with it, either. Considering all the things she's seen in the library, you'd think she could make headway, but it... resisted. We do think we know who might be attached to the grimoire. The sun goddess, Amaterasu. When Katie asked the grimoire, it didn't fight the idea. Now Amanda's on a tear, convinced we have to get with the Disciples and confirm. What about you?"

Sofia offered a tight smile. "Nothing quite so dramatic. Today we got the assignment for our first graduating class."

Jayne leaned forward, eyes sparkling. "Sofia, Cillian, that's incredible. Congratulations." But she sobered when she saw the way Sofia's smile wobbled. "You don't like it."

Sofia shook her head.

"I should've guessed. Sofia doesn't like any of her kids to grow up."

Sofia lifted her chin. "That's not true. You've grown up."

"That is still to be seen," Vivienne said haughtily, and Jayne laughed.

"It's going to be fine, Sof. Better than fine. Do you know what I'd have given for this chance at their age? To be instructed in magic, like Tristan and Vivienne? I might have power, but they have talent."

"*Merci,*" Vivienne said.

"When you were eighteen, you were nowhere near old enough to go out on your own," Sofia said.

Jayne burst out laughing. Vivienne ducked her head and let her hair cover her smile. Even Cillian chuckled. Sofia felt her cheeks heat. "Well, it's true," she said.

Cillian squeezed her calves. "Lass, people mature by being given the opportunity to mature," he told her. "Too young, and that's a bad thing. But too old is a bad thing, too."

"But Amanda wants to put them in the war," Sofia objected.

"And they are what? Seventeen? Eighteen? That is nothing. I am younger than many of them and have been taking missions for five years." Vivienne examined her nails, already world-weary.

"No offense, but I'm not looking to take mothering lessons from Gina Labelle," said Sofia.

Vivienne's eyes blazed, and for a moment Sofia thought she had gone too far. Then the girl sighed. "I think the whole world is grateful to you for that," she replied. Her voice was soft. Sofia bit her lip. This was exactly why she'd started the school. She wanted her kids to have good role models, good parental figures. A good start to the life they were inheriting.

An awkward silence stretched. "Look, those kids will be fine," Jayne said at last. "Amanda talks tough, but she's not going to throw them in the deep end. She wants wins, and she wants soldiers who survive from battle to battle. She'll know how to use them."

Yeah, use them, Sofia thought. She didn't want anyone *using* these kids. Using was what people like Ruth Thorne did to Jayne and Sofia. And where would Jayne be without Sofia's protectiveness? It was hardly wrong for her to want to advocate for those with a quieter voice.

The bell rang. Their food was here.

For the next few minutes all was chaos as they opened boxes and got out plates and forks. Sofia's stomach felt the wrong kind of hollow for food, but both Cillian and Jayne gave her a knowing look, and she admitted defeat with a smile, dipping her fork into her mapo tofu. She hadn't started feeling sick yet, though the food smells were more intense than usual.

"I don't suppose anyone's been keeping up with the footie?" Cillian said after a few minutes' silence.

Jayne snorted a laugh into her rice noodles. Sofia smiled. Cillian missed his football. He'd managed to put together a half-decent team at the school, but they had no one to play against—Seo-Joon preferred baseball and paintball, and Sofia trained them in kickboxing and martial arts, though she was happiest tucked up in a window somewhere, watching the game with a cup of tea.

Luckily, Vivienne came to the rescue. "It is a tragic day for anyone who hates the English," she said. "Manchester is set to win the cup."

Cillian mock groaned and shook his fist at the heavens. Vivienne giggled. As they launched into complaints about various coaches, players, and stadiums, Sofia nudged Cillian. He took the hint and stood up to switch places with Jayne.

Jayne sagged onto the couch with a fond sigh and swung her feet up, turning sideways and looking at Sofia over her knees. Sofia smiled. She couldn't remember the last time it had been just her and her sister. And maybe that was a good thing, she thought, glancing at Cillian. She couldn't remember the last time she'd looked for him and he wasn't there, either.

"So is Matthew in this first graduating class?" Jayne said.

Sofia nodded. Any thoughts of their stepbrother put a smile on her lips. "He's so quick, Jayne. He's so smart. And he's got the Thorne heart."

"I can't believe you haven't introduced me to him," Jayne groused.

Sofia's mouth thinned. She gave Jayne her best mothering look. "Whose fault is that? You know Matthew can't leave the Time Catch. Us being out of there for a night will translate to weeks for the kids. If I'd brought Matthew out here, his class would have moved on without him and he'd have fallen behind. You'll meet him when he reports for duty, like all the rest of the Aegis students."

"Ooh, you named the school for Athena's shield? Nice." She shoveled in some food. "What's he like? Besides quick and smart."

Sofia thought about this. She didn't know whether it was the food or the conversation, but things were feeling a little less dire. Cillian was happy, their students did have power, and they had as much training as Sofia could give them. And Matthew...

"He's kind," she said at last, taking some of the empty containers and heading to the kitchen. Jayne sighed and swung her feet down so she could follow with a stack of dirty plates. "He's always conscious of the younger kids, and when he makes a battle plan, he thinks about what they can and can't handle."

"So he's got a Sofia heart," Jayne said.

Sofia flushed with warmth at the compliment. "He's got a Jayne mischievous streak, too. He tried to pull wine out of the Torrent for a party once." She laughed softly at the memory of a dozen kids clutching their stomachs on the floor. "He nearly poisoned his whole class."

"So he succeeded?" Jayne said.

"Technically. It was the worst wine I've ever tasted. I think they distilled it in old shoes. It smelled like rotting grape juice.

But he's loyal. We know he had help to get it, but he never told us who."

Jayne stacked plates in the dishwasher with a grin. "Note to self: don't use the Torrent as a wine cellar." She sobered up for a moment and looked at Sofia. "Is he powerful?"

Sofia disliked the question. Matthew's worth wasn't intrinsically tied to his power as an Adept. But she knew Jayne didn't mean it like that. "Very much so. And he's got Guardian magic, too."

"From his dad?"

"Yes. Hans Kaufmann. He was the Guardian of the Geneva pocket, but his sister died there, and he left in a fury. Joined forces with Ruth. They had Matthew. So he's like us. Has Adept and Guardian blood."

"Who does?" Vivienne had appeared in the kitchen. She started raiding the cabinets. "Where is the coffee?"

"Check the freezer," Jayne said. "I tossed the bag in there before I left."

Vivienne wrinkled her nose. "You will ruin it. Who is this Matthew you are talking about?" she asked.

"Our stepbrother. Looks like you'll soon have friends your own age to hang out with, Viv." Jayne pulled her in and hugged her around one shoulder.

"Oh, yes." Vivienne tapped her lip. "You say this Matthew is powerful? And handsome? Maybe I will fall for him."

Jayne coughed. Vivienne's smile turned wicked. "It is only fair play, after all. You steal my brother, I steal yours."

"On second thought, let's keep you here with the adult team," Jayne said. She looked like she regretted bringing up the subject of Matthew at all. She opened the fridge. "Blueberry or peach?"

Sofia found a light dessert wine and some glasses, and poured herself some water. Jayne took the pies into the living room, and Sofia heard the soft rumble of Cillian's voice. A gentle warmth suffused her belly. This was how their lives were supposed to be—carefree nights to joke and catch up, and not worry about the fate of the entire world. Only Tristan was missing—*but he'll be back soon enough*. Even Vivienne, who had struggled the most to adapt to life with the TCO, was starting to loosen up a bit, thanks to Cillian and his ability to talk about sports when none of the rest of them could.

Sofia had just dug into the perfect crust when she felt her phone buzz in her pocket. At the same time, Cillian's beeped. Jayne's chimed. Vivienne's lit up from where she'd set it on the side table.

Jayne frowned at her phone. "Ruger?" she asked the others. They nodded. "I've got a bad feeling about this."

CHAPTER
TEN

Looking up from his book, Tristan realized the hospital staff had donned PPE. They looked like aliens behind the masks and gowns, their faces hidden, only their eyes showing through the plastic shield. The nurse who brought in his lunch and set it down on the side table winked at him. "Just being on the safe side," she said.

"Naturally," Tristan replied. His heart sank all the same. This was not good.

His arm itched, though he wasn't sure whether that was from the stitching of his wound or the magic that tied him to Blaine and the Wraith. He knew better than to scratch it, but sometimes it felt as though ants were crawling beneath his skin. At other times, prickling flushed over his body in a wave, so that every movement felt like rubbing a sunburn.

In the hospital bed next to him, Blaine lay completely still. They'd pulled back the curtains so Tristan could keep an eye on him, but the Kingdom operative had been unconscious since they brought him in. Occasionally he groaned. He'd been hooked up to a drip, but his skin looked dry and scaly, a red patch flushing over one arm in a pattern uncomfortably reminiscent of Jayne's leathery rash.

Today's lunch was a chicken sandwich from the TCO canteen. The bread was dry, and Tristan took a moment to mourn good French bread. And there was too much mayonnaise. Why did Americans slather everything in mayonnaise or ketchup?

He considered trying to read to distract himself from the subpar sandwich but opted not to risk besmirching the book with crumbs. It was *Arrows of the Queen,* one of Jayne's avowed favorites, and he wanted to be able to talk about it with her. He was enjoying it well enough, but he struggled to concentrate. His head had been feeling fuzzy since the attack. He smelled of sour sweat and old magic. He needed a shower and a shave. And his damn skin itched.

He heard a rustling from Blaine's bed and looked over. The big man's eyes were open and darting from side to side. "Welcome back," Tristan said, keeping his voice calm and neutral. "You're in the Torrent Control Organization hospital. You have been heavily wounded, and we are treating your wounds. Do not attempt to escape. Do not attempt any magic. You are under arrest, and you have a Custody spell on you. Fun little spell we cooked up so you can't hurt us. If you try to blast your way out of here, you will burn."

Blaine's lips parted, but no sound came out.

"Should I tell them that you are awake?" Tristan asked. "Perhaps you'd like to eat something?"

One shaking hand lifted from the bed. Blaine started to trace movements through the air. "Don't do it," Tristan warned, dropping his neutral act.

Magic flashed on Blaine's fingers.

Then he started to scream.

His back arched off the bed, then slammed down. He started convulsing. Tristan turned and slammed his hand on the panic button. The reddish scales on Blaine's arm began to grow darker, harder. The skin on his elbow split with an audible crack and a brownish-black fluid began to seep out. The scaling rushed up Blaine's neck, and he screamed when his jaw split, opening wider and wider. His teeth were growing long and thin. *Like a snake,* Tristan thought with horror.

But really, it was like a Wraith.

All of Blaine's skin had turned a burnished color by the time the doors slammed open and the medical staff rushed in. Tamara was the first at his side.

"His heartbeat's going nuts," she said. Cloth ripped as Blaine thrashed beneath the sheets, and Tristan caught sight of a clawed foot. But it looked...wrong somehow. Stubby, too short to support a real Wraith of Blaine's size.

Blaine's head turned toward Tristan. He saw the pain in the other man's eyes and recoiled at the sight of the rest of his face. Only half of his jaw had grown longer, leaving his mouth in a permanent state of lopsided openness. Some of his teeth had sharpened to wolf-like canines, while others were the human ones he'd always had. His tongue had grown into a long and flopping thing. He'd already cut it on one of his teeth, and it oozed blood that hissed and burned the sheets. Tristan choked on a putrid smell. It was as though Blaine was rotting from the inside out.

Another sharp note joined the stink. "Catheter's out," Tamara cried. She grabbed one leg, and two nurses grabbed another. They forced him down and secured him with leather straps that barely fit around his swollen ankles. Then they moved to the arms. Blaine fought, but he was weak and confused, and with the team's help, Tamara managed to secure him.

She looked over at Tristan. "What happened?"

"He tried a spell. I warned him, but he did it anyway."

Half of Blaine was nearly unrecognizable as human, but it

wasn't so far off from being a Wraith. Tristan recoiled, gripping the far side of the bed. The spell was more powerful than he'd realized. His mind whirled. Had the spell done this kind of damage? Or was there something else going on?

Only the most powerful Adepts and Masters were turned into Wraiths; perhaps Blaine had somehow triggered the transformation but hadn't been powerful enough to complete it. Was that the Kingdom's aim? Were they *trying* to become Wraiths?

Who would go this route willingly? Ruth Thorne should be a warning Klaxon, not an aspirational goal.

He forced himself to look into Blaine's eyes. They were filled with pain and desperation. Tristan knew with sudden certainty that if Blaine had chosen this, he had done so without understanding what it would mean.

The dripping, mutilated jaw moved. "Haa," Blaine groaned.

Help, Tristan thought.

God knows he'd want to be put out of his misery rather than turn Wraith. But this man was the enemy. He was everything they'd been fighting against. He'd killed, and maimed, and damn it all, he'd hurt Jayne. Tristan would rather kill the man than help him. Slowly.

And that would make you no better than them. You can show mercy.

The nurses were busy at the bottom of the bed, glaring at Blaine's monitor. Two of them lifted his body while a third pulled his soiled bedding out from under him. Tamara went to the other side of the room and took out her phone, looking grim. No one was paying attention to Tristan. He swallowed and forced himself to lean over, speaking too softly for the others to hear. "I can only help you end it. If you wish."

Blaine moved his head in a fraction of a nod.

Tristan thought. Blaine's heartbeat was still erratic, according to the machines. A Smothering spell would be best, one adapted to the heart instead of the lungs. He reached into the Torrent and sought out the right shape in his mind—something fluffy and gentle. An end to suffering.

He found it and opened his eyes to find the spell overlaid against his hand. He eased out of bed and carefully draped it across Blaine like a blanket.

He was rewarded by the sound of Blaine's monitors in a panic. The nurses went into uproar. Tamara dropped her phone.

It was the last thing he saw before he was overtaken by fire.

The sensation wrapped around him and squeezed tight. He flung himself away from Blaine, but nothing could give him relief. A high keening pierced the air, and he was too far gone to realize that it was his own voice. Fingers like hot iron rods pressed against his skin, and he ripped his flesh away.

Jayne, he thought desperately. This was not how he wanted to die.

CHAPTER
ELEVEN

"I do not have time for this," Amanda said in low tones to Joshua, her boss and the direct report to CIA director Isaac Fitzgerald.

Joshua looked grim. "You can't afford to snub Fitzgerald, either. Amanda, this is bad."

Like she needed him to tell her. She had an operative in the hospital with a contagious condition they couldn't identify, Wraith attacks the world over, and a grimoire they couldn't unlock. She had too many fires in her own house to justify coming over here to convince Isaac Fitzgerald that magic could be a force for good—again.

They paused outside of Fitzgerald's office. "Good luck, Amanda. I'll be with you the whole way."

"Come," barked Fitzgerald. Amanda swallowed, straightened her suit jacket, and went in.

Isaac Fitzgerald looked the way she felt. His short gray hair stood on end, as though he'd been combing it with his fingers for the past several days. His collar was stained with sweat, and his shirt was wrinkled. An empty glass stood on the desk; it stank of liquor.

"What are they?" he said without preamble as soon as Joshua closed the door. "In plain language, for us nonmagical folk."

His sarcasm was not lost on her.

Amanda sighed. "We call them Wraiths. They are rather dangerous, as I'm sure you've noted. And they can be seen by civilians, which isn't helping. They've been attacking the new Adepts as they emerge. And they seem to be in search of the same magical objects we are. They want the grimoires. Or, whoever is creating them wants the grimoires. We're not entirely sure what their motivations are."

"And why haven't you stopped them?" he said.

Amanda clenched her jaw. "They seem to be…impervious to most forms of magical attack and capture techniques. We have to battle it out with them one by one."

The director let out a harsh, ugly laugh. "Fantastic. *Fantastic.* Was this not the very reason my forebears created the TCO? To protect ordinary citizens from—this?" She was pretty sure he'd stopped just shy of saying *from people like you.* "And you can't even do it?"

Amanda tried to keep her voice even, measured. "We can do it, it's just—"

"From what you're telling me, a SWAT team could do your job better than you could. Even worse, we're losing allies." He started to pace back and forth. "The president of France has cut ties. As has the president of Spain. They think they don't need us. Why might that be, Newport?"

Because they're as backwards and foolish as you? "I'm sure I don't know, sir."

"I think it's best if we just show her the footage, sir," Joshua said from where he stood by the door.

Fitzgerald glared at her for a moment, breathing hard through his nose. Then he said, "Yes. Yes. Come over here and take a look at this."

He pulled up a news site covering the Wraith attacks. Around the conspiracy theories, discussions of powers, and timeline of attacks, Amanda spotted a video: *President Garnier of France Introduces New Wraith-Fighting Force.*

Fitzgerald hit Play.

Thanks to Katie Bell's French Dictionary spell, Amanda didn't need the subtitles. She watched President Garnier take the stage, surrounded by politicians and crowded by journalists. He cleared his throat and began, and Amanda translated.

"In the past day, we have seen an unprecedented number of attacks on French soil. The creatures known as Wraiths have targeted French lives and French national relics in a sweeping attack that targets the heart of our nation. We have reason to believe that these attacks are related to the sudden appearance of many citizens with certain...special powers.

"These powers are nothing to be ashamed of, and nothing to be frightened of. They are a part of France's future, and these blessed people who have found themselves with new and strange abilities may hold the key to defeating these Wraiths."

Amanda resisted the urge to glance at Fitzgerald. She hoped he was hearing what Garnier said. He could take a leaf from the Frenchman's book.

"But we must also understand the truth: that this is war. War against a dangerous enemy who seems to want nothing more than our complete destruction. We therefore have established recruitment centers, where anyone with newly developed powers can come and join the fight. You will learn how to develop and use your powers to protect your fellow citizens from this new threat. You will be safe, and all your questions answered. You will have the chance to be heroes for France."

She paused the video and chanced a look at the director. "A public callout isn't a horrible idea. We're training young Adepts in secret. To do so openly—"

"Keep watching," Fitzgerald snarled.

Frowning, she hit Play, and Garnier's voice sprang from the speakers again.

"Fortunately, we have had many heroes fighting for France from the shadows, for all these years. One has graciously accepted our request to step into the public eye and openly command our new warriors. She is our new face of freedom."

He stood back and extended his hand, motioning for someone to come in from out of the shot. A dark-haired woman in a gray suit approached. Her serious expression couldn't quite smother the smirk when she took her place behind the podium. "Good afternoon," she said, and Amanda's stomach dropped.

Gina Labelle.

CHAPTER
TWELVE

"How did the hell did Gina Labelle wiggle out of her war crimes charge?" Jayne asked, incensed. It was all-hands-on-deck, from all the departments, and Amanda's office was crowded. Jayne's boss was pacing back and forth behind her desk, clearly agitated. "The last we heard of her, she was being held for a trial at The Hague."

"I don't know, and I don't care," Amanda said. Her hand was at her throat, clutching the Guardian necklace her late husband, Karam, had given her. She did that whenever she was angry, or nervous, or both. "The point is, Gina Labelle is no longer a terrorist in charge of a few misguided Adepts. She's now the head of a state-sponsored magical combat division. This makes her more dangerous than ever. Additionally, it means that battle lines are being drawn on an international scale. Labelle has no love for the TCO or our philosophies surrounding magic. You can bet she'll be pushing the British to make the Kingdom *their* official magical branch, and other sects in other countries have the opportunity to gain power now, too."

"What about the Disciples of Gaia?" Jayne asked. "They

seem to be on our side in all of this. They have magical integrity."

"They're not exactly friends of their governments, either," Ruger said with a grimace. "Generally the Disciples have a more...anarchic approach to governance. And the way they operate, they'd all have to agree to be a part of a project like this. It's never going to happen." He stood stock-still, maintaining his cool. But she could see a tightness around his eyes. He was as wound up as Amanda; he just didn't show it the same way.

"Sofia, Cillian. Your job's about to get a lot harder," Amanda said. "Fitzgerald has agreed that the best way to react to this situation is to unveil the Torrent Control Organization and do a recruitment drive of our own."

"Whoa," Jayne said. "We're going to expose the TCO publicly? Doesn't that undermine everything we've been doing? I mean, covert is our middle name."

"Stop joking around, Officer. This is serious." And to Sofia, Amanda said, "You're going to get a lot of students soon. Is the Aegis Battle Academy ready for it?"

"We're certainly confident in the program," Sofia said. "But we need to make provisions for a school in the real world. The more people the Time Catch is supposed to hold, the more delicate the entire operation. It could collapse and take us with it. Before we throw hundreds more into it, I think we should build a real-world version."

"Noted. Vivienne." The girl jumped. She tried to look haughty as usual, but Jayne could sense her undercurrent of nervousness. "Has your mother tried to contact you since she's been released from the Hague?" Vivienne shook her head. "We'll be keeping you under surveillance, just in case. Tristan, too. You will let me know immediately if she reaches out."

"That's not fair," Vivienne burst out.

Amanda stopped to look at her. "No, it's not," she replied

coldly. "Welcome to life, Vivienne. Your mother may try to slip you a clandestine message. She might just want to take *you*. I'm not interested in missing valuable information or losing an asset. And your access to Jayne puts you in the crosshairs once again. We're not interested in the Kingdom or La Liberté breaking into the TCO again. Our priority is to decode the Man'yōshū manuscript fragment and access the totem. Until that totem is in Jayne, it's a risk."

She turned. Jayne tried not to flinch at the fire in her eyes. "That brings us to you. How long until you have the totem?"

Jayne's mouth was suddenly dry. She couldn't quite look Amanda in the eye. "I, uh, I'm not sure."

Amanda said nothing, but her jaw tensed and her eyes flared.

"That is to say," Jayne hastened to add, "that we've been trying. A lot. Right, Dad? Right, Katie?"

Henry Thorne and Quimby were mashed by the door. "No luck," Henry proclaimed. Katie Bell also shook her head. The librarian wore a fuzzy pink sweater and ancient pink Birkenstocks. She looked like she'd just rushed in from a bubble bath.

"The totem is your primary objective." Amanda sighed heavily and squeezed her necklace. "Actually, scratch that. The totem is your *only* objective. You sleep, you eat, but you do not leave the premises until you crack that totem. Any questions?"

"Yes?" Jayne said. Amanda's nostrils flared. "No."

"Right answer."

A soft knock came on the door, and a woman in nurse's scrubs came in. She handed Amanda a note. *Tristan,* Jayne thought with a sudden pang of worry. She craned her head. Amanda read the note and quickly crumpled it, but Jayne hadn't been named Most Likely to Read the *Oxford English Dictionary* for Fun for nothing in high school. "Condition stable? Whose condition?"

"Your job is unlocking the totem, not reading my private

messages upside-down," Amanda said coolly, but two bright spots of color appeared in her cheeks.

"It's Tristan, isn't it?" Vivienne said.

A sudden heat flushed Jayne. "What. Happened?" she growled. If Tristan was in trouble...

"There was an incident. It's been taken care of." Amanda let the crumpled paper fall into the wastebasket.

"What sort of incident?" Jayne balled her hands into fists to keep herself from summoning a spell and Blasting the truth out of Amanda.

Amanda took a deep breath, and for a moment, Jayne thought she'd spill everything. But in the end, she merely said, "Tristan's condition is now stable. That's all you need to know."

"No, it is not." Vivienne took Jayne's arm. Her dark eyes were full of rage. "My brother's life is in danger, and you would keep that from us?"

"Yes." Amanda slammed her hand down on the desk. "Your priorities are not the TCO's priorities, and you need to focus on what you've promised us. That may sound harsh, but it's the truth."

"Amanda," Ruger said softly.

Amanda straightened and brushed down the front of her suit. "Tristan agreed to give his life for the TCO, if necessary. We are doing everything in our power to keep that from happening. But you know he would be the first to tell you to focus on the totem. When the fate of the world is at stake, is one life worth all the others?"

"Yes," said Jayne without thinking.

"We are going to him," Vivienne told Amanda.

The director shook her head. "You are staying right here."

A moment later, a tigress stood where Vivienne had been. A nine-foot beast that came up well past even Ruger's head. As crowded as the office was, Jayne suddenly had room to move, room to breathe, as everyone shrank back. A paw the size of Amanda's head thumped down on her desk.

Amanda's eyes flickered with fear, then rage. She brought her hands up, flashing green with protective spells.

"All right, all right." Cillian appeared next to Amanda, gently pushing her behind him. He gave Vivienne a strict, no-nonsense look. *He must have been working hard on that at the school,* Jayne thought, impressed. "Stand down, Vivienne. Let's not do anything we regret, hey?"

"Let me heal him," Jayne said past Cillian, to Amanda. "Then I'll get to work on the totem. I won't rest until it's here." She tapped the side of her forehead.

"Jayne." Ruger sounded tired.

"You know you can't use your healing magic," Amanda said. "The consequences are too dire."

"Not to mention, the infection seems to get worse every time magic is used," Ruger added.

Amanda slapped her own forehead. "Ruger, stop."

"Might as well tell her. She's going to defy your orders and march her bony little ass over there the second you kick her out of this meeting anyway."

"What is it?" Jayne said. "And my ass is not bony."

"Fine. Fine!" Amanda collapsed into her chair. "Tristan tried a spell, and it nearly took him."

"He almost burned? And you didn't come get me immediately?" Jayne felt the totems on her forehead start to prickle, and the goddesses whispered inside her brain, *Calm, child. Calm,* like she was about to have some sort of nuclear meltdown.

"You really do need to learn how to control yourself, Officer Thorne," Amanda said coldly, but Jayne had seen the second spark of fear in her eyes. Between her powers and Vivienne's Rogue abilities, they were a formidable team. "It's some sort of infection, the Wraith magic. Tamara thinks that like any virus, there's an internal breaking point. If you can overwhelm the infection with your own power, you survive unharmed. If you can't...the infection absorbs it. It's why she thinks you escaped mostly unscathed. Your totems overwhelmed the infection."

Jayne's thoughts buzzed. Anger still fizzled beneath her skin, but she had the feeling she could direct it somewhere else now. "So I could heal him. By overwhelming the infection."

"And chance turning into a Wraith yourself? No, thank you."

"What if—" piped up a voice from the back of the room. Everyone turned. Quimby, who had squashed up against the coat rack when Vivienne shifted, was wide-eyed with mild panic at the advent of all eyes on her. She pushed her glasses up her nose and coughed. "Well, what if Tristan...could heal himself?"

The room was silent for a beat. "Go on," Amanda said.

Quimby swallowed. "We tried blood doping on Cillian when we needed to activate his Rogue abilities. And he's very in tune with his powers now. What if we gave Tristan some help? Maybe that would give him the power to fight the infection?"

Jayne fought to breathe. "Could it?"

"It might," Ruger said slowly. He didn't sound happy. "It might also get absorbed, and we could be dealing with an enhanced Wraith in the TCO. A Wraith of our own making."

Amanda looked at the message in the garbage can. "There have been no breakthroughs," she said quietly. "Blood doping might be our best shot."

"My way's safer," Jayne tried.

Both Amanda and Ruger opened their mouths to object, but it was Henry Thorne who got there first. "We simply don't know that, Jayne," he said.

Traitor, Jayne thought, furiously and unfairly. Henry ought to know something about fighting for a lost cause, considering how long he'd tried to save Ruth.

Jayne wanted to stand firm. She wanted to stand against the whole world for Tristan. But with even her father against her...

Henry continued. "In matters of urgency, making no decision is a form of decision-making. And it's often the worst form. I say we try Quimby's idea. We shouldn't have to alter it from our current experimentations, so a sample should be ready to order." He blinked anxiously at Amanda.

She considered for a long moment. Then she said, "If Tamara thinks it's a good idea, we'll do it. And *you*." Amanda rounded on Jayne and Vivienne. "Human, please." The tigress turned back into a disheveled and furious French girl. "I expect cooperation from the both of you, from here on out. We're trying to save the world. What would be the point of saving Tristan if he's living in Hell for the rest of his life?"

Jayne wanted to punch something, but she retained enough sense to know she couldn't punch anything in this room. She jerked her head up and down. The sooner she got out of there, the sooner she could let out her frustration. *And,* she told herself, *if Tristan isn't healed by this, to Hell with it. I'll break into the damn hospital and do it myself.* It wasn't as though anyone could stop her.

"Well. With that out of the way..." Amanda looked to Katie. "You and Jayne need to seek out other librarians. Unravel this grimoire puzzle before the Disciples of Gaia demand it back in Kyoto. If you can access another goddess and totem, Jayne, you will help sway the outcome of this war. And Katie, while you're at it, see how many librarians are sympathetic to us. We'll need all the friends we can get."

Katie nodded, twisting her hands together.

"Quimby and Mr. Thorne, the blood prototype. I want it ready by tomorrow."

"We could use more time for testing—" Henry withered under Amanda's warning glare. "Yes, ma'am."

"Sofia and Cillian, you will present yourselves and your

team to me in the morning, as discussed," she continued. The pair nodded. Sofia clasped Cillian's hands so tightly Jayne could see a white impression on his skin around her fingertips. "Ruger, you're with me. Dismissed."

They filed out. Jayne could barely look up. A ball of anger and grief was stuck in her throat. She wanted to scream it out until she cracked the very walls of the TCO. Tristan had been hurt and they hadn't told her. He could have died, but if she could access a totem, they wouldn't care. She had thought they were past this sort of nonsense. She thought Amanda understood.

Henry gave her a quick hug. He seemed on the verge of saying something, but in the end, he just squeezed her tightly and hurried to catch up with Quimby. Their low voices rumbled to nothing as they went around the corner. Sofia gathered Jayne up in a hug, holding her for several long moments. Jayne took a shuddering breath and held her tears in. She wasn't going to cry in the middle of the hallway. She didn't want anyone concerned that she was too weak or too distracted to do her job.

"See you tomorrow," Sofia whispered. Jayne nodded and stared at the wall, listening to her sister's retreat, quick footsteps to Cillian's easier, longer stride.

She was staring at the wall of stars. A bitter taste coated the inside of her mouth. How foolish she must be, to think they could all get out of this unscathed. Now she was imagining Tristan's name at the end, a brass plate polished once a week by someone who never even knew him. His legacy couldn't end here. He was too...*vital.* Vital to Jayne.

The floor creaked behind her and a gentle hand fell on her shoulder. "She'll do what she can to save him," Ruger said.

Jayne shrugged his hand off in a sudden wave of anger. She opened her mouth to snap back at him—*what does she care?*—but she managed to catch the words on the tip of her tongue. It wasn't fair to lash out at Ruger. And, if she could dig down past her anger, she knew Amanda had risked a lot and lost a lot. She forced her shoulders down and turned to Ruger. "What would she have done to save Karam, if she could?" she asked softly. "How far would she have gone?"

"Anything. Everything. That's why she went easy on you. Yes, easy," Ruger warned. "Threatening to kick every ass in the hospital could be misconstrued as treason. But we have a plan for Tristan now, and if his condition changes, we'll let you know."

"Unless it interferes with my focus on the mission." Jayne's voice was bitter.

Ruger opened his mouth to argue, then stopped. "*I'll* let you know," he promised.

He made to pat her shoulder again, but Jayne moved forward and wrapped her arms around his broad chest. He squeezed her once, reassuring. Then he said, in his gruffest voice, "To work, Adept. And remember, telephones exist. You can always call him."

CHAPTER
THIRTEEN

Ruth Thorne came back to herself with a gasp.

The room stank of blood and burnt magic. Something thick and coppery coated the inside of her mouth. She recognized the outline of her office. London. Home.

Her desk was reduced to matchsticks. The windows had been blown out, and stains and scorches obscured the wallpaper.

But the worst part was the bodies.

This was not the first time she'd lost control in her own home. But this was undeniably the most gore she'd woken up to.

Her taloned hands shook. She stepped back, and glass crunched under a limb that ended in more claw than foot. She couldn't even count how many dismembered corpses were in the room—at least five. Maybe more. There was Lars—his head, anyway. And next to him, Sean, a powerful and promising Adept who had risen quickly through the ranks. There was a woman whose name Ruth couldn't remember, and two more bodies were mangled beyond recognition. Their flesh was embedded under her nails, soft and sticky.

Without Lars to convey her orders, the Kingdom would be in shambles. Her life's work, utterly destroyed.

A dark and menacing voice spilled through her mind. *You don't need the Kingdom. I've given you power they could never dream of. You have me now. I am all you will ever need.*

She was starting to think the voice lied.

She looked around the room for any clue what might have happened. Had there been a Wraith attack?

She knelt stiffly and awkwardly next to Lars. He held a long knife in his hand, and his face was frozen in a rictus of horror. Tarry blood smeared the knife, and Ruth's arm suddenly throbbed. Memory returned like fragments of the shattered windows. Lars, plunging the knife toward her heart. *For the Kingdom,* he'd cried, his face transforming into something terrible. She'd caught his blow on her arm and returned it with all of her wrath. Overkill? Perhaps.

But they'd turned on her. Betrayed her. And in turn, she'd torn them apart, absorbing their magic for her master.

She ran one claw along the edge of the knife. She'd sacrificed everything for the Kingdom: a home, a family, a moral compass. And all for what? For the privilege of being a slave to a master whose agenda was not her own? She'd founded the Kingdom to secure freedom for her kind, to put them where they belonged. And now she was nothing more than a puppet for a power-hungry god. And she could do nothing to stop him.

In fact, there was only one thing she could do, if she wanted to thwart his plan. She wasn't fully under Odin's control, not yet. She could end things on her own terms. She could take Lars' knife and turn it toward her own breast. She knew her weak spots, knew just where she should press. And the knife was sharp. It would only hurt for a moment.

Do it, she told herself. *Just end this.*

But what was the point of being free if you weren't alive? What was better?

Do not dare! the master roared.

Her talon slipped. The knife sliced into the back of her hand and she gasped in sudden pain, in sudden fear, cradling the ruined hand to her chest. She couldn't do it.

"Come to me. Now."

The command reverberated through her entire being. She launched herself from the floor, through the broken window, and out into the dreary British rain. Away from her self-loathing. Toward her master.

CHAPTER
FOURTEEN

Jayne leaned against the wall of the laboratory, watching Quimby and Henry fiddle with some last-minute tech. A few extra magic boosts in case they ran into trouble, and a dozen medieval-looking spiked balls. "It's the same basic concept," Quimby assured her when she'd remarked on them. "But they're tipped with a milder form of Tiriosis, so don't let one nick you. It doesn't kill, and it wears off after a couple of hours, so if you do accidentally stab yourself, get somewhere safe and wait it out."

Katie Bell was rummaging around too, putting her own gear together.

Tired of waiting, Jayne pulled out her phone and dialed Tristan's number. She'd tried the moment she left Ruger's side, but he hadn't answered. This time, he picked up on the second ring.

"Jayne." He sounded relieved but tired. She didn't like it.

"Have you gone mad yet?" she asked.

"I find myself enjoying relaxation," he replied. "I think we should try it together sometime."

"Liar," Jayne said. She'd never known Tristan to relax. She

wanted to say something else light-hearted, like *I'll see you soon* or *Boy, this grimoire's a feisty one.*

"I miss you," he said, voice low, making her stomach clench. "Are you on assignment?"

The question wasn't loaded, it was their job, after all, but all she heard was *Why aren't you by my side?*

"I'm sorry. They didn't tell me what was happening. And now they *are* sending me away. I want to help you, and they refuse to let me."

"*I* refuse to let you. I forbid it."

"You're not the boss of me," she said.

"*Non*. But I am asking you, Jayne. I couldn't live if you were hurt trying to help me. I made it clear I didn't want you trying. They've respected my wishes. I hope you will, too. You are more important than my life, my darling."

Not. Fair. "Oh, now you go getting all romantic on me?"

"I will show you true romance one day. So you do not mistake heartfelt begging for *l'amour véritable*."

"I wish I weren't going," she murmured.

"*Mon amour*. By the time you are back, I'll be well. Do we have a deal?"

"You can't promise that, can you?" She hated the way her voice went up in the end, like a whine, bringing her close to tears again.

"I know they will try. And Jayne, believe me, that is something new. Do you know what La Liberté would have done?" He paused to cough. The sound squeezed her heart. "They would have abandoned me the moment I showed symptoms. But Tamara works tirelessly. And so I have faith. You should, too."

"I'll try," Jayne said, but the words made her feel heavy, like a stone in a pond. What if Tristan got worse while she was off somewhere far away trying to crack the grimoire? Amanda wouldn't tell her until the mission was done. He could die, and she might not ever see him again.

He seemed to sense her thoughts. "I will be fine," he said.

"Jayne?" Jayne looked up. Katie held a cross-body bag. She nodded.

"I have to go. I—I'll see you later." A wish, a promise. "I love you."

"I love you," Tristan murmured. His voice seemed so far away. "Try not to worry. Go save the world. I'll be here when you get back."

Jayne let him hang up first and put the phone away with barely trembling hands. That had felt too much like a final goodbye for her comfort.

"All right. Well, Quantum." Katie stuck her hand out, and Henry shook it. "I'll see you later. Don't forget you promised me tea and a chat."

A ray of suspicion pierced Jayne's fog of misery. *Quantum?* Her dad had a nickname? Wait. Was Katie Bell *flirting* with Henry Thorne? Amusement bubbled up inside of Jayne like a fountain. If she was, Henry was absolutely clueless.

"Naturally, naturally. Tea and a chat," he replied. He was already looking at a report, brow furrowed.

Katie waved to Quimby, who called, "Have a good time!" with only a trace of envy in her voice. Quimby loved her lab, but she also loved getting in the field and dirtying her hands.

As they set off down the hall, Jayne glanced sideways at her librarian friend. Katie was a little bit pink. And had she reapplied her lipstick before they went in? Her mouth was glossy and plump. And shockingly, gone was the perpetual frumpy Christmas sweater and clunky footwear. She wore a professional gray suit with a peach-colored blouse beneath that brought a warm glow to her skin. Her hair was swept up in an elegant chignon. Jayne doubted somehow that she was going so far to impress other librarians.

"So…you know my father," she said in a teasing voice.

Katie cleared her throat, and the color on her cheeks rose even higher. "Yes. Well, we were at Oxford together, you know."

"I didn't know," Jayne replied.

"We both studied physics." Katie opened the door to the portal room and nodded to the technician standing at the console. They were a few minutes early, and he was still working on the setup.

"I thought you did library sciences," Jayne said.

"Yes, well. Physics was my first great love. I was a military brat. Parents traveled the whole world, so the two constants in my life were flying and books. I wanted to be an astronaut. But the first time I visited the Bodleian, I activated a grimoire, and the Bodleian librarian came running out to see who was trying to destroy his collection." She smiled wistfully. "It was a grimoire he'd missed. Just sitting in the stacks. Or maybe he'd been too embarrassed to touch it." She glanced over her shoulder and whispered, "It was a book of rather erotic poetry."

She giggled. The light in her eyes made her look so young. It was hard to believe she and Henry had been at Oxford at the same time. Then again, Henry's years in the Time Catch had aged him differently.

"So that was that?" Jayne asked. "You and Bod became BFFs?"

"That was that. I fell in love with the science of containing magic. The Bodleian librarian spoke to my professors and a few of the college faculty, and I changed programs. I was supposed to follow in my mentor's footsteps, take over the Bodleian magical library and let him retire." She sounded wistful.

"And then you joined the CIA. Po-tay-to, po-tah-to," Jayne teased.

"Well, you didn't see the state of this place when I was recruited. It was *begging* to be organized," Katie said. "And, of course, the added perk of saving the world—it was all very romantic for a young girl looking to make her mark."

"It's ready," the technician said.

"After you, my dear," Katie said.

Jayne stepped through the portal and found herself somewhere warm and bright. The safe house had a tile floor, and a gentle breeze wafted in from an open balcony. The kitchenette was small and neat, with a blue counter and white cabinets, lacking an oven and stove but stocked with a kettle and a microwave. The air was warm, slightly salty, sharp with the tang of gasoline and city living. But when Jayne looked out the window she was greeted with the sparkling blue water of the Mediterranean.

A quick glance at a takeout pamphlet on the table told her she was in Egypt. "I didn't exactly brush up on my Arabic," she murmured.

Katie appeared a moment later and checked her watch. "Lovely. My associate should be here any moment. I'll put the kettle on." She rummaged around for some loose-leaf tea and set to boiling the water.

Jayne studied what she assumed was the Red Sea. It sparkled blue and gold at her, magic in its own right. "So if you were at Oxford at the same time as my parents, and you got recruited to the CIA directly, why didn't they?"

"Oh, George tried. George Garrett." Katie's eyebrows rose at Jayne's blank expression. "You don't know George? I suppose he was before your time. He came directly to Oxford to recruit me. I suggested the Thornes to him, but he didn't have any luck. Ruth already had other plans, and I'm afraid your father was always wrapped around her little finger..." She shook her head and found three small tea glasses. Jayne wondered if Katie was regretting the lack of recruitment or Henry's enthrallment with Ruth.

"Anyway, he's with us now, though it's a pity George didn't live to see the day. He was an excellent general in times of upheaval. Knew just what to do. Though he left us a good replacement. Do you know he recruited Amanda, too?"

Jayne shook her head. It was hard to imagine Amanda being recruited, somehow. She seemed like the sort of person who would have grown up in the TCO. Come to the desk fully formed and ready to fight.

"Oh, that was a day. We all knew she was something special. And she's doing her best, even though she lost her mentor and her husband, and many more. The director gives her hell."

She lost her daughter, too. Rebecca wasn't dead, but Amanda had given her to another couple to raise so the girl would be safe. Jayne's spiky anger toward Amanda softened somewhat. From what she knew, the last trouble between the TCO and splinter groups had been nothing compared to this. Amanda was at the top of the chain of command and facing another huge war. She knew she'd lose people, maybe even people she loved. She needed everything to go perfectly if they wanted a chance at winning. *That* was why Jayne needed to focus, to be at her best.

Maybe she ought to apologize to Amanda the next time she saw her. "What happened to Garrett?"

"Tiriosis," Katie replied with a grim twist of her mouth. "It was the first time La Liberté had used the magical poison out in the field. We had no idea what it was, or what it did—and he died before we could work it out."

New biological weapons. New tests and targets. Would the TCO really be able to fix Tristan?

Jayne watched Katie pour out the tea, the scent of warm mint spilling into the room. *Focus on the mission.* Then, when she'd succeeded, she'd blast down the hospital doors and heal Tristan. Damn the consequences; she'd take them.

A knock came on the door. "Perfect timing." Katie beamed and crossed to open it. A tall, slim woman with dark brown skin and an angular face ducked through. "Isra, *as-salamu aleikum.*"

"*Wa-alaikum as-salam,*" the woman replied. "It has been many years, Katie." She wore a black hijab and a pendant around her neck, a disc flanked by cattle horns. Jayne recognized the sign of the ancient Egyptian goddess Hathor. Her wide brown eyes were measured, friendly but not too open. She leaned in to give Katie a kiss on both cheeks.

"I don't get out much anymore, I'm afraid. But I hope you found the Zulu dictionary useful."

Clever girl, thought Jayne, suppressing a smile at the *Jurassic Park* reference. Katie was good at this, subtly reminding Isra of a favor she'd done her.

"It was just what we needed, and just in time. Many of the tribes of Africa have the skill to kill a Wraith, and we hope to learn much from them."

"You'll let me know if you need anything else, won't you?" Katie said.

Isra paused and took a long sip of her tea. "You did not come here to offer me anything I might need," she said. "You want something. And if you are already making plans to put me in your debt again, your request must be mighty indeed."

So Isra was clever, too. Katie didn't seem to mind. She opened the shoulder bag. "Luckily, I think the puzzle is something you'll enjoy. Take a look at this." She pulled out the glass plate with the Man'yōshū leaf.

Isra straightened. "It's powerful," she said, looking it up and down. She stretched out a tentative, long-fingered hand, then frowned. "Its wards are old. I do not recognize them."

"Exactly. We think the sun goddess Amaterasu is tied to this grimoire. But we can't access it."

Understanding passed over Isra's face, followed closely by suspicion. "So that is why you have come to me. Not because you need my help, but because you need *hers.*"

"Who?" Jayne said.

"She will not take kindly to you, Wraithling," Isra said, looking her up and down the same way she'd examined the manuscript.

Jayne felt a flare of irritation. She was no piece of meat to be studied for flaws at the butcher. "I'm no Wraithling," she snapped.

"Then what is it on your arm?" Isra gestured. Jayne hid the arm behind her back. How had the woman seen through her long sleeves? "Word travels fast among the Disciples of Gaia. I have heard of you, Jayne Thorne. I have heard good, and I have heard bad, and I do not know what to think."

"Let me vouch for her," Katie said. "Jayne has a good heart. She fights for the right side. And she's already wielding three totems in her quest to save the Torrent. Can you think of anyone else on this Earth who can wield even one?"

Well, there was Ruth. But that totem was being wielded by a monster. No, thank you.

"The truth is, I am not your ally, Katie," Isra said. "Help with this book is one thing. Granting another totem to the Americans is rather different."

"But you *should* be our ally, and you know it." Katie leaned forward. "We are going to stop Odin, and we need all the help we can get. You want to preserve the Earth. You want magic back. You want to eliminate the Wraiths and restore our planet to a state of harmony. Those goals align with the TCO's."

"And when the war is over?" Isra said.

"We shake hands and say goodbye, with a record of cooperative diplomacy in our files." Katie stated it simply, like an easy fact. But behind her eyes, Jayne spotted the uncertainty. She didn't really know what would happen when the war was over. Of course, who could? The whole world might be a Wraith breeding ground.

Isra shook her head. "The problem is, not all Disciples

believe that we need the TCO. Or the Kingdom. Or La Liberté. Or the Sons of Vishnu. Or any of the myriad magical groups that have a grand vision for the world. We want to safeguard this place, not change it."

"Well, it's changing whether you like it or not," Jayne said.

Isra paused to look at her. Now that she had this woman's attention, Jayne sensed that she had one shot to make it work between them. "The TCO is dedicated to eliminating Odin as a worldwide threat. If you have the same goal, we're on the same side. Of course we'll have to figure things out when the war is over. Magic has already spread through the world again, becoming something normal people talk about. We don't have to operate in secrecy anymore, any of us. But why don't we let the leaders talk that over when the war is done, and focus on making sure we have a world to come back to?"

Isra smiled sardonically. "Ah, but Jayne Thorne. The Disciples of Gaia have no leader. We must decide together if we wish to join you. And with that patch on your arm, I'm afraid the answer will be no."

"Unless we get Zahra's approval," Katie said.

Isra took another sip of tea. She tapped a lacquered nail against the side of her cup. "If Zahra aids her, that will sway many hearts. It is true."

"And it will stop the Kingdom from seeking the manuscript," Jayne added. "Win-win."

Isra's eyes lingered on Jayne's arm. Jayne resisted the urge to scratch it. "I cannot promise that you will pass the test. I cannot even promise that you will survive it," she said at last. "But, ultimately, the decision is not up to me. It is up to a much greater librarian than myself."

"And if she deems Jayne worthy?" Katie prompted.

Isra sighed and set down her tea. "Then I will do what I can."

CHAPTER
FIFTEEN

Sofia fought down a touch of nausea while scrutinizing the recruits one last time. Matthew, Rebecca, Rufus, Medina, and Zia were dressed in their best clothes. *They look like bank interns,* she thought. Well, everyone but Zia. Zia wore an electric purple skirt and a black tee that glowed with green squiggly lines in the dark. When Sofia had gently questioned whether it was the right attire for the CIA, Zia had just shrugged cheerfully.

"Let her," Cillian had murmured in her ear. "She'll sort herself out."

Sofia took a deep breath. *One more day,* part of her screamed. It would hardly even delay them in the real world. But her mother-hen tendencies were getting in the way of the mission. She had more children to mother back at Aegis.

"Are you ready to see life outside of Hogwarts again?" she joked.

Zia rolled her eyes. "Yes."

"Yes, ma'am," Rebecca said crisply, not cracking the slightest smile.

"I told you, Sofia. Nobody reads that anymore," Matthew said.

Just you wait, bucko, Sofia thought. Jayne would probably faint when she realized Matthew hadn't finished *Harry Potter*. Then she'd sit him down and fill his ears and eyes with the audiobooks and movies until he was muttering spells in his sleep.

Sofia nodded to Seo-Joon, and he opened a portal for them. Cillian went ahead to receive them, then the TCO's first graduating class stepped through. Sofia nodded as each one of them disappeared. When only Sofia was left, she turned to Seo-Joon and gave him a hug. "Keep them on their toes until we get back," she said.

"How do you think Amanda's going to react?" Seo-Joon nodded to the portal.

He was talking about Rebecca. Amanda's relationship with her daughter was somewhat fraught; she'd come to visit a few times since Rebecca had agreed to training, and their meetings always burst with a strained politeness. Amanda obviously cared for the girl, but she wasn't a natural mother figure and had no idea how to actually *talk* to her.

It made sense. Sofia had spent far more time with Rebecca than Amanda ever had. Not that she blamed the director. Amanda's line of work was dangerous and made Rebecca a target. Hiding her away with a foster family had been the best decision to preserve her safety. But the trauma was there, and it could not be fixed by a few visits over tea.

"She'll either pretend it's business as usual or try to disembowel me," Sofia joked.

"Don't tell me that was the plan all along, Thorne." Seo-Joon laughed, but his eyes held a kernel of suspicion.

"Of course not," Sofia replied, but when she stepped through the portal, she couldn't tell whether it was a lie or not.

AMANDA STOOD as the TCO's newest recruits filed in. They were all so big. It wasn't a total shock seeing them as adults, but it was surprising, considering only a few weeks ago they'd left the real world as children. She had their folders on her desk, with their official documents fudged to match their adult faces. New Social Security numbers, new birth certificates, new everything. As a familiar, red-crowned head came through the door, Amanda felt a jolt of nerves, but she met her daughter's eye and nodded, professional to professional. She forced herself not to stare. Rebecca was stunning. But their relationship was of secondary importance on the clock. She consciously did not look at Ruger, who was observing her quietly from the corner and probably reading every thought that crossed her face.

"Welcome," she said. "Thank you for joining us, and for joining your country to fight for the fate of the world. I won't mince words; we're in a difficult spot and we need the help. I understand you've been trained on Wraith fighting as well as combat against other magical Adepts."

Nods all around the room.

"You were selected by your teachers to be part of a team, to work together," Amanda continued. "Every assignment you receive from here on out will be a test of that teamwork. I expect you to work flawlessly, from this moment onward. You've had a lot more time to bond and to train together than anyone else in the TCO. You are privileged, and because I have been told you are ready, I expect you to be ready. Are those expectations misplaced?"

She looked from face to face. Rebecca was the first to say, "No, ma'am." She stared straight ahead, hands behind her back like a military cadet. As though she'd never seen Amanda Newport in her life.

Amanda tried to ignore the sting of that.

"No, ma'am," chorused the others. She was amused to see the girl in the purple skirt. She'd have to learn to dress unobtrusively, but at least she didn't look like a Fed, the way the rest of them did. They'd learn.

She handed them their corresponding manila folders. "Your mildly altered identities." Then she handed Sofia a dossier. "And your assignment. You'll be traveling to Ljubljana, Slovenia, by portal. A Kingdom operative was spotted there by one of our informants. He's low-ranking, according to our intel, which doesn't mean he's weak. He may well be stronger than we expect. The Kingdom always prized brute power over intelligence. You will apprehend him, interrogate him, find out what the Kingdom is after in Ljubljana, and why they sent him. Sofia and Cillian will be with you to monitor your process and ensure the mission doesn't go sideways. Questions?" Silence. "Good."

They exited the office awkwardly, trying to squeeze through the door without looking as though they were hurrying out. Amanda caught a gleam of excitement in Rufus's eye. Matthew and Rebecca had already begun talking quietly; she could see their lips moving as they walked down the hall. Sofia followed them, flipping open the dossier. A classic Thorne move.

Ruger shut the door behind them and turned to face her. "So?"

Amanda tidied up her desk. "So what?"

"So how does it feel, seeing Rebecca on the other side of that desk? Did you ever think she'd be doing what you do?"

He was trying to be gentle with her. "No," she said shortly. She didn't want gentleness. She didn't want this conversation at all.

Ruger folded his arms. "You can have complicated feelings about your daughter going out into the field."

"This is a bunny mission. My feelings aren't complicated."

"Amanda," Ruger warned. She looked up and opened her

mouth to tell him off. He was smiling gently. "It's still a big step. She's venturing into a new world."

A world that might kill her, they both knew. Amanda gripped her necklace tight. "I..." She swallowed the sudden lump in her throat. No, this was not the time to discuss it. "This is war. There's no time for feelings, Ruger."

"You say that, but you don't believe it," he warned.

"You sound pretty confident about that," Amanda said.

Ruger shrugged. "I know you."

And damn him, he did at that.

CHAPTER
SIXTEEN

The Bibliotheca Alexandrina was a short walk from the safe house, a curling building of glass and gray stone, decorated with scripts from languages both ancient and modern. It looked a bit like a waffle trying to get a suntan. Elegantly, though. This place was a treasure to all mankind. Jayne couldn't believe she was actually getting ready to pass through its doors.

Going in, Jayne texted to both Tristan and Vivienne. Vivienne had opted to stay behind, since her services were not needed and she wanted to be near her brother. Jayne could hardly blame her.

Bonne chance, Tristan wrote back a few moments later.

Inside, the library was a modern marvel. An enormous hall held table after table, shelf after shelf of books, neatly partitioned by wooden half-walls. Concrete pillars held up the glass roof, which let in plenty of daylight. It smelled of fresh paper and old books, and Jayne paused to take a deep, savoring breath. The barest murmur of sound went around the hall—the scrape of a chair, the turn of pages, the quiet conversation of a group of scholars. Jayne felt a piercing longing for simpler days when she could go to a place like this and sit for hours in quiet research.

At least no one was laughing at her for her librarian tendencies here. When she opened her eyes she saw Katie Bell staring around, eyes sparkling in wonder. Even Isra's mouth was turned up in the corners, a quiet expression of pride or satisfaction.

"The original library site fell into the sea, of course," the Disciple said quietly, leading them to a side door off the main hall. She produced an identity card from her pocket and pressed it to a magnetic lock. The door opened with a click. "We had to do a lot of shuffling to secure the old library to a safer new location."

"Secure the library? "Do you mean to say...that the ancient library still exists?" Jayne almost couldn't finish the sentence. A tingle started in her belly and flushed to her toes.

They were in a sterile white hall. The smell of books was washed out by the smell of industrial cleaner. Isra led them to a staircase at the end and began to descend. "You will see—if Zahra sees fit for you to see," she replied simply.

OMG, as Vivienne would say. No pressure. "Who is this Zahra?" Jayne whispered to Katie as their footsteps clattered on the hard stairs.

"She's a Guardian," Katie replied. "The current Guardian of the Alexandria pocket." She smiled and whispered, "I hope she likes you. I'd like to see it, too."

At the bottom of the stairs they came to a storage room, and at the back of that storage room, squashed against folded tables and chairs, sat a small desk with a book lying open on it. The whole scene looked as though someone had left for a break and forgotten to ever come back, letting the room fill up behind them.

"That book is the key." Isra nodded, then stepped back, folding her arms.

Jayne made her way through the furniture maze and sat at the desk. The book before her was a simple one, bound in blue linen, printed in Arabic, but she could feel the hum of power. She glanced at Katie, who nodded slightly, encouraging, then she set her hand on the book.

An odd sensation flooded her, like cold water flowing directly under her skin. A voice she'd never heard before said crystal-clear in her ear: "Who are you?" It was a deep voice, rich, like hot chocolate and cream.

"Jayne Thorne," she said. *Master of Magic. Keeper of Totems.* That rather felt like boasting.

"And to what are you loyal, Jayne Thorne?"

"Um..." Was this some sort of trick? Jayne glanced at Isra. The woman leaned against a box, arms folded. She was speaking quietly with Katie, who seemed completely at ease. Jayne trusted Katie, so if the other librarian thought Isra was trustworthy...

"I'm loyal to the TCO," she said.

The voice sounded amused. "Are you now?" Jayne winced. *Wrong answer,* she thought. "Are you truly?"

Maybe this strange voice was trying to figure out her weak spots. She was loyal to Tristan, of course, and to her family—everyone but Ruth. She tried to do what was right, so maybe she was loyal to...justice? She winced. That sounded corny as hell.

"Would you kill for your Torrent Control Organization?" said the voice.

"No," Jayne said immediately and was rewarded with a throaty chuckle. Her skin prickled with anxiety. She couldn't help feeling that she was going about this all wrong. "But I wouldn't betray them, either, so if that's what you're trying to do—"

"I am trying to understand you. I am wondering whether

you understand yourself. To what are you loyal, Jayne Thorne? Do not answer until you are certain."

Jayne let her fingers run over the weathered pages of the book before her. If she had to guess, she'd say it was from the early 1900s from the binding and the look of the paper. It was in fairly good condition, though she still winced inwardly at touching it with ungloved hands. Her senses told her it wasn't a real grimoire. It was more like a portal. A portal contained within the book, locked up until whoever was on the other side allowed it to open. *Elegant magic,* she thought. She'd love to get the chance to study it. When all this was over, if she still had a home and a life left to go to, maybe she could convince Amanda to put her in the research section for a while, traveling the world and investigating magical books. *Maybe books hold my loyalty,* she thought with a wry smile.

A moment later, she knew the answer.

"The Torrent," she said. She was loyal to the Torrent. She worked for the TCO because she wanted to protect the Torrent and its Adepts, as they did. But she'd butted her head against plenty of bureaucratic walls because her priority was the Torrent, and people, over the rules of the TCO.

Something seemed to lock on to her. Her limbs froze. Then the portal flashed open, and she was sucked inside.

Jayne blinked. She was no longer standing in a bare-walled, boring storage room. Instead she stood in a broad pillared hall, carved from sandstone, lined with high, neat wooden shelves divided into small squares. The air was hot in here and smelled like sand and sun. The tile beneath her feet showed a mosaic of a river—the Nile, she presumed—dotted with small boats. A man stood at the top of the river, exuding divinity.

"Serapis," said the same deep voice. Jayne turned to see the voice's owner.

The woman was smaller than Jayne had expected, slim and lithe as a cat and dressed in a pleated linen shift so thin that

Jayne could see the outline of her body when the sun shone through it. She had wide brown eyes framed by thick lashes, full lips, and a strong nose. Her black hair ran in tight curls over the shoulders of her dress.

She was looking at the mosaic with something akin to fondness. "He was a special god here, in Alexandria. Used by the Ptolemies as part of legitimizing their rule. A god of the underworld, of healing, and of the sun. Fitting, I think, considering the grimoire you carry."

"Yes." Jayne looked up. She could hardly speak. Her breath caught everywhere she looked. Scrolls filled the little alcoves in the shelves. Plain tables had been set up for reading. A wax tablet and stylus lay next to a scroll on one table, as if someone had been taking notes and left for a moment.

Jayne turned to the woman with shining eyes. "Is it real?" she asked. "Is it really *the* library?"

The woman nodded, smiling. "It is. And I have guarded this library since time out of mind, when it first needed to be hidden from those who wished to destroy knowledge. I am the Guardian of this place."

"Wow." Jayne looked around. *Wow* didn't even begin to cover it. The ceiling was vaulted to let the light stream in. Dust motes swirled and danced in a breeze Jayne couldn't feel. She wanted to touch everything at once—and she was afraid to touch anything at all.

"I am Zahra," said the woman, and extended her slim brown hand. "Zahra Hassan."

Jayne took the hand. "Jayne Thorne. But you already knew that."

Zahra laughed her throaty laugh. "Indeed. I suppose you're here for that?" She nodded to Jayne's shoulder bag, and the artifact within it.

"We need to unlock it." Jayne pulled out the grimoire once more and showed it to Zahra. The woman gently took it from her, caressing the edges. "I think Amaterasu and possibly the Spirit totem are locked in there. If I can gain the totem, we have more power to use against Odin."

"And what would happen if you didn't use the totem?" Zahra asked, cocking her head. Her fingers still fluttered lightly over the grimoire, but Jayne wondered at the wisdom of just handing it over. "What would happen if you kept it safe here?"

"The Kingdom would come for it," Jayne replied. "Or La Liberté. Or France would send Gina Labelle and her perverted magical soldiers. Or worse, my mother herself. Any of them—all of them, they would destroy the beautiful library you've been protecting for thousands of years. As long as I don't have the totem, they know there's a chance they can take it. And they won't stop until they've won and destroyed all of us."

Zahra looked thoughtful, but she wasn't convinced. "Please." Jayne stepped forward. "You know I'm loyal to the Torrent. I won't misuse this power."

"I cannot give it to you," Zahra said at last, and Jayne barely stifled her groan of frustration. How many hoops did she have to jump through?

Zahra laughed. "So impatient, little one. Try guarding the same Pocket for a thousand years or so—then perhaps you'll know the value of slowing down."

"I wish I had that luxury," Jayne muttered. "Wait. Is this pocket in a Time Catch?"

Zahra put her finger to her lips. "I cannot give it to you, because I am not the totem's keeper. But I can unlock the grimoire so that you may make your case to the goddess yourself."

She traced magic across the air in a flowing script. Her fingers moved so fast, conjuring golden spells from the Torrent that flickered and changed as she layered one spell over the next, Jayne could barely keep up. "Your hand," Zahra said, a strange urgency in her voice. Jayne's hand shot out. Zahra pressed it to the glass case holding the grimoire and conjured one final spell.

The world shifted again.

This one was a little more familiar to Jayne. She'd been in enough dreamscapes by now to recognize one. The dust-and-sandstone library had transformed into a neat garden. Verdant grass sprung up beneath her feet. Stones had been laid in a pleasing pattern to make a path for her, twisting between artfully trimmed trees and bushes. A small stone shrine was suffused with light, though she could not see the source. Jayne stepped onto the path, breathing the light perfume of wildflowers. The click of her shoes on the stones was the only sound in the garden. Even when she rounded a corner and saw the three figures at the edge of the pool, the only noise was from her own movement.

Two of the figures she recognized: one was clad in a simple toga, with brown hair and deep red eyes like fire, and laugh lines like a loving mother. Vesta. The other wore war gear, a breastplate emblazoned with hissing cats, a helmet of shining steel inlaid with gold patterns. Freya. Two goddesses who had given her their own totems. Their feet moved back and forth in the water as they looked at her. Next to them sat another woman, black-haired and pale-faced, with eyes that flickered from color to color. She wore a kimono as blue as the autumn sky, embroidered with glittering golden suns. Amaterasu.

"Little warrior, welcome," said Freya. "We have been waiting."

"You're late," Vesta said reproachfully.

"Sorry. There was some red tape." Jayne came over to the pool. Her shoes disappeared and her bare feet made imprints on the soft, cool ground. She hoped she'd get those Converse back; they were some of her favorites.

Amaterasu looked at her through a curtain of hair like a waterfall. "You have been blessed," she said, and Jayne felt her totems blaze on her forehead. The goddess's voice was quiet and measured, warm like a bit of sunshine on a cold spring day. "Yet you seek more blessings."

"Well, I've been told I'm sort of a big deal," Jayne joked. Amaterasu did not smile. Jayne coughed. "I mean...I've been told that I have the power to stop Odin. That's what I want. Anything that could help me...won't it help you, too? You know he must be defeated."

Amaterasu dipped her chin. "He must," she agreed. "And you are, perhaps, our best hope to do it. But what if you turn against us, Jayne Thorne? What of your mother, who bears the Water totem and serves the Allfather? Would you follow down her path?"

"Never," Jayne said with a fire that made all three goddesses lean back. A smile played at Vesta's lips. "Ruth Thorne loves power before anything else. I love people. And I want to protect the people I love."

The sun goddess blinked. Her mouth, painted in red, pursed. "Love is a powerful motivator," she acknowledged. "But it is not always a force for good. I loved, once, and lost, and the path through loss can be lonely and dark. If you lose the ones you love, what will you do? How can we know you won't burn in your grief?"

Jayne thought of Tristan, and Sofia, and Vivienne, and Cillian, and felt the scaly patch on her arm begin to itch, as though Amaterasu's words had woken it. She resisted the urge to scratch and summoned up her best smile. "Well, you know me," she told Vesta and Freya. "There's always someone else to save. I told you I love people, and I do. I want to make sure *everyone* has a chance in this world, both magical and nonmagical. I'd rather save my enemies than leave them to die. And I'd rather sacrifice myself than let someone else be sacrificed in my place."

The three goddesses looked at her. Amaterasu was examining her much the same way Isra and Zahra had, taking Jayne's measure. Jayne sat and dipped her feet in the pool. The water was cool and soothing; it seemed to pull all her aches out through her heels. She hadn't realized how much she'd been walking recently.

"You are telling the truth," Amaterasu decided after a long minute's silence. "And while no one knows what the future may bring, I believe it is in good hands with you."

She leaned over and pressed her fingers to Jayne's forehead. A flush of warmth washed through her, and she smelled heady roses and campfires and fresh air, a wave of summer in the midst of a cool dreamland.

"You have a difficult path ahead," Freya warned her. "More Wraiths are being formed every day. New Adepts are found, caught, and brought to Odin as a sacrifice to his power. And they will continue looking for you." She used her spear to stand. "You are perhaps the only person powerful enough to defeat Odin, Jayne Thorne," she said. "But your power makes you a beacon for him. He fears you and wants you in equal measure."

"We Thornes don't go down easy," Jayne said, pulling her feet from the pool. She felt reinvigorated. "It's in the name."

Freya and Amaterasu didn't smile. But Vesta did, an indulgent, maternal smile. She came over to Jayne and put a hand on her cheek. "Keep your humor, child," she said. "You will need it in the days to come."

"Do not make me regret this, Jayne Thorne," said Amaterasu. She lifted her hands, and on each palm sat a beacon of light that pulsed brighter and brighter, blinding Jayne, warming her skin like a summer's day, sending her mind spinning—

Until she opened her eyes in the storage room, with the Spirit totem blazing on her forehead.

CHAPTER
SEVENTEEN

Tristan was finding it hard to breathe. His lungs rattled, and his nose seemed to have closed up. When he tried to feel it, it seemed much smaller than it ought, more reptilian. And when he'd tried to lift his head, his world had spun until he gave up and let himself flop back on the bed. There was a slimy sensation in his mouth, and his teeth seemed smaller, rounder, with more of a gap between each one.

He became dimly aware of someone in the room with him. *Get away,* he thought. *Don't you know I'm contagious?* And he had enough of his wits about him to know that he was getting worse. Yesterday he'd been able to read Jayne's text and send a short one back. Today his fingers felt clumsy and the screen was too bright. He blinked heavy eyes that felt like they were packed with sand.

He heard the whir of his bed rising. With effort, he turned his head. A figure in full white PPE stood next to him, and he recognized Quimby's friendly eyes, crinkled up in a smile. "Morning," she said brightly from behind her mask. "Are you ready to feel better?"

"Yes," Tristan said. Rather, he tried to say it. What came out was more of a rasping growl.

"Good to know. We're going to do a little procedure to help kick-start your magical immune system. Henry and I developed it some time ago. We're very optimistic."

With effort, Tristan focused on a second figure at the end of the bed. Henry Thorne. He wasn't dressed in PPE, just a mask. But Tristan didn't need to see his whole face to know he looked far from optimistic. He looked downright worried.

Behind him, operatives stood to either side of the door. Tamara, Seo-Joon, a few others. They weren't wearing safety gear at all.

Get out, he thought desperately. *I could hurt you.*

Though perhaps that was the very reason they were here. Preparing to kill him, in case he turned full Wraith. He thought he spotted a sidearm at Tamara's hip.

"Do you like apple cake? There's an apple cake in the staff room, I'll save you a piece if you want. And I found a new coffee spot for you to make fun of with your sister. They make a *great* gingerbread latte."

Quimby was trying to make him feel better, Tristan realized. She set a gossamer silver net over his head. Trying to make him oblivious, perhaps, to the way her hands shook when she pulled out a needle and a vial of blood and checked his IV. He rolled his eyes for her benefit. Then he gestured to the blood. "What?" he groaned.

"A simple solution. Blood and some of the essence of our former Adepts. Remember we've been trying out blood doping? We want to make your magic stronger, strong enough to fight off the Wraith that's trying to form inside you." Quimby inserted the needle into the vial, filling it with solution.

Tristan shook his head dizzyingly. Didn't they understand that the magic only fed the Wraiths?

"We've run lab tests, and the power should push out the disease. I promise." Quimby's voice shook on *promise*.

But if she was so certain, what was a kill team doing here?

Quimby stopped with the tip of the needle against the IV. She was looking at him. He could say no, and he was pretty sure she'd walk away. Let him lie in the hospital bed until his feet were claws and his skin was scales, until he recognized no one and nothing, not even his own sister.

Or he could let her try. If it worked, he lived. If it didn't work, he might be spared a few days of agony.

He nodded his strangely contained head. Quimby sighed in relief and filled his drip with the doped blood.

For a few moments all was still as the IV carried the solution into his system. Tristan blinked, sniffed, flexed and clenched his hands. Nothing seemed different. "Maybe—"

Then his magic flared.

It rushed through him in raw power, more than he'd ever felt before. He was adrift in a sea of it, tossed wildly among ever-growing waves. It was as though the Torrent was no longer a place he had to reach for—it was there, in his mind, in this room, everywhere. The very air was shimmering with magic and the promise of spells.

But hot on the heels of the magic came the pain. Like fire bubbling under his skin, as if the new blood was poison trying to purge his insides. His muscles spasmed as one, and he screamed. "Get back," he dimly heard. His arms flailed wildly and without his consent. He smelled burning hair. Quimby screamed. Something smashed with a sound like glass.

"Get back!"

Just do it, he wanted to tell them. Something was rippling up his legs with a feeling like his skin shearing right off. *Just kill me now.* He didn't want to hurt anyone. And he didn't want this pain. *Please.* Then the roar of the fire reached his head, and he couldn't think anything anymore.

He was trembling when he came to his senses again. He blinked rapidly, and a tear slid from his eye. It stung fresh new skin.

He was terribly thirsty. "Water?" he grated, and he heard a half sob, half laugh in reply. Then a hand was tipping a plastic cup up to his mouth, sloshing water down his chin. It was cool and sweet, a balm on his skin.

Tristan looked down. His hospital gown was shredded. Beneath it he could see the pink of new skin, even where his Wraith scales had once been. All around the bed were flakes of ash, the remains of his old body. His feet were no longer gray, with sharp black nails, and when he flexed his fingers he felt all the motion of a master pianist. Green magic sparked off his fingertips.

Mon Dieu! He was cured.

Quimby stood at the end of the bed. Her mask hung off one ear, and he could see the edge of her open mouth. "How do you feel?" she gasped when she'd regained enough composure to speak.

"I..." *Better* somehow wasn't enough. Nor was *good*. The truth was, he felt better than good. He felt better than he had in a long time. He couldn't remember the last time his magic had felt so ready to take on the world.

He thought of the Torrent, and the river of stars materialized around him. He hadn't even needed effort. He pulled a simple Materialization spell from the Torrent and cast it over his legs, replacing the shredded hospital gown with trousers. Another spell cleaned the ash from around his bed. In fact, he could barely move without sparking off some kind of magic. It clung to him like pollen.

"Quimby," he said slowly. "What was in that vial?" He pulled the net from his head.

Quimby hurried forward to rescue it from him. "Blood. And ash. From powerful magicians. We'd love to study the effects, now that it seems to have worked..."

"Cool your jets, Quimby, he's still my patient. Tristan, I'll thank you to lie back down." Tamara came forward. She was looking slightly gray, and leathery around one ear.

"Someone needs an injection of her own," Tristan said.

Tamara cast him a sharp look. "Don't change the subject. You'll be discharged when I say, and when I'm certain all traces of the infection are gone. And then—only then—can you talk with Quimby and Henry about tests. Health first, geniuses."

But somehow Tristan knew that the Wraith infection was gone. It was as though he could locate every cell in his body at once, and he found them to be healthy. He summoned a local breeze to ruffle Tamara's hair. She glared at him.

Tristan shrugged and smiled. But his hands shook with excitement. Only one person he knew had this kind of power: Jayne Thorne.

And if Tristan rivaled her for magic now, that meant he hadn't just been healed by the serum.

It had turned him into a Master.

CHAPTER
EIGHTEEN

"I see the gods have smiled favorably upon you," Isra said.

"Again," Katie added, beaming. Isra looked slightly irritated at this, and Jayne suppressed a smile of her own. She was seeing the world in new ways. The two librarians in front of her had auras—Katie, a warm pink, and Isra a mellow gold. Both were pleasant to behold.

After a few minutes to fill them in, they'd left the storage room and headed back out into the city of Alexandria. Jayne's forehead no longer glowed, so she enjoyed the ability to stroll along the street without too many strange looks. Isra was an engaging guide. They stopped for koshari takeout along the way back to the safe house, then got a few supplies. They might be there a day or two more, Isra explained.

"I said I would help you if the goddess gave her approval," Isra admitted. "She has, so I will now call the heads of each clade of the Disciples of Gaia and summon them here. We will decide together whether we throw in our lot with the Torrent Control Organization."

"And it has to be unanimous?" Jayne said through a mouthful of koshari. The day's adventures had left her starving.

Isra nodded. "We must all agree," she said.

Katie played with her fork, pensive.

"What are our chances of that?" Jayne asked her.

Katie bobbed her head back and forth. "Not impossible. But I wish I'd been able to talk to a few more librarians first."

"Tomorrow night," Isra decided. "At the Bibliotheca. I can get us access to a hall. You will make your case, and then we will debate."

Jayne could only imagine Amanda's reaction to *tomorrow*. "Any chance we could do it sooner?"

"Enjoy your time in Alexandria, Jayne," Isra replied coolly. She stood and hugged Katie, then took her leave.

"I don't think she likes me very much," Jayne said as the door shut behind her.

"Well, you've given her a lot of work to do in a short time," Katie replied easily. "Do you know how many Disciples are going to be here tomorrow night?"

WELL OVER TWO HUNDRED, as it happened.

They were set to begin at nine p.m. The Bibliotheca Alexandrina had a 250-person auditorium, and it was filled nearly to the brim with Disciples wearing the traditional dress of their country. They left their weapons by the door, stacks of spears and swords and maces, a few throwing stars and nunchaku. Jayne thought of her own staff, tucked nicely away in the Torrent, and felt a little thrill of competition. What would sparring with some of these experts be like?

Jayne had called Amanda and Ruger to brief them on the situation, earning a businesslike "Congratulations" when she broke the news of the totem. "Now get us those Disciples," Amanda said.

"It's nice to know you're alive, too," Jayne had replied pointedly.

Ruger's voice cut in. "Jayne? Good luck. Win this for us."

She'd called Tristan next. He'd sounded cheerful. "The experiment worked. Tamara has proclaimed me completely healed. She'll be getting the procedure next. And Jayne...it's amazing, what I can do now. The new magic, it's remarkable."

"'New magic'? What's that supposed to mean?" Jayne had asked. But Tristan had changed the subject, leaving her an odd mix of worried and relieved.

Now she stood next to the stage, watching the Disciples greet each other and find their seats, and wished she'd brought Tristan over so that he could talk to them instead of her. He always had such a smooth, convincing tone. *That tone you found so arrogant when we first met?* she imagined him teasing her.

"Maybe you should do this," she said to Katie.

Katie squeaked. "Me? I run a library. I don't do crowds."

Jayne resisted the urge to point out that she was in the same boat. But Isra stood at the podium now, and cleared her throat over the microphone, and the chatter in the hall died down. "Thank you for coming," she said. "We have been troubled by Wraith attacks the world over, and from what we have seen, the Wraiths appear to be growing stronger and more numerous. Many of us have expressed concern over what that means, and how we might stop it. Yesterday, Jayne Thorne from the CIA's Torrent Control Organization came to this very library to seek our help."

"You know we don't trust the Americans," shouted a Spanish-sounding man from the third row. This was accompanied by a broad round of laughter, and a few cries of "He's right!"

"Jayne Thorne has earned the trust of goddesses," Isra replied, unflappable. "They have bestowed their powers upon her. And she has a proposal that I personally think is worth hearing."

She nodded to Jayne, who nodded back. Her mouth was dry and her head felt light. She focused on going up the stairs, one at a time. Then she focused on walking to the podium.

And then she was there, and Isra was adjusting the mic to her height, and now she had to focus on the actual task at hand. Isra nodded. *Good luck,* she mouthed.

"Yes. Wraiths."

Jayne had prepared some notes, and she dug her notecards out of her pocket. "A few nights ago, my team and I interrupted a Wraith trying to steal a grimoire from the Kyoto National Museum. This grimoire contains the soul of the sun goddess, Amaterasu. We intercepted the manuscript and have assured its safety. And I spoke myself with the goddesses and received their blessing." More murmurs. "The Wraiths are becoming bolder and more methodical. They're not mindless machines that want to kill us. They're working toward something, and I think we all know what that is. Domination of the world, by Odin Allfather."

Shock swept through the hall. Maybe they'd heard rumors, but no one had said it plainly before.

"We are going to take a stand against Odin," Jayne continued. "The Torrent Control Organization wants to take the fight to him and take him down. And if we have your help, we have a better chance of victory."

"What will you do with Odin?" said a burly man in the front row. He had wild hair that sprouted all over his head, and he was dressed in simple peasant clothing from Europe.

"We will end him," Jayne replied.

More laughter echoed through the hall. It didn't sound nice. "He is the Allfather. The most powerful magician in the world. And who in the TCO is powerful enough to do that?" the burly man called out.

Jayne closed her eyes and took a deep breath. She reached for her magic—from the earth, from the Torrent. Her staff appeared, covered in runes. The totems came alive on her forehead, glowing bright, the promise of four powerful Masters. Then she opened her eyes again. "I am."

The laughter in the hall cut off. For a moment, all was silent. Then a Japanese Disciple in a *hakama* pointed. "Amaterasu," he gasped. He fell from his seat to his knees.

Jayne recognized the Disciple Ruger had brought back to the TCO. "I have something for you," she told him, leaning away from the mic. She held up the grimoire.

He stared. Then he turned to face the rest of the auditorium. "It is as Isra says! She is beloved by the goddesses!"

Shouting broke out around the hall. Isra cleared her throat into a separate microphone, off on the side. "If there are questions, we will take them in an orderly fashion," she said.

And there were. How had Jayne gotten all the totems? She tried to sum up succinctly. What was she planning on doing with the totems once the war was over? She wasn't sure. What was the TCO planning to do when the war was over?"

"I don't know that, either," she said. "But we're asking for your help in defeating Odin. We're not asking you to become branches of the TCO."

"You know the Americans," said the burly man, seizing the mic from the woman next to him. "They ask for one small thing, then they start to take. And take. If we ally ourselves now, what will we be by the end of this? Will we truly still have our freedom?"

"Will you have your freedom if Odin conquers the world?" Jayne shot back. "We can make an agreement with you, draw up paperwork, shake hands. And we won't go back on our word. What other magical community can say the same? Do you trust the Kingdom to take care of the Torrent like you want? Do you trust La Liberté?"

"No," said the burly man. His lip curled. "But we don't trust you, either."

They had to convince everyone to join, Katie and Isra had said. Well, this one fellow seemed to be their biggest detractor. Three factions were becoming apparent among the Disciples: those who felt the TCO was the practical decision, like Isra; those who felt that Jayne was divinely blessed, like the Japanese Disciple Akio; and those who wanted nothing to do with them at all.

She spoke directly to the burly man, as though he were the only one in the room. "You can't sit out this war," she said softly. "It's coming for you, whether you want it or not. Making no decision is its own kind of decision, and it's the worst one. Because if you don't pick a side now, you won't get to pick later. So please. Choose a side. Choose our side."

The hall broke out into argument again. The Disciples began to move amongst each other, discussing animatedly. Isra trotted up the steps to the podium and took Jayne's arm. "I think you've done what you can," she said. She sounded sympathetic.

"Is that bad?" Jayne asked.

"Go back to your safe house. Get something to eat. The decision will be made when it is made, and I will deliver it to you."

Katie put one arm around Jayne's shoulders. "Thanks, Isra," she said. "We do really appreciate it."

"I hope you realize this favor is much greater than the loaning of a Zulu dictionary," Isra replied tartly.

"I owe you one," Katie told her. "Come on, Jayne."

Jayne nodded. It was out of her hands now. If she'd failed, well, Amanda and Ruger could hardly be angry, could they? They should've sent a politician to give a grand speech.

There was just one more thing. "Sorry, Isra? Which place in the city makes the best pie?"

THE BOOK OF SPIRITS

T̲h̲e̲y̲ ̲r̲e̲t̲u̲r̲n̲e̲d̲ to the safe house loaded with pastries, and Katie put on a pot of tea.

"All right." Jayne stretched out on the couch. "Favorite author?"

"You'll think me terribly pretentious, but Joyce," Katie said, blushing.

"A classic choice. It's Tolkien for me. I always did tend toward fantasy."

"What do you think of Mervyn Peake? He was rather good, wasn't he?" Katie plopped down in a modern egg chair across from her.

"He was. And his poetry doesn't get enough attention, I think." Jayne popped a sweet piece of *kanafeh* into her mouth and crunched.

"I never took you for a poet," Katie said, a little sly. Jayne shrugged.

The door opened. Jayne tensed, reaching for the Torrent. "It's me," said Isra's familiar voice, and Jayne's shoulders sagged.

"We should really have a password," she grumbled.

"Stop your grousing." Katie leaned forward, adjusting her glasses. "What did they say?"

Isra came into the sitting room and looked first at Katie, then at Jayne. Then she smiled.

"They said yes."

CHAPTER NINETEEN

Ruger held the door open for Amanda as they entered the interrogation room. The room was small and spare, sporting a table and three chairs. One of those chairs was occupied by a trembling, skinny man in magical handcuffs Quimby had developed to dampen an Adept's magical senses. Their newest, youngest team of operatives had been sent to apprehend the Kingdom operative in Slovenia and had succeeded brilliantly, bringing in the man with no wounds.

His eyes flickered between Amanda and Ruger. His lower lip trembled. His breath huffed loudly in and out in the silent room, adding to stale air.

He seemed scared to death. What had Sofia and Cillian been teaching those kids?

Amanda cleared her throat and sat, trying to push her misgivings out of her mind. There was a job to do. She could worry about methods later. "Let's begin," she said. "Your name is—"

"Brian," said the man in a clear Irish brogue. "Brian O'Connell. Age twenty-six, grew up in Dublin, worked as a mechanic before my recruitment."

Amanda paused. All of this information was in her folder. He might be pretending to spill his guts to get her to trust him, so he could feed her a lie later. Had he been a trap, all along?

If he was, he was a fine actor. He looked one jump scare away from fainting. "And what was your mission in Ljubljana, Brian?"

He shook his head, sandy hair flopping. "There was no mission. I was—I was trying to leave. Go underground. But I can defect. Are you looking for defectors? I'm happy to tell you whatever you need to know."

Amanda and Ruger exchanged concerned glances. Brian O'Connell was clearly too incompetent to be a spy. Eagerness and desperation wafted off him in equal measure. "You don't have to trust me," he said. "You can even lock me up."

Ruger folded his hands. "Now why would you rather be in prison than free and roaming the world?" he asked.

"Because." O'Connell's voice dropped to a whisper. "She's seen me. She knows me. And she's—she's hunting me."

"Who?" Amanda asked, leaning forward. She already knew the answer.

"Ruth Thorne," he replied with a visible shudder.

Amanda poured him some water. They worked slowly to coax a cohesive truth out of him, with Ruger taking notes in a little black book. The Kingdom had attempted a coup, and Ruth hadn't taken kindly to that. She'd thwarted the attempt and killed the people behind it. O'Connell had been the one to find them; he'd gotten a message from La Liberté and was taking it to Lars. Only to find Lars' head on the other side of the room from his body.

"All of them, destroyed," he breathed. His eyes took on a glassy look. "They were all—"

"Drink," Amanda told him. He took a shaky slurp of water, and she leaned over to Ruger. "We need the names of everyone in that room," she murmured.

Ruger nodded. "Brian," he said gently. "I have some photographs here. Do you think you could identify them?"

"It would greatly help your defection case," Amanda put in.

O'Connell set the water down and nodded.

Ruger pulled out photographs of high-ranking Kingdom operatives and showed them to O'Connell one by one. The names they knew, but O'Connell's most valuable insight was that all of them were dead.

"Were there others like you?" Amanda asked. "Innocents, caught up in this? Maybe some who ran?"

O'Connell snorted. "Loads. Some ran off to join La Liberté, since they're s'posed to be our friends and all. I just wanted out. I signed up to use magic. I didn't sign up to wage a war."

Then you picked the wrong side, buddy, Amanda thought, but she kept her opinion to herself. In all likelihood O'Connell hadn't been told the whole truth about the Kingdom's aims—and who knew what its goal even was anymore? If Ruth Thorne was slaughtering her followers, it looked like the problem of the Kingdom was resolving itself.

"So you just struck out on your own?" Ruger flicked through his file. "That's funny, because we have a photo of you in Geneva, with a known member of La Liberté. Are you sure you're telling me the truth, Brian?"

Brian's hand spasmed, knocking the water over. "I am, I swear. Don't send me back out there!"

Interesting. Not *don't torture me,* or *don't put me in prison.* The thing he was most afraid of was being alone in the world. A single target for Ruth Thorne's wrath.

"What were you doing with Angelique Dufort?" Angelique was hardly a high-ranking officer, but she'd been a loyal member of La Liberté since she was a teen, according to Tristan.

"I-I-I thought they could help," he said. "A group of us went to them together. They've even got the backing of the French government, right? Of course they could protect us. But that

Gina Labelle, she's flippin' bonkers. She thinks Wraiths are like Rogues. She thinks they'll join us if we offer them the right kind of freedom. I'm not touching those scaly bastards, not with a ten-foot pole. But she's got some big plan to get them all together and pitch her cause. Like a recruitment drive of some kind."

A recruitment drive for Wraiths. It did sound like Gina Labelle's brand of crazy. Amanda touched O'Connell's arm. He flinched. "It's all right, Brian," she said, soothingly. "We're going to take you somewhere safe now. Somewhere deep underground, where the Wraiths won't get you. But you have to tell us something first.

"How is Labelle summoning them?"

CHAPTER
TWENTY

Jayne sat on a yoga mat with her eyes closed and her hands resting lightly on her crossed legs, trying desperately not to squirm. Meditation had never been her strong suit. Her mind tended to wander, or dwell on the latest book she was reading (*The Vorkosigan Saga*) or remind her that she itched right at the small of her back. The Spirit totem made her jumpy. Distracting scents wafted through the city, practically assaulting her nose—her senses were much keener now. Cumin and sea salt were predominant, though she could smell the smoke from the charcoal braziers grilling fish and almost taste the lemon being squeezed on boiled prawns. She thought she could sense a hint of rain on the wind, too. It was disconcerting, to be tuned in so well.

When they'd come into the small training room above a fitness center in Alexandria, she'd been looking forward to a long workout where she exhausted her muscles. Instead, Isra wanted her to try sitting still, just for a bit. Who knew how easily she could exhaust her mind instead, just by trying not to think about anything?

"Your thoughts are deafening," said Isra in a disapproving voice.

"What, you can read my mind?" Jayne joked weakly.

"I do not need to," Isra said, which wasn't a *no*. Jayne opened her eyes. The Egyptian woman was watching her with her large, liquid brown eyes. "You will not settle. You shift and fidget, a sure sign that something is on your mind."

A lot was on her mind. Tristan, for starters. Jayne had fulfilled her mission, and now it was time to go home. Tristan might say he was fully healed, but she wanted to see for herself. *Besides, a little physical examination never hurt anybody,* she thought slyly.

She also wanted to know how Sofia's students had done in the field. Now that Matthew was out of the Time Catch they could actually get to know one another. She could be a middle child and enjoy watching Sofia mother someone else for a change. And, of course, there was the matter of her father. Henry Thorne was up to something, and she didn't like being out of the loop.

But what she said was "I don't think I completely understand. I'm establishing my contact with the Earth? I usually do that through my Earth totem."

"And now you will learn to do it the way the rest of us mere mortals do it," Isra said, mouth twisting in amusement. "We Disciples do not suffer when the Torrent is damaged or infected. Do you know why? It is because we draw our magic from the sun and the Earth. We respect the Earth and recognize it as a source of life and magic. And the magic we draw is cleansed of impurities."

"But...the Torrent is the source of all magic," Jayne said.

"Not so long ago the Torrent was here, on Earth, in the air we breathe, the sun shining down on the land, the land itself. All cohesive, all working together," Isra reminded her. "And now it is closer than ever to being healed, and all magic reunited. It is a complicated prospect, but it means that our own powers grow as the Earth takes more magic from the Torrent. But it is not an entirely blessed thing."

"Why not?" Jayne asked, shifting. Her butt was getting sore.

"The Torrent is sick. It has been corrupted by the Allfather, and if it fully merges with this plane, Odin will come here, too. His Wraiths can already slip through portals and fly among us, visible even to the common man. If Odin comes..." She shook her head. "Well, perhaps there will be no more Disciples of Gaia, because there will be no Earth to save."

She got to her feet, evidently deciding that their meditation was over, and Jayne was only too glad to hop up as well. Isra twisted her hands and a long saber rose from the earth, fitting to the palm of her hand. She raised it in salute. Jayne grinned and drew her own staff from the Torrent. The sword flashed and she swept the staff up just in time, knocking the saber aside. Jayne imagined the staff becoming slippery and slick, repelling all attacks, and drew a spell from the Torrent. It worked a little too well: when Isra swept forward with her next attack, Jayne flipped the staff to block it and it sailed out of her hands.

She conceded the round and retrieved the staff, stripping away the Slippery spell and trying for something more specific. "Draw from the Earth," Isra directed her.

Right. That was the whole purpose of this. Jayne took a deep breath. "So Odin. What's his deal, exactly?"

"Odin Allfather is a magician of immense power," Isra said, easily conjuring a spell to dull the edge of her blade for training. "To call him a Master would be like calling you an Adept. He is one of the old powers, the magicians who were revered as gods. And the power was all-consuming. He could take anything he wanted, and so he wanted everything."

"But other gods don't act like that," Jayne said, thinking of Freya and Vesta and Amaterasu. She nodded to the pendant half-hidden by Isra's hijab. "I'm guessing Hathor's not a power-hungry lady."

"These great Masters once kept each other in check," Isra said. "But rifts grew between them. Odin became consumed with gathering knowledge and power, and by the time anyone realized what he was doing, it was too late. He had already created the first two Wraiths."

"Are they still around?" Jayne found a Repel spell at last and laid it over her staff. It was weak, nothing like the spells she could pull directly from the Torrent. She grimaced as they faced off again. The Spirit totem was too ephemeral.

"Yes, they are still alive." Isra darted forward. Her saber slipped past Jayne's guard and slapped against her ribs. Jayne pushed Isra's arm hard to the side and brought the staff around to sweep Isra's feet out from under her. Isra pirouetted and the saber swung out again, slapping Jayne's staff aside and breaking the Repel spell with a crack. The blade tapped her shoulder. "I win again."

Jayne backed off, grinning. It had been a while since she'd sparred without Tristan or Vivienne. It was good to diversify. Isra was very talented. "You should be a warrior, not a diplomat."

"The power of the Earth comes with great responsibility. I would much rather talk my way out of a fight."

"And the Wraiths? How will I identify them?"

"You will know them," Isra said. "They are the largest Wraiths I have ever seen. Huginn and Muninn are their names."

"Thought and Memory," Jane murmured. The names of Odin's raven companions in Norse mythology. Myths were more real than people imagined.

"Legends say that they were created to gain knowledge, to preserve magical ways. But when he made them, Odin was already corrupted by his vast power. He used them as bludgeons to take what he needed. He used them to pick off other

Masters, one by one, killing them or trapping them in the Torrent. Others fled to hide in grimoires. And it was only with great effort that he was trapped in the Torrent himself, in a prison even you couldn't re-create, Jayne Thorne. Now, try again. Connect to the Earth. Bring forth your magic."

Jayne closed her eyes and reached for the power. It was difficult; the Torrent was like a beacon in her mind—*Pick me! Pick me!*—and she could feel the totems, too, pulsing gently. Medb's totem in particular seemed amused. "Feel like giving me any insight?" she muttered. "No? Didn't think so."

If the Torrent soaked into the earth, and the earth cleansed the magic, then maybe what she was looking for felt like the Torrent after all...just a smaller part. Jayne cast her senses out, trying to ignore the roaring river that had exactly what she wanted. How did Disciples *do* this?

There. She felt it, the barest trace of something, and reached for it. It was rooted in the ground, and she felt Medb stir as the Earth totem in her longed to connect.

And, well—would Isra really notice, if she got a little help?

Jayne activated the Earth totem. The magic flared, going deep, deep as a well, spreading like a tree underground. It was a network, Jayne saw in a flash, a network over the whole Earth, lines of magic that could draw on each other and refill each other.

Something in the network *rocked*.

Jayne reeled back. Suddenly she was in the training room again and falling. Isra grabbed her by the wrist and propped her up. "What is it?" The woman's brow furrowed.

"Didn't you feel it?" Jayne dropped to the floor and pressed her hand against the mat. No good. "We need to go outside. Something's happening."

Isra hurried her down to a garden dotted with statuary columns and palm trees. "Try not to look too suspicious," she said as Jayne knelt in the fresh dirt.

She let her fingers rest on the soil and drew on the power of the Earth totem; to hell with training now. She cast her mind down into the earth, feeling for the network. It was like veins, she thought, shooting out the world over. Her mind connected with the network.

She scarcely had time to appreciate its vastness before she felt it tremble, like an earthquake. *Find the source,* she demanded, and imagined a map of the world.

The rumble came again. It seemed to be coming from the south.

Jayne opened her eyes and brushed her hair across her forehead to conceal her glowing Earth totem. Isra looked shaken. "I felt it, too," she said.

"Any idea from where?" Jayne was already getting out her phone. Isra shook her head. Katie appeared at the edge of the garden, alarm on her face. She'd been enjoying a cup of tea while Isra and Jayne trained. Jayne could smell the crushed mint on her fingers.

"What's happening?" Katie asked.

"I don't know. I'm calling in." She dialed Ruger. For a moment she was tempted to portal right back and tell him in person—but she knew the main reason she wanted to do that was so she could see Tristan, and that reason wasn't good enough.

"Yes?" Ruger said. He sounded tense already.

"I've got the Disciples on our side, and now's a great time to show them how we work."

Ruger sighed. "What did you do?"

Jayne was momentarily thrown by a bout of self-righteousness. "Why do you assume I've done something?" she asked.

"Because I know you. I don't have time to deal with your problems, Jayne. We've got a massive Wraith attack in Wellington. I need you to get to New Zealand, now. Send Katie to the portal. She can come back first, and it will reset for you."

Wellington. Southward. Could the two things be related? "We're on our way," Jayne said. She hung up and turned to Isra and Katie. "There's a Wraith attack. We have to go, now."

Katie paled. "Not you," Jayne said fondly. "You get back to the library and pull everything you can find on Odin. I can handle this."

"You can't handle a Wraith attack on your own."

"I will go with Jayne," Isra said.

"But you'll need help."

"Do not worry. I will call for reinforcements, also. You are not prepared for war, I think, Katie Bell."

They hugged briefly. "Be careful, both of you," Katie said, already moving back toward the safe house.

At the portal, they saw Katie safely through, and when it glowed again, Jayne looked up at the elegant Isra. "Ready to tangle, partner?"

"I pray to the Goddess that I will not regret this," Isra replied and looped her arm through Jayne's.

CHAPTER
TWENTY-ONE

They tumbled out of the portal into a war zone. Wellington, New Zealand, was someplace Jayne had always wanted to go, but not like this. The sky was black, the sun blotted out by a host of flying Wraiths. The screams of civilians mixed with the cries of the police and the howls and shrieks of the Wraiths. Jayne stumbled over the bloody body of a La Liberté member, then threw up a Block spell just in time to protect Isra and several other Disciples as they ran through the portal. A Wraith's claws screeched against the spell, and it beat its wings to gain altitude, snarling.

Something whizzed past Jayne's ear and she ducked. "Bullets," she warned Isra. A few feet away, a policeman had his firearm out and was emptying it into a nearby Wraith. Not every bullet found its mark; the scaly hides of the Wraiths could deflect bullets if they struck the wrong spot.

The Wraith he'd shot spun to face him, seemingly uncaring that it had three new holes in its rib cage. It loped toward him on long canine legs. He squeezed the trigger, but an extra bullet to the shoulder didn't stop it. Jayne dove in front of him and threw up a Block for him, too. The Wraith smashed against it, and she felt her muscles tremble as the spell held. She reached for her staff and gave it a hard poke between the eyes. It stumbled back and spun to find a new target—an easy prospect. The ground was lousy with people.

Jayne turned to the police officer. He was looking past her, shaking, mouth slightly agape. He didn't even know she was there.

"Well, this is going to be a picnic," she muttered.

Three more portals flashed against the side of a large brick building, and Adepts began to pour through. Jayne recognized Ruger and Tamara. A moment later she felt a touch, mind to mind, and she turned to see Vivienne running toward her, transforming already into her tigress form.

Jayne, she said, breathless. *See—*

Jayne saw.

Tristan Labelle had traded his hospital gown for a pale blue collared shirt and black trousers. His dark hair was tousled, and color had returned to his fine-boned cheeks. His eyes blazed with health and something more—focus.

Focus on her.

God, he looked scrumptious.

He strode up to her as though she were the only thing in Wellington, as though a battle weren't raging around them. He seized her shoulders and pulled her to him, sliding his hand up her neck to cradle the back of her head. He kissed her, hard. She gasped, and he slid his tongue into her mouth. Heat seared over her, followed closely by a relief so potent she sagged against him. Tears sprang to her eyes.

She hadn't really believed he was well, she realized. She'd needed to see it for herself.

He pulled away and brushed at her cheeks with his thumb. *"Mon amour,"* he murmured. "I am here."

"You..." She ran her hand down his chest. She still couldn't quite believe it was him, even though his breath hitched when she caressed him and she felt his heart, strong and steady, beneath her palm. "Are you sure you should be out here?"

One side of his mouth came up in a roguish smile. Tristan slid one hand around her waist, and with the other sketched a quick spell out in the air and flung it at a Wraith. The Wraith sailed backward on a sudden draft of wind. Then Tristan pulled a medieval sword from midair.

Jayne stared. She'd never seen that spell before. And Tristan had conjured it with ease. She'd felt its power; a few days ago he would have been sweating with the effort.

"I should certainly be here," Tristan said.

"Mushy stuff later," Vivienne called. "Battle now."

"Right." Jayne took quick stock. Isra had summoned more Disciples of Gaia and they had fanned out, taking on Wraiths two to one. "We need to protect our new allies. What's our objective?"

"Defend civilians. Kill Wraiths," Tristan said.

Jayne looked up at the sky. There were too many of them to count. "Is that all?" she muttered.

Tristan went for a nearby Wraith with a snout like a crocodile and claws like a cat. He lopped off one paw at the wrist, then ducked as the Wraith clumsily swiped with another. Vivienne slammed into the Wraith and bowled it over, and Jayne hit it hard with her staff.

Protect Isra, she told Vivienne.

The tigress' lips curled. *I wish to protect my brother,* she said.

I'm with Tristan, don't worry. Protect Isra. Jayne turned in time to see Tristan charging after another Wraith. *Looks like someone got bored sitting in his hospital bed all day.* She ran after him.

He stabbed a Wraith through the heart, then slipped as it toppled over on him. Jayne grabbed him by the hand and hauled him out. "I am fine, Jayne," he said, bending down to retrieve his sword.

"You still need someone to watch your back," Jayne told him. "Whatever happened to you, you're not invincible. Right?" If Quimby had come up with an invincibility serum, then *that* would be something.

Tristan flashed her his rakish grin again. "To be fair, we haven't tested it. Down!"

He tackled her and they barely avoided the claws of a low-flying Wraith. A huge bird flapped after it, cawing. Vivienne, in a harpy eagle form.

"I thought you said you could take care of him," Vivienne screeched.

"I *said* protect Isra!" Jayne shouted. She whirled. Isra was backing away from two Wraiths, swinging her saber. She had a look of determined desperation in her eye, the look of a woman who was staring her death in the face.

Jayne ran, pulling a lasso from the Torrent. Her Fire totem blazed, and she imbued it with a Burning spell. She flung the lasso and it caught around the foot of one Wraith. Then she pulled with everything she had. It screamed, and she smelled sizzling flesh.

Isra plunged the saber into the fallen Wraith's neck, and the scream subsided in a gurgle. She looked up at Jayne and nodded —then an enormous hand swatted her away like a fly. She hit the side of an overturned sedan and slumped to the ground.

"No!" Jayne cried. The Wraith spun to face her. It was between her and Isra. Jayne bared her teeth and hefted her staff. The Wraith had a batlike face, with a squashed snout and long tusk-like teeth that dripped with something she hoped was saliva. Its wings snapped open and it roared.

Something pierced the roof of its mouth from behind.

A lithe shape jerked a short sword free, leapt down to the pavement and raised her arms. A shimmering bubble closed over Isra. Another Wraith slid off the bubble as it tried to snatch up the Disciple, and Jayne recognized a variant on the Slippery spell she'd tried earlier today. But this one was much more efficient and effective and complex. Who *was* that Adept?

Jayne found she could slip through the bubble, though it felt vaguely slimy on her skin. She knelt by Isra, who had opened her eyes and was looking dazedly after the girl.

"A friend of yours?" Jayne asked.

Isra shook her head and leaned heavily on Jayne while she got to her feet. "I thought she was with you."

A whole squad of new Adepts had entered the fray—Adepts who moved with deadly precision, wielding both weapons and spells as though they'd been training this way for years. They raised more bubbles over the fallen, enabling TCO medics to scurry from place to place to evaluate the wounded. Spells shimmered along their swords and spears and other weapons. As Jayne watched, one of them shook his hand, and an apple-sized piece of metal appeared in it. He wrapped a Fire spell around it, pulled the pin with his teeth, and hurled it into the sky.

Another Adept flung a Block spell the size of Jayne's apartment overhead. The grenade exploded, and a dozen Wraiths or more screamed as the projectiles pierced their flesh. Blood and metal bounced off the Block spell.

"Rufus!" shouted the boy who'd conjured the block. "I said no grenades!"

There was something familiar about that boy...but before Jayne could fully put her finger on it, she was helping Isra limp out of the bubble, holding up her staff, and looking around for her errant Rogue. *Vivienne, we are a team,* she said through gritted teeth.

And now one of us is with my brother, and the other with your Disciple. It is as you wish, Vivienne replied.

But it wasn't what I ordered. One of us has to call the shots in battle, Viv. Jayne handed Isra off to a TCO medic and spun back toward the battle. *And that person is me.*

I won't leave him, Vivienne said. Beneath her anger, Jayne sensed something more: fear. Vivienne had almost lost her brother. It was natural that she would feel protective of him, just as Jayne did.

"I know the two of you are arguing about me," Tristan said. His blue shirt was spattered in black blood. "I'm fine. I'm very well, in fact." He swung the sword and sheared off the claws of another Wraith. "So stop acting like I'm a bauble and start treating me like a soldier."

"No," said Vivienne succinctly.

Jayne couched it. "We're taking on the Wraiths two to one, and my partner's down for the count. Let's just work together for now, all right?"

But even with their new, strangely powerful Adepts, the battle was not going their way. For every Adept there were at least five Wraiths, and the Wellington police were getting in the way more than anything. The Adepts had to watch out for bullets as well as teeth and claws. They were going to need to retreat. Retreat or do something drastic.

Jayne spotted Ruger standing over a bloodied Tamara, swinging a mace that looked almost like a toy in his big hand. He smashed a Wraith across its jackal face. Jayne gave it a blow on the other side. It wobbled and went down. "What's the plan?" she said.

"The plan." What little color was left in his face drained away at the carnage. "We had no idea there were so many," he murmured.

Then his eyes widened. "Watch out!"

He shoved Jayne out of the way as a tail lashed toward them. The tail caught him in the chest and he went flying. Jayne tried to leap after him, but a thick, scaly hand gripped her forearm in a grip like concrete.

Jayne stiffened. This was the end of her arm, she knew it. But the Wraith leaned forward, black eyes rolling in its head.

Jayne caught the scent of rotting violets. Her breath hitched. *No.*

The black cleared, revealing two horribly familiar stormy gray irises. "Help me," Ruth Thorne whispered through a ruined mouth. Her grip slackened for a fraction of a moment, just enough time for Jayne to twist free. Her eyes went black again.

Jayne whirled the staff and dealt her mother a hard thwack. Ruth reeled away.

Help me. Did she think they could drive the Wraith out of her? *Could* they drive the Wraith out of her? Would Quimby's serum even do that?

Jayne had no time to ponder. The Wraith spun back toward her and grabbed her staff, wrenching it from her hand and flinging it wide. Jayne stomped hard on what passed for Ruth's instep, then delivered a powerful kick to the knee. She heard something crunch. Then a fist slammed into her jaw, and she went down.

Get up. She rolled over and stumbled to her feet, reaching into the Torrent for a weapon—any weapon. Two long knives appeared in her hands. Her vision was still spinning, and her jaw felt like it had been dislocated. She raised the knives and slashed out wildly. Ruth batted one away, then the other. She roared, revealing sharp, bloody teeth and a serpentine tongue. Her claws became a hand, and she reached toward her daughter.

Jayne felt a spark of panic. *She's going for the totems.* She scrambled back, searching for a weapon, conjuring a Block, a Shield, anything she could use to defend herself—Ruth would rip Jayne's head off and figure out how to get the totems out later.

Before she conjured the spell, a blur passed in front of her and materialized as a warrior. Tristan swung his sword to meet Ruth's hand. She screamed as the blade lodged in the flesh of her palm with a meaty *thunk*. He pulled the sword free and swung again. He moved forward in quick steps, jabbing, forcing her back. Giving Jayne some breathing space.

Jayne got to all fours, then stood. Her head spun, and she swayed. Ruth's attacks were becoming clumsy; Tristan had scored a hit just above her heart and another on her thigh. She was losing blood, and momentum. Perhaps enough of her remained in the Wraith to realize she'd been about to kill her own daughter.

Not something that's ever stopped her before, Jayne thought bitterly.

Ruth snarled one final time at Tristan, and took to the skies, trailing blood.

Tristan watched her go for a moment then reached for Jayne. *"Mon amour,"* he whispered, holding her steady. "Let us get you to a medic."

"I'm fine." Jayne squeezed his arm. "Thanks to you."

"You likely have a concussion, Jayne."

"I'll live. I'll have Tamara look at me when we get back," Jayne said.

"Don't argue with me," he pleaded softly, pressing his forehead to hers. "Not when you almost died."

He bent down and pressed his mouth to hers. She pressed back—

And felt him go rigid against her.

Warmth spread over her front. She pulled back and gasped. Long black claws protruded from his chest. His eyes were wide with shock. He began to tremble.

The claws withdrew with a sickening sucking sound and Tristan collapsed against her, unable to hold his own weight. Behind him, the Wraith that had been Ruth Thorne stumbled back, eyes flickering between black and gray.

A long, powerful shape hit her with a force that sent them tumbling over the wrecked road. Vivienne roared and slammed a paw against Ruth's head, then dug her teeth into the Wraith's shoulder. Ruth screamed. The noise seemed distant to Jayne. She sank beneath Tristan, lowering them both to the ground. Vivienne shrieked as Ruth swatted her off and leapt to her feet. Her eyes flickered one more time, and a look of horror came over her face. Then she turned and ran.

Blood bubbled from Tristan's mouth. His eyes were full of pain. "You're going to be all right," she whispered, choking on her own fear. She tore off her jacket and pressed it to his chest. It soaked through almost instantly. "Get help," she cried to Vivienne, and the tigress loped off.

Tristan's head bobbed back and forth, like he was trying to shake it. She took his hand, and his fingers spasmed around hers. "You're going to be fine. You're going to be fine." It sounded like a desperate prayer, a plea. Tristan's lips moved soundlessly, then he was racked by a cough.

A terrible hole opened up in her, and the air around her turned cold. It was as though her entire future were unraveling before her eyes. The life she'd always wanted with a man who was her equal and saw her as his. A life spent traveling together, saving the world together, raising children together. The daughter Henry had seen in the Torrent. It was all disappearing.

Gentle hands pressed on her shoulder. Jayne shook them off. Tamara knelt down next to her and put her hands around Jayne's where they pressed on Tristan's chest. "We've got him now," she said gently, but hissed when she drew the coat away and saw the long, angry, puckered wounds. "This is bad."

But it doesn't have to be. Jayne watched her work, determination slowly spreading to consume her numbness. Tamara moved quickly and efficiently, but the grim set of her mouth foretold the outcome.

Jayne put a hand on his arm. "Jayne, please," said Tamara. Then she called over her shoulder, "Can I get a blanket over here?" She murmured to another medic, and Jayne caught the words *girlfriend* and *shock*. "Jayne, you've done all you can."

"No, I haven't." Jayne closed her eyes and summoned the Torrent.

Jayne, no. Vivienne's voice rang in her head. *You cannot do this.*

Viv, we have to heal him. Of all people, Vivienne should understand.

Jayne, remember what it does to you. You'll die, or worse. Vivienne's voice was tinted with desperation. *Tristan will never forgive you for it.*

That was the thing, Jayne thought with a bitter smile. He'd be alive to hate her. And that was all that mattered.

She drew the Healing spell from the Torrent. It seemed to crackle in her hands, anxious to be put into use. She laid it over Tristan's chest and pressed down. Dimly she heard a shout: Ruger, calling her name, Tamara crying *no!* But she couldn't concentrate on that, because her entire body was on fire.

Flames burst to life beneath her skin. She threw her head back and screamed, feeling heat scorch her throat and crack her teeth. Smoke poured from her mouth, choking her, and every breath she gasped felt ice cold in comparison.

The center of the blaze was on her arm. The skin there seemed to rip in two, tearing from her with a roar, and she couldn't tell whether the roar was the sound of the fire or her screams or entirely within her mind. She focused on that hand, pushing down on the spell, on Tristan's chest. If this was going to kill her, it was going to damn well work in the process.

The pain became too great. She could feel herself slipping away. *Heal,* she thought desperately, and sagged over Tristan's chest, and the whole world faded to a gentle buzz.

She couldn't have blacked out for long, for when the dull throb of pain in her mouth and chest and limbs brought her back to the real world, she still heard the sounds of battle. People screamed, weapons clashed in a sound of ringing steel and smacking wood. Guns discharged in a rapid fire. Then someone gasped, "What the hell is *that*?"

Tristan shifted under her. "You are making my shirt wet," he murmured.

Jayne lifted her head. "Tristan?" she whispered in a voice like smoke.

He lay on the cobblestone ground. His blue eyes were clear of pain and the fading that came with death. His lips curved to look at her. Then they looked past her, into the air, and widened. *"Mon Dieu,"* he whispered.

Jayne forced herself to sit up. Her shirt hung in tatters, smoking and charred. What price had she paid for this healing? She pulled what remained of her sleeve away from her forearm, then stared in amazement. The flesh of her arm was as pale and soft as the rest of her skin.

"Jayne," Tristan said and pointed. "What the hell is that?"

A gray, scaly shape, larger than any of the Wraiths they'd battled so far, glided through the air on wings the size of an airplane's. Its tail whipped back and forth through the air, and its long neck wound about, looking for prey. It sighted and dove, a flashing silver spiral; its head darting out to snap a nearby Wraith on the wing. The Wraith screamed as its wing crunched. The new creature jerked its head back and forth a few times, then released the Wraith to plummet to the ground. The Wraith smashed into the roof of a car, setting off an alarm to add to the cacophony of destruction.

"I don't know, but it looks like it's on our side." Jayne ran her fingers over the new patch of skin on her arm. The scaly gray skin was gone. Whatever it was, she suddenly knew it was *hers*.

Could she...control it?

You may direct me, said a voice deep in her mind. *I control myself.*

All right then, Jayne thought, still slightly dazed. *Uh, kill Wraiths, I guess?*

The creature above roared. Three Wraiths tried to converge on it, but a rending of claws and teeth and white-hot flame left them screaming and limping away.

Tristan was looking between Jayne and the creature. "Jayne? Did you do something stupid?"

Jayne bent and pressed her forehead to his. The inside of her mouth tasted like smoke, and her teeth hurt like they all wanted to fall out, but she smiled. He was warm and blood-stained and sweaty and filthy. But—"You're alive, aren't you?"

Tristan grunted and she helped pull him to a sitting position. He tugged his blood-soaked shirt away from his chest, noting the holes in the cloth and squinting at the skin beneath. "I am going to take that as a yes."

Above them, Wraiths were scattering in panic. People were starting to venture out from behind cars and buildings and piles of rubble to watch them go. Isra sat open-mouthed against a wall. Ruger started barking orders. A number of Adepts in matching black clothing began to spin more spells, this time aimed at their opponents on the ground.

"Pierre," snarled Tristan suddenly, lip curling. La Liberté was here.

Tristan's former friend caught his eye. He raised his hand in a mock salute, which turned into a rude gesture. Then he summoned a portal.

"He can't get away," Jayne said.

"Go after him," Vivienne replied. She'd turned back into a human, and she knelt at Tristan's knees. "I will look after Tristan—"

"Oh, because you did such a good job in the first place?" Jayne snapped. It was wrong of her, but she'd just brought Tristan back from the dead, and she'd be damned if she would leave him now.

"He ran from me," Vivienne said, and Jayne heard the half-hysterical note in the girl's voice. Of course she'd be blaming herself. Of course she'd be angry.

"Here is a thought," Tristan said. "Both of you go and stop trying to babysit me."

"No," Jayne and Vivienne said at once. Then Jayne looked up. The new creature was still a dark shape in the sky, chasing the last of the Wraiths like clouds on the wind. *Can you recognize La Liberté Adepts? Can you...capture them without hurting them?*

I am part of you, the creature replied. *I can do what you do.*

Somehow my flights are only flights of fancy, Jayne thought.

Let's get them, she said to this new being.

It wasn't a creature, she realized as it dove. It was a freaking dragon, the sort of dragon she'd dreamed about riding when she was a kid and lost on Pern, with leathery bat wings and a sleek, elegant body. A dragon like the one she manifested the first time she used her magic at the Farm in Virginia, with Ruger standing on the ground shaking his head at her for showing off.

The dragon swept toward the ground, and Adepts from both sides of the battle scattered. Pierre swore and ran for the portal, diving through just in time. The dragon beat his great wings and alighted gently as a songbird. He now loomed between the portal and half a dozen La Liberté agents, leathery wings flapping.

They are yours, he rumbled in Jayne's mind.

"I think that will do," Ruger said, and motioned with his hand. The members of La Liberté were quickly surrounded. Faced with a dragon or powerful Adepts, their choice was clear. They put up their hands and allowed themselves to be magically bound.

Things had quieted down. The Wraiths were gone. The dragon landed, hard, and looked fearsome. Jayne smiled. Now that was one hell of a party trick. Everyone was staring at her like she'd grown wings herself and started flying around.

It was Ruger who came forward first. He didn't exactly bow before the dragon, but he certainly seemed subservient. "We are grateful for any allies we can get in this troubled time. But...will you honor us with your name?"

The dragon cocked his head, whether deciding to eat Ruger or comply, Jayne didn't know.

He cannot hear me, he said to Jayne with what felt like an eye roll. A name bloomed in her mind.

"His name is Hayden," she called over. Her voice had improved, but it was still hoarse, as though she'd run through a burning building. "He's with me." She coughed. Someone handed her a bottle of water and she drank, relishing the cold and metallic tang.

"I might have known," Ruger groaned, but a slight smile graced his features.

"What other surprises do you have in store for us, Jayne Thorne?" Tristan said.

If I am no longer needed, I will return to my rest, Hayden rumbled.

All right, Jayne said uncertainly. But a moment later she found out what he meant: He spread his wings, stretched out his neck and tail, and light spread over his body. It grew brighter and brighter until Jayne had to put a hand over her eyes—then, with a sound like a small implosion, the light was gone. And so was he.

"Mon Dieu," Tristan said again. He ran a finger up the inside of Jayne's arm, eyes wide. The scaly patch of gray was gone; the flesh there was now silver from her wrist to her elbow.

"What is it, a Wraith?" Vivienne asked. "Like, a good Wraith?"

"Technically speaking, I'm not sure," Jayne said, touching the strange new flesh. A ripple of something akin to joy moved through her. "But he's on our side." And he had come from her, so she wasn't turning into a Wraith after all. And Tristan was whole and well. She grinned. "And to think you told me I shouldn't heal people anymore."

"Jayne." Tristan's hand slid back down her arm, leaving a shiver in its wake. All she wanted to do was press her face to his, prove to herself that he really was here, and safe, and solid. But he was looking at her seriously. "You have done something beyond my knowledge. We are in uncharted waters here."

"Well, as long as the uncharted waters are badass," Jayne replied with a smile.

The air was full of dust and smoke and the acrid, choking smell of Wraith blood. Despite this, news cameras were already on the scene, cataloguing the devastation and interviewing panicked residents. Jayne wondered if the non-Adepts had seen Hayden the way they'd seen the Wraiths. The TCO began to walk among the rubble as well, finding officers and picking up weapons pulled from the Torrent. They ignored requests for comment from the sidelines. Jayne, Tristan, and Vivienne joined the search, retrieving Wraith claws and scales and bits of wing. Quimby and Henry would probably jump at the chance to study these.

As they inspected an overturned car for any civilians or magical artifacts, Jayne heard a familiar voice. "Rufus, Zia, remember you're a team. You've got to have each other's backs. Remember that one of you is always the principal in battle—the principal picks the target, and the secondary follows. You nearly got into trouble because you were both too busy running off to do your own thing. Matthew and Rebecca, good job. Next time, we're going to try a wider coordination with Rebecca taking over as principal. Medina—"

Jayne came around the car. Sofia and Cillian stood in front of the new powerful Adepts. Sofia was ticking points off on her fingers. *Of course,* Jayne realized. Their new allies were from the school. If every class was this powerful, the TCO would be in a good position, indeed.

Jayne looked closer at her sister. Something was definitely up. Her whole body seemed to glow, and Jayne could see something flashing on her hand. Her left hand.

Cillian caught her eye first. He gave her a little wince, but she grinned widely at him, which made him grin back. He nudged Sofia. "I'll take over," he said, gesturing. "You probably need to talk to your sister. Like, *talk* talk." Sofia turned. Her eyes widened.

"Jayne! Someone said—" Sofia looked Tristan up and down. "Have you ever been told that reports of your death were greatly exaggerated?"

"Thanks to Jayne, I am still here to hear it," Tristan replied.

"Are these your students?" Jayne asked. "Amanda had you bring them to a Wraith battle?"

Sofia grimaced. "It was all-hands-on-deck. Believe me, I wouldn't have chosen it for our second mission."

Jayne laughed. Motherly Sofia probably would have given them an ice cream run. She wrapped her arms around her sister, relaxing for the first time since the battle was over.

"Jayne?" Sofia pulled back. "There's something I need to tell you. I'd hoped for a more...private moment, but..." She held out her hand, and Jayne saw a beautiful antique diamond ring nestled on her sister's finger. She also saw a golden glow coming off Sofia's skin.

"You're getting married," Jayne said, a happy sob catching in her throat. "Oh, Sofia, I am so thrilled for you both."

"There's more," she said with a rueful smile.

"Yeah, kinda figured that one out. You're glowing. Actually, you're incandescent. Like you ate a lightbulb. I assume there's a little Rogue in the oven? I'm going to be an auntie?"

"You are."

Jayne hugged Sofia so hard she gave a little squeak of

protest. "This is the best news ever. I'm really happy for you guys."

A deep male voice interrupted them, calling from across the street. "Um, Sofia? Orders?"

She turned to the interloper, grabbed Jayne by the arm. "There's someone you need to meet."

She led Jayne away from Tristan and Vivienne. Vivienne started to follow, but Tristan put a hand on her arm and started speaking to her in low and rapid French.

"Matthew!" Sofia called. A tall, curly-haired boy looked up. "Come here for a moment."

He broke away from his friends and approached. He looked nervous somehow, like he expected Jayne's dragon to pop his head out of her arm and take a bite. His ice-gray eyes darted everywhere but Jayne.

She'd never seen him before in her life. Yet there was something so familiar about the tilt of his chin, the slope of his nose. His eyes... He glanced at Sofia and swallowed.

"Jayne, I'd like you to meet Matthew. Our brother."

CHAPTER
TWENTY-TWO

Jayne's breath caught in her throat. Matthew looked like he was trying to be as small as possible, no easy feat for a boy of nearly six feet. "Uh." He stuck his hands in his pockets. "Hi."

"Pleasure," Jayne said. She didn't know whether to shake his hand or hug him. God, he looked so much like Ruth it was freaky. "I'm looking forward to getting to know you, Matthew."

"Me too. Sofia says you're a badass."

"I'd say it runs in the family, considering that move you pulled with the Wraith. Nicely done."

"Don't think I'm nuts, but was that a dragon earlier?"

"Yes. His name is Hayden. He's...mine." She touched her arm and felt a strangely happy sigh from the silvery patch of skin.

Matthew grinned, and Jayne was thrust back in time to a vision of her mother she hadn't seen since she was a very small girl. She warmed for a moment, then the same icy eyes reappeared in her mind, tortured now, calling for help. Right. Like Jayne would help that bitch now, considering what she'd done to Tristan.

Jayne rounded on Sofia. "You didn't tell me he'd be here."

"Where have *you* been, Jayne? Gallivanting around the Middle East? We're both working in different branches of the TCO, so we obviously have different priorities. Especially when you were focusing all your worries on him." She tilted her head toward Tristan. "He's looking really good, by the way."

Jayne softened toward her sister. "Yeah." It *had* been a hectic few days.

"Besides, what sort of secrets are *you* keeping? You ready to explain the thing that popped out of your arm?" Sofia said.

Jayne opened her mouth, then closed it again. She couldn't explain. She didn't understand what had happened. Even Tristan didn't understand, it seemed. They'd have to scour the library when they returned to the TCO and try to figure out what Hayden was, exactly, and whether he had any similarities to the Wraiths that might make him dangerous.

Going back to the TCO sounded good, actually. Mainly because she wanted to shower, stuff her face with pie, then fall back in her bed and sleep until she couldn't feel the prickling of phantom flames under her skin anymore. She also wanted to talk. She had a good two decades of catching up to do with her brother. "I need pie."

"You always need pie," Sofia said.

"Who doesn't? I mean, come on. New Zealand loves pies. We love pie. Do you love pie, Matthew? Should we get some pie and have a chat?"

"Uh, yeah." His eyes darted nervously from side to side. "Pie sounds really good right about now."

"Sofia..." Cillian's voice held a note of danger.

The city had gone silent around them. The calls of people looking for survivors trapped under cars or rubble had cut off, and no one was moving around. The rest of the TCO was focused on a mass of bodies slightly obscured by the smoke.

"Pie sounds really good, like, right *now*," Matthew said again.

A policeman in black body armor and a rifle stepped out from behind a van. "Hands where I can see them," he barked. "No funny business."

"Why is this stuff never shielded from the normal people when you need it to be?" Jayne wondered, slowly putting up her hands. *You bulletproof?* she asked Hayden.

Hardly, he replied from within her.

"Team Aegis," Sofia said calmly. "Block spell."

They moved with perfect precision, so quickly Jayne hardly had time to think *Team what now?* A green-gold web shimmered over their group, growing larger and larger. The first bullet pinged off it.

"It won't hold a steady barrage, so let's get going." Sofia started to back up. Her students followed, holding up the spell as they moved. "Where were those portals?"

"Closed," said Tristan. "After the prisoner and medical transport. They're too hard to sustain."

"Peachy," Jayne muttered.

A hand grabbed her arm. "With me," said a voice she didn't recognize.

Jayne turned. There stood a man she'd never seen before, a tall man with a strong, chiseled face and dark hair pulled back in a ponytail. He held a spear stained black with Wraith blood, and beneath his torn shirt she spotted the edge of a Māori tattoo. Was he a Disciple?

"It's all right," called a much more familiar voice. She turned and spotted Ruger waving at them. "We can trust him."

"I'm near my source of power, so I'll have no trouble making a portal for us. Hold tight." The Māori man spun his hands, and a golden web appeared between them.

A Guardian, Jayne realized.

More bullets began to fly, with a harsh *pop-pop-pop* sound. The portal glimmered to life on the pavement behind them.

"Kids first," said Sofia and Jayne together. "That means

you," Jayne added to Vivienne as Sofia's Team Aegis trotted through the portal.

"I am much more trained than they are," Vivienne sulked.

"But you're not older. Go on," Jayne said. She lent her power to the Block they'd left behind, but she could feel it weakening as more bullets slammed into it. "You next," she said to Tristan, gritting her teeth, pouring power into the spell.

Tristan smiled, and a spell appeared in his hand. "You do not understand, Jayne," he said and laid the spell against the Block. The net around them shimmered and seemed to solidify. His hands glowed with power. "There is so much more I can do."

The police on the other side of the spell gasped and shouted as bullets began to ricochet. Tristan had strengthened the entire spell, a spell that five Adepts had spun together.

Ruger was herding the last of their team through the portal. "Let's go, you two," he said.

Jayne began to back up. "So who is this guy?" she asked Ruger.

"He's trustworthy. I'll explain everything," Ruger promised and stepped through the portal.

Jayne took Tristan's hand. When they left, the Block spell would collapse. She took one last look at the wreckage around them, then they leapt together.

And came out in a room dimly lit by a naked bulb. It was a plain flat, with a sitting room that sported simple white wallpaper and a riotously joyful color-block rug. A pressboard bookcase in the corner held a variety of Māori myths and history, and a small white coffee table held a nature photography book. A brown faux-leather couch sat in the middle of the room, crowded with bodies. The young ones were all trying to fit on it together, which meant Matthew was squashed somewhere near the bottom of the pile while the girls lounged on top.

Ruger leaned against the wall, while Vivienne and a half dozen other operatives sat on the floor.

"Okay," Jayne said. "We're all here. Now what's going on? Who are you?"

The big Guardian stuck out his hand. "Danilo," he explained and shook Jayne's hand gently. "I'm the Guardian of the Wellington pocket. And as much as I'd like you to stay, we'll need to get you out of here before we attract too much attention. I've been keeping this pocket away from Ruth and her thuggish friends, and I intend to keep doing so."

He glanced at Ruger, and Jayne didn't miss the slight stain that spread over Ruger's brown cheeks.

"And Team Aegis?" she asked. "You sent schoolkids into battle, Ruge."

Ruger cleared his throat. "*Agnes* Jayne Thorne, meet the next stage of our initiative. It's a continuation of the blood-doping experiment, the one Quimby conducted on Cillian, and later on Tristan. It saved his life and even boosted his power, so we've taken it further. The new alpha graduating class from the Aegis Battle Academy have all been given a shot of the serum."

Jayne glanced at Sofia. The TCO had tested this on kids, and she'd been okay with it?

"They are adults," Sofia reminded her gently. "They sign their own release forms now." But from the way her mouth thinned and her nostrils flared, Jayne knew Sofia would have liked to shred those release forms.

"And we're powerful," said a redhead girl who had to be Rebecca, Amanda's kid. Jayne didn't know how she hadn't seen it before. She had the same nose, the same standoffish and practical aura. "Much more powerful than we were before."

"Side effects?" Jayne said.

Tristan's hand was warm in hers. He squeezed. "None so far," he assured her gently. "Except...sometimes I remember things. Things that didn't happen to me."

"I know spells and formulas I didn't learn at school," Matthew added.

"We think that the Adepts whose ashes we used have been able to...pass on something of themselves to the subjects," Sofia said. "All good, so far."

"It sounds a little cannibalistic," Jayne said.

"It's practical and it's useful." Ruger pushed away from the wall and gave her a stern look. "And I won't have you alarming the kids. Now, our new Adepts and their power were something we'd been counting on in this battle. Jayne, do you have any explanation for that little surprise in your arm?"

Jayne put her hand over the silvery patch. It seemed to thrum warmly. "Not really," she admitted.

"I think it's a familiar," Danilo said. Ruger shook his head, skeptical, but Danilo nodded. "There are tales of powerful Masters who could call forth a familiar, an ultimate expression of their magic. Different than a Rogue. Familiars often appear in great times of need, when a Master's power and emotion mix together. With practice, you could call it forward at will, and not just in an emergency. Does it speak to you?"

Jayne nodded. "He does. Now, I mean. He hadn't before the battle."

Danilo sent Ruger a triumphant look. Ruger folded his arms. "It could be a familiar," he allowed. "It could also be a Wraith of some sort. Is it possible that instead of turning into a Wraith, she projects it out of her body?"

"But then why would it fight the other Wraiths?" Jayne argued, sitting down on the arm of the sofa. Zia moved her feet to accommodate.

"Wraiths are not inherently loyal to their own kind. If Odin doesn't control it, why shouldn't it fight the others?" Ruger countered.

"But it never went for us," Cillian mused.

Ruger scowled. But he was spared the argument when his

phone rang. He dug it out of his pocket, grimacing at the cracked screen. "Amanda," he announced, and took the call. "You're on speaker."

"Good." Amanda's voice was clipped and cold. Jayne and Sofia exchanged bracing glances. Amanda was going to eviscerate them for causing a scene, putting civilians in danger, summoning a *dragon*—

"Good work, everyone," Amanda said.

A shocked silence followed. After a few moments, Vivienne leaned forward. "Is that all?" she said.

"That's all. We needed the Disciples of Gaia on our side, and they're sitting in the break room, eating cake. We needed the school to produce working soldiers, and they acquitted themselves admirably in a difficult battle. In fact, in light of our success, I think we can start planning a *real* offensive. We've been on the back foot for too long. It's time to take control, and I have some ideas."

"Is everything, uh, clear?" Ruger said.

Amanda paused. "What do you mean?"

"We ran a mission without clearance, in a foreign country," Vivienne said for him. "Are we in trouble with the director?"

"Let me deal with the director. You deal with getting back to Virginia. The portal was damaged, but Quimby is working on it. It will be ready for you soon."

CHAPTER
TWENTY-THREE

The rest of the day went by in a blur. Danilo went out and returned an hour later with a feast of takeout, and after eating far more pie than should be healthy, Jayne and Tristan had pulled out the couch bed while Sofia and Cillian took the bedroom. "What about you?" Jayne yawned at Ruger.

"It's a double bed. Two people should take it, and you're the couple," Ruger said. Maybe he thought she'd miss the furtive glance he shared with Danilo. But Jayne was too tired to bring it up and didn't want to embarrass him in front of the entire team. She went to shower instead.

It wasn't exactly the romantic reunion she'd dreamed of from the hospital, but there was a comfort in snuggling close to Tristan, feeling his arms wrap sleepily around her. They were probably too tired for sex anyway, she decided half-glumly. Then she didn't have time to think anymore. Her exhausted body gave up and she tumbled into sleep.

She found herself walking on a rocky black shore, where smooth pebbles of volcanic glass tumbled in with the tide. To one side, the sea spread out, blue-gray and angry. To the other, the black beach gave way to mountains, green and verdant at the base, snow-capped at the top.

A beacon blazed in the distance, and Jayne found she was walking steadily toward it. Wind tangled in her hair and ran long fingers down her spine, making her shiver. When she rounded the small bay, she was unsurprised to see Vesta, goddess of the hearth, sitting at a cheerful fire with Freya and Vivienne. Amaterasu sat on a rock nearby, her shifting eyes and glossy black hair reaching almost to the ground. Jayne had to admit, the goddesses were looking better than she'd ever seen them. Maybe it was just the relief of battle.

"You are late," Vivienne told her.

"You always say that." The fire was warm. A flame tickled her palm.

"You have had a great victory today, Jayne Thorne," said Freya. "And as a warrior, you have reached the next stage of your abilities. The Spirit totem has allowed you access to your familiar."

"He will be important for you in the battles to come," Vesta said. The firelight painted her face in long stripes of shadow and red-orange light. "Odin is only growing in power, and this was but the first attack. He will keep coming, and you must be ready for him."

"Not just ready for him." Freya's golden sword lay across her lap, shimmering like water. "You must be able to surprise him. To keep him defensive. He is sending his Wraiths after the Guardian pockets. He wants to destroy the pockets and release the powers of the Torrent into the world. Your victory today has shown him that winning this war is far from assured, but that means he will redouble his efforts."

"But we have such power on our side. They would like to meet your dragon, Jayne," said Vivienne. She leaned forward. Her dark eyes were eager in a way Jayne wasn't used to from the overly cynical French girl. Then again, she liked impressing

Vesta, Jayne remembered. Vesta was the closest thing Vivienne had to a real mother.

All of them were looking at her. Jayne held her arm up to the light of the fire and considered the silver that glittered from her elbow to her wrist. "I, uh, don't have much practice calling him," she said.

"Child of fire and pain, come forth," Amaterasu commanded.

The rending wasn't so painful this time, and Jayne didn't know whether it was because she was in the dreamscape, or because the first manifesting hurt the most. It was the ghost of a pain, the memory of splitting in half. And then Hayden sat by the fire, curled up around a tree stump and much smaller than she remembered him in real life.

He was as gray as the Wraiths, but where their eyes were black, his were a shifting fire, orange and red with a heart of blue. He had a reptilian snout, and two paws upon which he rested his head. Jayne reached over and stroked his nose, and he flicked out a forked tongue to investigate her hand. His scales were soft and smooth as water. "Hayden," she said.

"It means 'flame.'" Vesta sounded approving. "Welcome, familiar."

Danilo had called him a familiar, too. Jayne looked between him and Vivienne. She had a familiar and a Rogue, but how were they different? *Can you, uh, be anything you like?* she asked.

I am me, he replied, and in this place, everyone could hear his mental voice. Jayne saw Vivienne's eyes widen in surprise. *I can be big if I like, or small if I like. I can be dangerous if I like, or safe.*

You can be a poet? Jayne suggested.

Hayden smiled, teeth glistening in the firelight. *I do like poets. Very tasty.*

"Hayden is a part of you," Amaterasu said. "You were found worthy, and he chose to reveal himself. You cannot transform him into an animal, like Vivienne, but you can call him forth. You cannot always make him do exactly as you like, just as sometimes your desire to do one thing fights your need to do another. In fact, it was your desire to heal Tristan battling your need to save yourself that brought Hayden into being. But he feels what you feel, and he will act on that. Unlike a Rogue, he is a part of you. Vivienne follows your commands, but Hayden will follow your instincts. I think he will be a...rather strong-willed and independent familiar."

Vivienne snorted. "It will be no more than you deserve."

"Thanks," Jayne muttered. But warmth spread through her that had nothing to do with the fire. Her own little—or not so little—dragon. *So, I mean, no offense...but what do you do?*

I fight for you, Hayden said, cocking his head so that one burning eye could regard her. *You can send me far away, and I will always know how to return to you. Or I can carry you, if you trust me. I cannot die, for if I am killed I will return to you to regenerate. I lose my life only when you do, little one.*

Carry me? Jayne said. *How could you carry me?*

Hayden uncoiled from his tree stump, and somehow he kept uncoiling. His body was much longer than it had been when he lay down, Jayne was certain. He smiled again. *Try me.*

Vivienne half stood. "*I* want to try."

Only she may ride, Hayden replied. Vivienne slumped back down with a pout.

Jayne stood uncertainly. *Did* she trust him?

"He comes from you," Vesta said gently.

"I wouldn't necessarily call that an endorsement," Jayne muttered, but went over to him. She stroked his scaly hide, smooth as a bolt of silk, and took a deep breath. *Do I trust myself?*

The dreamscape smelled of woodsmoke and hot metal and sage. Jayne clambered up on his foreleg and slung one of her own legs over his long body, wondering how she was going to hold on. At the thought, long black spines emerged from the scales of his back. She hesitated, then grasped the one closest to her. It was smooth and supple, like cartilage.

Hayden surged to his feet. Jayne slid to the side and had to squeeze tight with her thighs to keep from falling. She felt a rumble of amusement from beneath her. *You did that on purpose,* she accused.

What, don't you trust me? he said in reply.

There was no point in answering. His great wings pumped and they lurched into the air.

There was no wind in the dreamscape. Hayden flapped, and they rose until the goddesses and Vivienne became little spots around a bright dot of fire. To one side of them, the beach stretched blackly, glittering as shards of obsidian caught the moonlight. White foam divided land and sea, and in the water, Jayne spied the smooth backs of seals and breaching whales. The sharp, jagged edge of a volcano appeared on the horizon.

Something tickled the back of Jayne's mind. *Iceland.* They were in Iceland. Or at least, a dream of it.

Shouldn't it be day here? Jayne asked. If it was night in New Zealand, Iceland should be sunny and bright.

It should, Hayden replied. *But we are in a dream, so perhaps things are different.*

The goddesses controlled this space, so was it their choice to make it dark here, or was it something else? They were tangled up in the Torrent, so could the Torrent's current state have something to do with the gloomy view?

Something is wrong, Hayden said abruptly.

It seemed her familiar was more attuned to magic than she was, for it was several more seconds before she felt it, too. A tugging on that extra sense of magic, as though the river of power at her fingertips was being redirected away from its natural flow.

It was moving inland. Without prompting, Hayden turned

to follow it. They swooped over emerald hills and fast-flowing rivers, over lava fields and forests. As they flew, Jayne started to feel a strange, oily, sickly feeling in the current around her. Another kind of magic was swimming in the Torrent, a strange and corrupted kind. Hayden shivered and rippled in the air. This new magic was oddly sticky; Jayne felt a scrap of it attach to his hide a few inches from her knee. His muscles twitched in an attempt to dislodge it. Jayne summoned an easy Clearing spell and wiped it away. But no sooner had she done so than she felt another bit stick to his tail, and another to the edge of his wing. The corrupted magic was filling the sky, the Torrent, growing thicker, dragging on Hayden's wings. An acrid stench filled Jayne's nose. Not unlike the smell of her mother's magic, she realized—but when she forced a deep breath, she smelled no violets—just rot. Perhaps that was what corrupt magic smelled like.

There, said Hayden, out of breath. His wingbeats were slow and ponderous. Jayne could feel his struggle to fly forward. Ahead of them stood a mountain, wide at the base and tapering like an arrowhead.

Just float, she told him. *We'll be there soon enough.*

I am you, Jayne, he admonished. *I fight to the last.*

We're not fighting, Jayne said. *We're conserving our energy for the right moment.* She could almost hear Ruger laughing at her. *How the tables have turned.*

Hayden relinquished his struggle and focused on keeping his wings light and steady so that the Torrent could bear them along. Every so often he tried to flick some of the sticky, corrupt magic off part of his body when it threatened to weigh them down. Jayne helped where she could, but a Shield spell didn't seem to do much against the magic, and she couldn't wipe off anything that she couldn't reach.

The mountain drew closer and closer, a dark ridge against the sky. As it did, a light at the base of the mountain grew ever larger. It was this light the Torrent moved toward, and as they got closer, Jayne's misgivings grew. Small shapes swarmed back and forth like mosquitos in that light, buzzing around a central figure.

The Icelandic pocket. Odin's hideout and fortress. The mosquitos were the Wraiths, Jayne realized with a jolt. Hayden jerked up, shaking the poison magic from his wings with some effort and breaking free of the current that tried to pull them down.

Can we get any closer? she asked. *It's just a dream, isn't it? They can't see us?*

We will try. But I know as much as you do, Jayne, Hayden replied. He began moving in wide circles, angling down with each pass, trying to keep up his momentum so that they might make an escape if it turned out the Wraiths could access them.

It looked like the Wraiths had enough to worry about, though. They were smothered in the corrupted magic, their skin and eyes dull. They looked as though they were slowly suffocating. Hard to believe they were once human—they growled and swiped at each other like animals. Jayne remembered the light in Ruth's eyes as it had flickered and died.

The central figure around which they flew was larger than they were, a gigantic silhouette with broad shoulders and a muscular frame. He turned and looked up, and Jayne spotted a grizzled face with a bent nose, sharp chin, and one cold, cruel blue eye. The other was hidden beneath an eye patch that slashed through his face like a scar. Odin Allfather. Master of the Wraiths.

For a moment Jayne thought he was looking straight at them, and her heart sped up so much that Hayden flapped upward in alarm. But Odin was looking past them, toward a figure that barely avoided them as it swooped down. An enormous Wraith, winged and clawed like a bird. It held a small body in its arms.

A child.

Come on, Jayne urged. *We have to save him.*

Hayden didn't move. *We are not here,* he reminded her simply. *We sense the magic, but we cannot touch the child.*

The Wraith landed in front of Odin Allfather and held the child up like an offering. The Allfather's broad hands took the boy—for it was a boy, Jayne saw—and set it gently on the ground. "Huginn, my Wraith of Thought," he said in a deep voice that seemed to resonate across the base of the mountain. "You have served me well. I can sense the power in this one."

The boy was awake. He stumbled to his feet, and Odin steadied him by putting his gargantuan hand on the boy's head. His fingers wrapped all the way down the child's skull. The boy froze, trembling in fear.

"Yesterday, you were nothing. You were ordinary." Odin's voice took on a soft, almost singsong quality. "Tonight, you are reborn. You will serve a cause greater than you could ever serve on Earth under your own volition. And so I humbly accept your offer of power. My newest Wraith."

His fingers blazed with magic. The boy began to scream. Jayne reached for the Torrent and her fiercest spells, but the magic was weak and flickering. *We aren't here.*

There was nothing they could do. Nothing but watch.

The boy grew, shooting up beneath Odin's hand, bones cracking and skin splitting as wings unfolded from his back. His skin turned gray and leathery. Claws shredded his boots and dug into the ground. His arms grew long, his fingertips razor-sharp. He opened his mouth and let out a high, keening sound, a sound of rage and pain and loss. At the same time, Jayne saw a surge of magic gather in his chest, over his heart, and burst out. It hit Odin Allfather with its full force, and he staggered back. Light fizzled and crackled over his rib cage, but as the glow faded the magic seemed to soak into him, filling him with an energy that Jayne could feel even from where she was. He pushed his shoulders back and stood tall once more.

He removed his hand from the new Wraith's head. As it reeled away, another Wraith landed in its place and offered up another boy. "Welcome to the new world," he said and looked up to the sky. And this time, Jayne was utterly certain he was talking to her.

She didn't need to tell Hayden to get them out of there. His powerful wings flapped and took them up, up, until they could clear the top of the arrowhead mountain.

Jayne gasped. On the other side of the mountain, the entire landscape was gray—the gray of scales and leathery skin, of wings and claws and dark, ruthless eyes. It was an entire Wraith army.

And it stretched as far as the eye could see.

CHAPTER
TWENTY-FOUR

Jayne woke shivering, covered in a sheen of sweat. The goddesses and Hayden were gone, but the images of Odin's massive army, of how he was making Wraiths, made her bolt upright.

Next to her, Tristan rolled over, chest rising and falling with the deep of sleep. For a few moments, she stared at him, trying to sort out her thoughts amidst a residual terror muddled by the haze of sleep. Her heart thundered at the memory of long claws poking through his chest. She still couldn't believe he was alive. She would never unsee the bloom of blood on his chest, the agony on his face as his life burned low in him—they were clear as photographs in her mind. She knew now how deeply she had fallen for him. That brief moment when she was willing to lay down her life for his because living without him was unthinkable. It made them both weaker, because their love could be used against them by their enemies. But together, they were an unstoppable force.

And now he slept in a borrowed gray T-shirt with WELLINGTON stamped across the chest, one muscular arm beneath his ear. His breath tickled her arm. She tried to focus on that breath, such a precious thing that was so easy to overlook. The battle was coming for them. She didn't know if they would both survive, and that thought pierced her heart like an arrow.

Well. She wasn't going back to sleep—not that she'd trust her dreams if she did. Jayne slipped out of bed and took advantage of the fact that it was five-thirty in the morning to take another shower without worrying about who was waiting to use it next.

When she came out, Danilo and Ruger sat at the kitchen table. A pot of coffee was full, and the men each had a steaming mug. Ruger's was black, while Danilo had doctored his with plenty of cream. They were speaking quietly, but when she came into the kitchen they stopped abruptly. There was a certain guilty air around them that made her narrow her eyes.

Danilo spooned sugar into his cup from the bowl on the table. "Ruger tells me you like tea," he said. "I've only got builder's tea, but it's in the cabinet above the toaster."

Builder's tea—strong, bitter black tea made with the sweepings from the factory floor—was better than nothing. Jayne found the electric kettle and splashed some milk into a cup while she waited for it to boil. Good tea didn't need milk or sugar, but builder's tea needed both. Or maybe she just needed both this morning.

She snuck a glance at Ruger while she puttered about. She wanted to tell him about her vision, but Danilo was practically a stranger. *A stranger who saved us from being shot by Wellington police and put us up in his safe house,* she reminded herself. Still, was it wise to trust him too much, and too well? On the other hand, Ruger needed to know and know now.

"I've got toast and Vegemite," Danilo offered. Jayne's mouth twisted involuntarily, and he laughed. "Ruger ate the last of the jam. I didn't expect to put up half an army, I'm afraid."

"It's fine. I'm sure we'll be out of your hair...soon?" Jayne glanced at Ruger.

Ruger took a long drink of coffee. "The portal is nearly fixed. We're to head back to the TCO as soon as possible. There's only so much we can do over the air, and Amanda needs help building a battle plan." He fixed Jayne with a stern look. "Can I count on you to make a breakfast run?"

A walk and an errand seemed like the perfect thing to dispel the last of her dream jitters. She knocked back the last of her tea and spread her arms. "Come on, Ruge. This is food we're talking about. Have I ever let you down?"

"Ruge?" Danilo said. He looked back and forth between them, eyes sparkling with amusement. Suspicion sparked in Jayne once more. He seemed too comfortable with Ruger, somehow—leaning on the table as though they'd spent many mornings like this, easy and comfortable in this space.

Ruger caught her looking, and a blush stained his cheeks. "Go on, Agnes," he said gruffly.

Danilo said, "There's a bakery on the corner that has the best cruffins and hot jam donuts you'll ever eat."

"Cruffins? Hot jam donuts? I'm game. But hey, before I go?" She leaned against the wall. "Listen. Odin is building a Wraith army. In Iceland. I saw it in a dreamscape last night. Ruger, it's massive. We're going to need a bigger boat."

Ruger and Danilo looked alarmed. "Danilo, since you're a Guardian, maybe you could brief us on the Iceland pocket? I think that's where this was."

"I'll put something together. Remember, we're rather siloed."

"Another thing we need to tackle. We can have all the battle plans we want, but if the various factions don't start sharing their individual knowledge about the magical world, we're sunk. Trust me. Odin's numbers will overwhelm us. We have to find a path together. And with that...I'm off like a prom dress."

Ruger groaned. "Ignore her," he said to Danilo. "Her sense of humor is not for everyone."

But Danilo was laughing. Jayne grinned at him and stopped by the bed, where Tristan still slept. She paused, breath catching, but she saw the rise and fall of his chest and pressed her fingers against the silver mark on her arm and reminded herself: *Everything is fine.* Tristan was alive; she wasn't turning into her mother. When you thought about it in those terms, things were actually going well. Sure, the world was being overrun by Wraiths and a master of evil was corrupting the Torrent and trying to take over the Earth. But it could be worse. She grabbed her backpack and found the bakery Danilo suggested.

By the time she staggered home with bags full of pastries and savory pies, everyone else was up. Tristan and Vivienne nursed coffees and spoke quietly in French, while Cillian and Sofia enjoyed the builder's tea. Sofia was scolding Rufus, the scrawny one, as Jayne came in: "—can't take fifteen minutes in the bathroom when you're sharing it with a dozen people."

"I needed to do my hair," Rufus muttered defensively.

Vivienne broke away from her conversation to look him up and down. "Darling, nobody can tell the difference."

"Enough out of you," Sofia said as the others snickered.

Jayne laid out the pastries and pies—brisket and peppers, Moroccan chicken, mince and cheese. "Well done," Ruger sighed happily and picked up a brisket. Jayne dumped out a bag of napkins, Sofia conjured up some juice for the kids, and Danilo found a battered pack of paper plates at the back of a cabinet. They scattered around the flat with their breakfasts.

"Game plan," Ruger said when they'd all had a chance to finish their first pies and the teens had gone back for seconds. "After breakfast, we set up a portal and head back to the TCO. We need to be out of New Zealand before the authorities can link the CIA to what happened here. I know Amanda said she'd talk to the higher-ups, but we don't need to make her job more difficult than it already is."

The teens groaned. "Can't we take half a day? I want to see Hobbiton," Matthew wheedled around a bite of chicken.

"That's up near Auckland, mate," Danilo told him. Matthew shrugged as if to say, *So?*

"We're not tourists," Ruger said sharply. The kids deflated, and Jayne felt a pang of sympathy. Who wouldn't want to visit Middle Earth if they got the chance? "We're soldiers," the big man added. It was a smart move. Jayne saw shoulders pull back and spines straighten. "We're on the job. You all did excellent work yesterday, but after action comes regrouping and reaction. We need to debrief on what we experienced, what we saw, and did"—here he nodded significantly to Jayne—"and make a plan for what's next."

"Why were the Wraiths here?" Vivienne asked. "I know La Liberté wanted to recruit new Adepts, but why pick Wellington?"

"It's an island?" Jayne suggested. "Damage control?"

"There is a pocket," Danilo said. He looked down. His broad fingers drummed on his thigh. "La Liberté knew they would be here, trying to break in."

And they'd probably want to turn the Wraiths from their original plan. Odin would want to control the pockets before emerging from the Torrent completely. The more power he had before coming, the more assured he was of victory. Which was why...

"We need to take the fight to Odin. Now," Jayne said.

Danilo sat back, crossing his arms. "Jayne," Ruger warned.

"Every moment we wait, he grows more powerful." Jayne traded glances with Vivienne. The girl nodded slightly. She'd had the vision, too, and she was agreeing that they needed to speak up. "Like I told you earlier, Ruger, Danilo, we saw something terrible."

Jayne tried to lay out her vision clearly, full of facts and devoid of emotions. Vivienne supported her, adding details where relevant. When she got to the part about flying Hayden, she heard a snort from the teen section. She broke off and glared. "Something to say?"

"It's just..." Rebecca paused, trying to tame her wild curls into a ponytail. "It sounds like a dream. Maybe it was lifelike and everything, but..."

"It was a dreamscape, not a dream. You all saw him emerge yesterday. You know he's real." Jayne gestured to her arm. "And what I saw was real, too. Doesn't it make sense? We're bringing children in, the Kingdom's trying to recruit, too, and we know Odin's on the hunt for powerful Adepts he can turn into Wraiths. The longer we wait, the more Wraiths we have to contend with when we finally do clash. If we act, we might be able to catch him off guard. Especially with this." She tapped Hayden, feeling a sleepy inquiry in the back of her mind as he stirred.

"We barely prevailed." This came from Sofia. Jayne glared at her, and she put her hands up in a gesture of surrender. "I'm just saying, Jayne. Our victory was hardly decisive."

"But we did prevail. If we gather our allies and make our move now, we might be able to catch Odin with his pants down. So to speak."

"We should do it," said the youngest looking of the teens, Zia. She was leaning forward, eyes shining, legs folded in a butterfly position in front of her.

"No," Sofia said immediately.

"But Sofia—" Matthew said, but she cut him off.

"This was what, your second mission? This wasn't what we agreed to when we decided to put you in the field," Sofia told them. Her nostrils flared and the skin around her mouth tightened. She turned to Jayne and Ruger. "They're not ready. They have almost no field experience, and less life experience. They need support."

She nudged Cillian. He scratched the back of his neck,

looking guilty. Across the wall, the five teens broke into protest. "Come *on*—" "Good test scores—" "Stronger than anybody out there—" "Kicked ass—"

"Oy," Cillian said loudly, and they subsided, grumbling and nudging each other. "You've passed our tests, which means you are field ready. But Sofia's right. There's a difference between being ready for your first assignment and being ready for war."

An awkward silence followed. Rufus muttered something but was elbowed by Medina. Sofia's mouth was a thin line, and she was staring at Jayne as though this were all her fault. Jayne almost longed for the days when their arguments were about her, and her alone.

"For what it's worth, I'm with you," Danilo said at last. He sat back on the couch and gave Ruger a significant look. "I have a pocket to guard, and there's no magical organization in New Zealand that can pledge for you, just me. But I'm honored to be an ally."

"Right. And we've got the Disciples of Gaia with us, and they recognize that the Wraiths are a threat for *now*," Jayne said. She saw Sofia's jaw tighten.

"Enough, Thornes," Ruger warned them. "You don't work for a democratic organization. You have a boss, and she calls the shots. If Amanda wants an offensive, an offensive she's going to get."

IT TOOK them another hour to finalize the portal and get everyone organized. In the end, Danilo and Ruger worked together to send them through two at a time, starting with Zia and Rufus and moving up. As Jayne took Tristan's hand, still marveling at the warmth of it, Ruger tapped her on the shoulder. "Tell Amanda I'll be along shortly."

"You're not coming now?"

Ruger's eyes flicked to the side, where Danilo was busy pushing chairs back into place and putting pillows up again. "We still have a few things to discuss regarding New Zealand's commitment," he said.

Sure you do, she thought. "I'll try not to crash a dragon into the TCO while you're gone," she teased. Ruger shook his head.

And then the Torrent was all around her, and a moment later she stood in the TCO, before the wall of stars.

The rest of the team had gathered off to one side. Amanda stood before them clutching a manila folder that she held in front of her like a shield. "Is it working?" she asked as soon as Jayne and Tristan stepped free. "The totem? Is it integrating properly?"

A strange way to put it, Jayne mused, but she nodded. "I have a familiar. I healed Tristan, and when I did, he came to the fore. His name is Hayden. The Spirit totem allowed me to access him. He's very powerful. A dragon."

Amanda stared at her incredulously. "Familiars are just legends."

"So were Rogues. And Odin, for that matter. We're living in a brave new world, Amanda."

Amanda smiled, a real, genuine, hopeful smile, the likes of which Jayne had never witnessed. It was dazzling. "Good work, Jayne," she said.

Jayne wasn't sure what to say to that. She'd just been complimented by Amanda twice in two days. She had the sudden urge to check if the world was ending.

Oh, right. It was. Possibly.

"All right, people. Listen up. We will be pursuing an offensive on the Allfather," Amanda announced.

Sofia's jaw clenched and the hand at her side curled into a fist. Jayne saw Cillian wrap his fingers around her hand, a gentle reminder and a comfort. Their protégés, on the other hand, exchanged excited glances. Zia bounced on the balls of her feet.

"Tomorrow you will return to my office for your personal assignments," Amanda told them. "Spend today training and studying up on Iceland, Odin, and the Wraiths. I expect everyone to be ready tomorrow, in body and in mind." At this last, she fixed Sofia with a pointed look. Sofia glared right back, disentangling her hand from Cillian to fold her arms.

Amanda turned and strode off. Sofia leaned against Cillian's shoulder. He wrapped one arm around her and shooed at the kids. "You heard her. Practice time. Work on your sparring and your coordinated spells."

Jayne approached cautiously. Her sister seemed angry with her, and she wasn't sure why.

"We can do this, Sof," she said.

"Yeah. *We* can." Sofia twisted to face her. Her eyes were red and a tear glistened in the corner of one. "What about them? They think they can do so much, but they're kids. Kids who grew up in a magical wonderland where no one ever wanted to hurt them. And you want them to throw their lives away."

Jayne recoiled. "You know I don't." She cast about for a way to apologize, but Sofia went on before she could think of anything to say.

"Do I? You're so obsessed with stopping Odin, with stopping Mom—what are you willing to sacrifice to do it? Them? Me? Us?"

Bile rose in Jayne's throat, along with her anger. Sofia had always been protective, but now she was going too far. "I've never wanted to give up one human life, not *one*," she hissed. "You didn't see what I saw. What about the kids Odin's turning into Wraiths right now? Don't they need to be protected?"

The rage in Sofia's eyes faltered. "I have to take care of the children under my protection first," she said. "I'm not going to let you put them in an army. They're my world now. Ever since you..." She took a deep, shuddering breath.

Ever since Jayne stopped being her world. The words cut, even though she'd known for a long time that she wasn't the center of Sofia's universe anymore. Hell, she'd been trying to gain independence since she was eighteen. But to see it like this...

"Thorne women," said Tristan dryly to Cillian, who nodded. "Both obsessed with saving the whole world. Come on, Jayne."

"But I..." She couldn't leave things like this with Sofia. She needed to make up. She needed Sofia to see the truth: that she could adopt kids to care for, but she couldn't protect them forever. Everyone grew up, and took risks, and made mistakes. They had the right to want that.

And that those kids had the right to do dangerous things, just as Jayne did.

Cillian shook his head. *Later,* Tristan mouthed to Jayne. And Jayne felt another invisible thread sever between her and Sofia, the thread that bound them closer to each other than to anyone else. Cillian knew Sofia better now, well enough to know when she was too distraught to have a real conversation. Maybe it was just hormones. Yeah, she should tell her sister *that* and watch her take off like a rocket.

Jayne let Tristan pull her down the hall toward the portal door to her Nashville flat, waiting until they'd made a couple of turns before speaking. "She has to know that she can't keep them on the sidelines. What did she even train them for?"

Tristan stopped at her door and dug out his keys. "*Mon amour,* your sister is who she is and does not wish to change. Just as you do not."

"What do you mean?" Jayne crossed her arms.

"You are stubborn, and think you can save the world your way, even when we tell you to make sacrifices. You tried to kill yourself in healing me after promising to leave that power alone."

"But it wasn't like I—"

"That is hardly the point," Tristan said. His eyes blazed and kindled a heat deep in Jayne's belly, a heat that spread like fire as his fingers circled her wrist. He came closer, slowly, and each step sent a new flush of desire over her body. "You are and always will be willful, convinced of your own righteousness, and guided by an invincible moral compass. You are strong, and powerful, and you will always be the thing I want most in this world."

He opened the door and pulled her inside.

CHAPTER
TWENTY-FIVE

They stayed in bed until it grew dark, first making love with an emotion-filled urgency, fueled by their days apart and the aftermath of Jayne's fear that Tristan was gone forever. Then they held each other beneath her quilt. Jayne ran her fingers over Tristan's hip, along his thighs, enjoying the way he shivered at her touch and marveling at the wholeness of him. Tristan stroked her arm, feeling the silvery patch where it met her skin, brushing the pad of his thumb over her wrist in a way that made her breath catch. She enjoyed the sensation, half asleep after their efforts, and was startled awake when he said, "Why did you do it?"

His curls were a shadow on her pillow. She tangled her fingers in them and cupped the back of his head. "You were dying."

"Do you think I would have asked you to save me, had I the words?" Tristan murmured.

"You were dying," Jayne said again, and pulled him closer, wrapping her leg around his waist. He twitched against her thigh and she felt an answering pulse within, something deeper than want. She needed Tristan Labelle, his strength, his unflappable knowledge of what to do in any situation. She pushed him, rolling him over so that she straddled him.

Besides, she thought, bending down to kiss him, she'd summoned a dragon and turned the tide of the battle. Everyone else was quite pleased with the results of that.

"Promise," he whispered against her mouth. He broke the kiss and looked into her eyes. His own eyes seemed to glow, blue and beautiful and serious. "Promise you won't do something like that again. Don't risk yourself for me."

In reply, Jayne lifted her hips and guided him into her. He gasped and began moving automatically in a slow, sensuous rhythm, and for a few glorious seconds, they were lost together. Then he gripped the back of her thighs and stopped. "Promise me," he said hoarsely, his voice thick with desire.

Jayne pressed her nose to his. "You know I can't," she said. Couldn't promise him, couldn't lose him. "You will always be the thing I want most in this world, Tristan Labelle. I will protect you until my dying breath."

She moved his hands up, pinning them next to his head, and started to move again, reveling in his hitched breath, the feel of him beneath her, bringing them both to the edge of forever.

WHEN JAYNE WOKE a few hours later she didn't feel like lying in bed and watching Tristan breathe. He was alive and whole, and he'd proven that well enough. Now she had a buzzing energy. She needed a workout.

She pulled on her exercise clothes and snuck out of the apartment with her shoes in hand, putting them on in the drab corridor of the TCO. Part of her wanted to knock on Sofia's door, see if her sister was willing to pretend that their fight had never happened. But she was afraid of what she might say or do if Sofia tried to confront her about it. Her wounds were still raw from Sofia's words, and in the wake of her time with Tristan she was feeling strangely vulnerable. She'd spent the last six months and more trying to save everyone she could, trying to save the whole *world*. She'd been called selfish many times. But never callous or uncaring. It was weird. Her sister seemed much more emotional lately. More protective. Fiercely protective. She wondered how much of that was tied to her pregnancy, and how much was the attachment she must be feeling toward the children she'd been shepherding through their magical upbringing. Training them for war.

Jayne sighed. Sofia's world was going through a great upheaval. Greater than Jayne's. She deserved grace.

Jayne trotted down the hall toward the training rooms. At the very least she could land a few punches on a bag. But before she reached the gym, she spotted a flickering at the end of the hall, like a portal activating. She changed route without thinking and started toward the light.

A portal was indeed active, and the broad shape of Ruger emerged in a flash of white. He was smiling to himself, a broad, personal smile, as if everything was going exactly his way.

He was also wearing a clean shirt. A clean button-down shirt, in his size. "Have you been in New Zealand all this time?" Jayne asked.

Ruger jumped. His smile disappeared, like it was a jewel he only brought out for special occasions and Jayne didn't make the cut. "What are you doing here?" he snapped. Color rose in his cheeks. His voice had a sandpapery quality to it, like he'd been up all night.

"Taking a walk. What are you doing?"

"Returning from our tactical liaison," he said, but he wouldn't look at her.

"Your shirt's buttoned wrong, Mr. Tactical Liaison." Jayne

folded her arms. "And I bet if you had hair, you'd have bedhead."

"What, like you?" he shot back, fingers fumbling at his shirt.

He ducked his head so that Jayne could just see the corners of his smile. He couldn't keep it in, even when embarrassed. "Well, maybe taking a break in...tactical discussion...is good for you," she teased. "Did you have a good time?"

"I'm not in the habit of discussing my private life with subordinates," Ruger said.

"How about friends?" Jayne offered.

He stopped, thumb and finger on his collar. Hesitating just long enough that Jayne was starting to feel insulted. "Pie and wine?" she said. He looked like he needed a shave and a nap, but that was how all good nights out ended, wasn't it?

"What is it with you and pie, anyway?" said Ruger. "If you're offering, I'll accept. If you've got something with chocolate."

Yes! She resisted the urge to pump her fist in the air. Doing so would probably tempt Ruger to change his mind. "Pie is excellent. And it's made with fruit, so it's a healthy dessert. At least, all the best pies are made with fruit. But I bet I could find something chocolatey for you."

They ended up sneaking through her Nashville apartment to find an all-night diner that served chocolate silk pie. They sat in a squeaking-leather booth that smelled like cheese and burnt coffee and ignored the odd looks of the waitress while she took their order, listening to a playlist clearly inspired by the best of Johnny Cash.

Jayne dug into a slice of traditional apple with ice cream, watching Ruger across the booth from her. For a moment he closed his eyes, lost in the bite. He washed it down with a swallow of coffee. "You look as though you had a satisfying reunion yourself. Though do spare me the details."

Jayne laughed. Telling Ruger the details of her love life was tantamount to telling her own father. "Tristan's angry," she said, surprising herself. "So is Sofia."

"Everyone was ready to be angry with you for that stunt. Healing him could have gone sideways, and you know it." Ruger put his fork down and pinned her with a frank gaze. "You disobeyed a direct order and used your power for something we all thought would destroy you. The fact that it didn't doesn't change that you thought so, too. Amanda's too busy to discipline you for it, and I think she doesn't see the point, since it turned out so well. But Tristan's well within his rights to be angry with you. Just like Sofia is. Just like I am. We all care about you, Jayne. We want you to be safe."

Why was he allowed to use that argument on her when she wasn't allowed to use it as a reason to save people? Jayne pushed a slice of apple into some melted ice cream. "But do you really believe that some lives are more valuable than others? That some people should be allowed to die in this war because they're less important?"

Ruger was silent for a moment. He took another sip of coffee and wiped his mouth, delicately folding the napkin over and tucking it under his plate. "I don't believe so. I *know* so. It's unpleasant, but it's a fact of war that people do die. And as awful as it is to think of our officers as weapons...it's also what you are. And you are the most powerful weapon we have right now. That makes you the most valuable, whether you like it or not. Self-destructing to save a less valuable weapon is a bad idea. I know it, Tristan knows it. Even Sofia knows it."

"Well, maybe if he thought of himself as a human being—"

"Jayne." Ruger leaned over the table. "The problem is that you value everyone's life equally except for one: yours. You deserve to live just as much as anyone else. And we need you."

"And I'll never change, and I'll never accept that," Jayne replied with a smile.

"Hm." Ruger pursed his lips and sat back. They were silent

as Jayne finished her pie, washing it down with her tea. "I confess that I sympathize with your position," he admitted grudgingly. "It's not easy having a loved one in this fight."

"I didn't realize you and Danilo were so serious," Jayne said.

She'd meant it as a lighthearted jab, but Ruger's mouth twitched and for a moment, his face seemed lit from within. Then the smile faded to something more somber. "I didn't mean for it to get serious," he admitted. "The last time I had a real relationship in the TCO, I regretted loving anyone at all." Jayne raised a brow. "Oh, it was long before your time. I was young, and naïve, and stupid, and I thought everyone believed what I believed. It ended badly. So I decided not to mix business with pleasure. And, well, if you want to keep the two separate in our line of work, there's only one thing you can do."

"Get a *Men in Black*–style neuralyzer?" Jayne joked.

Ruger smiled back. "Be a spinster."

Jayne put a hand to her heart. "You can't mean that, Ruge."

Ruger shook his head. "Looks like I can't, at that. Take Amanda. Lost her husband, gave up her kid—and if you'd been anyone but you, Jayne, you'd have lost Tristan, too. We are devoted to magic, but sometimes I wonder if she is too harsh a mistress."

They lapsed into silence again, sitting that way until the waitress brought the check. It was nice, really. Jayne didn't feel like she'd failed Ruger, or like he had to understand her point of view. They understood each other.

Ruger took the check. "I know what you make, and I do better," he said with a smile and stuck a couple of twenties behind the bill.

"I hope you won't let your fear stop you," Jayne said in a sudden rush. She probably shouldn't have spoken—Ruger's eyes raised in challenge—but she found she couldn't hold back, either. "I like Danilo. He seems very brave, and very cool. I hope the two of you can make it work."

He chewed over this for a few long moments. "I don't know what I hope," he admitted. "Then again, I don't have to know, do I? If we fail, it will hardly matter. If we win, we can sort out the details."

Not the worst philosophy, Jayne decided as they grabbed their coats and started over the sticky black-and-white linoleum. "Here's to the details," she said as Ruger held open the door and they stepped out into the night.

"Here's to the details," Ruger agreed.

CHAPTER
TWENTY-SIX

Jayne didn't get back to sleep until the sun was peeking over the horizon, and it was far too early when Tristan shook her gently awake. "My love," he whispered.

"Nngh," she grumbled. The inside of her mouth tasted sour. How was that possible, when the last thing she'd put in it had been so delicious? Her eyes refused to open, and all her limbs felt heavy.

"Amanda needs to see you now."

Jayne swatted at him and missed. "Tell her I'm busy."

"You're only busy if I make you busy," Tristan growled in her ear, in a voice that woke up every part of her at once. Then he pulled back. "And even I am too afraid to put Amanda off for *le petit morte*."

"You're a tease," Jayne grumbled, flopping over.

Tristan grinned wickedly. "A tease who would be happy to help you out in the shower, if it will get you on your feet."

And that, Jayne decided, was the best compromise she was likely to get.

One delicious, too-short shower later saw Jayne headed down the hall of the TCO, past the wall of stars to Amanda's office, hair still damp against her jacket. Amanda sat at her desk, impeccable as usual with her slicked-back hair and a gray-and-salmon suit. She was glaring at an open manila folder. "Good afternoon," she said as Jayne shut the door.

Drama queen. It was only half past nine. "Odd night. Sorry." Amanda pursed her lips, as if to challenge her, but Jayne wasn't about to explain further. She didn't owe Amanda the details of her love life, and talking about Ruger felt like a betrayal of his confidence. "Did I miss the briefing?"

"Everyone's getting their assignments personally, for now. Here's what you need to know: we're moving on the Allfather this week, so be prepared to hop through a portal when I say go. You'll need to work with everything you've got: Vivienne, your new pet, and all your totems." Amanda tapped the manila folder on her desk and eyed Jayne's forehead as if she could see through the skin to the totems themselves.

Jayne felt a prickle of irritation from Hayden. "He's not a pet," she said.

Amanda waved a hand. "This is your assignment while we prepare. And I want to see you in action, maybe with one of the geniuses around to help us understand what we're supposed to be looking at."

It's as though she doesn't trust me, Hayden grumbled.

She doesn't trust anyone. Don't take it personally.

Jayne asked Amanda, "So where are we going to fly an enormous dragon without the world noticing?"

Amanda smiled. "That is the easiest question I'll have to answer all day."

JAYNE HAD NEVER BEEN in the Aegis Battle Academy's Time Catch. She felt like a bad sister for not visiting, even though trips to the school were heavily restricted, and their time had been so compressed in the real world. The TCO couldn't have the Kingdom or La Liberté trying to infiltrate the place, after all. Jayne felt odd going in without telling Sofia first; then again, they hadn't spoken since their argument. Maybe Sofia wouldn't want her here.

"This is government property," Amanda said when she asked, smoothing back her red curls. "And it's the best training ground we've got."

"I like it," said Vivienne. The natural setting was, Jayne had to admit, much better for shapeshifting practice than the mats and blocks of a training gym. All the same, she was a little nervous. She'd be multitasking on three levels: working with Vivienne, directing Hayden, and wielding the power of her totems all at once. And if she failed, well, it was only the fate of the world at stake.

Jayne looked around with a critical eye. "How much can we alter the landscape here?" The hilly countryside, dotted with rocks and copses of trees, must be fantastic for students practicing for a general all-terrain battle. But she didn't want an all-terrain battle. She wanted to know the field of their exact battle as well as the Allfather would himself.

A quick internet trawl had revealed to her the location of the Iceland pocket and Odin's base. It was known as Kirkjufell, or Church Mountain. The mountain itself sat in a waterlogged plain ringed by plateaus. There wouldn't be much tree cover on the approach to the battle site, so the best chance they had at ambush would be portaling in en masse. Wraiths would have a distinct advantage with their wings, so the element of surprise when they would be awkward on the ground was paramount.

And, of course, once they did get in the air, Hayden and Vivienne could take the fight to them.

Jayne glanced at Vivienne critically. The girl caught her look. "Whatever you are thinking, no."

"Do you think you could turn into a Wraith?" Jayne asked.

"*No,*" Vivienne repeated vehemently.

Amanda was close behind. "We don't know what that might do to her. What if she started feeling Odin's pull?"

"If you turn into a chicken, will you be tempted to eat worms?" Jayne said.

"Perhaps only tempted to peck out your eyes," Vivienne replied sweetly.

Jayne threw up her hands in surrender. "*Fine.* No Wraiths. What about a dragon?"

Vivienne thought about it. She closed her eyes. Jayne could see the flickering image of something bigger, something winged, then Vivienne stamped her foot. "*Non.* It is not working."

"That's okay. We can practice. How about the terrain?"

"We'll know in a moment," said Amanda, and nodded. In the distance they spotted a lanky figure trotting over a hill. Seo-Joon.

They stood in awkward silence. When he was within earshot, he called an easy greeting. He wasn't even out of breath when he reached them, and he nodded professionally to Amanda, gave Vivienne a half hug, and shook Jayne's hand. "Welcome to the gym." He grinned. "Far cry from the little room in the TCO."

Jayne would hardly call the training room of the TCO "little." Then again, what wasn't little compared to this place? "How hard is it to alter?"

"Depends. What do you want?"

"Iceland," Jayne told him.

Seo-Joon looked through the pictures on her phone, whistling. "At its heart, this is all an illusion, so it could be reshaped. It'll take a lot of power." He snapped his fingers. "Good practice for the team." He pulled his phone from his pocket. She was amazed—for all intents and purposes, this Time Catch had all the elements of the real world.

Jayne felt a prickle of anxiety at the orders. Would Sofia be angry with her about this? But when he hung up, Seo-Joon was his cheerful self. "Some students are on their way. It'll be good to use the arena like the real battlefield anyway, and now you can get an idea of their skill sets," he said to Amanda, who nodded approvingly. Jayne tried not to wince in front of them. Sofia *was* going to be angry.

Fifteen minutes later, all the students were there. Some of them had loped in as Rogues turned into horses or lions or, in one case, a preening griffin. Others had walked. They gathered in little groups and argued, discussed homework, or practiced spells while they waited for their assignment. More than one looked at Amanda, Jayne, and Vivienne curiously.

They were all so young. A pang went through Jayne's heart. No wonder Sofia was so protective of them. Twelve-year-old kids *should* be arguing about homework and movies and sports. *And will they be able to do that if Odin takes over the world?* she reminded herself. Besides, these students wouldn't be rushing off to battle. They'd be safe here, having helped win the war through this illusion.

Seo-Joon divided them into teams and gave each group a task. One had to make the mountain itself, while another team was in charge of the plateaus. Yet another was in charge of the field surrounding Kirkjufell, which was bisected by a thin asphalt road. One team had water features, and a final was responsible for the inclement weather.

"There's only so much we can do," he admitted as they got to work. "I don't think any of them have ever even been to Iceland, though we've got a Norwegian boy who has some experience with fjords and the like." He nodded to a white-haired boy of twelve or thirteen.

"It will do very well," Amanda said.

It took another half hour or so, but it was so fascinating to watch that Jayne forgot to worry about it. The ground mossed over in browns and greens, becoming soft and spongy. The landscape rippled, and with every ripple the little hills seemed to grow a little smaller, while one hill before them grew larger and larger, taking on a crook like a witch's hat. The kids in charge of Kirkjufell stopped to check photos frequently, arguing and adjusting. A sudden cold breeze lifted Jayne's damp hair from the back of her neck, and she turned to see herself surrounded by the stark stone walls of plateaus. The sea wound its way in, finding corners and nooks to fill, and the air took on a briny scent. Vivienne shivered.

Changing the landscape at will like this reminded Jayne so very much of the training facility in the Kingdom's Time Catch that she felt her heart race. So much had happened since that time, so many changes. She was barely magical then, and now... The weight of responsibility her new powers imbued was intense. Everyone was counting on her to be able to overthrow Odin. What if she couldn't?

We will, Vivienne said in her mind, vehemently. *We will.*

Boundaries, Viv. I'm wallowing.

Amanda interrupted her thoughts. She smiled and beckoned the students in. "I'm impressed with your work," she told them. "Do you know why we wanted you to make a corner of Iceland here in your training grounds?"

She started talking about pockets, and the Torrent, and the war. Jayne moved away and swung her arms to limber up. Time to call forth the dragon. *You awake?*

I am awake when you are awake, Hayden reminded her. *And stop wallowing. This is important.*

"Okay...how do I bring you out?" Jayne muttered. Vivienne cut her a glance. She felt a bit like a crazy lady who talked to plants. She turned toward Kirkjufell, staring up at the mountain. Was it as big in real life as the students had made it here? It seemed impossibly high. Then again, no one was trying to scale it. Though portaling to the top of the mountain and ascending in a wave might not be a bad idea…

"Come forth, child of fire and pain," she intoned, holding out her arm. Hayden snorted but didn't budge. "Well, it was worth a try. That's how Amaterasu got you out."

Focus. She was no strategist. She was a weapon, as many people were keen to tell her. What had brought Hayden forth in Wellington?

Desperation. Complete and utter despair. An inability to believe that Tristan could be gone. Not exactly feelings she could re-create here, nor was she eager to re-create them on the field of battle.

You wanted something, and you were willing to give your whole life for it, Hayden reminded her. *Perhaps it was this selflessness that drew me forth.*

Selflessness? Ha. Saving Tristan had been the epitome of selfishness, an utter refusal to think of life without him. But Jayne focused on the first part. She'd wanted something. She'd wanted it more than she'd wanted life itself. She could work with that.

She wanted to defeat Odin Allfather. She wanted to defeat Ruth Thorne before the Wraith-woman became even more powerful and terrible. She wanted the Torrent to be what it was before, a place of light and learning where magicians could go to explore, to take refuge, to discover. And was she willing to sacrifice herself for that cause?

Yes. Absolutely, she thought, and she felt an answering roar in her mind.

Pain rippled up her arm, first a prickle like a bad sunburn, then a sharper pain, as though someone had taken a flaying knife to her skin. *Don't scream in front of the kids,* she thought and gritted her teeth. A whimper escaped her anyway. The pain intensified, and black spots appeared in her vision. She clenched her fists, trying to focus on the way her nails bit into her skin, the way her tendons stretched over her knuckles, anything but the feeling of her arm pulling away from her own body.

And then she was aware of cool air on her sweaty skin, of a gentle breeze across her arm, still burning with pain. Gasps went up from behind her. *"Holy—"* Amanda said.

"Language," Seo-Joon reminded her, though he seemed barely able to say it. "There are kids present..."

Hayden was somehow even longer than she'd remembered him, speeding upward like an arrow, silver tail lashing. Maybe he was showing off. It was what Jayne would do, after all. His long gray body undulated sleekly through the air, scales flashing in the artificial sunlight. His wingspan was as large as a 767, and his tail added an extra twenty feet, easy. He opened his mouth and roared.

"Can we get on with it?" Vivienne was looking at her nails, the very essence of a bored teen.

"Right." Jayne grinned. "I forgot you're not impressed by anything. Why don't you try changing? We'll need all the help we can get in the air, so something with wings? Maybe you could try again at being a dragon?"

"*Non.* That is his domain now." Vivienne shook out her hair, then leaped into the air—and kept leaping. Feathers seemed to fold out of her skin, turning brown and gray and white. A moment later, she was a huge harpy eagle, and took to the sky, screeching in triumph. Hayden bellowed a greeting back.

"Wow," whispered one of the kids. Right. Jayne had an audience. Trying to bury a sudden burst of self-consciousness, she picked up a stone. "Hayden, Vivienne. Let's try working in tandem. How about a game of catch?" She tossed the stone into the air.

Vivienne caught it easily, carrying it on an updraft until Jayne told her to release. Then she dropped the stone.

Hayden was nowhere to be found.

Excuse me? Jayne tapped her foot. *Familiar mine?*

I was curious as to what is on the other side of this mountain, Hayden replied.

That's not where I told you to be, Jayne replied, irritated.

No. But you *were curious, thus I was curious. And there are too many people over there.*

Her familiar wasn't something she could order around, she reminded herself. It was part of her innermost being. Which meant that if she wanted Hayden and Vivienne to work together, she had to focus and forget about her audience. *All right, come back down here,* she ordered. *I'm going to take a ride.*

Maybe it was because she could visualize what she wanted. Or maybe Hayden *would* obey her commands and could tell how annoyed she was. He landed in front of her, claws digging into the spongy ground, and cocked his head. His eyes were the same fiery hue they'd been in her dream. It was reassuring, she found. He had life and light, not the black depths of despair and coldness that she saw in the eyes of Wraiths.

He extended one foreclaw and she clambered up onto his back. It was lumpier than it had been in her dream, and the scales were sharp around the edges. When he flapped to take off, she was nearly thrown free, and she had to grab onto one of his spines to steady herself.

What did you expect? He sounded a little smug. *Gravity exists in real life.*

Jayne decided she didn't love this part of herself so much. But she looked down at the scattered group of faces, turned up in awe, and smiled. So maybe there were perks to having a familiar.

She had Hayden pick up another large stone, and this time he tossed it to Vivienne, who caught it easily. She threw it right back, and Hayden had to make a quick turn to catch it, almost throwing Jayne off again.

Maybe a little more warning next time? Jayne said, trying to catch her breath and her courage at once.

Battles don't come with warnings, Vivienne replied. *Come on!*

If that's the way you want to play it. Hayden hurled the stone so that it sailed past Vivienne, curving up into the air, and she had to spiral after it. She batted it back to him, and he swatted it with a quick flip of his tail.

It soon became a game of who could outwit whom. Vivienne was more maneuverable, thanks to their difference in size, but Hayden could use his wings, tail, and even head to catch the stone, whereas Vivienne was more restricted. Once, Jayne even caught it in her hand. After they'd been working for twenty minutes, they changed the game again: Vivienne started to become different winged animals on Jayne's command, catching the stone and playing a sort of keep-away.

Another twenty minutes had passed before Jayne realized she was exhausted. Though she'd physically done little, she was out of breath, and her mind buzzed from managing two different conversations and concentrating on what Hayden needed to do. She wasn't sure how she was going to direct him, and Vivienne, and tap into her totems, all at the same time.

Maybe you don't have to, Hayden said. *I can see what you need and act before you even put it into words. Is that not a great advantage?*

Jayne knew what Amanda would say: That Hayden was a soldier, and he should follow orders, not Jayne's whims. But Hayden came from her, and he echoed her inner sentiments. He would do what Jayne *needed* to do, not what she'd been told. In the heat of battle, what must be done must be done.

No general behind the lines can anticipate a need from moment to moment, Hayden told her. That was true enough. But if she had to make a choice again, between saving someone she loved or killing the Allfather...

It won't come to that, she decided, and the swell of determination bolstered her and the dragon both.

She brought them down to claps and cheers from the students. Vivienne looked flushed and pleased when she turned human again, and Hayden bowed. He kept his head low as Amanda stepped gingerly over the soggy ground.

She studied him from a few feet away, pressing her hands together as though she wanted to touch him but didn't quite dare. Jayne had to admit that was fine with her; strangers caressing Hayden felt odd, as though they were touching an inner part of her.

"You understand me," Amanda said to the familiar. He dipped his head.

"But he can't speak to you, except through me," Jayne added.

"You fly elegantly together," Amanda told her. Jayne waited for the added criticism, but the other woman let her eye rove along Hayden's flank. "I understand what Ruger meant now."

"What did Ruger tell you?" Jayne was instantly suspicious.

"He said I'd have to see it to believe it." Amanda smiled. This time it wasn't a disapproving or sarcastic smile. She seemed genuinely pleased. "Keep at it. This will be a potent weapon against the Allfather."

"I think we're finished for today," Jayne admitted. The blue spark at the center of Hayden's eye seemed dimmer, his iris yellow with no hint of orange. His wings drooped, and even though he tried to hold himself proudly, his jaw was slightly parted and Jayne could just see the tip of his purple forked tongue. "I'll do some totem work," Jayne said in response to Amanda's questioning look.

Amanda nodded. "It's past time I checked in on how the school was going, anyway. Seo-Joon!" She turned, and Seo-Joon straightened considerably. "Let's see what else your students have got."

Hayden lowered his snout even further until it touched Jayne's arm. He seemed to unravel, pulled by a thread back into her body, and a cooling sensation spread over her like water.

Jayne was bone tired. She'd flown for almost an hour; perhaps she shouldn't be surprised. And she'd separated herself into two different entities.

She found a rock that would keep her dry and sat down. Then she closed her eyes. She heard Vivienne stomp toward her, muttering as her shoes sank into the soft earth. "Now what?" the girl said.

"Now I pay a little visit to a goddess."

CHAPTER
TWENTY-SEVEN

Jayne reached down and felt her magic touch the Spirit totem of Amaterasu. A moment later she stood not on a low plain in front of a mountain but in a neat garden. The grass here was long and verdant, dotted with cheerful crocuses and snowdrops. In front of her was a small pond lined with smooth gray stones. A low bench sat in front of the pond, and the sun goddess sat on the bench. "Welcome, my totem-bearer," she said, and spread an inviting hand.

Jayne sat. "We're going in," she said. Telling the goddess felt almost like making a promise. She looked down at the pond. It was full of yellow koi, but yellow was too bland a word. Sun-colored, star-colored, glowing. Almost too bright to look at.

"And how do you feel?" Amaterasu said.

"I feel..." Jayne hesitated. Her feelings were difficult, really. She was excited, but not in a happy way—in an anticipatory way. She wanted the battle to happen because she wanted it to be over with. Yet she knew she wasn't ready. "I feel like I need you. All of you, with me."

"And so we have given you our gifts." The warm voice came

from off to her left, and Jayne turned. Vesta stood, clad in her toga, regal as a queen. "We will be with you."

I need more, Jayne wanted to say, but she knew she wouldn't get it. She looked at Amaterasu, at the black fall of her hair, at the solemn sadness that seemed ever-present on her face. "I need to know about the Spirit totem. I know it helped me manifest Hayden, but I don't know what else it does. What sort of magic can I do with it, like I can with Earth and Wind and Fire?"

Amaterasu slipped from the bench and knelt at the edge of the pond. "Very well." She dipped one hand beneath the water and the koi flocked to it, nudging her fingers with their lips. She picked one up. It didn't flop and flail in her hands but lay calm, still as a statue. "I am the goddess of the sun. The sun makes things grow." She caressed the fish with one long-nailed finger. At her touch its tail lengthened, a fin feathering out in bright red and orange. Its body grew larger, fins extending and growing cartilage until they resembled wings. The fish's face sprouted a snout, eyes moving to the front of its head. Two legs pushed from its body and split into talons at the end. Skin pebbled over the legs. The animal flopped and wriggled until it had turned over in her palm. Amaterasu cradled it for a moment, loving as a mother, then lifted her palm and tossed a bird into the air. It flew away with a joyful snap of wings. "We bring forth the true nature of things," she said. "My totem summons light and warmth, promise and memory. It will help some evil to remember that perhaps, once, it was good."

She reached into the water and picked up another fish. "If used correctly, you can draw out the knowledge of spirits past, the memory of things you have not known and have not done." The fish in her hand took a slow, deep, shuddering breath of air. She kissed it gently and replaced it in the water. She picked up another fish. "The sun can also be dangerous. It burns, hotter than anything on Earth. My totem can burn too, though you must be mindful of what it costs to do so." The fish glowed, brighter and brighter until Jayne had to look away. Heat seared her face and crinkled the edges of her hair. Then the light was gone. She took a breath of still-scorching air and looked back. Amaterasu let a pile of ashes trickle from her palm into the water.

"These skills can help destroy the Wraiths that have invaded your world. But use them carefully, or you might lose yourself, to fire or to memory."

"How do I activate it?" Jayne said.

Amaterasu smiled. "It is as simple as picking up a fish," she replied and pressed a middle finger to Jayne's forehead.

CHAPTER
TWENTY-EIGHT

Gina Labelle's arm was on fire. She was lucky she hadn't lost it, as a bad-tempered La Liberté doctor had told her more than once, but that hardly helped her mood. She might not have lost her arm, but she'd lost the faith of her people.

After the disaster in Wellington, they'd regrouped in a neat villa in the countryside outside of Toulouse, tucked away from the obnoxious interruptions of the outside world. The once-elegant house had done little to lift spirits, and soon the scent of pine and fresh flowers was replaced with that of blood, medicinal fluids, and the sharp reek of alcohol as the villa became a field hospital. In every room lounged disconsolate and injured people, both from La Liberté and from the Kingdom. Gina herself had spent most of her recovery time in a small library that she used as an office, drawing up a secondary plan of attack. It felt like hiding, and when Pierre appeared in her doorway flanked by Kingdom and La Liberté officers, she had the sensation of being a mouse, staring out of her nest into the eye of the cat.

"Have you spoken to the president?" Pierre asked.

Gina rubbed her temple with her uninjured hand and

leaned on the strong oak desk. "Not yet." Getting President Garnier to endorse her had been a coup, a ticket out of The Hague's prison in the chaos unleashed by the sudden unveiling of magic. But Gina wasn't used to answering to someone else, and Garnier was furious that she'd gone to New Zealand without so much as briefing him.

"Well, I have." Pierre moved into the room, and Gina stood to keep from shrinking back in her chair. She would not be cowed by her son's friend, a man barely out of childhood himself. *I ought to have expected the betrayal,* she thought bitterly. "He's furious, as if that would shock you. He did not ever sanction an attempt to unify with the Wraiths, nor to go to New Zealand in order to do so."

"Garnier doesn't understand the needs of the magical community," Gina replied coolly. "Nonmagical men rarely do. Surely that doesn't surprise you?"

"Except now I agree with him. And so does everyone else," Pierre said.

Gina knew that was a lie. Plenty of La Liberté still stood with her, mostly the old guard. The defected Kingdom operatives were less enthusiastic, it was true—after witnessing Ruth Thorne's transformation into a Wraith and hearing of her murderous exploits in London, they'd fled to La Liberté for protection, among other things. But Labelle wasn't in the business of protection.

"We should never have tried to work with the Wraiths," Pierre said. His face was pale and bisected by three angry slashes, a souvenir from the New Zealand fight. They were neatly stitched, but Gina knew they would scar. "They're abominations."

"Like Rogues?" Gina suggested quietly, menace in her tone. That surprised Pierre, enough, at least, for him to fall silent. She came around the desk, walking slowly. She'd always known how to command a room. "I didn't think you needed reminding that my own people were enslaved, subjugated. What did you Adepts used to call us? Abominations, wasn't it? Lesser, mostly. Servants, if we were lucky. Rogues were long forced to serve Masters we hated. Why shouldn't we see the Wraiths as something like us?"

"They are *not* Rogues." Pierre clenched his fists. "They are Adepts—corrupted Adepts. Your blind hatred for the TCO and the Americans has clouded your judgment, and now we have to answer to the authorities."

Gina waved his complaint away, looking with amusement from face to angry face. "Are you so furious about that? I'll get on the phone with Garnier now. The Americans do things like this all the time, and since they arrived in New Zealand, it will be easy to overshadow our presence with accusations of CIA interference. What we need to do now is deflect, present a unified front, and begin recruitment as the premier European training facility for promising new Adepts. Garnier will be happy to redirect. He doesn't care what I do, as long as I make him look good doing it."

Pierre stared at her, and for once Gina paused. She'd dealt with anger from within her institution before, most recently in the form of her own son's defection. But Pierre wasn't merely angry with her now. He hated her.

"*I* care what you do," he said. Behind him, the cronies nodded. *His* cronies, Gina realized. They were no longer allied with her. "Tristan and Vivienne were right about you. You're unhinged. Unreasonable. I joined you because I wanted freedom for Adepts. I wanted justice for Rogues. I didn't want freedom for Wraiths, or whatever magical horrors we don't even know about yet."

"You called Rogues horrors, once, too—" Gina started.

"The Wraiths are evil, and everyone can see that but you," Pierre snapped. "And now that magic is back, I don't need you anymore. I've got what I wanted. La Liberté is obsolete. As are you."

"Careful, Pierre." Gina raised her hand. She might be injured, but she was still a formidable Adept, and if she went up against Pierre she'd bet on herself any day, even fighting one-handed.

Pierre shook his head. Behind him, two men spun Block spells into being, ready to throw up against her. Behind him, more figures stood in the whitewashed hall, and she doubted any of them were on her side. No, Pierre had gathered his little army before confronting her. Too weak and cowardly to oppose her himself. Lars had done the same to face down Ruth Thorne. It hadn't gone so well for him, either.

"So now what?" she asked silkily. "You'll stage a coup, imprison me in some Time Catch or cell, and tell Garnier the problem has been contained? You'll run La Liberté? I think you'll find it a harder job than you ever gave me credit for."

Pierre's shoulders drooped. A sorrow uncoiled in the man, and Gina realized with a jolt that it was the melancholy that came with leaving a life behind. "I don't need a coup," he replied. "La Liberté is done. We fought to bring magic back to the world, and it is back. All I need to do now...is walk away."

Her arm twitched. She wanted to hurl her spell in his face, preferably followed by a slash of her lioness claws. A matching set of scars would look good on him, she decided. But a Shield spell shimmered over him before she could make a move.

"I don't want to fight, and you don't want to lose," Pierre said. He turned.

"You can't just leave this war behind," Gina flung at his back. "You can't leave us behind! You'll regret this!"

But whether her words made an impact, she couldn't say. Pierre didn't turn. He walked back down the hall, and Gina watched half her forces fall in line behind him.

CHAPTER
TWENTY-NINE

Jayne felt light-headed when they left the Aegis Time Catch and went back to the TCO.

She was still exhausted, but strangely energetic. Power filled her to the brim, warming her fingertips, shining from her forehead. The students had stared, even when Seo-Joon clapped for their attention.

Less than five minutes had passed in the real world, but Jayne was ravenous. She'd barely had time for breakfast after her shower with Tristan, so she turned to Vivienne and said, "Canteen?" Vivienne nodded. "Amanda?" Jayne offered.

"I have more briefings and too many reports to read," Amanda said, chagrined. "Return to the Time Catch as you need to. Use it as your main practice field. I spoke to Seo-Joon about adding in a few more obstacles that might represent the Wraiths, so you'll have plenty of challenges. And keep your phones close by. When I say we move…"

Jayne nodded.

They headed for the canteen. As they walked Jayne sent Tristan a quick text: *Breakfast?*

The reply was immediate. *Again?*

You try spending all day in a Time Catch. Jayne had to admit she'd often wanted a few extra hours in the day—more reading time—but her body was utterly finished and it wasn't even noon.

"Canteen coffee," Vivienne grumbled, but when they got there she wasted no time filling her cup. Despite the day's workout, she still looked impeccable, her glossy black hair in a high ponytail and her cat-eye makeup unsmudged. Jayne had never been so put together at seventeen.

Jayne selected a bag of generic Earl Gray and made it palatable with extra milk. Maybe she should have just taken them back to Nashville for lunch, where she had a great selection of takeout and excellent loose-leaf teas.

What the TCO canteen lacked in drinks, it made up for in breakfast, and Jayne filled her plate with waffles, fresh fruit, maple syrup, granola, and hash browns. They sat, and she dug in. "What's the smallest thing you could turn into that could still make a big difference?" she asked Vivienne through a bite of waffle.

Vivienne made a face at her coffee and forked in some hash browns, bobbing her head back and forth in thought. "I think it depends," she said, swallowing. "Like, is my enemy allergic to bees? Could I have a month on the field ahead of time? Then I could be a mole and dig lots of little tunnels for people to fall and break their ankles."

"Let's roll with this bee scenario. Say we're in the midst of battle and we want to take down a Wraith," Jayne said. "I don't know, could we alter your bee venom so that it delivers a dose of Tiriosis?" She sipped her tea and tried not to make the same face Vivienne had at her coffee. "Bags, man. Just so blah."

"You would have to ask your father. But is chemical warfare not illegal?" Vivienne replied.

"You may have a point." Besides, if they were facing a Wraith army in the tens of thousands, how much good would it do to have Vivienne buzzing around one Wraith at a time? "Maybe we can do something with the stone game, make some kind of weapon we can throw at them?"

"Maybe. But for now, I am going to eat my breakfast. And I think you should eat, too." Vivienne took another bite to illustrate her point.

Jayne *was* starving. But she found it hard to focus on the food. Her energy wouldn't go away. Her movements were quick and darting like a hummingbird. Everything seemed laced in a golden light, and she couldn't tell whether it was the outside world streaming in through the windows along one side of the canteen, or the sun peeking through her.

She felt Tristan before she saw him. He looked disheveled and slightly sweaty, eyes moving automatically from side to side, checking for danger before moving further into the room. Beneath his T-shirt she caught the fluid movement of muscle, a reminder of how powerful and dangerous he could be—both with and without magic. She swallowed.

"Keep it in your pants, Thorne," Vivienne said, but her voice lacked rancor.

He sat without taking a plate. "Did it go well?"

Jayne nodded. "The school grounds are incredible. I really should congratulate Sofia," she said, and bit her lip. That didn't sound like the worst opener to a reconciliation. She could assure Sofia that her work was valid, that her students were competent and smart, making a difference while staying safe.

She took another bite of waffle. Both Vivienne and Tristan were looking at her. "What?" she said through a full mouth.

"You seem..." Tristan frowned.

"Your head is somewhere else," Vivienne told her. Jayne hid a smile behind her hand. She could always count on Vivienne to be blunt.

"I've had a long day already. And the totem..." She stopped. Trying to explain felt impossible, like trying to explain the tide to someone who had never seen water. She trailed her fingers through the air, half expecting to see gold trails of sunshine following after them. Vivienne looked unimpressed. Tristan, on the other hand, had a wrinkle in his brow. She recognized that wrinkle. "Don't worry. I'm fine." She was better than fine, really. She was...renewed. In a war where everything she'd done felt barely adequate, she was gaining new power, which meant a new fighting chance.

"You seem even less down-to-earth than usual," Tristan replied, and though his tone was lighthearted, the wrinkle in his brow didn't go away. "Did something happen?" He looked at Vivienne. "Did she hit her head?"

Jayne captured his face between her hands. "I'm fine," she repeated, feeling her heart stutter. When had someone other than Sofia last noticed her like this, and cared? Even Henry Thorne wouldn't have realized something was off with his daughter. Jayne leaned in and pressed her forehead against his. "Thank you for caring," she murmured.

"Of course I care." Tristan sounded baffled.

She kissed him. It was supposed to be quick, a sort of peck that could manage to be affectionate but professional enough for a work setting. But something seemed to hook behind her new totem as their lips met. It pulled, drawing down through her mouth and flowing into Tristan.

Her heart began to patter. She twisted against his lips and broke away with effort. The golden sheen that touched everything seemed to concentrate in him, burnishing his skin, gilding his hair. Jayne glanced at Vivienne.

"What are you doing to my brother?" Vivienne whispered. Her fork was halfway between her plate and her mouth, forgotten. So she could see it, too.

Tristan's blue eyes grew brighter, then brighter still. His pupils flared like the sun behind an eclipse. He drew in a sudden breath, like a gasp—and he began to speak.

But it was not his own voice that emerged from his mouth.

"The bombs were coming," he said in a low voice. It was tinged with a Midwestern US accent. "I could see, in that moment. I could watch them come, and the whole world would die. Or I could do something to stop them, and I would die." He looked at his long, slim fingers. "I know I died. I know these aren't my hands. But what I don't know is...did I do it? Did I stop the bombs?"

People all around them were falling silent. Jayne stared. Tristan's face had gone oddly slack, and he wasn't in control of his own body anymore.

Vivienne picked up her knife and held it like a weapon. "Where's my brother?" she said. "Who are you?"

"Your brother is here," Tristan—well, not Tristan—told her gently. "He says not to worry, and that he is interested in meeting me, too."

"I don't believe you," Vivienne growled. She half stood. "Who. Are. You?"

"My name is Calvin Carver. I am...I *was* the director of the Torrent Control Organization."

Calvin Carver. Jayne gasped. "Viv, come on." She grabbed Tristan's limp hand. His feet moved sluggishly. Vivienne jogged after them, still holding the knife as if she could actually use it for something more difficult than cutting pancakes.

"Tristan is interested in the spells I developed to repel ballistics," Carver/Tristan said in his odd voice. "It is more powerful than your usual Block spell. He thinks it could be handy for repelling...Wraiths." His face contorted. "I have seen a few Wraiths in my life, missy. You're not about to tangle with them, are you?"

That settled it. Tristan really had given his mind to someone else. He would never even think of calling her "missy."

She pulled them to the wall of stars and headed all the way to the end. There it was: the largest star, etched in bronze, fixed below the portrait of a middle-aged white man with gray hair parted to one side, hands folded on the desk that now belonged to Amanda. *Calvin Carver,* read the star. *First Director.*

Vivienne's mouth fell open. "How?" she said.

Jayne didn't know. But she knew how she was going to find out.

~

Quimby sat Tristan down in the examination chair she used for the blood-doping experiments. "Tell me again?" she said.

"My name is Calvin Carver. I was born in 1906, and my parents were Dorothy and Tim Carver. I discovered my magical abilities in 1924 at New York University. I traveled the world by portal, looking for other Adepts who could help me understand my power, and returned to the USA in 1939 after Adolf Hitler invaded Poland." He tapped the arm of the chair. "I was in Warsaw, you know. Wanted to go right home and join up...of course, then we didn't actually enter the war, so I had to wait. Nearly killed myself overseas trying to heal up my unit, and when I came home I got drafted to join the new magical association. The United States Paranormal Forces Unit. We were looking for anyone with power, assessing whether they were a threat to American security, and neutralizing that threat."

Vivienne snorted. "Typical Americans," she said. "But where does it come in that you possess the spirit of my brother?"

Something flickered in Tristan like a light, and for a moment he was unmistakably himself again. It was in the way he held his shoulders, his mouth, in the way his eyes moved from face to face, focusing first on his sister, then on Jayne. "I am here, Vivienne," he said. His voice was warm, accented in the pan-European way that made Jayne melt a little every time she heard it.

Then his face twitched, and Calvin Carver was back. "Satisfied?" he asked.

"Hardly," Vivienne told him coldly. "What's to stop you from taking control whenever you like?"

"Well, he is. Your...brother, is that right? He's a strong one. You can think of me as his guest, little lady. I'm in the house, but he makes the rules."

Quimby tapped her chin thoughtfully. "Henry?"

Henry Thorne stood next to the blood centrifuge. They'd taken samples from Tristan the moment Jayne had dragged him in, and now Henry was putting tiny drops onto microscope slides. "I have a theory," he said.

"It could be bunnies?" Jayne suggested, recalling her favorite musical episode of *Buffy the Vampire Slayer*. Four faces turned to her, ranging from confused to unimpressed. She held up her hands. "All right, all right." Just once, it would be nice for someone to get her reference and reply in kind.

"Tristan, you were given a transfusion including the ashes of a powerful magician in the hopes that it would boost your power in fighting off the Wraith serum." Henry blinked owlishly behind his round glasses. "Quimby, do you recall whose ashes we used?"

Quimby's eyes flared. *"No."* She hurried over to the shelf at the far wall and pulled out a thick blue binder. She set it on the table and began to flick through pages. "I've got it here...transfusion of B-positive blood, including an extraction of urn number...201." She looked up. "201 is not Calvin Carver. He's 102. Oh God, Henry. Could the records have been wrong? Did we access the wrong ashes?"

"Perhaps."

"This is unacceptable. We'll have to cross-reference all of the samples with the mausoleum records."

Henry smiled. "What are we waiting for?"

"You seem quite okay with this mistake."

"Henry's eyes had taken on the happy glow of a historian. "It's a good mistake. Look at all we can learn!"

"What does all this mean, exactly?" Vivienne looked from Henry to Quimby to Tristan. She still clutched her butter knife. Her face could have been set in steel, but Jayne thought she saw something else behind the strong and angry exterior. The same thing she'd seen when Tristan was in the hospital: fear. Something had happened to her brother and she didn't know what.

Jayne put an arm around her shoulder. Vivienne was stiff for a moment, but Jayne felt her decision to relax, to push her shoulders down and lean into Jayne's side. She listened intently as Jayne said, "When Tristan was in the hospital bed, they used Adept ashes from the mausoleum to save his life. They think those ashes were Calvin Carver's, which would explain why Calvin's talking through him." She frowned. "Though it doesn't explain why Calvin's been quiet until now."

"Maybe it took him a while to wake up?" Quimby shrugged. "Now quiet—I have to make a phone call."

One call to the mausoleum confirmed it: Tristan had been doped with a sample from urn 102, not 201. Calvin's ashes. Quimby was steaming mad and muttering to herself. "I should have taken the sample myself, what a mess, how could they transpose the numbers, didn't test using a master's ashes—"

"I suppose it's good to be of some use," Calvin interrupted dubiously, looking down at himself. "And if I'm honest, the body's an improvement. But did he have to be French?"

His face flickered, and Tristan was back. "Americans," he grumbled.

Quimby plopped down on a chair. "Can we re-create the situation that called him out? Did you have control over it from the start?"

"Um." Jayne cleared her throat, feeling a heat spread up her cheeks. She didn't think of herself as a prude, but she wasn't interested in a makeout session with Tristan in front of her father. Besides, they'd kissed plenty of times post-hospital visit, and none of them had resulted in this. "Are we supposed to go back to the canteen, or...?"

"There has to be a reason it happened now. Tristan, have you felt him before?"

Tristan shook his head. "Only the power. But now...did you know he diverted and neutralized a nuclear missile *midair*? It killed him, but the sheer power to slow time, to create a Block spell that acted as a sphere strong enough to contain a nuclear explosion..." He shook his head. "No wonder he could repel a Wraith for me."

Jayne's totem burned on her forehead. She gasped. *That was it.* "Spirits," she whispered.

They all looked at her. Tristan took her hand and she squeezed his fingers. "I carry the Spirit totem now. I was thinking about the sun, and how it makes things grow, and change, and I must have drawn Calvin out of you." Her gut twisted, and she grimaced at a sudden new thought. "Is that going to happen every time we..."

Tristan laughed, and he sounded entirely like himself again. "I don't think so, *mon amour*. Mister Carver is gone, for now. I can't even feel him." He spun a light spell between his fingers. "I can still use his power, though. *Mon Dieu,* the man was a powerhouse."

That was a relief. Jayne could think of few things worse than hearing *little lady* in the middle of a night with Tristan. They had enough blocking their way, between Jayne's link with Vivienne and fights that put them in the hospital. All the same... "What other side effects can we expect?"

"Given that this is the first time any of us are experiencing something like this? No idea." Quimby was still steaming mad, but there was a spark in her eyes. *She always gets so excited when presented with a mystery,* thought Jayne. Scientific anomalies were Quimby's version of a really good book. "But the kids might have the same side effect. That will freak them all out. I have to do some research."

Henry checked his watch. "Sofia should be getting back from a mission now. I promised I'd meet her." He carefully set his slides in a small refrigerator under the shelving unit. He turned and smiled at Jayne. "You should come, too. It might be the last Thorne family gathering before we go to war."

Jayne hesitated, but Tristan pressed her hand and nodded. He was right. She needed this. It had been weighing on her, and perhaps her father could be the intermediary they needed to make peace.

CHAPTER
THIRTY

They all left the lab together, but Quimby split off to head to the mausoleum. "I'm going to get a head start on cross-checking Adepts to ashes," she said, eyes sparking. "We don't need any more mistakes."

"Dad," Jayne began, but she wasn't sure what to say. The Thorne sisters had always relied on each other for advice. Henry had been out of the picture for so long that it was hard to imagine him doling out wisdom the way fathers did in books.

But for all his absence, he was still their father. And he cared about them. He patted Jayne's shoulder. "You start by telling her you're sorry, and you go from there. Life's too short to spend it fighting. And an apology can bring down a lot of walls. Trust me."

Especially now, Jayne thought.

They arrived at the portal to find Amanda, Ruger, and Seo-Joon already waiting. Jayne half expected Amanda to scowl and tell them to get back to work, but her boss was busy reading a thick file and barely spared them a glance. It occurred to Jayne that she ought to brief Amanda on this new development—but she wasn't sure where to start. Besides, at the moment, it looked more like a curious side effect than something that would have a big influence on the battle to come. She and Tristan could tell Amanda later, once Quimby had assembled all the data.

Seo-Joon greeted them jovially, and Ruger nodded. Jayne smiled at Ruger, who gave her a cautious smile back. Then the portal flashed and he turned toward it, ready for business.

It opened. For several long seconds, nothing happened. Jayne was just starting to wonder if they'd all got the time wrong when they heard a loud *bang!*

A Shield spell was up and shimmering over the assembled officers before Jayne had time to think. Tristan spun a quick Support spell, layered with a Strengthening spell—*when did he learn to do that?* she thought—and the shield took on a thick green glow. It was so intense she almost didn't see the figures as they scrambled through. One of them sent a spell ricocheting back through the portal. *Rufus,* Jayne thought. Two more stumbled through soon after, with a third suspended between them. Matthew, Sofia, and Cillian were last. The portal closed with a pop.

Tristan let the spell dissipate and Amanda ran forward. Ruger had his radio out and was paging Tamara in a low voice. Medina and Rebecca fell to their knees, letting an unconscious Zia fall between them. Her back was soaked with blood.

Jayne ran forward and dropped between them. "Heal," she murmured, putting her hands over Zia's back. The girl's T-shirt had been shredded by long claws. Jayne's palms began to itch.

"What happened?" Amanda demanded. "Did you get the Rogue?"

"Does it look like we got the Rogue?" Sofia snarled.

"Sofia." Cillian's deep voice was full of pain. He cleared his throat and said to Amanda, "We tracked him to Glasgow. He spotted us there, got into a scrap. He's a powerful one, but we were holding our own."

"Until the Wraiths came." That was Rebecca's voice, just off to Jayne's right, but Jayne couldn't see her. Pain was starting to turn her vision black. *You did it before. You can do it now.* She gritted her teeth and tried to focus on Zia.

"They wanted him, too. There were five of them, seven of us...they're just too powerful." Whatever Cillian said next was lost to Jayne, who succumbed at last to the pain; fire spread beneath her skin, up to her eyelids, behind her fingernails. She felt the stinging pull when Hayden broke away from her skin and hissed, then collapsed.

When the black spots cleared from her vision, she saw Hayden, small as a cat, perched on Zia's back, seemingly heedless of the blood smearing his belly. Zia's breath rose and fell regularly. Her eyes were closed in sleep.

Feet surrounded the girl, and medics lifted her onto a stretcher. "She'll be all right," Jayne called, trying to rise. Dizziness overtook her, and she slumped back to the floor.

"She's lost a lot of blood." Tamara's face swam in her vision. "She'll need a transfusion at the very least. And you need some electrolytes, Jayne." She ran a hand through her military crop. "Thorne!" All three Thornes looked up. "Genius Thorne. You're with me. You put doped blood in Zia before, right?"

"Correct." Henry hurried over and they started toward the hospital wing, deep in conversation already.

"Oh God, Jayne." Sofia tackled her, taking them both to the ground. She was sobbing. She smelled like dirt and sweat and tears. She wrapped her arms around Jayne's shoulders and shuddered.

"It's all right." Jayne winced as Sofia squeezed. She rubbed her sister's shoulders and upper back. "It's okay. She's okay."

"It's not okay. She almost died, and you almost died healing her—"

"I didn't," Jayne protested.

Sofia looked up. Her gaze was so fierce it reminded Jayne of Freya the warrior goddess. Even Amanda leaned back when Sofia turned it on her. "Everything went wrong in this mission," she said. She was still holding tightly to her sister. Just behind Jayne, Tristan knelt, and she felt his cool touch against her elbow. "We were undermanned, inexperienced, and lured to a city we didn't know."

"You were on that Rogue seven to one." Amanda's voice was strained. "We didn't anticipate Wraith interest."

"There's a lot you didn't anticipate," Sofia spat.

"Watch your tone, officer," Amanda told her coldly. "Everyone who was on the mission, with me. We need to debrief in my office."

A fresh wave of tears rolled down Sofia's cheeks. Jayne pulled her close. "I'm so sorry," she murmured.

Sofia gripped her as though she were afraid to let go. "I can't," she wept into Jayne's shoulder. Jayne ran her hand down her sister's back in long, soothing strokes. She swallowed sudden tears of her own. She couldn't remember having ever played mother to Sofia before. "I can't."

She took a deep breath and looked up at Amanda. "I can't," she said, more clearly this time. Amanda raised a brow. "I can't just do this. Debrief like it's a regular mission. Plan the next one."

Amanda looked as though she wanted to snap, but she glanced at the kids, clustered together as though numbers would afford them protection. Their eyes were wide, their shoulders hunched. They were scared. "We need to debrief precisely *because* this was an irregular mission. We need to talk about what went wrong and how to fix it, so that next time—"

"There will be no next time." Sofia took one more deep breath, clearly steeling herself. Then she let Jayne go and got to her feet. "I wanted to teach these children how to use their powers. I wanted to provide a safe space for them. I *didn't* want to get them killed."

"Officer, you are taking liberties," Amanda said softly.

"Yeah? How's this for liberties? The Aegis program is finished. I quit." And with that, Sofia spun a golden portal of her own and stepped through it.

CHAPTER
THIRTY-ONE

Living in the Torrent was cold. Like standing in an icy river for centuries and centuries on end. Eventually, you became numb to it, forgetting that there was ever such a thing as warmth. Then you felt the tingle of the outside world, and it was like the glow of fire.

Odin Allfather sat on his throne, letting little eddies and currents of magic run over his freezing feet, dreaming of that fire. On his finger glimmered the ring Draupnir, a relic that helped to magnify his powers.

The Allfather was beset by problems, but the one that plagued him most was power. He lacked it. Enough of it, at least, to break free from the Torrent. And he was tired of being patient. Tired of building up his army and sending his Wraiths out into the warm, beautiful world. He belonged there, not they.

Something howled from outside of the Icelandic pocket. A moment later a Wraith entered the torrent, carrying something in its black claws. A body, a body that thrashed and shifted like the stories of Tam Lin the fairy prince. This moment it was a serpent, that moment a horse. Odin felt a spark of curiosity. Did the creature have any control over its shifting, or was each shape born of desperation?

"And what is this? An offering?" Rogues were rarer than Adepts or potential Guardians, and more complex; Odin had yet to turn one into a Wraith. Yet why shouldn't he be able to? He twisted Draupnir on his finger and felt his magic grow.

The ring didn't multiply his power, not really. It was more of a lending factor. He would have to give power back to Draupnir, at some point. But *some point* was always so nebulous, and today beckoned. He took the swell of power within himself and put a clawed finger on the Rogue's chin.

The Rogue was human again. A man, trembling and enraged. He reminded Odin of a cornered lion, a predator realizing that for the first time in its life, it was prey. The point of Odin's claw dug into his chin, just shy of breaking the skin. And through that claw, the magic wound. It wrapped around the Rogue like the threads of a cocoon. *You are mine. You bend to my will. You do my bidding.* Odin conjured an easy spell of Subjugation and flung it against the cocoon. The Rogue thrashed, broke the spell. Odin bared his teeth. This was a powerful fellow. He reached for more magic and felt the telltale burn.

His skin steamed with effort, and a burning smell filled his nose. He fought to dominate the Rogue, his magic stretching to the limit, then stretching more. He let forth a low howl, a sound of rage and refusal. He would never admit defeat.

The Rogue snapped and went limp.

Odin let up, dipping his arms into the icy Torrent. It was good for some things, after all. Then he straightened. The Rogue stood like a doll, a vacant thing with eyes as black as midnight, as black as his Wraiths. "Cut yourself," he told it.

One finger transformed into a slim sickle blade and ran down the Rogue's other arm. Blood sluiced from the cut. Odin leaned forward and caught a bead on his claw, lifting it to his mouth, and smiled.

There really was nothing like fresh blood.

CHAPTER
THIRTY-TWO

Sofia sat at her desk in the headmaster's office, knees pulled up to her chin. Her blonde hair hung limp around her face, and her eyes were sore and red from crying. She toyed with her engagement ring. Across from her sat Cillian and Seo-Joon, both looking serious. "I just can't," she murmured.

Seo-Joon shook his head. "Sofia, students are pouring in. Anyone with even a drop of magic wants to attend America's only magic school. They're calling it real-life Hogwarts."

"That's because they don't understand what it does." She stared at her cup of tea, long turned cold. "You have to stop enrollment. You have to tell them to go home."

"How?" Seo-Joon spread his hands. "For some of these people, we're all they've got. And do you know how dangerous an untrained Adept can be? They can try spells that are too ambitious and set themselves on fire. You wanted to start this school to protect children, and that's what it does."

"Not at the expense of their lives. We're training them to die! Amanda said they would have easy assignments—"

"Come on, Sof." Cillian put one massive hand on the edge of the desk, as though reaching for a peace offering. "Amanda thought it would be an easy assignment. Don't blame her because something went wrong. It wasn't as though she planned it. They acquitted themselves well in the Wraith attack. Zia will be okay."

"But she knew it could go sideways in a heartbeat, didn't she? She's seen how people can die in the field. More than either of us. And she let it happen anyway? She sent her own *daughter* out there?" Sofia shook her head. She couldn't do that to her own child. Never.

No, it didn't matter whether Amanda had known or suspected that things might go wrong. She *knew* their deaths were possible, and she didn't care. Anything to further the TCO's goals. She understood Jayne's earlier reluctance to go all in with the TCO now.

"Sofia, I do understand where you're coming from." Seo-Joon ran a hand through his short hair. The shiny black was peppered with gray, his face lined in a way it hadn't been when she'd met him a few months ago in the real world. Well, she no longer looked thirty herself.

Do you understand? she wanted to ask. Seo-Joon had never had children of his own, nor any siblings he'd had to parent the way she had. But she forced the words back down her throat. Seo-Joon took this job seriously, thank the Goddess, which meant he *did* understand where she was coming from. He'd shepherded the kids through homework and heartbreak, too. "I know," she said.

He rubbed at his face. He looked sad, and tired. "The program has been a runaway success. People all over the States are applying to send their kids to us—and people from Canada and Mexico, too. The benefit of training a new generation of Adepts, out of the shadows...honestly, Sofia, how different would your life have been if you hadn't been part of a great secret? Maybe even Ruth Thorne wouldn't have turned out the way she did."

Was that really possible? Ruth *had* resented the way Adepts had to hide their powers, and she'd tried to get Sofia to resent it, too. Would she have sent Sofia off to a boarding school in the hopes of making her daughter more powerful? Or would she have tried to hoard Sofia's power for herself? Would she have still wanted complete control, the kind she could only get through seizure?

"We talked about next year's enrollment at the last board meeting," Cillian said. The Aegis board was currently made up of Cillian, Amanda, and Amanda's direct superior, Josh. "We've made offers for about 80 percent of the applicants we felt had a high enough magical threshold to need intensive training. The others were referred to sister programs that are getting underway in London and Shanghai. I'm not sure we could shut the program down if we wanted to, Sof."

If they wanted to? "Whose side are you on?" she accused, reaching for a tissue.

Cillian got up and made his way around to her chair. He knelt, putting a hand on her knee. It was warm, comforting. His big blue eyes met hers, clear and honest. It was one of the things she loved most about him—the simplicity of his truth. Cillian had always, *always* been truthful with her. Now he said, "I'm on your side," and she knew that was no lie. He'd always been on her side. "But Seo-Joon's right. We can't close the program down. People are relying on us."

"Then we have to change it." Warm fire spread through her belly. "Surely most of these parents aren't keen for their children to go to war as soon as they've got an education, either."

"That's...not really their decision, is it?" Cillian asked gently. "You made this choice for yourself. Jayne made this choice for herself. Matthew and the team, Seo-Joon and I...we walked into this knowing it was dangerous. Aye, for some of us that was part of the attraction." He chuckled. Then he turned serious again. "Part of the problem with magic is that the danger seeks us out. We have to make sure our students are prepared."

"We can do that. We can also just...teach them self-defense only. No attacks."

"You know Amanda's not going to swing for that," Seo-Joon said.

"And so what?" Sofia bit out. "What does Amanda know about this?"

"Sofia." Cillian moved his hand from her knee to her cheek. She closed her eyes, letting tears slip out to be wiped away by the pad of his thumb. She couldn't get the image out of her mind—Zia's back arching as a Wraith slashed up her spine. Lying in a pool of her own blood, lips moving soundlessly. Her body spasming as shock set in.

If Jayne hadn't been right on the other side of the portal, Zia would be dead. An eighteen-year-old girl, dead. And for what?

"Don't beat me up for saying this, but you're a wee bit emotional right now. You might not be thinking clearly. Eighteen-year-olds sign up for war all the time. They join the military academies, they enlist. If they want to fight in this war, you can't take that right away from them. Is it hard, and unfair, that they're going to face war immediately upon graduating instead of just a possible threat of it? Yes. But this is our reality, love. By teaching them to fight, we're giving them the best protection. Without it, Odin will take them for himself."

Seo-Joon spoke gently, steepling his fingers. "He makes a good point. And don't forget, this is a TCO facility. As the director, Amanda decides what to do with the school and what's on the curriculum. And remember that she's our boss too, Sof. She can put you back in the field or on another assignment if she thinks you're not doing what the TCO needs. Is that what you want? To be moved? Or would you rather stay here and make a difference to them? Teach them to care about each other and the world as much as you do? Because compassion will absolutely help them in battle."

There was no way to win. Sofia knew that. How could she have been so naïve when she'd started on this journey? But Seo-Joon was right. She could choose to run from this as a mistake or take responsibility for it. And Cillian might be right, too. Her hormones were on overdrive. Nothing that put any child in danger would ever feel right, but especially now, when she was trying to protect her own tiny creature.

An old rotary phone rang on the desk. It was a direct line to the TCO. Seo-Joon leaned over and answered it. "Aegis Battle Academy. This is Seo-Joon."

A crash sounded from the other end and he held it away from his ear, wincing. "Hello? Who's speaking?"

A tinny voice spoke in garbled syllables on the other end. Seo-Joon's face turned white. "We're on our way." He set the phone down and looked at Sofia and Cillian.

"It's Zia."

CHAPTER
THIRTY-THREE

Quimby could hardly keep herself from running to the mausoleum. This changed things completely. That Tristan, already one of the most knowledgeable members of the TCO, was now a Master *and* held the memories of one of their most esteemed predecessors? He could tell them things about lost code names, experimental spells...they could fill in so many gaps with Carver's knowledge. He'd come into his own during a time with unfettered access to the Torrent, before it had closed itself off. They'd lost so much just from that...and he could help them get so much back.

And think of what all the other dead Masters might teach them.

We'll have to be a little more discerning from now on, of course, she thought, swiping her key card to get into the mausoleum. In a perfect world, they'd match Adepts and old Masters carefully, maybe studying skill sets, temperaments, and more, but she knew better than to suggest that to Amanda before they'd won the big battle. Such assessments would take months, and they had a few days at most. Amanda's finger was already hovering over the proverbial button, ready to push *go* and get Adepts like

Tamara, Seo-Joon, and Amanda herself transfusions. Which meant that Quimby, in turn, had a major report to write on Tristan's new pal.

The mausoleum attendant, an Adept well into his seventies named Gerry, met her in front of the mausoleum's doors and allowed her in, with a little resentment for disturbing his peace. The mausoleum itself was a neat and tasteful room in white plaster with blue trim at the top, with little alcoves dotting the walls. Each alcove was lit from below and held a stainless-steel urn. Brass plates fixed just below the urns contained a serial number. For extra safety on top of all the other magical protections of this room, the serial numbers correlated to the magicians' names were hidden behind several layers of encryption, magical and technical. There had been a series of mausoleum hacks a decade ago when Quimby was a newbie at the TCO. Someone, they assumed the Kingdom or La Liberté, had managed to get past the extensive firewalls, but the hack had been stopped before any information was leaked. Knowing what she did now, she could only imagine what they were after. The blood doping was her idea, but Goddess knew what their enemies had planned.

"How are we doing, Gerry?" Quimby smiled.

Gerry was not the smiling type. "All this excitement around the dead is unhealthy, Miss Quimby."

Quimby suspected he was irritated that he couldn't sit with coffee and a crossword, with only the dead to keep him company and the most menial of tasks to fill his day. "Would you believe you're one of the most important men in the TCO right now?" she said.

Gerry lifted his nose. "I never doubted my worth, Miss Quimby, but I've never lied to myself either. Don't *you* start lying to me. You haven't got the years to make it convincing."

Quimby laughed and handed him a note. "Like I mentioned when I called, there was an issue, some numbers got transposed. We used a Master's ashes instead of a powerful Adept. Carver's ashes, to be specific."

Gerry paled. "But...how...I didn't..."

"It's okay. I assume the hack messed things up somehow, so we're going to have to cross-check every set of ashes with the database and files to be sure it doesn't happen again."

"What did happen, exactly?"

"We used them in an experiment and it's taken a *fascinating* turn. Carver came...alive, using Tristan Labelle as a conduit, of sorts. He can share his knowledge with us. We just thought we could access the Adepts' power. I never thought the actual person's memories could be accessed. I need to do some research to see exactly who else we have down here."

Gerry scowled. "I'll have to verify your identity."

Quimby flapped a hand. As if Gerry didn't see her at staff meetings and in the break room. "Go ahead." She handed over her key card and her badge.

As Gerry fiercely typed in her information, one agonizing keypunch at a time, she looked around. "Have you ever wished you could hear the stories of all these people?" *Because maybe soon, you can.*

Gerry was silent, concentrating on his task. At last, the computer beeped and began to run her credentials. "I took this job so that I didn't have to talk to anybody." He turned, and a green spell spun in his hand. "So no."

He threw the spell over her. It hit her like a blanket of water, cold and wet and somehow...slimy? She gasped and rubbed furiously at her face, only half surprised to discover that it, like her sleeve, was dry.

"Sorry. Checking for illusion or glamour spells is part of the protocol."

"You're not sorry in the least," she grumbled, and he cackled. Ah well. She didn't usually manage to make Gerry smile, and today was a great day. He should share in it.

He pulled up the name database and searched for the serial numbers one by one, painstakingly writing the name of the dead magician next to each corresponding number. Impatient, Quimby wandered from urn to urn, letting her eyes rove over the lines of alcoves. Imagine being practically brought back to life! Ordinary people tried to leave something of themselves behind after death in the form of a legacy. But these powerful magicians...they could bring their knowledge and wisdom to new generations, could boost the power of hundreds of Adepts. She'd made Tristan's serum with just a small sample of Carver's ashes. How many people could actually use Carver's power? And would they somehow be linked to each other? The possibilities were staggering. She knew Jayne liked to get her knowledge from books, but this was a first-of-its-kind program for accessing the knowledge firsthand. If only they weren't covert, she could win a Nobel for figuring all this out.

"Here we are. Six numbers, six names. I take it that's all you need?"

"Yes. I'll leave you alone now." Quimby tried not to snatch the paper from him in her excitement. She grabbed his hand, too, and shook it. "Gerry, you have no idea how much you're helping the cause of science as it relates to magic."

Gerry disentangled himself and shook his hand to loosen his fingers. "If you want to butter me up, coffee's better than words." He tried to scowl, but she could see the hint of a smile hiding behind it. "Make that coffee and a croissant."

"You know what, Gerry? I'll do that," Quimby promised.

Out in the hall, she stopped and pulled out the note. She simply couldn't wait. Her eyes roved down the list. Carver they already knew about, thanks to Tristan. But they also had someone named Lorraine Docker, a Russian by the name of Markov, whose name made her wonder if he'd fled the revolution, a Sergio Urbina, Dayo Abioye, and...

Quimby's elation slid off her like Gerry's slimy spell. "Oh

no," she breathed. Grabbing her phone, she shoved the note in her pocket and started toward the lab at a fast walk.

Henry's phone rang through. "Come on," she muttered and called again. Again, it rang through. She tried a third time. Then a fourth.

He finally picked up. "I'm busy," he said, sounding annoyed.

That in itself was unlike Henry. Sometimes he was so deep in his work that he didn't hear his phone, but even then he was genial enough. And she knew for a fact he was supposed to be having tea with Sofia.

"This is an emergency. Who got transfusion F3916?"

"Zia," Henry replied, far faster than she'd expected. He sounded grim. "And I just gave her another as you were ringing the speaker off my telephone. It's not easy to handle a needle when I'm constantly being startled—"

"You gave her *more?*" Quimby shouted, startling an officer going in the opposite direction.

"Ah, you weren't there. Zia suffered significant injuries in the field and had to be given an emergency transfusion."

"But those are Aaró's ashes!"

Silence on the other end of the line. Then, *"What?"*

Then something crashed, and Henry shouted, "Shi—", and the phone call ended abruptly.

Quimby stuffed the phone in her pocket and took off at a run.

ALARMS BLARED.

"JAYNE THORNE TO THE HOSPITAL WING. REPEAT, JAYNE THORNE TO THE HOSPITAL WING."

Jayne, Tristan, and Vivienne tore through the hospital waiting room, joining Amanda and a team of newly arrived

Disciples as they headed for the hall. "What is it?" Jayne shouted at Amanda. "Is it Dad?"

Amanda didn't answer.

But Jayne didn't have to wait long to find out. She saw where she was needed immediately, as an Adept was tossed out of a room and into the hallway in front of her. He hit the plaster on the opposite side hard enough to leave a dent and slid to the floor.

Amanda stopped and checked his pulse. "Get in there," she snapped, jerking her head. The Disciples of Gaia fanned out behind Jayne, pulling weapons and spells from the Torrent.

The hospital room was complete chaos. Beds, chairs, and gurneys had been overturned; privacy curtains had been torn loose. Tamara lay on the floor, unconscious. Henry crouched beside her, using one of the beds for cover. "Dad!" Jayne shouted.

He whirled, eyes wide. "Jayne! Get back—"

Only the quick thinking of a Disciple stopped Jayne from being blasted into oblivion. A Shield spell sprung up in front of her face just a moment before an Attack smashed into it. Jayne summoned her staff and her best Roundhouse spell and looked for her enemy.

In the center of the chaos stood Zia. Her thin chest heaved and her eyes darted from side to side, wild, furious. "I said you'll never take me alive."

Her voice was different. *Like Tristan when he was possessed.* It was harsh and angry. Zia flung another spell, and Jayne spun a Deflect along her staff before batting it away.

"You're confused," Jayne said, pitching her voice low, trying to soothe. "That's understandable. A lot of things must seem strange to you right now."

Zia's mouth twisted strangely, as though she were fighting the motion and losing. "I'm not confused. I know exactly where I am." Her lips drew up in a sneer. "I'm at the Torrent Control

Organization. That bastard Ruger stole what was left of me and brought me to the last place I'd ever want to be."

"Who are you?" Jayne asked. Zia didn't answer.

We bring forth the true nature of things, whispered Amaterasu in the back of Jayne's mind.

Good idea. Thanks.

Jayne summoned the Spirit totem and imagined it washing down her staff. Harsh golden light filled the room as the staff began to blaze with a nonconsuming fire. Henry winced. Zia threw a hand over her face to shield it. Jayne motioned toward the girl, and the light followed her command.

It moved strangely around Zia, as though it couldn't tell how tall she really was, nor what she really looked like. If Jayne tilted her head she could see the possessor like a shadow: another person entirely, the magician who controlled her. Red glinted in his hair, and his pale limbs moved as though he were summoning a spell.

Oh, shit. She'd been up against this one before. He was mega dangerous, extremely powerful, and the reason she'd joined the TCO in the first place. Aaró.

"Bring Zia back," Jayne said in a hard voice. "This is your final warning."

Zia raised her arms. Sweat trickled down her brow. "Well. If I'm here, I might as well leave you with a little something to remember me by."

She started to tremble. A scent of smoke and burning flesh filled the room. "She's going to immolate," Henry said urgently.

Jayne couldn't think of what else to do. She leaped forward and hit the girl on the head with her staff, hard.

Zia dropped to the ground. The smell of strange magic and burning skin retreated. Through her totem, Jayne couldn't see Aaró's spirit anymore. Zia seemed like herself again, just unconscious.

Jayne knelt by Tamara, who was struggling to sit up. "What happened?" the medic asked.

Henry peered at her. "You likely have a concussion."

"I think we'd all like to know what happened," said a hard voice from behind Jayne. It was a Disciple—the big Disciple who'd been reluctant to join the TCO. He looked no less reluctant right now. In fact, he looked somewhat murderous. "What sort of magical experiments are you running? Explain!"

"Let's go back to my office, Augustin," Amanda began, but Henry interrupted.

"It's all quite simple," he said, pushing his glasses up his nose. "You see, we discovered, somewhat by accident, that making a serum from the ashes of a powerful magician could increase the power of an Adept, exponentially."

"Thorne," Amanda warned in an iron voice.

"And what do you do with this serum?" the Disciple asked softly. His voice was filled with such menace that Jayne took a step back before she knew what she was doing.

But poor Henry Thorne was oblivious to the danger. "We inject it, usually with a blood transfusion. It's a simple process once you get the serum right—"

"Outrageous," spat the big Disciple.

"Augustin, let's talk about this," Amanda began again.

"I don't think I need to talk," he replied, whirling to face her. His weapon was still out, and he was easily twice as wide as Amanda and a good foot taller. But the woman didn't back down. She folded her arms and looked at him, frank and unimpressed.

"I agree with Augustin," said Isra from next to him. She sheathed her sword. "And when we take this news back to the rest of the Disciples, they will agree, too. This is an abomination."

"It's just science," Henry said. "Science that is allowing us access to the secrets of these magicians. We can learn our history in ways we never could before."

Isra's eyes were flashing in fury. "Magicians are sacred. Masters even more so. They are the ones who came before. When the Torrent flowed, we could ask dead Masters for an ounce of their wisdom at any time. But you would tether a dead magician's spirit to an untried girl? Without his consent, or hers?"

"Oh, she certainly consented," Henry said. "I'm afraid Aaró couldn't consent, on account of him being dead—"

"Henry Thorne, *shut your mouth,*" Amanda snapped.

Henry stopped, shocked. It was hard to say who looked more surprised, actually. Jayne looked from Henry to the Disciples, who looked murderously angry. Sparks formed on her fingertips unbidden. The way the big one was looking at her father, she might have to take him down, quickly. *That* would really help their magical cooperation.

"This is an utter travesty," Augustin spit out. "We won't work with it."

"*This* is an unfortunate necessity if we want to have the power it takes to win this war," Amanda replied.

"Then you can win this war without us," Augustin said. "Our agreement is cancelled."

He turned and strode down the hall, his Disciples trailing behind him.

CHAPTER
THIRTY-FOUR

Jayne, Vivienne, and Tristan helped Tamara to her feet, then righted the room. Jayne found Hayden unconscious in a corner and gently fed him back into her arm. *I was having a nice sleep,* he grumbled at her before mentally rolling over and going back to it.

Yeah. Very helpful, she thought.

They lifted Zia onto her hospital bed and fastened magical restraints around her wrists and ankles. "I'm sure she'll thank you for the headache," Tamara said when Jayne briefed her on the fight.

"I've healed worse than concussions. And maybe she *will* thank me that she's not a pile of ashes."

Quimby crashed into the room. "Am I too late?" she panted.

"You're in time," Amanda replied. "In time to avoid being a civilian casualty. And maybe you can help us with our latest predicament." She gestured to Zia. "How are we supposed to stop Aaró from taking her over again? If he's there every time she wakes up, we have a huge liability on our hands." She looked over at Henry, who was still pale with shock.

"We may have to research how we can reverse the serum," he said.

"Is that even possible?" Jayne asked.

Henry shook his head. "I don't know," he said softly. "When we discovered what it could do... Tristan had no ill effects, so we thought it was safe. We didn't think about side effects, or about what might happen when someone wanted to, well, go back to normal..."

He looked a little lost. Quimby put a hand on his arm. "We'll figure it out," she assured him. "We're the geniuses, right?"

"Genius must be steered by compassion and morality," Henry replied.

"So maybe our doping plan isn't so solid. And now the Disciples have flown the coop. Jayne, what did you do to convince them before? Think you could it again?"

Quimby was such an optimist.

"I'll try. Don't break anything else, okay? Tristan, Vivienne, you're with me."

THEY FOUND the Disciples in the portal room, being watched over by a terrified young officer who looked as if he'd seen a cadre of ghosts parading by. The Disciples were intimidating, Jayne gave them that. They were conversing in low voices and broke off when she approached. Augustin stepped in front of the others. He held his spear proudly, crossed in front of him like a sort of challenge.

"Don't waste your breath," he said.

"You don't even know what I'm going to say." Jayne put one hand on her hip.

"I'll take a guess. It has something to do with how we don't have time, and we have to pick a side, and even indecision is a kind of decision. Isn't that it?" Augustin's lip curled.

"Well, he has us pegged," Vivienne said and flopped down in a chair.

Tristan tried next. "War is difficult. Sometimes it's unpleasant. I've done things I wish I hadn't had to, but I did them because the alternative was far worse."

"We fail to see how Odin will be worse than you. *That* is the problem." Augustin pounded the floor with his spear. "You say that Odin will enslave humanity, but what have you done with the former magicians' ashes? Have you asked their permission to be reanimated into someone else's body?"

"Their spirits are still here. In the mausoleum," Jayne said. "We didn't take all of the ashes, just a tiny bit."

"That makes no difference. You've already disturbed their rest. And when I think of the fact that not only do you have the ashes of your dead, but also that of your enemies?"

"It's tradition to keep the ashes of the powerful when they've fallen."

"That is *your* tradition," he spat. "We know that when a magician dies their spirit must pass into the Torrent. It keeps the river of stars alive. You and your *tradition* are holding them all hostage. We had no idea you were so reckless." He was shouting now, and Isra put a calming hand on Augustin's arm.

"It is hard to regret helping you, Jayne," she said. "I think you have promise and potential. But if you use it to subjugate others, you are no better than those we are trying to fight."

"I don't know why you thought she was worth it in the first place." Augustin pointed at Jayne's arm. "She's Wraith-touched. She's corrupted. This was all a mistake from the beginning."

"I'm not—" Jayne began.

"Enough. I will not speak with you. If you wish to engage me, you may engage me in battle." Augustin swung his spear around so that the tip was an inch from Jayne's throat.

Tristan's palm was out in an instant, a Slap spell smacking

the spear away. "You watch what you say to her," he said, bringing up his fists. His eyes blazed. He was ready for a fight. Part of Jayne was, too. But she knew what Amanda would say if they got caught brawling in the portal room.

She also knew how she could end this fight, easily. "You think you could take us?"

"You may be a Master, Jayne Thorne, but you are not invincible," Augustin said. "We are four on three, not bad odds."

"What if I made that four on four?" she said and reached for her familiar.

Get big, she told him and clenched her fist until her nails left crescent marks on her palms.

I was still sleeping, he grumbled, unwinding from her arm, stretching out to fill the space. The portal room was suddenly very crowded, and Hayden growled a little, shifting his wings. Then he lowered his head until it was level with Augustin's and stared at the man. Curls of smoke rose from his snout. *Is this why I was disturbed? What am I supposed to do, eat him?*

Jayne sort of wished everyone could hear what her familiar was saying. It might put the fear of the Goddess—or at least of Jayne—into them. But looking at the Disciples, she realized that perhaps she didn't need to. At the appearance of Hayden they'd gone completely white.

"It can't be," Isra whispered. "I thought I was hallucinating."

"It's..." Augustin swallowed. "Impossible." The bluster was gone. He sounded downright reverential.

The other female Disciple behind him fell to her knees, eyes wide and liquid as they fixed on Hayden. Next to her, the last man raised a trembling finger. "She's a dragon rider!"

Jayne looked at Tristan. "A what now?"

Tristan looked smug. "A dragon rider. Long ago, the Disciples of Gaia had familiars, too—those who were powerful, and pure of heart. They rode their dragons into battle. It made them feared, and respected, for a dragon rider only ever fought on the side of good. Not for nations, or programs, or people. For the cause of justice. What do you have to say now, Augustin?"

Augustin couldn't take his eyes from Hayden's magnificent snout. "We have always revered dragon riders," he said, sounding astonished.

"Every time I think you cannot surprise me anymore," Isra murmured.

"I promised you a deal," Jayne said, flushing with satisfaction. *Don't let it go to your head,* she thought, and couldn't tell whether it was her own or Hayden reminding her. "We hear and understand your concerns about the spirits of our ancestors, and we are willing to find a way forward that is right for all of us. But we must stop Odin. The fate of the world relies on it. We have to fight him together, or we lose everything. What do you say?"

"Nice speech," Tristan murmured in her ear.

"You...serve a just cause," Augustin replied in a trembling voice.

"We cannot deny it," Isra added.

"The Disciples followed the dragon riders until there were none left. Which means that you..." Augustin was lost for words for a moment. Then he looked past Hayden to Jayne. His eyes were filled with a strange light, but one as bright as anything her totem of spirit could call forth. It was the light of devotion.

"Now we follow *you*, Jayne Thorne."

CHAPTER
THIRTY-FIVE

Sofia kicked her sandbag as hard as possible, sending it spinning across the air of her Nashville apartment. As it swung back her way, she punched it full on, imagining it to be Aaró's face. A knee to his imaginary groin, a palm to his hypothetical nose, thumbs to his unreal throat. She was about to stomp on an illusory instep when Cillian's punch to the sandbag from the other side sent it swinging toward her and brought her out of her fervor.

"Need to talk?" he said.

"No." She brought her foot down and lashed out again. "Nothing to talk about." She was going to train until she collapsed, right here on the living room floor, then sleep off this horrible day.

"Sof, it's okay. Of course there's a lot to talk about—"

"No, there's not. What happened to Zia is not going to happen again. Quimby's going to stop the doping experiments, simple as that. And *don't* tell me that you understand it's hard."

She stopped. Sweat dripped from her hairline, pooling in her collarbone and beading on her upper lip.

"I wasn't going to," Cillian said. He handed her a towel and she wiped her face. "But I was going to say that you can't make Quimby stop. Amanda's the one giving orders. Amanda's the one you have to convince."

And Amanda wanted her super soldiers.

"Then we'll tell Amanda that the experiment is over."

Cillian chuckled ruefully. It only made Sofia angrier, but she pushed that anger down. It wasn't useful right now.

"I love your protective streak. You're going to be such an amazing mother."

"Don't try to change the subject, Cillian."

He grinned. "It's true, though. But seriously, in my experience, *telling* Amanda doesn't get us anywhere. We have to appeal to her. We've got to make her tell *us*."

"Yeah, well, I don't feel like appealing." Sofia kicked the sandbag again.

"We can do it your way. But I think she'll say no," Cillian warned.

"So what if she does? What is she going to do, stop us by force? We're stronger than her."

"Aye, Sof." Cillian rubbed the back of his neck. "Amanda isn't in charge because she's the most powerful. She's in charge because she understands the big picture."

"Well, I don't *like* the way she's understanding this big picture." Sofia punched again. Somehow Aaró's face had morphed into Amanda's, and the *thwack* was almost as satisfying. "And if we don't want to follow her rules, maybe we need to be in charge to change them."

"Like a coup?" Cillian raised a brow.

"It wouldn't be the first CIA coup, would it?" Sofia said.

Cillian was silent for a long moment. "You don't sound like you, Sof," he said.

"I'll protect those kids any way I can. If it means pushing Amanda out and taking power myself, I'll do it."

"Like Ruth was willing to take power for her own ends?" he asked.

Rage flushed through Sofia, filling her with both energy and a blaze of magic. She wrapped a Cut spell around her fist and slammed it into the sandbag, slicing through the tough fabric and releasing a stream of sand over the apartment floor that swung in a pendulum pattern. "I'm *nothing* like her."

"Everyone who does what you're suggesting claims to have a good reason. That's what we all tell ourselves, whenever we do something bad. I've been there, Sof. Don't you remember? I worked for the Kingdom once, and every bad thing I did—tailing your sister, stealing your dad's journal, committing petty crimes all over Dublin—I did it because I thought it was for a good cause."

"Well, how else am I supposed to save them?" Sofia shouted. "How else am I supposed to protect them?"

She kicked the sandbag, hard. Sand exploded out, and it fell from its hanger to the floor with a thump. But she wasn't done with it yet. She stomped on it, then set to it with her fists again.

"Sofia," Cillian said from above. Sofia couldn't stop, couldn't listen to him. She needed to kill something. She needed to remember that she was powerful, that she could fight and win for the sake of someone else.

She'd always been the protector. She'd always been the mother. No one would take that from her or make her impotent, not even Amanda Newport.

Cillian's arm came down, blocking her punch and diverting it to the side. "Sofia, listen to me." His voice was urgent.

Well. If that was how he wanted to play it. Sofia went to shove him in the shoulder, a light sparring blow. He turned that aside as well. One fist snaked out, lightning-quick, and tapped her side. A point. "We can still help them."

Sofia moved inside his guard, tucking her leg around his

and throwing him off balance. She shoved him onto the couch. "Help them what? Help them die?"

He rolled and she sprang over the arm of the couch. "Help them grow up. No matter what, they grow. And they'll leave the nest, and you'll have to let them."

"I don't have to condemn them." She was short on breath, her chest heaving.

Cillian clambered to his feet and came toward her slowly. Arms out. "Then we'll talk to Amanda. Together. Discuss our concerns and see how we can keep our students as safe as possible."

Talk to Amanda. She knew he was right. But she just... couldn't face it. What if Matthew was next? What if a Wraith got to him, and Jayne couldn't heal him in time? Why did he have to be involved in this fight? Why did any of them?

Because of you, she told herself. *Because of your stupid school idea. It was supposed to be magical and wonderful and healing. It wasn't supposed to be Adept boot camp. And now you're pregnant, you idiot girl. You're going to send your own child into the fray eventually.*

Energy raced through her again. But now she didn't want to hit Aaró or Amanda. She wanted to hit herself. She threw herself at Cillian, aiming jabs at his ribs and stomach and shoulders. He turned her blows until she snuck one in to his stomach. "Sofia, Sofia—*oof.*" He took a half step into her guard and swept her feet from under her.

She grabbed his shirt. They went down together.

Their mouths met in a clash of teeth and lips. Her energy quickly redirected itself as Cillian moved atop her, pinning her to the floor and grinding his hips against hers. She let out a growl, half rage and half anticipating. Her fingers tore, trembling, at the buttons on his jeans. His hands were surer but slower as they pulled up her tank top and worked at the bra beneath. Her breath quickened as his thumbs danced at the sensitive skin under her breasts. She yanked his jeans down, then wiggled out of her own leggings. All the while his lips were a searing heat on hers. His tongue slid between her teeth, stroking, and she arched into it. She growled again when he moved one hand from her breast, but the sound caught in her throat when he hooked a finger around her panties and tugged them gently down.

He made to move away, to free their legs, but Sofia couldn't let him. If he broke the spell, she'd have to think again, and then all she would think about was how stupid she'd been. She kicked off the last of her leggings and wrapped her legs around his waist.

He broke the kiss. His breath was hot and quick on her cheek, and his forehead was pressed to hers. "This doesn't change anything, Sofia," he murmured.

"Don't," she begged him. "Not now."

He hesitated, then relented. He started out slow, but Sofia moved with urgency, trying to outpace her feelings. And for a small glorious while, it worked: she felt the frantic panting of his breath on her neck, the thunder of her heart, the trembling of her legs. And the pleasure, of course, mounting until it became unbearable and broke like a dam, and all her anger broke with it. Cillian shuddered against her, then went still.

He collapsed next to her and pulled her against his side. She didn't realize she was crying until she couldn't breathe. He didn't say anything; he ran one hand up and down her arm, calm and sure, patient and loving.

"I can't," she said when she could muster enough air to speak. "How can I just let them go? How can I just abandon them?"

Cillian's other arm encircled her, and he rolled over to face her. She focused on his chest, the comforting solidity of him. "I know this is about more than the kids at the school. We will protect them the only way we can, Sof. We teach them everything we know. We're not abandoning them, especially if you stay to shepherd them. They're just...growing up. They have to. And when they do, we can't save them anymore. They'll have to save themselves."

CHAPTER
THIRTY-SIX

Jayne's phone pinged with a message from Amanda. *Briefing, 5pm. Bring the Disciples.*

"Why yes, I did get them back on our side, thank you very much," she muttered. "Good work, Jayne. You achieved the impossible—*again*."

"You whine more than I do, and I am French," Vivienne said.

Tristan snorted, then shrugged as Jayne glared at him. "Sorry, *mon amour*. It is somewhat true."

"Somewhat?" Vivienne and Jayne replied in outraged tandem.

They trained, they ate lunch, they sat. At four-thirty Sofia and Cillian came through the portal, looking rumpled. Sofia's eyes were red, and there was a melancholy about her that Jayne recognized all too well. Her sister was fixated on something. Jayne could guess what. She cared for the students of Aegis as if they were her own children.

They headed to Amanda's office at five minutes to five. Augustin and Ruger stood outside already, talking quietly. There was something slightly amusing about the dichotomy between them: two equally massive men, one in a trim suit, well-shaved and professional, the other looking like a hippie from the Middle Ages.

Ruger's face washed over with relief. "I was worried you'd be late.

"We're in plenty of time, Ruge." Jayne made to punch him in the arm, but he leaned away. "What's wrong?"

"This is serious," he told her.

"We're in the CIA. Everything's serious."

Ruger straightened his suit jacket and stared ahead. "Not like this."

The door opened.

"I'm glad we could come to an understanding," Amanda said, looking at Augustin. Her red hair was frizzy like she hadn't brushed it at all today. Her suit was wrinkled, too, Jayne noticed. When had this woman last slept?

"We have conditions for helping you," Augustin said. "We have spoken to your librarian, Katie Bell, and we understand now that you made a mistake out of ignorance and not malice."

Amanda's mouth thinned. "A what?"

Jayne ducked her head so that the director wouldn't see her smile. When had Amanda last been told she'd made a mistake?

"The ashes of powerful magicians are not playthings or scientific experiments. Among the Disciples, the ashes of Masters were given the highest respect. We preserved them, tended them, nurtured them. Legends go that in times of need, we could even call upon the familiars of the dead Masters to help us in battle. Many of our traditions were lost when the Disciples were forced into obscurity and hiding, and many of the ashes we once cared for have been lost. Your office may have access to the greatest collective magical memory in the world. We can help you access it...but only if you promise never to make another such serum."

Amanda looked down at her desk, one brow raised. Zia's file was open on it, Jayne saw. "A few months ago, Jayne was the most powerful Master in the world. Yesterday, six other Adepts rivaled her in power, and all because of this serum. You can't expect me to shut down a program that constitutes our greatest hope in defeating evil."

"I'm with him," Sofia said.

Amanda closed her eyes briefly. Jayne suspected that if she were a little less professional, she might have rolled them. "Of course you are," she muttered.

"The serum was not properly tested before we started human experimentation," Sofia continued. "Tristan ended up okay, but Zia was possessed by a malevolent former Adept."

"Quimby's report suggested that it was the nature of that Adept, which we can easily avoid in the future, mixed with a second transfusion that made him temporarily stronger. There's no reason to think he could take over again."

"Until the next time Zia gets hurt," Sofia said.

Amanda rubbed her forehead. "Naturally, more screening should have taken place as to the nature of the ashes used. Quimby's also putting together a profiling and matching system—"

"Irrelevant," Augustin cut in. He crossed his arms. *He looks like a bear,* Jayne thought, or as close to a bear as a non-Rogue could get. "Either the Torrent Control Organization agrees to stop the experiment at once, or you can win your war without the Disciples."

Amanda's jaw moved back and forth. Finally she said in a low voice, "And you think you can call out more dragons? More familiars from these dead Masters?"

Augustin nodded once.

Amanda's shoulders sagged. "Fine. We'll move the work with the mausoleum in a different direction. But that means you're with us for this operation, and *that* means I'm in charge. Understood?"

"We cede to you," Augustin replied.

"Right. We've got three teams: Guardians, Disciples, and TCO. According to our sources, the Icelandic pocket sits at the base of Kirkjufell mountain." She nodded to Jayne. "We don't have a good enough insight into the mountain's terrain, so we'll have to portal in at the base. We should still have the element of surprise. Augustin, you'll be in charge of the Disciples. I'll lead one flank of Adepts, and Tristan, you'll lead the other."

"Me?" Tristan raised an eyebrow and glanced at Ruger. Ruger looked impassive. He must have known this would come.

"You're a Master now, Tristan. We'll need your power, especially to protect our flank. Now, the Guardians have the best shot at containing and controlling the pocket, so the Disciples and the TCO need to clear the way for them. We're on Wraith duty: detain and destroy. The Disciples are well-versed in Wraith combat, so I have faith in you. While we begin the fight, the Guardians will hang back, providing protection spells along with our youngest Adepts."

Jayne felt Sofia sag with relief next to her. She squeezed her sister's hand.

"Sofia and Cillian: I want you up in the air, if possible, taking down Wraiths as they fly. Jayne and Vivienne, you too. The plan is to draw Odin out of his pocket by targeting his two favorite Wraiths, Huginn and Munnin."

"What do they look like?" Jayne asked.

Amanda smiled humorlessly. "Birds, if birds were designed by Salvador Dali and forged in Hell. They were the first Wraiths in Odin's thrall, and he prizes them above anything else. I think if we take one down, his rage will be too much and he won't be able to resist coming after us."

"That's a big gamble," Jayne said.

"If you have a better idea..." Amanda raised an eyebrow and pursed her lips. When Jayne was forced to shake her head, she breathed out through her nose and continued. "Keep a lookout for Huginn and Munnin. Until you see them, you focus on any

Wraith you can reach. Quimby says she's been developing something that we can use in aerial tactics. She sounded overwhelmingly excited. In fact..." Amanda checked her watch. "We're due at the Genius Lab in two minutes."

"And when do we move?" Tristan asked.

"Tomorrow afternoon," Amanda replied. "Midnight Icelandic time."

They filed out of her office together and headed for the Lab, stopping at the portals to pick up a cluster of Guardians. Danilo waited, ready in a camo suit that barely contained his large Māori frame. He spotted Ruger, and his face lit with a smile. "So this is the CIA, is it?" he said.

Jayne and Sofia hurried toward a small, proud brown woman with braids of pure white. "Xiomara!" Sofia hugged the woman hard. Xiomara hugged back until Sofia squeaked. The Guardian of the Patagonia pocket was unyielding and tough as nails and had gotten both Jayne and Sofia out of more scrapes than Jayne knew.

Xiomara pulled away. "What have you done to yourself?" she half scolded, tucking a strand of gray hair behind Sofia's ear. "It took me sixty years to look the way I do. And you're with child, too. Look at your glow. She will be very powerful."

"Back to the war now, troops, please," Amanda said, but her eyes held a deep warmth.

Zahra Hassan, the guardian of the Alexandria pocket, came forward. She looked Augustin up and down. "Did they need a gorilla to stamp and bellow the Wraiths into submission?" she asked archly.

"I suppose your plan is to bore them to death with one of those stupid books," Augustin replied in his rough voice.

Jayne's gasp was only half fake. "There, there," Tristan said drily and drew her away.

Augustin shook hands with Danilo, too, and bowed to Xiomara. It made sense, Jayne supposed, that the Disciples all knew the Guardians, but she was surprised somehow to see it. And pleased that they all seemed to get along. As more Disciples popped through the portals, the hall filled with chatter. It was almost like a meet and greet. *Should have catered canapés,* Jayne thought, and felt Hayden rumble in agreement.

The portals flashed once more, and more bodies stepped through. Heads turned to greet the newcomers. Then silence spread like ripples in a pond. No one seemed to move, but suddenly there was space around the portal, isolating the small group of men and women who stood at its mouth.

They looked ragged, as though they'd been traveling without much. Their modern clothes distinguished them from the Disciples immediately, but they were no Adepts that Jayne recognized.

She frowned. Or maybe she did...

The man at the head of the group raised his arms in surrender. Three long, angry welts stood out on his face. "Please," he said in French-tinged English. "We mean no harm."

Jayne felt a flash of recognition from her Rogue. Vivienne snarled. She dropped to all fours, assuming her tigress form. "Easy," Jayne murmured.

"I will not be easy. What is that *traitor* doing here?"

Tristan had gone still next to Jayne. His eyes were hard and unforgiving as a stormy sea. His muscles tensed. "Pierre." He drew the word out in a long growl. He moved, shouldering people out of the way. Vivienne stalked behind him.

"I knew you would be here," Pierre said, and now Jayne remembered. The last time she'd heard his voice, he'd been furious, arrogant, utterly devoted to La Liberté. So what was he doing here?

"Then why did you come?" Tristan asked softly. "I am a traitor, am I not? To my own blood, and to the cause?"

"I...we..." Pierre looked wretched. "She is insane," he whispered. "Your mother is sick. She wants to join with the Wraiths, she thinks she can liberate them...But I have looked into their eyes, and I know they have no minds of their own. They serve a terrible master, and I will not share their fate. *We* will not."

"And so you want forgiveness? As simple as that?" Tristan's mouth twisted.

Pierre looked at the ground. "No forgiveness is simple, brother. I only want to fight with you. I dedicated myself to dying for a cause long ago. But I want it to be the right one."

For a moment, the air between them was thick with all the things they'd said in anger and all the things they might have said after. No one spoke. Then Tristan took the first step. He grabbed Pierre by the shoulders and brought him into a hug.

Pierre straightened, shocked. Then his arms came around Tristan, too, and he squeezed back.

"We need all the help we can get. Welcome back to sanity, brother." Tristan smiled.

"This is not sanity." Vivienne was back in human form, still scowling. She flipped her hair behind her head. "And I do not welcome you."

"And *I* would very much like to talk to you," Amanda cut in. "All of our new...companions. The rest of you, I believe we're late for a demonstration."

She led Pierre and his comrades away, probably toward an interrogation room to stew. Everyone else funneled into the hall that led to the Genius Lab. Jayne let herself be buffeted along by the crowd and found herself next to Ruger and Danilo. "This is amazing," she said. "It might actually work."

"I'm glad you have faith. It being your idea and all," Ruger replied.

CHAPTER
THIRTY-SEVEN

"Oh-*kay*." Quimby rubbed her hands together. Next to her, Henry pushed his glasses up his nose. They kept slipping down.

Jayne leaned over to Sofia, who'd found them in the crowded lab. "Does he look sweaty to you?"

Sofia cocked her head. "You know, he does," she replied after a moment.

"Welcome, everyone. We're so excited to have you in our army, and we've prepared a few things to help us win the fight against Odin Allfather. First up, the world's greatest magical physicist will be presenting his concept for Wraith grounding. So without further ado: Henry Thorne!"

The applause was enthusiastic, but Henry didn't smile. He coughed, rubbed the back of his neck, and pushed his glasses up again. "Yes, um. Yes. Great to see you, everyone. Xiomara, you're looking well..."

"I'm not, and you know it," Xiomara called back. Laughter rippled around the room. "Get on with it, Thorne. I'm hungry."

"Right." He leaned over and checked his notes. "So Wraiths, uh, sense magic. That's how they can show up whenever Adepts or Disciples or Guardians are making a big use of their magic. Or, for example, when an Adept child first discovers their magical powers and begins to explore. So we've made a sort of magical stink bomb." He held up something that looked like a grenade. "And it, um. Stinks. Magically speaking." He blinked and looked out over the crowd. "Any questions? No? Over to you, Quimby."

"How does it work?" Jayne called when Henry, relieved, turned back toward his papers.

His throat bobbed. "Work?"

"Is it going to hurt us? Make it difficult to use our own magic?" asked Zahra.

"Ah…" He looked at Quimby, panicked.

Quimby stepped in for him. "It's in grenade form. You pull the pin and throw it, simple. It releases a gas that is completely harmless to humans and Rogues, though it does stink a little." She wrinkled her nose. "But it has some pure essence of the Torrent in it. This can actually do two things: it might give you a little boost of magic where you need it, but enough used in force will overwhelm the Wraith. Just like cinnamon or peppermint overwhelms a dog's nose, the sense that a Wraith uses to detect magic will be put on overdrive. The confusion should throw them off-kilter and, we hope, force them to land. Then you spell them with your enhanced magic, and the war is won!" She beamed around the room. "More questions?"

They moved on to the next tech, electrified bolas. These were for the Disciples, who had more practice fighting with physical weapons. "Throw it around the Wraith, activate by remote, and you get a charred monster," Quimby said cheerfully.

There were a few other things that quickly went around the room: booster vials for temporary magical assists, shock prods that had been adjusted to hold spells at the end, and a sticky spray that could blind a Wraith. "Just be careful with those,"

Quimby warned them. "They're permanent and will work on humans just as well."

She and Henry handed out bags according to teams—one bag for Ruger, another for him to pass along to Amanda, one for Tristan. One for Augustin, who studied the contents of his for a long time before stomping off as though they were wholly inadequate. One to Xiomara.

Jayne got a couple of boosters and a shock prod. "We're not sure if Hayden will be affected by the stink bombs," Quimby admitted.

"If he can't come loose, I'll just hop on Vivienne and we'll ride, like Sofia and Cillian," Jayne said.

"If you think I'm taking you on my back, you're sorely mistaken," Vivienne sniffed.

Sofia was eyeing Henry Thorne. "Pretty impressive, Dad. Was that what you've been working on all this time?"

"What?" Henry looked up guiltily from his computer.

"The gas?"

"Oh. Um, yes?" He scratched his neck. He didn't sound certain.

"It was his idea to modify my original plan for the boosters." Quimby sighed. "One day I'll be a genius like him."

"You already are," Jayne assured her. She was rewarded with a classic Quimby smile, but the other woman shook her head before moving on to answer a Guardian with a question.

Sofia tried to lean around the desk. "So what's on the computer?"

Henry shut the laptop with a snap. "Notes," he said. "Lots of numbers. Boring stuff, really. Anyway, I'd better go. Always need a good night's sleep before traveling."

"Traveling? Traveling where?" Jayne asked.

Henry looked truly baffled. "Iceland," he said. "Haven't you been listening, Jayne?"

Jayne and Sofia exchanged glances. "Dad, you're not coming with us, are you?" Sofia said.

"Of course I am." Henry shoved his laptop into a case, stuffing papers in after it. "Biggest fight of my life."

For a guy who doesn't fight at all, Jayne thought. Sofia was retying her ponytail, scowling.

Henry seemed to realize how fishy all this sounded. He clutched the laptop case to his chest and smiled tightly first at one daughter, then the other. He opened his mouth, but apparently couldn't find anything convincing to say, for he shut it again and scurried off, skirting the side of the room and disappearing through the door, dodging questions and congratulations along the way.

"What's wrong with him?" Jayne asked Quimby, but the other woman was busy explaining the shock prod to Augustin.

Sofia's brow was knitted. Jayne knew that look. "You can't mother your own father," she said, nudging Sofia with her hip.

"You know as well as I do that putting him in the field is a bad idea. He'd only be a liability, and he knows that. He's too distracted to be of any use. So what's his real aim?"

Jayne didn't know. And the more she thought about it, the less she liked it.

CHAPTER
THIRTY-EIGHT

Everyone piled into the canteen for dinner. The atmosphere was cheerful and the food was excellent. Amanda must have warned the chefs—and maybe even gotten them a time-stop kitchen—for the tables were piled high with chicken and rice in a spicy tomato sauce, salads and veggies of every shape and size, mashed sweet potatoes, potatoes gratin, and a whole table of desserts. Jayne felt a certain satisfaction in the size of the crowd. *We did this,* she thought. They'd brought the leaders of the magical world together. Maybe, after the fighting was done, they would have a true coalition of good guys.

Dinner wasn't quite as relaxing as she'd hoped; she sat with Sofia and Cillian and Tristan and Vivienne, hoping to talk all things baby and wedding, but Disciples kept coming up to her to ask about Hayden. Some were shy, others in awe, and Jayne quickly grew weary of having to explain it around bites of rice and sips of floral jasmine tea. When she was finished with dinner, she grabbed Sofia's arm. "Dessert in Nashville?" she muttered.

"You're on." They collected a plate full of cake, cookies, fruit and cheese and snuck out of the canteen together.

"I think we've actually got a shot," Jayne said as they entered her apartment. She kicked off her shoes, sighing happily at the familiar place. *Home.* She put her plate on the coffee table and went into the kitchen to make a nice lapsang souchong.

"When you get everyone together, we're more than I expected, too. I didn't realize there were so many Disciples," Sofia admitted. "But I was watching Amanda at dinner. She didn't exactly look confident, you know?"

Jayne hadn't noticed. She'd been too busy with her Disciple fan club.

"Amanda is a realist," Tristan said. "She is worried because in this war, she will lose a lot of people. The Allfather is more powerful than any of his Wraiths, and no one has tried to go up against him yet. He is an unknown quantity."

"And what happens after?" Cillian added.

Tristan nodded. "Indeed. If my mother has truly been warped, as Pierre says, perhaps she is simply waiting for us to fall in this war so that she can take power. It is not just a question of being ready for battle tomorrow. It's a question of surviving long enough to retain control the day after."

"You are all very gloomy," Vivienne said. She took a bite of chocolate cake and sighed.

Sofia came into the kitchen and started putting mugs on a tray. "Well, at least we have one last night to be sisters," Jayne said.

She'd meant it as a joke, but it came out soft and serious. Sofia stopped, closed her eyes. Tension simmered in her. Then she swallowed and looked over her shoulder toward the living room and Cillian. "Yes," she replied. "No matter what tomorrow brings."

"At least your charges will be in the back, right?"

"Most of them." Sofia looked Jayne up and down, and one half of her mouth came up in a smile. "You'd have to be crazy to think I'm not still trying to take care of you, sis."

"Right." Jayne watched her take the cups into the living room. She seemed so...melancholy. *And why shouldn't she be?* The danger they'd faced before was nothing like what lay ahead. And no one knew what the day after tomorrow held for them.

The cake was gone criminally soon; it was delicious, but Jayne couldn't face going back for more. Sofia and Cillian inched closer and closer on the couch, and Jayne felt her own restless energy begging to be channeled. She could always train more...but she knew what she'd rather be doing.

Vivienne rolled her eyes and hopped off the pillow she'd put on the ground. "People in love make me sick," she declared. "I'm going to sleep. Put up your mental barrier." She pointed at Jayne.

"We'd better go, too," Sofia said, standing. Her fingers were tightly twined in Cillian's, her knuckles white. "Thanks for the tea, sis."

Jayne hugged her, breathing in her scent, as though she could memorize it. The glint of the diamond on her finger, the liminal glow of her body, was enough to center Jayne for the upcoming fight. She had to protect her niece, too. Assuming Xiomara was right. Which she probably was.

"I'll see you tomorrow for the saving of the world."

The door clicked shut behind them, and then the apartment was quiet.

Tristan's arms wrapped around her from behind. "Saving the world," he echoed. "What a life we lead."

Jayne leaned into him. The faint vanilla-and-soap scent of his magic was strong, overlaid with woodsmoke. She wished she had a Time Catch. They could slip into it and take their time, memorize each other. Not for the first time, she felt a little envious of Sofia and Cillian. They'd been given years together at the school. What might Jayne and Tristan have done with all that time? Had a child, traveled the world? Maybe Jayne would learn some of the lore Tristan always seemed to know. Maybe he would read more of her favorite books.

His hand slipped under her shirt and caressed her belly. "What would you do with your last night on Earth?" he whispered in her ear.

Jayne turned in his embrace and pressed herself against him. He picked her up, and she wrapped her legs around his waist and let him carry her into the bedroom.

Their lovemaking was sweet and slow. Jayne tried to focus on every sensation, the way his skin brushed hers, the shivers that ran down her entire body when he kissed her neck. It felt as though he knew this would be the last time, for he rushed nothing. Her pleasure mounted, and she begged him. He just grinned wickedly and stroked her cheek.

They climaxed together, then lay pressed together in a tangle of sheets, quiet. Jayne could almost convince herself that Tristan was sleeping, except that his breathing was too even. One finger tapped pensively on her shoulder. "What's on your mind?"

The finger stopped. Then Tristan propped himself up on his elbow. His eyes were serious, his lush mouth red from kissing. "Jayne, if I die tomorrow, will you let me?"

Ice struck her heart and flowed outward with her blood. "No," she said. "I won't allow it. It should be me."

"We need *you*, Jayne," he said, quietly, calmly, insistently. "The whole world needs you."

"Well, I need *you*," she replied before she could think better of it.

Tristan raised a skeptical eyebrow. "Jayne Thorne, you do not need any man."

Jayne put a hand on his heart. She didn't want to fight, but why was Tristan being so hard-headed? "Nothing bad happens to me when I heal people. It's all right, Tristan. I can keep you safe."

"You use up your magic and exhaust yourself," Tristan said. "You need to save that magic for other things. If you die, or hurt yourself healing, your dragon, your magic, your totems—they're all gone. We're counting on you to use all your power to defeat the Allfather. Not to protect me."

"What if I can do both?"

Tristan ran a finger down the line of her jaw. "In war, we must make sacrifices. I'm ready to sacrifice my life for yours. For our cause. For all we've built." Jayne shook her head. He put a finger to her lips. *"Mon amour,"* he warned when she snapped at it. "I have always known that I might be asked to give up my life for the cause. I am ready. You must let me make my own decisions, Jayne. And I would rather die saving you or Vivienne than for any other reason."

"You won't die," she promised him and pulled him down for another kiss, just to shut him up.

CHAPTER
THIRTY-NINE

Amanda stood at the mouth of the portal. She'd swapped her suit for tactical gear, complete with Kevlar vest and body armor. An arsenal of Quimby's magical tech was hooked to a belt around her waist, and she carried two weapons for the Wraiths: one sword, double-edged and long as her arm, and a short crossbow that could tuck into a holster on her thigh. As the TCO's best markswoman, she was confident in her ability to bring down a Wraith from the sky.

Their army had been assembling all day, wearing their own battle regalia and bearing their own weapons. Amanda had decided that the La Liberté defections were genuine. Pierre and a few others had agreed to join the battle itself, while others had preferred the TCO's holding cells to a muddy Icelandic field. And they needed all the help they could get, so she'd divided his forces between flanks. Tristan would keep an eye on his old friend.

Augustin was on the phone, coordinating with Disciples of Gaia who would portal directly to Iceland from wherever they were. Xiomara paced, tight-lipped. The Aegis students, or super-Adepts, as Amanda had taken to calling them, huddled in a corner. They were already one down; Zia was still under observation and would sit out the fight. They didn't need Aaró popping up in the midst of battle and wreaking havoc.

Amanda saw them glance her way every so often but spared them no more than a professional nod. They were TCO officers now. There was no use coddling them. She couldn't help but smile in pride at Rebecca. The girl was fierce, and a credit to her father's memory.

"Fifteen minutes," Ruger said. "No eyes on the Thornes."

"I'm here," said a breathless voice from behind him. Henry Thorne peered around Ruger's bulky frame.

"Doctor Thorne, I'm still not convinced that your presence is necessary," Amanda said.

"Oh, it's vital." His eyes darted back and forth. "I'll be working with the medics in the back. I won't be in the way. New ideas for healing and so on."

He smiled tightly at her. *That man is hiding something,* Amanda thought. If he jeopardized this fight...

She didn't have time to confront him. Jayne and Sofia Thorne were here, at last, dressed in combat boots and camouflage. Sofia kept tugging at her shirt. "Looking good, sis!" Matthew called, and she gave him a disapproving glare.

"Lock and load, everyone," Amanda shouted.

THE NOISE of the room subsided. Serious, pale, sweaty faces turned toward Amanda.

Jayne couldn't help herself; she took Sofia's hand and squeezed on one side; Tristan's hand on the other. Both squeezed back.

"I don't have to tell you how important this mission is," Amanda said quietly. "We've all been on the defensive since Odin initiated his takeover. Many of us have lost people we care about to Wraiths. But today, we're going to turn the tables. We have the element of surprise, and we've been learning Wraith technique and style. We've put aside our differences and started on a path of reconciliation. I would dearly love to find out where that path will take us. But that means surviving today."

That got a few grim chuckles, at least. "We have to move fast," Amanda continued. "We go through the portal in teams of five. Advance scouts say that when the Iceland pocket is closed, there are only ever a few Wraiths flitting around it. We need the pocket to open if we're going to get to Odin and draw him out. We need to make him desperate. We need to make him think that he *has* to open the portal."

She looked around the room. "Five at a time," she repeated. "We'll begin with the aerial team, but try for stealth, you four. Fly high and fly fast." She fixed Jayne with such a stern stare that it brought out another laugh around the room. Jayne smiled grudgingly, trying to ignore the way her stomach had started to flop. *You've been in lots of battles,* she told it. *Calm down.* But none of the battles had ever been like this. The earlier ones had been reactive. They were going on the offense now. Shock and awe, that was the only way they were going to win.

Amanda finished briefing the order of attack, and they broke. People started finding teammates, shaking hands. A lot of whispered wishes for good luck, and a lot of melancholic smiles. Jayne tried to look everyone she passed in the eye. It might be the last time she ever saw them.

Her feet brought her back to Tristan, who was checking his equipment. He looked up, and their eyes met. It wasn't the place to throw her arms around him, so she settled for a single finger on the back of his hand, stroking from his wrist to his knuckles. "I wish we were going through together," she said.

He hesitated. She knew what he wanted to say, because she wanted so badly for him to say it. *We will see each other again,* or *I will be with you.* Or reassurances that they would do this, that they would win the day. But after last night's conversation, the whole idea felt hollow. They both knew the risk they faced.

Vivienne appeared at Jayne's elbow. She had no compunctions about throwing her arms around Tristan, and he wrapped her up and squeezed her tight.

"Be fierce, *mon soeur*."

She released him, and he looked between her and Jayne. His eyes shone suspiciously bright. "My warrior women." His smile was as sure as ever. "I will do anything to protect you."

Jayne leaned in and gave him a searing kiss. To hell with propriety, she was on the edge of death today and she deserved a break. She broke away with the feeling of him still on her lips. Then she squeezed his hand one last time and turned to rejoin Sofia and Cillian.

"We are going to have to keep him from doing something stupid, aren't we?" Vivienne said.

"I'm afraid so." Jayne held up her pinky. "Protect Tristan Labelle?"

Vivienne hooked her pinky around Jayne's and shook. "Protect family," she said. They smiled at each other.

Sofia and Cillian were pale, but Sofia looked determined. "Cillian will transform as soon as we're through the portal. We were thinking griffin. How about you?"

Jayne nodded to Vivienne, giving her the ropes. "A hawk, to start," Vivienne replied. "Since Jayne has her own ride. I can fly above the battlefield and provide you with intelligence."

"Good plan." Jayne hugged Sofia. "We're good?" she murmured in her sister's ear.

Sofia squeezed her back. "We're good." Jayne felt a weight lift from her heart, leaving her so much lighter she had to fight the urge to cry.

Jayne hesitated, then hugged Cillian as well. She hadn't done much touching of the big man since their breakup; it had all seemed too weird. But she'd forgotten, too, that for him it had been many years since they were together, and there was no hesitation when he hugged her back. "Good luck out there," he rumbled.

"Luck of the Irish?" she suggested.

Cillian laughed. "Not sure I'd like the luck of the Irish in battle. But let's ask for the luck of the Rogue." He winked.

Jayne took a breath. She grabbed Sofia's hand, then Vivienne's. Sofia took hold of Cillian. "Ready?" Jayne said.

"Ready," Vivienne replied.

"Ready." Sofia nodded.

"Ready," Cillian said.

"Ready," said Henry Thorne.

Jayne's head whipped around. *"Dad,"* Sofia groaned from her other side. Henry had resolutely taken Vivienne's hand. The girl looked as though she didn't know whether to shake him off or endure it.

"I said I was going with you." Henry pushed his glasses up his nose with his free hand. He was dressed in camo gear that was at least a size too broad for him, skinny in his combat trousers and steel-toed boots. He looked like a boy playing dress-up in his father's uniform. Only he was Jayne's father, and that made the whole thing a lot less funny.

"Dad, it's combat. You promised to be in the back. You need to steer clear."

"Agnes Jayne Thorne, I know what I'm doing," Henry said, in a voice so stern it made her shrink back from habit. "And as the father in this situation, I'll thank you to let me do it."

"And what are you doing, Dad?" Sofia cut in. She fixed him with a blue-eyed stare that made Jayne shiver. It was a little too much like Ruth. "Do you have the same goal as the rest of us?"

Henry tilted his chin, but his eyes slid guiltily to the side. "I'm dedicated to winning the fight against Odin. And you won't convince me to stay out of it. And now we're holding up the line, so we'd better go."

"Thornes!" barked Amanda, as if on cue. "I told you not to be a problem for me today."

Jayne took a deep breath. Henry started moving toward the portal first, pulling the rest of them along. What was he hiding? What was he plotting in that oversized brain?

He's an adult, and he can make his own choices. And at least he's on our side, she thought. But she couldn't shake the feeling that Henry Thorne wasn't telling her his plans because he knew she'd try to stop him.

She took a deep breath, and they stepped as one through the portal.

For a moment Jayne was enveloped by magic, then the whole world turned dark. The air was fresh and smelled of sea and sulfur. The ground beneath her feet was spongy and soft, and close by she could hear the trickle of water over stones. In the distance, the crash of waves signaled the ocean. The sky above them was cloudless and dotted with stars. It would almost seem peaceful.

Except for the long slash of light like a crack in reality at the base of Kirkjufell mountain.

"This is some real 'Bad Wolf' stuff," she muttered. She glanced at Sofia, who was outlined in gold. "Shoot, sis, you're like a freaking flashlight. Can you dampen the Guardian mama stuff? You're like a beacon."

Sofia concentrated, then twisted her fingers over her head. The glow disappeared.

"Nice one. Okay. Let's do this. And team? Be careful."

"Now, Cillian," Sofia said softly. There was a rustle, then a thump, and Cillian took on his griffin form. Sofia slung a leg over his back and looked down at Jayne. "I'll do a patrol of the mountain, let you know if I see anything weird."

Jayne nodded. "Viv, do your thing."

Vivienne leapt into the air, transforming into her gray and

black harpy eagle, and shot toward the sky. She disappeared into the clouds. *Your turn now, mighty Jayne Thorne.*

Jayne had to do one thing first. "Dad, please."

Henry held up a hand. "You won't change my mind." His eyes glinted with a familiar steel, the same steel Jayne and Sofia had in spades when they chose to bring it out.

Jayne swallowed all the things she wanted to say, and said, "Be safe," instead.

Henry nodded. "I will."

The ground flashed green as the portal opened behind her again. It was time. Jayne rubbed at the scaly patch of skin on her arm. "Let's do this."

Hayden solidified like smoke in the air. It *was* getting less painful to bring him forth, Jayne decided, though she still welcomed the cool air on her arm. He tipped a foreleg, and she scrambled up onto his back. *How many Wraiths so far?* he asked.

Let's go find out.

They lifted from the ground. The world beneath them became a tapestry of dark greens and browns. Silver glistened on the water, and moonlight shone over the rocks. A chilly breeze tousled Jayne's hair and made her eyes water.

She focused on the pocket at the base of the mountain, looking for the telltale signs of Wraiths. At first she couldn't see much; the pocket was bright against the black mountain, and it was hard to look at. But gradually she began to make out dark shapes slipping through the air above the pocket. *What do you see?* she asked Vivienne.

A dozen Wraiths, maybe. Nothing to worry about, Vivienne said. *No traps.*

So Odin hadn't known they were coming. It was nice that the evening was starting out their way, at least.

The ground around Kirkjufell lit up like fireworks as the TCO forces portaled on site, five at a time. From above Jayne saw the Disciples of Gaia coalesce, felt a ripple of magic as they all reached into the Torrent at once for their weapons. Moonlight gleamed off the blades of swords and axes and knives. Jayne wished, for a moment, for the solidity of her staff. But she had Hayden's teeth and claws and tail to contend with, and a staff wasn't exactly a dragon-friendly implement.

She scanned the right flank as it joined up with the Disciples. *Viv? Any sign of Tristan?*

I will locate him, Vivienne said, and a moment later a sleek body streaked past her, headed for the ground.

A crack rang out over the plain like a thunderclap. Everyone stopped in their tracks. The wild slash in reality that led to the entrance of the pocket was bigger now, with tattered edges like pieces of ripped cloth.

Was it already working? Were they going to lure Odin out just like this?

With another almighty crack, the gap widened again. An enormous Wraith thrust his head through the gap, growling.

The rest of his body soon followed. He tumbled to the ground but landed feet first. Then he straightened. He was nearly twelve feet tall.

Jayne's hands tightened around Hayden's spikes. The dragon had balked at the sight of the Wraith and now undulated his wings in the air, keeping them in place. "Piece of cake, huh?" she murmured.

Another Wraith followed, one with the head of a bear and the body of a spider. Then another Wraith, and another. Soon dozens were pouring through the portal. It was time for action.

Jayne remembered what Amanda had said about Huginn and Munnin. They were more like birds than the other Wraiths, and larger—a thought that made her gulp when she looked at the twelve-foot monstrosity that stomped over the plain toward the Disciples now.

Would Odin send them out as advance troops, to direct the battle against the TCO? Or would he hold them back as protectors, using them only as a last resort if the battle didn't go his way? Jayne squinted at the pocket and scanned for her quarry. Below her, the first sounds of battle began: the clash of steel and wood against scale and leathery bone. A dizzying array of scents wafted in the air as everyone's personal magical signatures mixed together.

A hand she recognized came over the pocket's side.

It was as gray and scaly as the other Wraiths', but the fingers had a length and elegance that matched Jayne's own. The horned head shook back and forth as the Wraith landed on the ground, and her eyes flickered between stormy gray and black. As did the Water totem on her forehead. Jayne's totems flared in response.

Ruth Thorne looked up. Her eyes locked with Jayne's.

I've found him, Vivienne reported.

Great, Jayne said and leaned forward. *Keep an eye on him. I've got a little business to attend to.*

CHAPTER
FORTY

Jayne leaned flat against Hayden's neck. *Let's finish this,* she said. The fear that had flipped her stomach over and over had been replaced by a singular fury. The last time she'd seen Ruth Thorne, the monster had been pulling her claws from the chest of Jayne's love. Maybe Ruth should see how it felt to get *her* heart ripped out, for a change.

The Wraith formerly known as Ruth launched into the air. With three great beats of its wings, it rose to meet them. One claw wrapped around Hayden's before he lashed out to strike, and his roar became a hiss of pain as Ruth squeezed.

Jayne pushed a Release spell at her mother, and the claw let go. Hayden gained some altitude, and Ruth followed. Jayne pulled out the shock prod. Not enough range. She cursed and threw a hasty Block spell that knocked the Wraith end over end through the air. For a moment, it looked as though Ruth might keep falling, but she righted herself with a flip of her wings. Then she rushed back in.

Hayden and Ruth met in a clash that nearly knocked Jayne off her seat. The thud of Ruth's head into Hayden's chest sent a reverberation all the way down his skeleton. Jayne gritted her teeth and tried to swing around to get a clear shot. But Hayden and Ruth grappled fiercely. Her claws dug into his neck, eliciting phantom stings in Jayne's own, working between the scales. His claws pierced her shoulders. He bit down on one arm and worried at her like a dog. She howled in pain. But she wouldn't let go.

Viv? A little help? Jayne called.

No sooner did the words leave her lips than another Wraith rammed into Hayden's rib cage, and she went flying off his back. The sky above her was a tapestry of stars, and below her, the earth was a swirl of mountains and rivers and a wave of people—her people. *I suppose there are worse things to see while I die,* she thought.

She hit something, hard, and the breath was driven out of her. But not the life.

She realized she was lying on her back, and the stars above her still twinkled, oblivious to the turmoil here on Earth. A shadow she would recognize in her sleep bent over her. "Agnes Jayne Thorne, you will *not* do that," Sofia snapped.

Cillian growled in response, hovering over her in the sky, his wings flapping gently.

"What happened?"

"Cillian caught you in midair and dropped you onto a granite shelf on the side of the mountain."

Jayne grabbed her sister's shoulder and pulled herself up. She shot Cillian a smile. "Thanks for the ride. Mine has a couple of mommy issues." She sent a thought out to Hayden. *Bring her down to the ground. We'll finish her there.* "Drop me off and I'll catch my ride again."

"Any sign of the big ones?" Sofia asked as Cillian swooped toward the ground.

"Not so far." Amanda would tell her to remember what was important, to ignore Ruth Thorne and focus on taking out

Huginn and Muninn. And Jayne would—she just knew what she had to do first.

She had to free her family from the shadow of Ruth Thorne. And she needed that Water totem.

A Wraith rammed its hand into Hayden's chest, piercing the skin. He shrieked and disappeared in a dazzle of green light. *Jayne*, he gasped, voice fading.

The Wraiths he'd been fighting screamed in frustration at the disappearance of their prey. Ruth cast about, claws out, teeth bared. The water totem on her forehead blazed.

Jayne called her rune staff to her and ran her fingers down its length, bringing the spells carved into it shimmering to life. Ruth's eyes locked on the staff, and Jayne grinned. "Come and get it," she said. Riding Hayden was exhilarating, but this was the sort of fighting she was trained to do.

The Wraith barreled toward her. She brought up her staff and flicked a Shield spell around her, backing up. At the last moment, Ruth seemed to trip midair, stopping her powerful descent and plowing into the earth right in front of her.

Jayne didn't stop to wonder. She moved in and jabbed, hitting her mother hard on the shoulder. Ruth shuddered. Jayne followed up with a swift blow to the head that made her grunt. The third blow should have landed true, but the Wraith turned her head at the last moment, catching the staff on the side of her horns. She lashed out, grabbing the staff. Jayne sent a Heat spell down the staff. Ruth howled but held on. She jerked on the weapon, and Jayne jerked with it.

Ruth Thorne lifted her head. She blinked, and for a moment the black cleared away, leaving Jayne a clear view of those cold gray eyes. "Jayne," she rasped. Her voice was ragged and deep, like two stones sliding against each other, and her mouth was a broken ruin of jagged teeth. "Jayne, please."

Another wave of anger rolled from her heart out to the rest of her body. She arced her hand in a slashing Cut spell, and a shadowy line of blood appeared across Ruth's chest. "You can take your *please* and shove it up your—" She grunted as the Wraith shoved the staff back into her solar plexus. She hit the ground hard, and the Wraith threw her staff to the side. Its eyes were black upon black again. It lifted one foot, and Jayne rolled to the side, scrabbling at her belt. When the Wraith lifted her foot again, Jayne leaned up and jammed the shock prod against her arch.

White flashed over Ruth's skin as an Immobility spell spread over her body with the electric shock. She fell heavily to the ground.

Jayne scrambled up. Her mother—what was left of her mother—lay sprawled, wings extended, chest moving erratically. Her skin steamed. Now was the moment. "You tried to take everything from me," Jayne whispered and reached into the Torrent for a new weapon. Ruth Thorne was responsible for the shamble her life had been for so long: moving from place to place with Sofia, missing her parents, wondering what life might have been like as an ordinary girl. And then, when she'd found a purpose and a duty and even a love...Ruth had tried to take it all away again.

Jayne found the shape of a wickedly sharp dagger and pulled it from the Torrent. It was all so clear cut. The Wraiths were their enemies, and Ruth might just be Jayne's biggest enemy of all.

So why couldn't Jayne kill her?

Ruth's eyelids fluttered, and the ice gray was back. "Jayne," she murmured.

"Don't," Jayne growled. A tear slid from her eye and trailed down her cheek. The dagger trembled in her hand.

"You have to do it, Jayne," Ruth breathed.

Jayne blinked. "What?"

The Wraith head lolled from one side to the other. "You have to kill me," her mother said.

The words were like a shock prod to the heart. "I..."

I do have to kill her, Jayne told herself. It was her duty. Ruth Thorne had chosen the evil side of this war, time and time again. Yet Jayne had never killed someone as they lay prone on the ground. She'd never killed for fun, or even on purpose. And she'd never killed someone who'd asked her to, and somehow that made it all worse.

Jayne's voice shook. "If you come quietly as a prisoner of war, I'll spare you." She half hated herself for even suggesting it.

Ruth shook her head weakly. The laugh she made grated against Jayne's soul like nails on a blackboard. "There will be no prisoners," she said. "Now, while I am weak...do it. Take the totem. If Odin takes it in your stead, his power...there will be no stopping him."

Jayne knelt. Maybe she was looking for some trace of her mother in the Wraith's features. Maybe she was just looking for some trace of humanity. "If you don't want to serve Odin, then don't serve him. Join us instead."

"I...can't." Ruth began to blink rapidly. Her claws spasmed. The Wraith in her was taking over again. "He controls...everything. Can't...keep him out long. Jayne..." One claw worked its way toward her and gently squeezed her hand. "What do I have to live for, anyway?"

A mercy killing. A sacrifice from both of them, to save the world. Jayne could do that, surely. "Mom," she whispered, and sudden sorrow choked her voice. She hadn't used that word in such a long time.

Nearby a Disciple screamed as a Wraith impaled him on a long claw. The smell of his magic, fur and wood herbs, turned sour as life fled his body. Jayne looked over, hands itching with the sudden need to heal. And in the distraction, Ruth's Wraith took over again.

In a moment Jayne was flat on her back, pinned by one massive Wraith hand on her chest. The Wraith's head bent close and a lizard-like tongue flicked out, running over her forehead where the totems were hidden. She squirmed. "Mom," she begged. But her mother wasn't in there anymore.

The Wraith leaned back and brought its claws up. *It's going to rip my head off*, she thought dizzily. Rip her head off and present it to Odin.

Who would then control all the totems.

What have you done, Jayne Thorne? she thought. As final words went, it wasn't exactly what she'd hoped.

The Wraith stopped.

Its face contorted. Its head flopped and it brought a trembling hand up to its chest. It looked as though a piece of moonlight emerged from its heart. Black blood spilled from around it, spattering over Jayne, stinging where it made contact with her skin.

The moonlight pulled free, and the Wraith fell forward, pinning Jayne beneath it. From behind the Wraith's shoulder, Jayne saw Sofia, pale hair fluttering in the wind. She held a broadsword easily. And though she was dressed in modern-day camo, to Jayne she was every warrior heroine of every fantasy book young Jayne had ever read.

Ruth's eyes flickered one last time. "The totem," she whispered. She sounded relieved.

Jayne pressed her palm to Ruth's forehead. *I'm sorry*, she told her mother silently.

Sofia sheathed the sword and knelt. She grabbed the Wraith by the shoulder and rolled it off her sister. Jayne reached for her. "Sofia—"

"The totem, Jayne." Sofia's voice was flat, strangely calm. "That's the most important thing now."

Jayne brushed her fingers over Ruth's rapidly cooling forehead again. "Let's do this, Master of Shadows," she said. *Before I have to think about what we've done.*

She wasn't sure what she was supposed to do. Ask nicely?

Find the grimoire? She closed her eyes. Maybe she only had to search for the truth...

Pale light like sunrise illuminated Ruth's face, and even the twisted Wraith visage seemed more peaceful in death. Jayne focused on the Water totem and felt it reaching for her. For anyone, perhaps, but her fingers danced over it, and she invited it in.

Power swelled in her like the sea. The skies rumbled and a sound like a thunderclap echoed over the plains again. Around her, the sounds of fighting diminished as Wraith and human alike paused to look around. A cool sensation broke over her skin, like summer rain.

Jayne blinked. She could feel the groundwater in the field, the humidity in the air. And she could feel Sofia's hand in hers, still trembling.

"How many times have you lost her?" Jayne asked softly.

"Too many to count." Sofia's voice was small, childlike. She was remembering, perhaps, the first time, the time Jayne couldn't remember, a time when Ruth was there in body but not in spirit. "At least there's some closure in knowing this is the last time," she said.

Jayne looked down. She couldn't help wondering how life might have been different. If Ruth Thorne had chosen family over power. If she'd taken just one different step, somewhere along the line.

Their father would be devastated. He'd only just acknowledged that Ruth couldn't be rehabilitated, and Jayne suspected he'd always held out some hope for a change of heart. Some things just weren't meant to be.

Vivienne landed, waves of sorrow pouring off her body. *Jayne, are you okay?*

Am I?

Something flashed at the base of Kirkjufell. Jayne and Sofia looked up. *Odin,* Jayne thought, but no new Wraiths were emerging from the pocket at all, much less one like Odin. Their original quarries, Huginn and Muninn, were also still absent.

"Vivienne?" Jayne said. "What was that?"

There was a pause as Vivienne took off toward the sky. *Jayne,* she said softly after a moment.

Vivienne never took a soft tone with her. *What?* Jayne said, feeling the pit in her stomach grow.

I'm sorry, Jayne. It's...it's your father.

No. Jayne stumbled to her feet. "Jayne?" Sofia called, but she couldn't answer. She had to spare all her breath for running. She sprinted across the field, ducking the swiping tail of a Wraith, searching within for her dragon. Hayden was silent in her mind; he was wounded, might be out for the rest of the battle. Soon enough she heard her sister following her, still shouting.

The closer they got to the pocket, the more intense the fighting. The Disciples had tried to push their attack inward, to force the Wraiths on the defensive before they were even entirely through. The front of the pocket was a writhing mess of bodies as Wraiths thrashed and bit and tore their way to freedom. Henry had somehow gotten around that mess and hiked halfway up the mountain. Now Jayne could see a smaller slash of light, neatly made, as if a scientist had taken his scalpel and cut.

Which, she realized, was exactly what Henry Thorne had done.

He'd found the back door to the Torrent, and he'd opened it.

Henry stood before it, frowning as though he were back in the Genius Lab and stuck on a difficult theoretical problem. He held a box in his hand that looked like some kind of transmitter.

"Dad!" she screamed. She was still too far away. She darted around a Disciple with an ax and slid in the mud, landing painfully on her backside. Sofia hauled her to her feet and they took off again. This time they screamed it together: *"Dad!"*

Henry looked up at last. "Ah," he said with a small, sad smile.

Jayne started clambering up the rocks. "Come down, Dad."

He shook his head. "I'm going in," he said. "Your grandmother is waiting for me."

"You can't," Sofia cried. Tears shone on her cheeks.

"There's nothing you can do. I can hear her calling." He tilted his head, as though he really could hear her. "I have to go to her."

"*No,*" Jayne shouted. She'd lost one parent already today. She wasn't going to lose them both. She heard a roaring, twinned with a voice that sounded far away. She was so close she could almost touch Henry, and if she touched him she could pull him back.

Henry looked up, then back at his girls. "Trust me," he mouthed, and dove sideways, into the pocket. *No,* Jayne thought again, agony splitting her heart. For a moment she felt unmoored and ungrounded by the sudden loss of her father, floating in the air. Then she smashed into Sofia and hit the side of the mountain and she realized she *had* been ungrounded.

She rolled over, clutching her ribs. Above them Cillian whirled in griffin form, beak clacking. His eyes blazed with fury, and one talon was raised and dripping with black blood. A Wraith beat its wings lopsidedly in front of them. It had a shred of Jayne's shirt in one talon.

It was the Wraith's roar she'd heard. Cillian had impaled it just before it had picked her up. The Wraith lunged for Cillian and he reared up, beating his wings to keep balance. The Wraith stiffened and gasped, then went down in a buzz of electricity. Tristan stood behind it, shock prod at the ready. Vivienne shifted into her tigress form and pounced, bringing her teeth to the Wraith's throat.

It is disgusting, what I do for you. She came up with glistening black jowls. *They taste terrible.*

Tristan pulled Jayne to her feet. "Are you all right?" His eyes were frantic. He ran his hands along her arms, legs and chest.

"No," Jayne said, numb. She couldn't stop looking at the side of the mountain. Yet the neat slash that had opened the Torrent to the world had disappeared again, sewn together so that no one could follow Henry.

Her father was gone.

CHAPTER
FORTY-ONE

Tristan held Jayne tight, and she sagged against him. In body, at least, she seemed healthy enough, though she clung to him as though he were the last thing she had left.

"We need eyes on the battle from above," he said. "Sofia?"

Sofia nodded, palming at her cheeks. She was strong, that sister, though one day she would break from being strong for everyone else. Tristan could only pray that that day was not today. He watched her mount Cillian, and they took to the skies.

"Your dragon?" he said. When she didn't respond he shook her lightly. "Jayne?"

"He took a hit." Her voice seemed far away.

"I think we need to get her back to the TCO," he said to Vivienne.

"No." Jayne took a deep breath, and Vivienne let out a mournful cry. "We have to finish this. It can't all be for nothing. Odin?"

"No sign yet." But it shouldn't be long. The battlefield was looking...good. Wraiths were hard to kill, but the TCO-Disciple-Guardian alliance was strong and had better numbers. Five Adepts could take down one Wraith if they were creative about their combat. And their training was showing. Sofia's Adepts were blocking most attacks from the sky, so Wraiths had to land if they wanted to engage. They'd expected to see Huginn and Muninn by now, but he supposed it was possible that Odin had sent them out on an errand and they'd been unable to return.

He couldn't see *any* Wraith leaders, actually. Perhaps the Wraiths weren't suited to being directed like an army and Odin couldn't appoint commanders the way Amanda had. But if Odin was commanding the Wraiths himself, he was being sloppy about it. Tristan's flank had been nearly untouched for most of the battle, while Wraiths seemed to go for individual opponents instead of seeing the army as a whole. Their magical scent bombs had worked wonders as well, driving Wraiths to distraction and making it easier to bring them down. And not once had Odin tried to attack the young Adepts whose shield so severely impaired the Wraiths and their ability to fight.

Vivienne soared up to Sofia as a peregrine falcon. "She says the Wraiths are starting to disband," Jayne said. She straightened, and Tristan felt suddenly cold when she left his side. "They're becoming...aimless? It's like they don't want to fight."

"A retreat." Tristan felt a fizz of frustration. That wasn't how this was supposed to go. Odin himself was supposed to make a stand. Did he think to bide his time in the hopes that they'd weaken, that their alliances would fall apart?"

"But they're not trying to pull back, either." Jayne looked toward the pocket. "It's more like they're abandoning it."

"Do you think it has to do with your father?" Tristan asked.

Jayne's mouth tightened. "I don't know. He told us to trust him. Maybe?"

The soldiers on the field were looking around now, gradually lowering their weapons. One by one, the Wraiths took to the sky. Cheers went up around the field, and warriors hefted their blades in triumph.

One notable wasn't celebrating. Amanda looked around the

field, her crossbow and her sword held ready. She was frowning. She thought something was wrong, too. They knew Odin had more power, so why wasn't he using it?

Something slammed against Tristan's mind, so hard it wiped out any other thought. It was a word, a command, a single wish:

Come.

The pocket blazed, drawing his focus. He turned toward it. Something was in there, and he had to find it. Nothing else mattered. The sounds of the world grew distant in his ears. A query. A name that he almost remembered as *his* name. A quick scream. What had he even been doing?

Something hard fell against him. He caught it—her—without a second thought, and the world slammed back into focus. Screams rose from the field in panic. His Jayne, his warrior, leaned against him. She cried out. "Viv!"

Jayne. Tristan focused on her, fighting to scrub the curious blankness from his mind. It felt like someone was trying to wallpaper over his mind, erase his life. "Jayne?" he mumbled. She'd been panicked. She'd called out a name.

His sister's name. Jayne pulled away from him to stumble down the mountain, staring up at the sky. Tristan began to follow.

The voice stopped him in his tracks. *COME,* said the voice. It filled every pore, made every bone in his body vibrate. Tristan's mind bent toward the pocket. Everything that was everything sat inside it.

No. He wrenched at his mind. He had a full life out here, and he would not forget it. Everyone he cared about was here. Jayne, Vivienne, the people worth protecting. And he was trying to protect them from the pocket itself. Fear took the place of the strange, deep voice. He held on to that emotion, sharpened it to a needle point. He knew what lived in that pocket, and it was no friend.

"Jayne," he said. The air felt thick around him, as though he were trying to speak from under water. Jayne needed him. He had to be strong for her.

"It's Vivienne," she gasped, and the fear in him grew from a needle to a sword. "She won't listen to me..."

Tristan scanned the battlefield. Vivienne had plummeted to the ground. Now, in tigress form, she prowled toward the pocket, green eyes glowing and fixed on its light. "Vivienne, stop," Jayne shouted, squeezing her eyes shut in concentration. She was trying to exercise her powers of command, Master to Rogue.

Masters could make their Rogues do anything. Stop fighting, shift into a shape they didn't want, even lay down their lives in battle. But even as power rang through every syllable of Jayne's cry, Vivienne didn't hesitate. She moved slowly, steadily, transfixed. Away.

"You don't feel it?" Tristan asked.

"Feel what?" Jayne turned to him. Her eyes were wet and wide with despair. "Tristan, what are we supposed to do?"

Jayne didn't feel the call, but Tristan and his sister did. He looked out over the battlefield, just in time to see a small shape streak toward the pocket and vanish within. Another form ran after it, pulling up short, putting his hands to his face in despair. Pierre. It must have been a La Liberté Rogue fighter.

Jayne quickened her pace, sliding haphazardly down the mountain slope. Tristan scrambled after her. "We have to stop her from going in," Jayne said. Her voice was panicked. She ran toward Vivienne, conjuring a Wall, and threw it up before the girl in a shimmer of green. Vivienne batted it with an enormous paw, and it shattered like glass. Tristan grabbed a Push spell from the Torrent and shoved at the mud in front of Vivienne, churning it beneath her feet and pulling her backward. At that, her eyes finally broke away from staring at the pocket and slid to him. She snarled. The sound cut through his heart. His sister had never done anything like that to him before, not in seventeen years.

"Vivienne," he said softly, knowing her cat ears would pick it up. "Come back to us."

She growled. The sound was utterly inhuman.

"I can't hear her," Jayne cried. "It's like she's—gone."

The voice. It must have filled Vivienne's head, made it impossible to think about anything else. But why her? And why did it affect her more than him? "Ropes," Tristan said.

A scream from overhead made them stop. A huge shape swooped low, and Tristan barely heard a *"No!"* before Sofia was shaken loose from Cillian's back. She landed hard on her side and lay still. Cillian hit the ground with an earth-shaking thud, talons furrowing the soil and sending up chunks of mud and grass. He whirled, lowered his eagle head, and started toward the pocket at a run—

A bright green rope looped around one talon and pulled taut. He fell to the ground, thrashing. A scream tore from his throat, and Tristan winced in pain.

Jayne held the green rope fast. Sweat beaded on her forehead and trickled down her neck. In her other hand she held a second rope, leading to Vivienne. Tristan reached for a strengthening spell to layer over her rope. "More," he shouted to the stunned warriors nearby. "Subdue them!"

Cillian. Vivienne. The Rogue from the La Liberté splinter. And Tristan...but only he'd been able to shake off the call. *It's Rogues,* he realized. The Rogues had lost their minds. Rather, Odin was taking them over from inside the pocket. And the stronger the Rogue magic within, the harder it was to disobey. That had to be why he could break free and the others could not. He had his mother's genes but had never manifested her magic.

"Cillian!" he called. He had to try something. "Remember Sofia. You love her." Would it be enough to pull Cillian away from the voice? "Think of the kids. The school. Your baby. All you have done and everything you care about."

The griffin seemed to be beyond understanding. His wings whirled in a frenzy. His talons slashed. Jayne set her jaw and pulled hard. Other Adepts were trying to throw ropes over Vivienne, but she shook them off, tearing them free with her teeth.

Another wave of power came from the pocket and nearly sent Tristan to his knees. *COME.* At that, Cillian gathered his talons beneath him and launched himself—straight at Jayne.

Tristan didn't even think. He diverted all his power into a Shield that he spun with one hand, while he pulled Jayne behind him with the other. Cillian bounced off the Shield and rebounded. He clacked his vicious beak.

A shimmering net of woven green and gold fell over him. He crashed to the ground. His wings were pinned, and though he snapped at a thread with his beak, the magic was strong. From above, the five young Adepts came running down the mountain, headed by Seo-Joon.

"Sleep spell," Seo-Joon shouted. "And stay back from him."

"Jayne." Tristan turned and put a hand on her cheek. "Are you all right?"

She was trembling, whether from exhaustion or adrenaline he couldn't tell. "Yes, I'll be—Viv!"

They spun together, just in time to see an orange-and-black streak bound past. Without Tristan's spell to strengthen the magical rope, she'd easily severed it, knocked several Adepts out of the way, and dashed for the pocket.

"Vivienne," Tristan screamed in a raw voice. She had to hear him, she had to turn back—

But she didn't even look. She leaped, and there was a flash, and she was gone.

The whole world tilted. Tristan didn't feel his knees give out, but suddenly he was on the ground, staring numbly as the Adepts and Seo-Joon fought to contain Cillian.

He'd vowed to protect Vivienne with his life. His sister, his family. He'd lost her once, and it had taken him so long to get her back. And now she was simply...gone again. To the stronghold of their greatest enemy.

Come, said the voice once more. It was gentler, fading. The Allfather had what he wanted. The light from the tear in their world began to dim.

And Tristan knew what he had to do.

He knelt next to Jayne, who sat half-dazed on the ground. "My love, I must go."

"What?" She turned to him with eyes full of pain and confusion.

"I will bring her home." *Or I will not return at all.*

"Tristan, you can't." Her hand found his wrist, tightened around it. "What if you can't come back? What if you become a Wraith? What if..." She swallowed. "I can't, Tristan. I can't think I'll never see you again."

He tucked a stray dark hair behind her ear. "You will see me again, *mon amour*. I know you will save us." He pressed his lips to hers, a gentle promise. "After all, you are Jayne Thorne." No Master more powerful existed, on Earth or in the Torrent.

"Until we meet again," he whispered, and pulled free of her disbelieving fingers. Then he turned, and ran, and dove through the seam, feeling it close up behind him.

FOR A MOMENT JAYNE couldn't breathe. She couldn't think. The world was suddenly dark. The pocket had closed, and people she cared about were trapped inside. Lost.

You are Jayne Thorne, whispered the ghost of Tristan's voice in her ear.

Not lost. She got to her knees and put her palm to the earth. She was a Master, and she held the power of five totems. She conversed with goddesses and pulled captives from within grimoires. She had defeated Wraiths and brought forth the only familiar of her generation. And now people were counting on her to win this. To bring them back.

She called on her totems. All of them.

The ground rumbled and the wind tore through the plain. The sea crashed against the rocks, and thunder played like drums in the distance. A meteor streaked overhead, trailing fire. *Find the pocket,* she thought. *Burn it open.* Her magic moved like a wave over the ground, searching for the truth. The few Wraiths still trying to fight were knocked over, dazed by the force of it.

There. She felt a pull ahead of her, a place where the Torrent was trying to connect and seep through. But something was holding it closed, like a giant hand that had the pocket's entrance fisted shut. Jayne directed all of her magic toward it. She would pry up those invisible fingers one by one, force it open, and go in to do battle with Odin herself.

A tiny glimmer of light appeared, like a shaft of sunlight through a hole in the attic roof. Jayne seized upon it, pulling and pushing. The hole became the size of a fist. Her heart spasmed; she was forgetting to breathe. Sweat pooled in her collar. Her muscles burned, and the familiar heat of too much magic flushed under her skin. But she wasn't going to stop. She kept pushing, and sent a tendril of magic through the hole—

Something pushed back, so hard she was knocked into a backward somersault and smacked her head on the ground. As Jayne gasped for breath she felt the hole close up again. "No, no, no," she moaned, rolling to her side and getting back up on her knees. She put out one final blast of magic.

It dissipated in thin air. There was no more light, no more pocket. And when she reached for more power, it felt like scraping at the bottom of an empty bowl. She had nothing.

Freya? Vesta? Amaterasu? she tried. *Medb. Please!* The

goddesses didn't answer. *Hayden?* But even her dragon familiar was silent.

She had failed.

People were calling out around her, moving to each other in the aftermath of the battle. But she heard none of it. Master of magic Jayne Thorne, armed with all the totems and a dragon, couldn't defeat Odin Allfather.

And if *she* couldn't defeat him, what could?

CHAPTER
FORTY-TWO

Henry Thorne stumbled into a dark world.

The sudden change from the brightness of the pocket threw his eyes into disarray, but he knew he was at Kirkjufell by the smell of the grass and the sea, and the overpowering scent of magic. *Good.* The problem with experimental magic like pockets was that you never knew what sort of side effects awaited you—for example, whether you went *in* and came back *out* at the same place.

"I need to get back to the lab," he muttered. His vision began to grow used to the dim light. He looked at the moon. Judging by her position, he hadn't been gone long. He could hear the TCO army, too, though the sounds of battle were thankfully gone. Henry smiled ruefully to himself, running his thumb over the gadget in his hand. He was certainly no fighter, Sofia and Jayne were right about that. But this opportunity was not to be missed, and he'd learned so much from it. He had so much to share. And so much to do.

Portals began to flash into existence. Henry saw medics running through, carrying stretchers with limp forms. Fear undulated in his belly. How much had he missed? Had they won or lost? Had one of the girls been hurt? He got to his feet and hurried down the mountain, taking note of blast marks and claw marks. The field was ruined. The battle had been mighty. But judging by the lack of living Wraiths on the field, did he dare hope they'd won?

"He can't go through the regular portal," said a voice he vaguely recognized. Sofia's friend, Seo-Joon. "We'll need a special one. Not to mention a containment of some kind." He sounded weary. Henry saw him a moment later, disheveled, with his combat vest shredded. He stood well back from a glittering green net spell. The creature within it scrabbled and snapped, but it was growing tired. And it was too colorful to be a Wraith, Henry thought. Unless Odin was getting creative...

"Goddess," he whispered, realizing who it was. Cillian, in griffin form, still fighting like hell.

Sofia sat not far from her Rogue. Someone had wrapped an emergency blanket around her. Her blue eyes stared at nothing.

Henry knelt in front of her. "I'm here," he said softly.

She blinked slowly. She seemed to have trouble focusing. "Dad?" she whispered, as though she could barely believe it.

Henry leaned over and wrapped her in a hug. He half expected her to burst into tears, but Sofia couldn't even do that. "I killed her, Dad," she whispered. "I killed her, and it was all for nothing."

"Killed who? Goddess, not...?" Had there been some terrible accident? Was Jayne gone?

No. No, it couldn't be. Sofia would never hurt her sister. If Henry just found her, his fears would be alleviated. They could all go home. He looked among the wounded waiting for transport, but she wasn't there. Then he cast his eye out over the field. Desperation started clawing its way up his throat. "Is she here? Did she already go back through?" He grabbed the nearest arm. "Is Jayne here?"

The arm belonged to Amanda Newport. She pulled his

fingers off her with an iron grip. "Sofia took out Ruth Thorne. And last I saw Jayne, she was by the pocket." Amanda looked him up and down. Her face was streaked with dirt and she stank of burnt hair. It had been singed off along her left side. She looked weary and defeated and bitter. "Welcome back, Doctor Thorne," she bit out. "I hope your experiment was successful enough to keep you out of a world of trouble."

Henry had stopped listening. He set off over the field at a run, stumbling over bodies, making his way back to the base of the mountain.

He recognized Jayne easily by the glow on her forehead, and he nearly collapsed from relief. She was seated, which was a good sign. She too stared into space, though it was the mountain that kept her gaze. The opening that allowed the Wraiths access to the field had disappeared.

"Jayne." He crouched beside her. "It's going to be all right, Jayne."

"He's gone," she said quietly. "I lost him. He's gone."

Henry looked around. Understanding broke over him in a wave of sorrow. He'd hoped to be unlucky enough in love for the three of them. "Come," he said, and took her by the elbow. "I'll take you home."

EPILOGUE

It's so odd, Jayne thought. She sat on the couch, watching her tea grow cold. At some point the Nashville apartment had stopped being hers and started being theirs. The guest room had a bed permanently made up for Vivienne, and her clothes hung in its closet. Tristan's art graced the walls. Jayne's battered copy of *Catch-22* lay on the side table next to his favorite chair, a leather bookmark keeping his place. Now it was strangely silent, empty even though Henry and Sofia had spent the last three days here. None of them had been able to do much; they'd survived off the food in Jayne's freezer, which wasn't hard. No one had much appetite. Now Jayne sat on the sofa, with a kitten-sized Hayden curled in her lap and a Pern novel that she couldn't find the energy to open sitting on the side table.

The door opened. She was too tired to tense up, to worry about whether it was a Wraith who'd found her apartment, or Ruger coming to give her bad news. But she heard the telltale tread of Sofia and the clink of her keys on the front table.

Her sister flopped heavily on the couch. Jayne looked over. Sofia just shook her head. Their conversation needed no words:

Sofia had been to visit Cillian. There was no change in his condition. He hadn't shifted back into human form since the battle, but had gone from animal to animal, independent of Sofia's command. First he'd tried to be a mouse, a fly, anything that might be able to escape the pen they'd made for him. Then he'd turned into the fiercest animals he could: a polar bear, a rhinoceros, a dragon. But he hadn't been able to break the walls of the enclosure, either. He'd settled on a wolf, and stalked the enclosure, snarling. He was possessed, it seemed. Poisoned from within by Odin himself.

The news from outside their little world was grim, too. Though the battle had been going in their favor, when Odin called the Rogues to him, all was lost. Wraiths were being spotted regularly. Cities had repurposed emergency sirens to warn of imminent Wraith attack, and people were staying inside. Adepts with newly discovered powers were being kidnapped, turned Wraith themselves, then sent back to their cities and families to wreak destruction, and Jayne had heard reports of at least two more Rogues falling under the Allfather's spell. Amanda had sent them just one message—*Wait*—and for once, Jayne was content to do just that. After all, there was nothing else to do. They'd failed.

Henry came in from the kitchen. "I thought I heard the door," he said, offering Sofia a weak smile. She didn't return it. "Anyway. I'm glad you're here. It's time to talk." He took a seat across from them, in Tristan's favorite chair.

"About how I killed Mom?" Sofia said tonelessly.

Guilt and sorrow lanced through Jayne's heart. Sofia had killed Ruth Thorne because Jayne hadn't been able to. Her sweet and soft sister had shown remarkable courage, and it was hurting her so badly. Jayne had hesitated when she should have hardened her heart. Sofia had protected her again.

Henry put his mug down and leaned over the coffee table. He held out a hand. When Sofia didn't take it, he cleared his throat pointedly. He was still their father, after all. With a sigh Sofia leaned forward and rested her fingers lightly in his palm. "I don't blame you for killing Ruth," he said gently. "She chose to worship power long ago, and it was the power that killed her in the end. Not you."

He squeezed. "But...what if you didn't kill Ruth?"

"There would be one more Wraith in the world," said Jayne in her own attempt to be comforting. Her voice was listless. Emotion was a step too far.

"This isn't a hypothetical question." Henry stood and began to pace. It was a small sitting room, so he could only take three steps before he had to turn and walk back, but he tucked his hands behind his back and blinked at them as though he were giving a lecture to a full hall of students. "There is one more thing we might be able to do. Something I've been working on ever since I developed the Time Jumper. Something I couldn't research without going through the back door of the Torrent, to see your grandmother again. The Time Reverse."

"The...what now?" Jayne said.

"Are you talking about turning back time?" Sofia said.

"A time turner!" Jayne pressed her hands together. Possibilities clashed together in her mind. Cillian, whole in mind and body. Tristan and Vivienne, here and well. "Tell me that Grandma knows how to make a time turner."

"What?" Henry stared at her. Sofia smacked her lightly on the thigh.

"It's a thing... Never mind. Time stoppage, blah blah, please continue."

"Yes, I'm talking about turning back time. When I managed to stop time, it was an important first step. Of course, as you know, the Time Jumper works for a very limited number of seconds, and we're talking about stopping and reversing on a much larger scale.

"Girls, this is my life's work. All of my initial forays into time and Torrent research were geared toward saving Alexandra, who was lost a long time ago. But thanks to my recent journey into the heart of the Torrent, I've found concrete proof that it's possible. We can save not just your daughter, Jayne, and not just my mother. We can save everyone. We can keep it all from happening in the first place."

Jayne and Sofia exchanged glances. Saving Tristan, and keeping Cillian and Vivienne from losing their minds? Jayne would lose the totems as well, but that was nothing in comparison to getting their family back. And who knew? Ruth Thorne had given her life for a good cause once. She might be persuaded to do so again.

She looked to Henry again. "We're in. How do we do that?"

"Yes, well." He blinked rapidly. "That's the problem. I don't know."

Her hands became fists. Of course. Hope was for fools. She'd done nothing but fail, and now they were up against a wall no one had yet scaled: time.

Hayden stood up on her lap, arching his back in a stretch like a cat. He yawned, then twisted his head in Henry's direction.

You do not know how to turn back time? he asked.

"No," Jayne replied for her father.

Curious. Hayden sat upright, curling his tail around the base of his claws. *Because I do.*

Dearest Reader,

Wipe away those tears, friends, because there's still another adventure ahead.

I can't wait to share the final installment of this series, THE SCROLLS OF TIME, with you. Stay tuned to my newsletter for more exciting details on the release, and flip the page to get your pre-order in place.

In the meantime, if you're interested in more from Jayne's world, I suggest checking out the short stories in this series, which give some background and history.

I am so grateful for your time and support. Thanks for reading, and for being a part of my magical world!

Blessed Be,
Joss

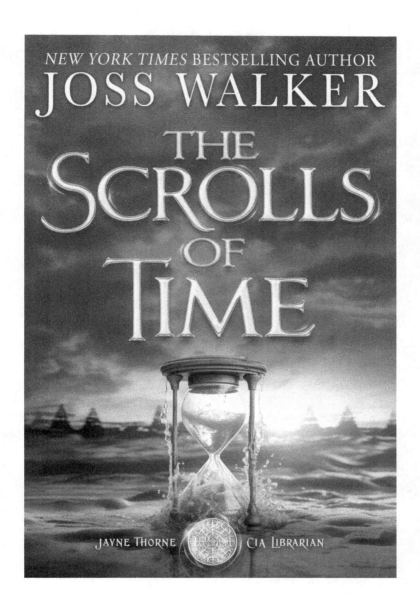

ACKNOWLEDGMENTS

A penultimate book in a series is probably the most important of all. Years of work has built to a crescendo, and all of the threads, all of the magic, has revealed itself. You know the story now, just as I do. The players. The stakes. You know where we're headed, at last. The final book is coming soon, and you will be riveted.

I need to give a massive shoutout to Claire Bartlett, who helped take my vision of the finale of this story from outline to draft with courage, good humor, and an inventive spirit. You've been a dream to work with!

More thanks to the usual suspects: my agents, Laura Blake Peterson and James Farrell, who kindly shepherded this novel through the audio process; Erin Moon and the fine folks at Tantor Audio, who bring Jayne et al. to life; Kim Killion, artist extraordinaire, who leaped at the chance to reimagine Jayne's world and created beautiful new covers that genuinely reflect the spirit of the series; Phyllis DeBlanche, who has copyedited all of these books and created the most majestic style sheet I've ever seen. My teams at Ingram and Amazon, as well, for all the help over the years getting these books into your hands. And my friends at Poisoned Pen, Murder by the Book, and Parnassus Books, who love to hand-sell these beauties—I adore you!

To my besties, Laura Benedict, Ariel Lawhon, Lisa Patton, Patti Callahan Henry, Paige Crutcher, Jayne Ann Krentz, Barbara Peters; thank you for holding my hand through this process! Thanks to my parents who love these books as much as I do; my exceptionally cool team of beta readers gave such incredible feedback and really helped this book level up, especially Jennifer Jakes, Sherrie Saint, Sara Weiss, Erin Alford, Carol Brandon, and Joan Huston; and my Readers and Rogues FB group are the best!

To my Tristan, Randy. You are my soulmate, my one true love, and my favorite magician.

ABOUT JOSS WALKER

Photo credit: KidTee Hello Photography

Joss Walker is an award-winning fantasy author and the alter ego of *New York Times* bestselling thriller author J.T. Ellison. Through her fantasy works, Joss delves into her passion for the genre and crafts stories of extraordinary women discovering their power in the world.

With the creation of Jayne Thorne, CIA Librarian, Joss has developed a captivating contemporary fantasy series that appeals to lovers of books, libraries, romance, and, of course, magic.

For more, visit josswalker.com or follow her online.

ABOUT TWO TALES PRESS

Two Tales Press is an independent publishing house featuring crime fiction, suspense, and fantasy novels, novellas, and anthologies written and edited by *New York Times* bestselling author J.T. Ellison, including the Jayne Thorne, CIA Librarian series under J.T.'s fantasy pen name, Joss Walker.

To view all of our titles, please visit

www.twotalespress.com

~

Printed in the USA
CPSIA information can be obtained
at www.ICGtesting.com
CBHW022020091124
17119CB00036B/369